'I will not marry him.' Kate's face was deathly white and her whole body shook but her voice, though low, was absolutely firm. 'I've done nothing wrong. I've got nothing to be ashamed of.'

'Right. Then if you won't marry him, get out.'

'David!' Too late Dorothy protested.

'Let me deal with this, Aunt Dorothy.' He turned to Duncan. 'Are you willing, lad?'

Duncan nodded stupidly, still dazed and unable to assimilate all that was going on. Five minutes ago he had thought he was going to be beaten, arrested, thrown out on the streets, and now his dream was coming true.

'I will not marry Duncan.' Kate's voice was still steady.

'Then pack your bags.'

Anne Vivis was brought up in Fife, Scotland, where all her books are set. *The Heather Loft* is her fifth novel; her first four, *Daughters of Strathannan*, *The Lennox Women*, *The Rowan Tree* and *The Provost's Woman* are also available from Mandarin. She now lives in Warrington, Cheshire.

Anne Vivis

The Heather Loft

ARROW

A Mandarin Paperback
THE HEATHER LOFT

First published in Great Britain 1997
by William Heinemann
This edition published by
Mandarin Paperbacks
an imprint of Reed International Books Ltd
Michelin House, 81 Fulham Road, London SW3 6RB
and Auckland, Melbourne, Singapore and Toronto

Copyright © Anne Vivis
The author has asserted her moral rights

A CIP catalogue record for this title
is available from the British Library

ISBN 0 7493 2322 1

Typeset by Intype
in 12 on 15 point Bembo
Printed and bound in Germany by
Elsnerdruck, Berlin

ONE

The massive wooden doors of Drumlinnie prison creaked open, spat out an ant-like creature then clanged shut, the noise reverberating along the sleeping street. Dwarfed by the looming walls, Matthew McPherson shoved his hands in his pockets and stood blinking in the early morning sun. He felt no desperate urge to get away from the place but rather a faint sense of loss. Almost reluctantly he picked up his bag and walked slowly up the soot-blackened street. At the corner he turned for a last glimpse of the institution which had kept him safely confined for the entire period of the war.

Funny how things turned out for the best, he mused as he made his way through streets littered with the detritus of tenement living. Despite the fact that he was what could only be described as a habitual criminal, Matty had learned his lessons early and, after a particularly unpleasant period in a reformatory, had been sharp enough to avoid further brushes with the law. Trusting no one, working strictly on his own, he had embarked on a series of relatively minor but occasionally violent crimes which had provided him with an easy living. Inevitably, his success had brought him to the attention of the Glasgow underworld where his iron nerve and willingness to deal brutally with unexpected difficulties had made him a much sought-after accomplice. For three years Matty had clung doggedly to his independence. But, as for many a villain before him, greed was his eventual undoing. Lured by the bait of serious money, seduced by a dream of life in more exotic climes, Matty abandoned his principles and joined three other men in a grandiose but ill-fated attempt to rob a bank.

That had been back in 1939. Matty had gone to prison a bitter man but within three months he had had every reason to be grateful for the King's hospitality. Having not the faintest desire to serve his country in her war with Hitler, he counted himself lucky to be beyond reach of the call-up and settled down to build his own little empire within the prison walls.

Matthew McPherson knew that reputation was everything; that the way he handled himself in the first weeks of his sentence would make the difference between relative comfort and hell on earth. At a little over five foot five he compensated for his lack of stature with a hardness which, even in that barbaric enclave of society, marked him as someone to be wary of and ensured his rapid elevation to the top of the prison hierarchy. He was supported there by a group of equally vicious thugs who exercised more control over the prison population than the guards themselves.

Now, seven years later, he found himself ejected from the place where admiration and respect had been his and, at the age of thirty, facing a world in which he was nothing, a situation he was determined to remedy in the shortest possible time.

He strolled on, making for the city centre, seeing for the first time the uncleared bomb sites which, although the country had been at peace for several months now, sent a shiver of disquiet through him as he realised just how much had changed. But no one looking at this apparently confident young man would have guessed how uneasy he was, how vulnerable he felt now that he was outside the vast walls of the jail. Deception had always been one of Matty's greatest talents and he wore each of his various personae with consummate ease. This morning, fresh out of jail, he blended perfectly with the young, working-class Glaswegians who were starting to throng the pavements, making their way to honest jobs. Stocky, dark to the point of swarthiness, to a casual observer there was nothing remarkable about Matthew McPherson. The unnerving coldness in eyes of a shade of brown more normally associated with warmth was hidden by heavy lids which gave a misleading impression of indolence, or on better occasions, suavity. Few people had been unfortunate enough to witness the mad glitter of violence which lurked in those inky pupils, but then few people knew the real Matthew McPherson.

Under the cloak of nonchalance which Matty had consciously donned to greet his freedom, his soul was as bitter and twisted as it had been since his first brush with crime as a ten-year-old. Matthew chose to lay the blame for everything that had since gone wrong with his life at the door of other people. And the person he blamed most of all was his sister, Meggie.

Thinking of her, Matty made his way to a small public park and sat on a bench, pondering his next move. In his pocket he had the address of an organisation dedicated to helping released prisoners such as himself. But though he had been advised that they would help him to find accommodation and perhaps work, he wouldn't go to them for help. He was too proud for that. Nor would he make any attempt to renew old acquaintances from the criminal world. His name and face were known to the police and he was wise enough to realise that any return to his old haunts would have him on the list of suspects for every crime committed from the hour of his release. Matty McPherson's ambition lay in a very different direction. East, well away from Glasgow. Home, to Strathannan, the county of his birth. Strathannan, and his sister.

TWO

It was a cosy scene, one which would be familiar in many homes as, the day's work over, the adults settled down to enjoy a restful evening. The farmhouse parlour was a homely place, crammed with good, solid furniture, some of it almost as old as the house itself and all in perfect harmony with the warped doors and beamed ceilings; doors and beams which added character, draughts and bumped heads in equitable proportions. In the midst of this rural domesticity, Henry Brebner and his wife Dorothy sat, one on either side of a roaring fire, a matched pair, rotund, robust and ruddy, quietly digesting a huge dinner.

The brief post-prandial peace was shattered by the door crashing open. Two equally matched, golden-haired children raced into the room, followed by a slightly harassed looking older girl.

Faintly irritated to have her favourite radio programme interrupted, Dorothy Brebner nevertheless smiled fondly and held out her arms. 'Come on then, give Mummy a kiss.'

Eight-year-old twins, Victoria and Edward, freshly scrubbed and polished, pressed against her with bodies damp and smelling of bath water.

Just, thought Kate, watching indulgently, like a couple of little angels. Which only went to prove how misleading looks could be. Left to their own devices the twins were a pair of wee devils who competed for everything, including their parents' affections, with a ruthlessness which sometimes shocked their elder sister. Yet she, a witness to the very worst of their tantrums, tricks and winsomeness, was every bit as susceptible to their charms as everyone else.

'Now, say goodnight to your father.' Dorothy detached herself carefully, and prodded the twins toward the trousers, slippers and stubby fingers which were all that was visible of her husband behind the defensive screen of his newspaper.

The paper rustled and folded in on itself. 'Well, then. Time for bed, eh?' Henry failed to keep the note of relief out of his voice and only just got the paper on to the side table before two solid bodies plonked themselves down, one on each of his substantial thighs. He ruffled each blond head and tweaked two rosy cheeks before finally accepting the damp kisses proffered by his offspring.

As usual, exasperation at their constant disturbance and energetic demands was tempered by love. But how much easier if they were brought up the way he had been – unseen unless invited, silent in the presence of adults, polite, tidy and civilised. The trouble, he thought glumly, was that he and Dorothy were simply too old for this sort of thing. The twins had arrived the day after Dorothy's forty-second birthday, just weeks before he celebrated his own half century. A miracle, no less, but a shock just the same when they had both resigned themselves to raising only Kate, an altogether different mould of child. The delivery of twins at this late stage of her life had been an extremely painful experience for Dorothy and one for which she held her husband entirely responsible. Refusing to risk a repeat performance she had banned him from her body forthwith, an embargo which was still in force despite the fact that she was now of an age when conception was no longer a biological possibility. It was an unsatisfactory situation and accounted for much of Henry's irritability, and for a certain restlessness which came upon him without warning two or three times a year. Where many men in similar circumstances turned to other women, Henry, a thoroughly decent character, indulged in nothing more objectionable than hard work and brisk walks.

'Get them off to bed then, lass. You too. Work in the morning.' He turned to his eldest daughter with a fond smile, pleased that she at least was turning out to be such an obedient, hard-working lass, and a pretty one at that.

Seventeen-year-old Kate returned his kiss gladly, knowing that no matter how lovable her brother and sister were, her place in her father's affections was secure. Then, as she did every night, she bent to kiss her mother and got, in return, a half-averted cheek, quickly withdrawn as soon as her lips brushed across it.

'Goodnight, Mother.'

'Goodnight, Kate.' Dorothy's reply was toneless as she turned away to adjust the dial on the radio, her message plain.

It was always the same. Though Dorothy's patience was notoriously short, it was obvious that her tenderness was reserved for the troublesome twins. Her attitude towards Kate was, if not quite cold, then certainly remote. Kate was unhappily aware of the stiffness in her mother's manner, but it had not always been this way. She had vivid memories of comforting cuddles, of stories being read, of country walks, and games and songs in the evening. Before the twins were born. A lesser person might have felt resentful, but Kate couldn't find it in her heart to be jealous of her siblings. Instead she carried her hurt tight inside herself and wondered what she had done to make her mother so determinedly displeased with her.

Half an hour later, at a little after nine o'clock, Kate slipped gratefully between her own comforting sheets. Within five minutes she was fast asleep.

The alarm clock rang, assaulting her ears with its terrifying cacophony only minutes later, or that was how it felt as she fumbled desperately for the switch at just after five-thirty the next morning.

Sighing, she threw the covers back and went to the window, stretching and yawning. The effect of the view was immediate. Set on a faint rise, the farm commanded a patchwork of undulating fields, some green and rich from the spring rains, others darkly brown with fertility, waiting to be impregnated with the new season's plantings. The front of the house overlooked a gentle vista of agricultural countryside which sank slowly towards the distant slash of the river Forth. From Kate's room at the back of the building, it was possible to see the hills of Perthshire, faintly hazy at this hour of the morning but still with the power to awe her. A few miles to the west, Inverannan, the county town of Strathannan, nestled in a clutch of lesser hills, its sandstone buildings catching the early morning sun, the castle ruins and the town clock clearly silhouetted in the spring air. In between were uncultivated fields, rough and hummocky, with sheep peacefully browsing among exposed rocks, clumps of gorse and patches of heather. Kate felt the sleepiness lifting from her, her spirits rising as they always did in response to the sheer perfection of the place.

The protesting creak of a floorboard on the landing warned her that her father was already up and would be expecting a cup of tea before he set about his day's work. Kate hurried to the bathroom, splashed cold water over her face and hands, and then pulled herself quickly into the trousers, shirt and old sweater which comprised her working clothes. Looking at her reflection in the mirror as she scraped her long, dark hair back into a rubber band she felt a familiar pang of dissatisfaction. Her nose was too strong, particularly in profile and her mouth was far too wide. Why was it, she wondered, that the twins had such neat, attractive features while she, by comparison, looked . . . well, plain? Intent on her critical self-examination, she completely overlooked the fact that her generous mouth displayed enviably white and even teeth, nor did she appreciate the upward slant to her eyes which, with her high, clearly

7

defined cheekbones, combined to give her an unusual, faintly exotic appearance. Nor did her workmanlike attire detract from the essential femininity of her figure, which was undeniably that of a shapely young woman. Her limbs were strong and lean while her eyes and skin were bright and clear from days spent in the crisp country air. Only her hands, rough with ragged nails, really let her down, but working on a farm there was little she could do to protect them. Kate gazed solemnly at her own reflection for a few moments longer, then, not given to self-pity, she pulled a grotesque face at herself and giggled, feeling foolish.

Wide awake and cheerful, she ran lightly downstairs. There was no sign of her father, who would have gone straight outside to the privy. Despite the addition of a modern bathroom and the protests of his wife, Henry Brebner clung to the old ways, washing in the scullery and insisting on his weekly bath in the tin tub in front of the kitchen range. Kate opened this monstrosity's fire door now, tossing coal into it before setting the kettle on the hob. By the time Henry came in it was steaming merrily.

They drank their tea in companionable silence, broken only by the chorus of birds and the impatient lowing of cattle in the home field where they waited to be milked.

'Right, lass.' Henry swallowed a second cup of tea in one long gulp and strode into the yard.

Kate abandoned the rest of her own tea, shoved her feet into her boots, placed ready by the door, and hurried after him. While he disappeared into the dark depths of the milking shed she ran across the yard, past various barns and outbuildings, and leaped nimbly over the wooden gate into the field. The cows, as well used to this routine as she, milled in the trampled mud round the gate, watching her with huge, placid eyes. When she opened the gate they went through it without urging, heading unhurriedly for the milking shed.

'Braw morning, Kate.' Duncan Auld, who lived in a tied cottage in the farmyard, gave her this same greeting each morning, no matter what the weather.

'Aye, it is that,' she responded cheerfully, waiting until the last animal was safely inside before closing the doors.

It was Kate's task to fill the feeding troughs and then clean the animals' udders, ready for her father and Duncan to attach the milking machines. She had been helping on the farm since she was five or six years old and, like everything else, she did this without having to be told.

While the men attended to the cattle, Kate hurried back across the yard and into one of the many small sheds where she busied herself mixing chicken feed. This she scattered liberally over the chicken run then chased the squawking, flapping birds out of the coop before gathering the newly laid eggs and taking them into the kitchen. Working deftly, she sorted through them, putting aside for the family's use any that were broken or irregularly shaped, and packing the rest ready for delivery to Hough's, Inverannan's finest grocer. Hardly pausing between the routine tasks she hurried back to the milking shed and set about cleaning the equipment while Duncan drove the relieved cattle out of the building. Henry settled the churns at the shed doors, cursing her loudly but without real anger when the hose she was using to rinse off the floor sent a splattering of filthy slime over his trouser legs.

Duncan, who only ever moved at the one, slow pace, sauntered across the yard, whistling tunelessly between his teeth.

'I've left them back in the home field,' he told her, grinning. 'You can shift them after breakfast.'

Kate stifled a surge of exasperation at Duncan's reluctance to do more than the absolute minimum. Once on the move the cattle would have carried on quite happily to the better grazing of the lower fields where they spent the day. Now she would have the trouble of gathering them up again and moving them on, wasting valuable time. 'Thanks, Duncan, that's a real help,' she snapped, glaring at him. He just grinned and walked away.

The Aulds had been labourers on this land for as long as the Brebners had farmed it, son following father for more than five generations with the inevitability of the seasons. Kate and Duncan, he just a year older than she, had grown up together, tending the cattle, helping with the vegetable crops, working side by side with their fathers after school, in the holidays and, occasionally – at harvest and planting time – taking a week or more away from lessons, their education a clear second in importance to the work of the farm.

Watty, Duncan's father, had worked here until the last week of the war. The same amiable aversion to work which was so apparent in his only son had been Watty's undoing. Dozing unconcernedly in the shelter of a tree when he should have been repairing a breached wall, he had failed to hear the ominous rumblings of an approaching storm. His rest was rendered permanent by one brilliant shaft of lightning. The day after his frazzled corpse was consigned to the local churchyard, Duncan had taken his father's place, receiving his wages at the end of the week and living on in the little cottage alone, without the need for comment from either himself or Henry Brebner.

The smell of frying bacon wafted temptingly from the kitchen. Kate, her stomach bubbling with hunger, swithered for a moment, knowing she should move the cattle on now, before they got settled. Hunger won and she followed the men into the fragrant kitchen.

Dorothy Brebner, a crossover pinafore making huge mounds of her breasts, turned from the range when she heard them approaching and stationed herself solidly in the doorway, permanently on guard against the mud which still managed to smear the flagged floor, watching as they rinsed their hands at the outside tap and kicked off their boots.

'You're not coming in here in that state,' she informed her husband, looking pointedly at his soiled trousers.

'Och away, woman,' he retorted. 'There's nothing there as will do any harm.'

She reached up to the wooden clothes airer which swung over their heads. 'Either put these on or you can eat in the yard like a pig,' she ordered, flinging a fresh pair of trousers at him.

Henry grunted, stuck his feet back into his boots and took himself off to the privy to change.

Satisfied, Dorothy returned to the range. The kitchen was her empire and was where she spent most of her day, preparing the filling meals which, seeming to take no heed of the continuing rationing, ensured that her family were healthily nourished. A woman from the local village came in for a couple of hours each day to attend to the mundane housework. Anything else, including washing the supper dishes and caring for the twins after school, was Kate's responsibility. The girl rarely had a free half-hour and Mrs Brebner, who had seen the way the local lads eyed her daughter, intended to keep it that way. Kate was too valuable about the place to risk losing in an early marriage.

Thick slices of home-cured bacon landed on top of crisply fried, home-baked bread, followed by two fresh eggs apiece, their yolks a rich, golden yellow. They ate with the application of folk who have better things to do with their time. Henry, whose paunch was large enough to get in his way, pushed his empty plate aside, sat back and patted his stomach before Duncan and Kate were more than half-way through their meal.

'Braw,' he declared, getting to his feet. 'Hurry it up youse two. Time's getting on. We've to make a start on planting the tatties this week. Then there's the turnips to be got in.'

Kate groaned. Potato planting was bearable, if boring, her job usually being to sit on the back of the tractor, guiding seed potatoes into the automatic feeder, one of the few modern contrivances on the farm. Setting out the turnip seedlings was another matter altogether, involving hours of back-breaking hand planting.

'Right then. Duncan, you take the eggs into town. Kate and me'll make a start on the tatties.'

Dorothy disrupted his plans. 'Kate'll have to go with Duncan. I'm needing her to fetch me some messages,' she insisted.

'Duncan'll do that.'

'No, he can not.'

Their eyes met and there was a brief, silent battle of wills before Henry looked away. 'Aye, well, just make sure youse're quick about it,' he growled, stomping out into the yard.

Duncan grinned at Kate. 'I'll fetch the truck round.'

Kate nodded and ran upstairs, more than happy to break the dull routine of work with a trip to town. Quickly she stripped off her working clothes, slipped into a blue skirt and flowered blouse then ran a brush through her hair so that it fell in shining waves around her shoulders.

'What's this?' Dorothy asked when Kate ran back into the kitchen. 'What did you want to go and change for?'

'Mum! I can't go into town in my working clothes.' She had done that before and suffered agonies of embarrassment at the way folk looked at her.

'You're getting above yourself, my girl. Fancying yourself up just to go to the shops.'

Further argument was averted by a furious honking on the truck's horn. Kate grabbed the first lot of eggs and carried them outside. 'What do you want me to get for you?' she asked, coming back for the rest.

Dorothy simply handed her a list and some money then turned back to her chores.

★

Though Inverannan was little more than six miles away, Kate rarely got the chance to go there unless her mother was with her. Now, leaving Duncan to deliver the eggs, she hurried to buy the few items on her list and then indulged in fifteen minutes of window shopping. When a lad, unloading meat from a flesher's van, whistled at her she coloured with embarrassment but, walking quickly away from him, pretending she hadn't heard, she felt a little spasm of pleasure in her stomach. Even Duncan's bad temper at being kept waiting couldn't destroy her happy mood.

They drove back along the country lanes in silence. When they reached the farm he parked the truck alongside the milking shed. As she opened the door to jump down she found herself facing a large, muddy puddle. 'Duncan!' she protested. 'I'll ruin my shoes.'

Never moody for long, he chuckled. 'Och, stay there a minute. I'll help you down.' Swinging easily from his own seat, he waded into the middle of the puddle and stood laughing up at her. 'Come on then,' he invited, holding up beefy arms.

There had been many times in their shared childhood when he had lifted her from trees, across fences, over streams. Without giving it a great deal of thought now, Kate allowed Duncan to put his strong arms round her and help her down, resting her hands on his shoulders to steady herself. But even before she reached the ground she sensed something different about him, saw it in the way his eyes never left hers, felt it in the way he held her against him, her breasts jammed against his chest, keeping her there with the power of his arms. Until this moment Kate had never thought of Duncan as anything more than her everyday companion, the lad she had romped and played with for as long as she could recall. Now, suddenly, she saw him as other girls did and this tall, muscular young man with hazel eyes, a thatch of sandy hair and a fairly recent moustache was suddenly a stranger. For a moment longer he held her, looking into her eyes with disconcerting intensity. Then, interpreting her lack of resistance as encouragement, he clamped his face on to hers and tried to worm his tongue between her stiff lips.

For a moment Kate was shocked into even greater stillness, then, horrified by the realisation of what he was trying to do, yanked her head away. 'Don't!'

'Och, Kate . . .' he murmured, slobbering wet kisses over her averted face. He still had his arms around her and was trying to pull her even closer to him, to get her pert little breasts pushing up against his chest once more. Until recently an unhappy combination of crippling shyness, late development and limited intelligence had severely limited Duncan's contact with the opposite sex. But for the past year he had been more aware of Kate's developing body than she had been herself. He took every opportunity to watch her covertly, enjoying the way her working trousers defined the gentle swell of her hips, feeling a gratifying stir of excitement in his groin as some innocent movement caused her shirt to tighten across nipples which sometimes stood proud against the rough fabric. In bed at night he found himself in a sweat of excitement, imagining how it might feel to grasp those firmly rounded breasts, to feel her lips warm against his. Now, with her so close that he could smell the sweet freshness of her skin, frustrated lust rose up and obliterated everything else.

Clumsily he pinioned her against him and lowered his hot face to hers again. She struggled, wriggling against him, unwittingly increasing his excitement until, quite violently, he slammed a hand against her buttocks and pressed her hips against the area of his own body which was straining for release.

'*No!*' Kate wrenched her head free.

'Please, Kate, you know I like you,' he mumbled, rubbing himself against her, oblivious to her distress, his excitement mounting until all he was conscious of was the feel of her. One hand slid to her breast, kneading it through her shirt.

And then came the dreadful, humiliating release as inexperience betrayed him: a hot explosion which left a shameful dark stain on his trousers and loosened his hold on her. Tension gone, he was suddenly aware of just how wrong he had been. He dropped his hands and stepped back, releasing her so abruptly that she stumbled into the puddle which had started all this.

'I'm sorry . . .' he mumbled.

Raised on a farm, Kate had seen enough bulls put to cows to understand the mechanics of the mating process, and she knew precisely what had happened. Anger and disgust rendered her speechless but the look she gave him was so full of contempt that Duncan flushed a brilliant red then turned and ran, crashing through the door of his own cottage and slamming it on the scene of his mortification.

Kate tugged her dishevelled clothing back into place. Then, splashing through the puddle, she reached into the truck, hauled out the messages for her mother and raced to the house with them.

'Don't you dare come in here in that state!' Dorothy's strident voice stopped her on the doorstep, forestalling Kate's desperate plea for comfort and reassurance. Her gimlet eye settled on her daughter's soggy feet but completely failed to see that Kate was upset.

The words dying on her tongue, Kate kicked her shoes off, dumped the shopping on the kitchen table and ran upstairs. In the bathroom she cleaned her teeth, scrubbing at them as if to scour away the taste of him. That done she washed, rubbing her face vigorously with the coarse flannel. Then Kate drained her incipient feelings of shame down the plughole with the dirty water. Not for one minute would she consider herself to blame for what had happened. Her overriding emotion was one of anger, but mixed in with that anger was a sense of loss. The easy companionship which she and Duncan had shared for so long was soiled and she would never be able to feel at ease with him again.

Kate dropped the hoe with which she was unearthing weeds from between the barely established turnip plants and, with difficulty, straightened her back. She had been in the fields since just before seven that morning, with only a half-hour break for lunch, and she was weary and thirsty.

She turned, looking along the unending green lines of vegetables, dismayed by how much was still to be done. As she stood there, flexing her shoulders, a hand rubbing the small of her aching back, Duncan, working just a few feet away, also stood, giving a soft groan as his own muscles protested. Their eyes, which had been studiously avoiding each other for the best part of six weeks, finally met.

Duncan, who had been suffering agonies of regret but had been unable to find the words to apologise, smiled self-consciously. Kate, suddenly aware that in rubbing her back she was causing her thin shirt to stretch tautly over her breasts, flushed slightly, grabbed her hoe and, turning her back on him, went back to work.

Duncan watched her for a moment, then, quickly checking that Henry was still in the other field, gathered his courage and walked over to her. 'Kate?' He stood, looking at his hands, not sure exactly what he was going to say.

Kate, who could feel his presence behind her like a small fire, drove her hoe into the ground and succeeded in uprooting two healthy turnip plants. Furious with herself, she ground them into the soil with her heel and rounded on Duncan.

'What?' she demanded hotly.

'I . . . that is . . . I just wanted . . .' He was forced to jump smartly aside as her hoe stabbed into the ground, missing his foot by a whisker's breadth.

'You're in my way.' Again the hoe flashed towards him, though by now he was standing between the rows. His calloused hands shot out and grabbed the handle. Kate, who had put a lot of energy behind that thrust, was unable to stop herself. Carried forward by her own momentum she collided ignominiously with the handle and took it with her, collapsing in a sprawling heap at Duncan's feet, banging her forehead against his steel-toed boots.

Fury rendered her immobile. For several seconds she simply lay there, a mass of untidy, soil-encrusted limbs, and gaped, her mouth working silently, like a fish. Suddenly realising how ridiculous she must look, she snapped her mouth shut and struggled to disentangle herself. Uncoordinated by humiliation and bad temper she tripped over the abandoned handle and fell again, landing squarely on her behind, looking up into Duncan's face.

'You . . . you . . . you pig!' she spluttered at last. Propelled by rage, she shot to her feet and gave him a huge shove.

Duncan staggered for a moment, striving for balance but shaking with laughter. 'Och, if you could just see yourself,' he chortled, doubling over and holding his sides.

For the second time Kate gaped at him, watching as tears poured from his eyes. Though she tried with all her might to hold it back, a small giggle escaped her.

Duncan looked at her, still quivering with mirth, meeting her eyes, challenging her not to laugh again. Then they were both convulsed until, weak from the effort involved, they sank to the ground and sat side by side among the turnips, still chuckling.

'Och, I've not laughed like that for weeks,' he sighed.

'Me neither,' Kate agreed, lifting a hand to wipe the water from her eyes and smearing mud all down her face.

'Wait.' Duncan reached out a hand to rub it away, his fingers rough on her skin.

'Don't!' She jerked her head away.

Duncan shifted uneasily, kicking heedlessly at the maltreated turnips with his feet as he sought the best words for what he had to say. Clearing his throat, looking pointedly away, he muttered, 'I'm sorry.'

Kate seemed not to hear.

'I said, I'm sorry.' He almost shouted it at her now.

'I heard you the first time,' she retorted.

'About . . . you know . . . when I kissed you,' he went on, determined now to have his say. 'I shouldn't have. Not like that . . . Like I say, I'm sorry.'

'Aye,' she agreed vehemently. 'So you should be.'

'I know that fine. But I couldn't help myself, see.'

'You frightened me!'

'I didn't mean to. I just wanted to kiss you.'

'You did more than kiss me, Duncan Auld.'

'Aye, well, you're right bonny, Kate.'

'You still shouldn't have done it,' she insisted. 'You had no right.'

He fiddled with the soil for a full minute while she sat in silence, then finally blurted out, 'I really like you, Kate. I want to walk out with you.'

'No!' Relieved though she was to be back on speaking terms with him, the thought of embarking on a more intense relationship was repugnant. But Kate had never deliberately inflicted pain on another human being and seeing the way his jaw tightened with badly concealed disappointment, added, 'I don't think Mum and Dad would let me go out with a lad,' trying to make the rejection less cruel.

Duncan was well aware of Dorothy Brebner's over-protective attitude. 'No,' he agreed slowly. 'I s'pose you're right.'

'Oy! Youse pair! What do you think youse're doing?' Henry's voice carried clearly over the still field.

They shot to their feet, looking sheepish as he came striding towards them. 'We were just having a wee rest,' Kate defended herself quickly.

'Time enough for lazing about when you've finished for the day. Now get on with it.' He cast a worried eye at the horizon where clouds were gathering darkly.

Kate retrieved her hoe and went back to work. Duncan, taking his time, eventually did the same. Henry stood and watched them for five minutes before turning away and heading back to his own tasks.

'Hey!' Duncan hissed at her and she looked up. 'Friends?'

'Friends,' she agreed, barely pausing in her work.

Duncan's little cottage was the end one of three in the farmyard. The others, unoccupied for many years, sheltered nothing more than a thriving colony of cats and bags of fertilizer. From the window of his kitchen Duncan had a clear view of the back of the farmhouse and he sat there, waiting until the light in Kate's bedroom was extinguished. Then, his heart thumping uncomfortably, he jammed his cap on his head, fastened his newly polished boots, straightened the tie which was threatening to throttle him and let himself out.

'I wanted to have a wee word with you, Mr Brebner,' Duncan muttered when Henry answered his knock.

'At this hour?' Henry snapped. 'Can't it wait?' He had been dozing contentedly in his chair and resented the disturbance.

'It's personal.' Duncan kept his voice low, keenly aware of Kate's presence above, hoping she was asleep.

Henry grunted and walked away, leaving Duncan to close the door and follow him to the parlour.

Dorothy's eyes flew to Duncan's feet and she didn't greet

him until she was satisfied they were clean. 'Don't stand there blocking the light, lad,' she said. 'Sit yourself down.'

Screwing his cap in his hand, Duncan perched on the edge of a chair and seemed trapped in silence.

'Well?' Henry barked, glancing at the grandmother clock.

'I . . . I was wanting a wee word with you,' Duncan stammered.

'Aye. So you said,' Henry responded unhelpfully.

'About Kate.' There! He had said it. Duncan, placed his cap on the floor and waited.

Dorothy smothered a smile and looked firmly at her hands.

'What about Kate?' Henry asked.

Duncan swallowed noisily. He had hoped they would know what he meant without the need for lengthy explanations. 'I'm wanting to take her out.'

'Och, you are, are you?' Henry fixed the unfortunate lad with his most intimidating stare.

Duncan nodded. 'Aye.'

'So what's stopping you?'

Duncan gulped. 'You.'

'Me!' Henry was enjoying this now.

'Aye, well, that is . . . well I asked her, see. And she said she didn't think she'd be allowed. Not to go out with lads.'

'And neither she is,' Dorothy confirmed it coldly. 'There's plenty of time for that. She's only seventeen yet.'

'Aye, I know. But it's not as if you don't know me. And . . . and I'd look after her. Bring her home on time . . .'

Henry let go of a huge, bellowing guffaw. 'Aye, you would that, or you'd have me to answer to.'

Duncan brightened perceptibly. 'Can I then?' he asked, his eyes alive with hope.

Henry looked across at his wife. 'Well, hen, what do you say to it?'

Dorothy looked less forbidding in the soft yellow glow of

the standard lamp but when she spoke her voice was hard. 'I'll not have Kate getting herself a bad name, hanging round with lads at her age.'

Duncan's heart plummeted, only to soar wildly as she went on.

'Still, so long as you have her home here by ten o'clock, and not one minute later, I don't see as it would do any harm.'

'Braw!' Duncan scrambled to feet, beaming.

'But – ' Dorothy fixed him with a penetrating gaze – 'Just one night a week. Saturday night.'

'Aye, Mrs Brebner.'

'And no carry on, mind. No sneaking into corners. You bring her home on the ten o'clock bus from town, and straight back to this front door. I'll be watching for youse.'

'Aye, Mrs Brebner.'

Dorothy nodded, satisfied that he was sufficiently terrified to behave himself. 'Right then.'

'Well, who'd have thought it?' Henry mused, coming back into the room after seeing Duncan out.

'Only you could have missed it,' his wife answered sharply. 'The lad's been making cows' eyes at her for months.'

Henry shook his head. 'Can't say I've noticed. And they've always been friends. More like brother and sister.'

'Aye, but that was when they were just weans. They've grown up now. You be sure and keep an eye on them, Henry.'

Henry recalled the way he had caught them fooling around in the field that afternoon. 'Aye,' he agreed grimly. 'I'll watch them all right.' He sat thoughtfully for a moment then added, 'I'm surprised at you though, agreeing to it.'

'Och, Duncan's maybe not awful bright but he's a nice enough lad. And better him than someone we don't know.'

'Aye. I suppose you're right. You usually are.'

'Aye.' She put her knitting aside and tidied round, ready for bed, a thin smile on her lips. Duncan and Kate? She might have wished for someone with more prospects, for the girl's sake, but this could work out very nicely, given a little encouragement. Married to Duncan, if things went that far, Kate would still be available to help about the house and farm, to look after them in their old age. And that, after all, had been the whole point of getting herself a daughter.

THREE

The jubilation Duncan had felt on gaining the Brebners' approval soon dissipated under Kate's adamant refusal to go out with him. A martyr to his raging hormones, he simply couldn't get her out of his mind, and had Kate known just what he did to her in his fevered imagination, she would have had good reason to be frightened. Nursing a crush that bordered on obsession, Duncan lost no opportunity to work beside her, his already slow pace further retarded by the amount of time he spent watching her. Despite her increasing coolness he managed to convince himself that it was only a matter of time and persistence before she agreed to walk out with him.

Irritated by his repeated invitations, made increasingly uncomfortable by the way his eyes followed her wherever she went, Kate – unaware of her mother's plans for her future – resorted to ignoring him completely.

'I don't know what's wrong with you these days.' Dorothy launched her attack one afternoon while Kate, her work in the fields finished for the day, supervised the twins, who were supposed to be doing a few simple sums for homework. 'You've no need to be so snappy with Duncan. The lad's soft on you, anyone can see that, and you won't even give him the time of day.'

Kate ignored her mother and concentrated on the children. 'Eddy, look at the mess you're making. If you make a mistake, cross it through with just one line, like the teacher told you to. Don't scribble it out like that.' She did her best with a rubber, then shoved the book back across the table. 'Come on. You know how to do this. It's only adding up. It's easy.'

'Eddy's stupid, Eddy's stupid,' Victoria chanted, finishing off her own neat work and jumping down from the table to display it proudly to her mother.

'Aye, very good.' Dorothy gave it no more than a passing glance but kissed the child fondly.

'Let me see it, Vicky. We'd better make sure it's right.' Kate held her hand out for the book.

'It is right,' Vicky insisted sulkily. 'It's Eddy that's stupid. Stupid Eddy, Stupid Eddy.'

Edward jerked out a foot and landed a sharp kick on his sister's shin, grinning with satisfaction when she howled in pain.

'*Stop it*! Stop it this instant,' Dorothy complained. 'Kate, make them behave.'

'Hurry up, Eddy. Just finish that last sum and then you can play out for a wee while,' Kate promised him.

The boy cheered up instantly and finished the sum with apparent ease.

'All right. Go and get changed.' Kate released them thankfully, then tried to make her own escape. She was thwarted before she reached the door.

'And where do you think you are going?' Dorothy demanded.

'I need to wash my hair.'

'You've not got time. *You* promised the twins they could go out to play so *you* can be the one to keep an eye on them. You know fine they can't be trusted in the yard.'

Kate knew that only too well. Strictly forbidden excursions into the various outbuildings had resulted in cuts, scrapes and sundry damage; not to mention the time when they had hidden in the chicken coop, terrorising the hens so much that they had refused to lay for a full week, or the time during the war when they had opened a gate, letting the cattle stray into a field of precious wheat where they did untold damage.

'If you've nothing better to do while you wait, run the iron over my clean pinny.' Dorothy pointed to the laundry basket.

Sighing, Kate plugged the iron into the light socket and waited for it to heat. Sometimes she felt like a servant; an unpaid one at that. For all the work she did about the house and farm she was given nothing more than pocket money. She yearned for a proper job, and had wanted to be a teacher, but an office or shop, or even a factory would do; anywhere where she could meet other girls and make friends. So confined was she to the farm that she had even lost touch with her ex-classmates.

'Now then.' Dorothy settled back in the big wooden chair by the range, watching her daughter closely as she returned to her original theme. 'I'd have thought you'd be glad of the chance to go out with Duncan. You're always complaining that you never go anywhere.'

Kate attacked the crumpled apron as if it were her personal enemy. 'I told you. I don't want to go out with him.'

'He's a nice enough lad.'

'Is he?' she asked caustically, thumping the iron down hard.

'I don't understand you, Kate. I really don't.' Dorothy shook her greying head in exasperation.

Kate turned flashing dark eyes on her mother. 'I don't want to go out with Duncan. I want to go to town on Saturday nights with the other lassies,' she cried passionately. 'I want to go the pictures, to the dancing. Anywhere! I just want to have some fun.'

'You're far too young.'

'But not too young to go out with Duncan? What's the difference?' she demanded angrily.

'The difference is' – Dorothy rose majestically from her seat and faced her daughter with her formidable bulk – 'We know Duncan. We trust him to behave himself.'

'Well, I don't,' Kate snapped. 'And I am not going out with him.'

'Then you'll go out with no one, not until you're twenty-one.' Dorothy saw all her plans collapsing.

'That's not fair!' Kate faced her mother with her mouth agape, hardly able to believe what she had heard. 'I'm seventeen years old. You can't treat me like a child any more!'

'All the time you live in this house, you'll do as I say. Is that clear?' Dorothy itched to slap the angry face which glowered back at her; to tell this ungrateful girl a few facts which would make her truly beholden to them; to tie her here with dutiful gratitude. She restrained herself with difficulty.

Kate's furious retort was aborted by the arrival of the twins who, for once united, stood wide-eyed with uncertainty in the doorway. Open disagreements were rare in this household, where their mother's word was law.

'Why are youse shouting?' Victoria asked, looking from her mother to her sister with undisguised amazement.

Kate yanked the cable from the light socket and dumped the iron on the hearth to cool. 'Do you want to play out or not?' she barked.

They nodded, too astounded at this display of temper from their sister to indulge in their usual horseplay.

'Get your boots on then.'

They went out, slamming the door behind them and leaving Dorothy fuming in her chair.

Kate perched on the home field gate, watching as the twins raced around, hopefully exhausting themselves in the process. An unremitting routine of hard work left her little free time in which to ponder her situation, but for the last year, since leaving school really, she had become increasingly restless, longing for some of the excitements girls of her age took for granted, for the first taste of independence, to be allowed some choices in her own life. Now, depressed and unhappy, she resented the way her mother was pressurising her into a relationship she did not want.

'Cheer up, lass. You'd think the end of the world was nigh from the look on your face.'

'It probably is,' she retorted glumly.

Henry rested his paunch against the gate and looked at her thoughtfully. 'It's not like you, lass, to be so down in the mouth. Has something happened?'

'Nothing special.'

'Aye, well then, if it's not special you'll not mind talking to your old dad about it.'

Kate sighed. 'It's Mum.'

'Oh aye?' he chuckled.

'She wants me to go out with Duncan. And if I don't I'm not to be allowed to go out anywhere until I'm twenty-one. I'll be too old to enjoy myself by then!'

'Too old!' Henry stifled a chortle of amusement and sucked air noisily though a gap in his teeth. He wasn't unaware of his wife's plans for Kate and in truth it would be reassuring to know the lass would be around to care for them in their old age. Duncan might be a wee bit slow-witted but at least he had none of the fancy ideas that were filling the heads of the young 'uns these days. Aye, he thought, gazing out over his fields, Duncan Auld would stay on the farm, like his father before him, until the day they carried him away in a box and Kate, a country lass through and through, would be safe and well enough cared for, if only she would see sense. Still, the way Dorothy was going about it, trying to force them together, was likely to have the very opposite effect.

'Look, lass, your mother's only saying go out with Duncan,

not marry the lad. And you do want to get out and enjoy yourself, don't you?'

'Aye, of course I do! All the other girls were allowed into town even before they left school.'

'So, maybe you should compromise. Let Duncan take you out, enjoy yourself. Your mother will be happy because she knows she can trust Duncan and you'll be out among the other young 'uns.'

'I do not want to go out with Duncan,' she repeated, enunciating each syllable separately.

'Why not?' he asked. 'What's wrong with the lad? I thought youse were friends?'

It was much too late to tell him exactly why she couldn't feel safe with Duncan. 'I don't like him that way,' she muttered.

'Och, go out with the lad a time or two. By the time you both decide you've had enough of each other, well, I daresay your mother will have got accustomed to the idea of you getting out and about a bit.' But with any luck at all the two of them would hit it off, he thought. Though better not to let Kate guess the way his mind was working. 'And who knows,' he went on. 'You might meet other folk to pal about with. I hear the Palace Ballroom in Inverannan is a fine place for you young 'uns meeting up.' He looked ahead, not meeting her eyes and so missing their appalled expression.

Why, she wondered, was everyone so anxious to pair her off with Duncan? Even before that ghastly episode she would not have considered going out with him. He had no ambition, was lazy to the point of idleness and frequently stank. And surely her parents must know that Duncan's brawny good looks disguised a meagre intelligence. At school he had been teased for being backward and the way he moved around the farm with slow, plodding steps, always waiting to be told what to do, even with tasks which were repeated day after day, was a fair reflection of his mental abilities. For her parents to want to pair her off with him was insulting. Did they really have so little care for her future, she wondered disconsolately? She stared blindly out across the field, immersed in her own dismal thoughts until Henry's furious roar made her jump.

'Get off that wall,' he bellowed at his son, who was systematically pushing stones from the top of the carefully built drystone wall that divided the fields. 'Little bugger. Needs his backside tanning.' But it was said with affection.

Edward, who had been so absorbed in his task of destruction that he had not noticed his father, jumped, appeared to lose his balance and fell with a shriek, landing out of sight in the other field.

There was a moment of stillness while they watched, fully expecting Edward's tousled head to reappear. When nothing happened Kate and her father exchanged one frantic look.

Bloody hell!' Henry rushed to open the gate while Kate jumped down, raced across the grass and clambered over the wall.

'Oh no . . .' Her heart seemed to stop at the sight of the inert figure. 'Edward,' she said gently, bending over him, 'can you hear me?'

Henry landed beside her with an awkward thump. When he saw his son's still form his face went grey. 'Don't move him,' he ordered. 'Away back to the house and call for an ambulance.'

Kate hesitated for a just a second then turned and scrambled back over the wall, tearing the skin on her hands in her frantic haste. On the other side she was stunned to find Victoria in the grip of uncontrollable giggles. A horrible suspicion formed in her mind. Cautiously she peered back over the wall to where her father, looking ready to collapse with shock, was kneeling with his face in his hands. Eddy was still unmoving and Kate felt fresh panic well in her chest. But then, just as she was about to run to the house after all, he opened an eye and, finding her glaring at him, couldn't hold back a triumphant grin.

'Got youse!' he chortled.

Henry jerked up as if he had been shot in the behind. While Edward still giggled he grabbed him by the scruff of the neck and walloped his backside with a plank-like hand. The laughter sharpened into shrieks of pain.

'Try another trick like that and you'll not sit down for a year,' Henry promised, thrusting his tearful son away from him. 'Now away back to the house and get to bed the pair of youse.'

Needing no second invitation, Edward scaled the wall like an agile monkey and the twins pelted away.

Henry sank back on to the grass and thumped his chest. 'Bloody stupid trick,' he said, still looking decidedly shaken. 'Could have bloody killed me.'

A big, blustery figure who, in his late fifties, still managed more physical work than many a younger man, Henry had seemed solid, immutable, like the very land he farmed. Now, his face the colour of putty and a slight tremor to his hands, he looked fragile, vulnerable.

A shiver started in Kate's scalp and prickled its way along her spine. 'We'd better go in. Mum'll wonder what's been going on.' She helped him to his feet, feeling him lean on her as he heaved himself up.

FOUR

A week later, in the early hours of the morning, the event which was to change the lives of everyone at Brebner's farm occurred without anyone being aware of it.

Sometime between midnight and five forty-five – when his wife woke with a start to berate him loudly for allowing his alarm clock to ring and ring – Henry Brebner simply stopped breathing.

'Kate! Kate . . .' Dorothy's anguished wail was so unlike her usual strident roar that Kate raced along the landing half-dressed. Dorothy, in tent-like flannelette nightdress and pink hairnet, but minus her teeth, stood at her bedroom door. Unable to speak, she merely pointed, then stood back and waited for Kate to see for herself.

Kate hovered in the doorway, unable to bring herself to go into the room, terrified of what she might find. From where she stood she could see her father, a huge motionless mound under the barely disturbed covers. Her heart in her mouth, she tiptoed across the room and gazed down at him. His eyes were closed, his mouth slightly open, as if he had been snoring, and he wore an expression of unusual contentment. Kate extended a trembling hand and touched his face. It was cold, the skin flaccid.

'Do something!' her mother implored from the doorway.

Kate, fighting for self-control, managed to find the words. 'I don't think there is anything I can do. I . . . I think he's dead, Mum.'

'No! No, he's not. Of course he's not. Don't be so stupid, Kate. He's just slept in, that's all. He'll waken in a minute. You'll see. Away downstairs. Get the kettle going. He'll be ready for his cup of tea soon.'

Kate, who felt on the edge of hysteria herself, exerted all her will-power and forced herself to appear calm. 'No . . . Mum, look, here're your clothes. Get yourself dressed.'

'Aye,' Dorothy laughed. 'I can't go around the house like this, can I? Och, what would folk think of me? Aye, I'll get my clothes on. You away and infuse a nice cup of tea.'

Kate waited until she was sure her mother was actually dressing, trying not to hear the way she carried on a one-sided conversation with her dead husband. Then she went to her own room and dragged on her working clothes before racing downstairs and ringing the doctor.

He came quickly, the collar of his pyjamas visible under his shirt, his face still flushed with sleep, his fair hair tousled, a haze of light stubble on his chin. Kate met him at the door.

'Your father?' he asked.

'Aye,' she nodded, feeling strangely detached now, as if this horror was happening somewhere else, her emotions suspended by the weight of responsibility thrust upon her.

He smiled at her gently and put a light hand on her shoulder. 'Show me where he is,' he said softly.

His kindness was almost her undoing. Sudden tears flooded her eyes, blinding her. 'Upstairs.'

He ran ahead and she followed. 'In here?'

He opened the door on a scene of such absolute normality that for a moment Kate wondered if she had imagined the whole thing. Her father was still abed, apparently sleeping, while her mother was sitting at her dressing table, counting the strokes as she brushed her long grey hair, as if this was any ordinary day.

The doctor examined his patient with quiet efficiency while

Kate watched and Dorothy progressed to pinning her hair into its customary tight bun.

'Mrs Brebner? I'm Doctor Torrance.' He addressed her directly, forcing her to look at him.

She smiled. 'Doctor Torrance. I heard there was a new doctor at the surgery. How kind of you to call. I'm afraid Henry must have been overworking. He's very tired this morning and having a wee lie-in.' There was something brittle in her voice and her eyes were too bright.

'Mrs Brebner.' He took her hand and held it. 'I am afraid it's more serious than that. I'm very sorry but your husband has passed away.'

Dorothy didn't move. Not a single muscle twitched while she looked into the doctor's sympathetic eyes.

'You do understand what I am saying, Mrs Brebner?' he asked, sliding his fingers gently to her wrist and unobtrusively checking her pulse.

Dorothy nodded and then seemed to fold in on herself. Torrance moved quickly but she was a great deal larger than he and he struggled to stop her slipping from the stool. Kate rushed to help him.

'She can't stay here. Is there another bed she could go to?' he asked.

'My room.'

Together they heaved and dragged Dorothy's inert form along the landing and finally managed to get her into bed, where she groaned gently then opened her eyes.

Torrance delved into his bag and produced a bottle of tablets, which he handed to Kate. 'Best give her two of these. They'll knock her out until we've tidied things up here. Then let her have one at a time until you think she's starting to cope.'

Kate took the bottle and turned it over and over in her hands. 'Thank you.'

'I can let you have some too,' he offered. 'Just until you're over the worst.'

For a moment she was tempted, wanting nothing more than to emulate her mother, crawl into bed and sleep, to wake up and discover it had all been a terrible dream. But common sense and an awareness of her responsibility prevailed. 'No, I can't. There's the children, the farm, people to be told.' And it all seemed to have fallen on her shoulders.

'All right. See to your mother then. I'll wait downstairs.'

Kate persuaded Dorothy to swallow two of the tablets, then leaving her with her face turned to the wall, weeping quietly, she crept out of the room.

Doctor Torrance was waiting for her in the hall. When she came downstairs he stepped forward, put an arm around her shoulders and led her into the parlour. 'Is it just you and your mother in the house, Miss Brebner?'

Kate made a great effort, managing to sound fairly composed as she said, 'My brother and sister are still in bed. They're eight.' As she spoke she realised that the twins must surely be awake by now. She was glad of her mother's discipline which absolutely forbade them to leave their rooms in the morning until called.

'You'll need someone to help you.'

'There's Duncan.'

'Ah, a young lad with a moustache?' Gavin Torrance had seen Duncan hovering in the farm yard, obviously wondering what was going on. 'I think I saw him outside.'

'He lives in one of the farm cottages.'

'I see. But he's not very old, is he? Isn't there an adult, an aunt or uncle you could ask to come and stay for a day or two?' His pale blue eyes smiled softly into her brown ones.

'My uncle and cousins.'

'Are they far away?'

'Up by Pitochrie.'

'Can you contact them? Have they got a telephone?'

She nodded.

'Right then. That's the first thing to do. Your uncle'll know what to do. I'll call back this afternoon just to make sure everything's all right.' He gave her hand a squeeze and stood up. 'Now I'll have to get back. Are you sure you'll be all right?'

She raised her head and gave a brave smile. 'Aye. Thank you, Doctor.'

'My advice is to get on with things as normally as possible.' Doctor Torrance had visited many farms in his one year in general practice and knew that cows had to be milked regardless of human tragedy. 'Better to keep busy.'

'Aye. I suppose so.' She followed him to the door and watched him drive away, a leaden, hopeless feeling in her stomach.

'Kate?' She jerked round at the sound of Duncan's perplexed voice. 'What's going on? Why have you not fetched the cows down? Where's your Dad?'

Kate looked at him, tears streaming unchecked down her face. Her words emerged, choked by huge sobs. 'He's dead. Dad's dead.' Desperate for comfort, she flung herself into his arms and clung to him as though frightened to ever let go. Over her bowed head, Duncan smiled.

Bernard Baillie Brebner arrived the next morning, striding into the house and immediately taking charge, insensitive to Kate's grief and ordering her around as if she were a skivvy. The twins, old enough to understand that they had lost their father, found their sister distracted, their mother unapproachable and their uncle terrifying. They retreated into miserable silence and stayed in their rooms.

Bernie was a very different type of man from his late brother. Overbearing, loud-voiced and plain spoken, he ordered Dorothy to pull herself together, yelled at Kate to stop that bloody greeting, and roared at Duncan to get off his lazy arse, alienating all three. Profitably farming his own acres, just south of Pitochrie in the north of Strathannan, he was openly critical of his dead brother's less ambitious approach. He organised the funeral and other formalities with the same ruthless efficiency with which he ran his farm. Within a week Henry Brebner was tidily consigned to the ground in Inverannan cemetery and the family was gathered in the parlour for the reading of the will.

Bernie, who as executor presumably had some foreknowledge of what was to be revealed, insisted that even the twins were present for this solemn occasion, a decision deplored by Kate whose job it was to control them. Irked by the restrictions of the last sorrow-filled week, Edward and Victoria, uncomfortable in their funeral clothes, were full of unburned energy. While the adults waited for the solicitor in a strangely expectant though subdued manner, they fidgeted, whined and bickered.

'Please, Edward, sit still for just a little while longer,' Kate pleaded.

He continued to swing his legs, banging his stout shoes heftily against the chair legs in the most irritatingly noisy way.

'I'm bored,' he complained.

'I know. But it won't be long now.'

The legs continued to swing and Victoria, equally disgruntled, joined in, rattling her own feet in an ever faster rhythm, competing with her brother for her share of attention.

'Kate, keep them quiet for goodness sake,' Dorothy snapped. Though she had rallied well from the original shock, the funeral had been an ordeal and the strain was clearly visible on her face.

Kate understood the confusion the twins were feeling but her own nerves were dangerously stretched and she rounded on them furiously now, scolding them soundly and succeeding only in reducing them both to noisy tears.

'Now look what you've done!' Bernie vented his fury on Kate then turned on the twins. 'If I'd my belt . . .' The threat was enough to bring instant silence. They glowered briefly at him then sat with their blond heads lowered, sniffing and rubbing at their watery eyes.

'I'm sorry to have kept you waiting.' The solicitor, round and shiny from the top of his bald pate to the tired material of his dark suit, took his place in the centre of the room.

It was as expected. The farm, including the house, was to go to Edward when he came of age and Dorothy was to be guaranteed a home there for her lifetime. In the meantime the business would be administered by a trust composed of Dorothy herself, Bernie and the solicitor. Kate, who judging from the economical ways of the household had always assumed that there was not a lot of actual cash in the bank, was mildly surprised to hear that there was a sizeable personal bequest for her mother, and even more startled to learn of a very generous one for Victoria.

'To Duncan Auld, the cottage in which he now lives, to be his, rent-free, for the rest of his life.'

Duncan, standing uncomfortably by the door, looked up, clearly surprised, and then grinned his delight.

'To my son, Edward, my watch. To my daughter, Victoria, the silver candlesticks which were my own mother's. To my brother, Bernard, my gold cuff-links and tie pin.' Kate listened, painfully aware of the omission of her own name. But she was his eldest daughter, his first-born child. Surely her father would not have left her out? No, it was unthinkable. He had loved her, she knew that. She waited while the solicitor ran on through a list of minor items, dividing Henry's personal property among his family; small mementos for everyone, even his two nephews.

And then, just as she was starting to believe that he truly had forgotten her, she heard her name.

'And lastly, to Kate Brebner – ' Kate looked up, feeling relief flood through her – 'the sum of fifty pounds.'

The solicitor folded his papers and fell into quiet conversation with Dorothy and Bernie. Kate merely sat, rooted to her chair, the pain visible on her face which was white with shock.

'Are you sure?' she asked at last, feeling every eye in the room turning on her.

The solicitor looked at her kindly. 'Aye, lass, I'm sure. In fact this latest will was drawn up less than a month ago so we can all be certain that it exactly represents the late Mr Brebner's wishes.'

It was later that evening. The twins were in bed. Kate, going about her tasks quite automatically, kept her mother, uncle and two cousins supplied with tea and washed piles of dirty dishes, feeling like an outcast. Shock had given way to a dreadful feeling of rejection. She had, in fact, expected nothing from her father's will, but to be left a mere fifty pounds when Victoria was the recipient of a sum fifty times as great was a terrible blow, an indication surely of some failure on her part. But in what way had she disappointed him for him to treat her like this? She had always worked hard, tried to be a dutiful daughter; had not argued when forced to leave school at fifteen when she knew she could easily have stayed on and won qualifications which might have led to her becoming the teacher she had always secretly yearned to be. Nor had she complained about the way she was used around the farm, doing the work of a labourer as well as acting as household skivvy and nursemaid.

She took a final tray of tea into the parlour and, over-sensitive now, felt that her mother, uncle and cousins behaved as if she wasn't there, taking what she offered without so much as a 'thank you.' Helping herself to a cup of tea, she sank wretchedly on to a chair in the very corner of the room and sat there as if invisible.

Finally Bernie stood up. 'David will bring his things down on Sunday. The girl and young Duncan can keep things ticking over until then.'

Dorothy nodded. 'Aye. We'll manage fine until then, Bernie. And thank you.'

'Just doing my duty,' he replied gruffly. He and his two strapping sons went out to where their car was parked in the yard. Again it was as if Kate no longer existed.

Fighting back tears, she waited until her mother came back into the room and said, 'I'm going to bed now, Mum. I'll see to the dishes in the morning.'

Dorothy frowned. 'Do them now, Kate. You'll not have time in the morning. You and Duncan will have to manage on your own for a day or two. You'd best set your alarm half an hour early.'

Wearily Kate gathered the dirty cups and plates. Never had she felt so unloved, so out of place. Rare self-pity sent tears coursing down her face, blinding her so that she fumbled, knocking a half-empty cup over, spilling the dregs on the carpet.

'For goodness sake! Be careful,' Dorothy snapped.

It was the last straw. Kate crouched over the spilt tea and wept, great wrenching, gasping sobs. Dorothy, still in her chair, made no move to comfort her but sat waiting until, gradually, the tears began to ease.

Finally exhausted, Kate looked up and was further hurt by the way her mother was staring at her. 'Why?' she choked.

Dorothy sighed. 'Well, you had to know sometime I suppose.' In truth this was something she had hoped to keep from the girl for a good many years yet, but then no one had expected a big, hearty man like Henry Brebner to pass away so abruptly.

'Know what?' Kate pleaded. 'What have I done? What did I do wrong?' She knelt, resting on her heels, unable to get up, her face blotched with misery. 'Why did he leave Vicky so much but only leave me fifty pounds? What did I do to upset him?'

Dorothy cursed her husband for being so inconsiderate as to die and leave her to sort this out. He would have dealt with this so much better than her – when the time was right. She turned her anger on the unfortunate girl. 'Self, self, self. Is that all you can think about at a time like this?'

'No!'

'Henry Brebner was a good man. He raised you, fed you, clothed you and treated you like his own. How can you be so ungrateful?'

Kate felt a strange emptiness fill her head. 'I'm not ungrateful,' she stammered.

'Seventeen years. And all that time nothing but love. Good food, new shoes, everything you needed. And we didn't have to do it. We weren't obliged to have you. We could have left you where you were. Aye,' she snorted. 'Oh aye, things would have been very different for you then. All from the goodness of our hearts we did it. And now you throw it back in my face and complain because he's left you fifty pounds!'

'Left me where?' Kate whispered the words, feeling the room spin around her as her world collapsed.

'We took you in when you were just three days old. Took a real chance on you turning out right.'

'I don't understand . . .'

'You are adopted. Not our flesh and blood.'

Kate closed her eyes, feeling the words echoing round in her head as if in some great void. 'Adopted?'

'Aye. And now you know.'

'But why?'

'Why! Why? Because your own mother didn't want you, that's why. Because she'd no husband to give you a name. A wee bastard, that's what you were, and if it hadn't been for us taking you in, that's what you'd be known as now. Mind you,' Dorothy confided with heedless cruelty, 'it was Henry who wanted you. I always said it wasn't the same. Not like having one of our own.'

It explained so much. 'Then why did you take me?' Kate whispered, knowing that she was offering herself for more pain but desperately needing answers.

'Och, we'd been married a while and no sign of bairns of our own. Henry, well, he always wanted children. Wanted a lad really, he did, but I wasn't having that. A lad wouldn't have been content to stay on the farm knowing that it was going to Bernie's lads in the end. I said if he wanted a bairn it'd have to be a girl, so's you could grow up to be a help around the house. Then, of course, I was blessed with weans of my own after all and Henry got his son to carry on the farm after him.'

'Is that all I am? Unpaid help?'

Dorothy looked at her daughter's anguished face and seemed to relent a little. She would need to be careful; if she upset the girl too much she might just up and leave and then it would all have been for nothing. 'Och no, lass, of course you're not. But every mother wants a daughter. And all lassies help around the house.'

Kate had a piercingly clear picture of just what her role was here. 'I always thought you loved me,' she said, dangerously close to tears again.

'And so I do,' Dorothy lied. 'Och, lass, don't go upsetting yourself over nothing. I'm maybe not awful good at showing it but I'm right fond of you and I don't want you to feel hurt by this. Your father knew you wouldn't need much money of your own. You've a job and a home here with me. I'll feed and clothe you just like I always have. Until you get wed. And the way young Duncan feels about you, well, maybe that's not too long away, eh? That's why he made sure of the cottage for Duncan, see. So's you'd always have a home here. Och, you've no need of money, lass. But for all Henry knew, by the time Vicky gets to your age I could be dead too and that money will be all she has.' She got up and lifted the cup from the floor. 'Now away to your bed, Kate. I'll see to the dishes. You'll see the sense of it in the morning.'

Perhaps she did. Sometimes Kate felt she understood, but at others she felt the terrible emptiness growing inside, threatening to swamp her.

David Brebner, a faithful imitation of his father and the younger of her two cousins – only he wasn't really her cousin now – had come to take charge of the farm. It was clear, from the day he arrived, that he was fully aware of Kate's unfortunate start in life. He made it quite obvious that he regarded her as nothing more than a charity case, someone who should be eternally grateful for the generosity of the Brebner family. Dorothy, intimidated by his overbearing manner and still mourning the loss of her husband, seemed glad to surrender the decision-making to her nephew, and, though aware of her daughter's unhappiness, couldn't find the energy to intervene and make the girl's life easier.

Sometimes, Kate thought despondently, leaning on her hoe and staring blankly over the green fields, it was as if Henry had never existed, so completely had David taken over. The routine of life went on: the same chores, the same paltry payment, the same lack of appreciation. But now it was as if she didn't belong here, as though she were no longer a part of it all.

Kate was so lost in her sad thoughts that she failed to hear David until it was too late. His foot kicked out, knocking aside the hoe she had been leaning on, causing her to stumble.

'You're not paid to stand around and watch while other folk break their backs. Now get off your fucking arse and do some bloody work.'

Henry Brebner had been a stern taskmaster, but always fair, and never would he have used such language to a woman.

Kate's temper flared dangerously. 'I don't get paid at all,' she retorted, scrambling to her feet and facing David, her eyes boring into his. 'And don't talk to me like that!'

'Ungrateful little bitch,' he snarled taking a threatening step towards her.

'Leave her alone.' Duncan, working a few yards away, ran across the field, trampling plants beneath his booted feet and imposed his sturdy frame between them.

David's face flushed puce. A vein bulged alarmingly in his forehead and for one dreadful moment Kate believed he would actually hit Duncan. 'You little bastard,' he snarled. 'I'll have you off this farm and out of that house – '

'You can't. Mr Brebner saw to that,' Duncan said, squaring up, ready to fight if necessary.

Like most bullies, when challenged, David backed down. 'Aye. Which just shows what a stupid old man he was,' he muttered, stepping back.

'Don't!' Kate spluttered, shoving Duncan aside furiously. 'Don't you ever criticise my father. He was a good, kind man . . .'

David snorted. 'Aye, Kate, but he wasn't your father, was he? And don't you forget it. This family doesn't owe you a thing. If you want to keep a roof over your head you'd better start earning your keep. Now get back to bloody work. Both of youse.' With that he turned and walked away.

'Bastard!' Duncan hissed.

Kate stood, her shoulders hunched, staring at the ground.

'Och, don't let him upset you. He's nothing. He gets paid to work here just the same as we do. Besides, he's a right arse.'

He stationed himself just behind Kate's shoulder and waited for some response, aware that he still had to be careful in the way he approached her. Then, to his horror, he realised that her shoulders were shaking. 'Don't cry, Kate,' he said, bringing his deep voice to as near a whisper as he could manage and setting one cautious hand on the top of her arm.

'It's Dad,' she sobbed suddenly. 'I miss him. I miss him so much.'

'I know,' he murmured, seizing his chance to gather her into his arms.

Kate sank her face against his broad chest and felt his arms go round her. Thank goodness he had got over his childish crush on her, she thought. At least there was still one person she could turn to.

Duncan held her as tightly as he could, stroking her hair and murmuring words of comfort into her ear. As his chin came to rest on her head, he was grinning broadly and, though he was careful not to let her feel it, there was the familiar surge of hopeful heat in his groin.

FIVE

In Inverannan, Meggie Laing opened her eyes to the sound of torrential rain. At five o'clock on an early autumn morning the bedroom was pitch black. Shivering, she got out of bed and negotiated her way round the room on instinct, gathering her clothes and taking the utmost care not to wake Oliver, who did not need to rise for another two and a half hours.

Half an hour later she parked her little Ford outside the nearest of her two general stores. Dashing through the rain, she unlocked the door and went straight through to the back room, where she set a kettle on the gas stove, ready for her early morning cup of tea, a smile of contentment hovering around her mouth.

Although Meggie employed capable staff, she made a point of keeping a personal eye on her business, making quite sure that her high standards were maintained. But only here did she play an active role in the day-to-day running of the business. Set on a corner, half-way up a steep hill of stone-built, terraced houses, a mile or so from the town centre, this particular shop had been the first of her acquisitions and Meggie still derived enormous pleasure from working here, dealing with customers she had known for more than fifteen years, maintaining the personal links which made this little shop such a happy focus of the community.

'By, it feels like winter already.' Ronnie Sandys hurried in with the morning delivery of papers, dumping them on the counter ready for her to sort out.

'Aye, it does,' Meggie agreed, smiling at him. 'Have you time for a cup of tea this morning?'

'Not really,' he grinned. 'But I'll have one anyway.' He leaned against the counter and waited, puffing on a cigarette, until she handed him a steaming mug.

They drank in companionable silence. Meggie had known Ronnie since she had first taken over this shop, sixteen years ago. He and his wife, Sally, were her greatest friends. Red-haired, round-faced and freckled, Ronnie gave an impression of irrepressible cheerfulness. Perhaps his hair was a little thinner and his stocky figure slightly less round than it had been before the war, but on the whole, she thought as he sipped at his tea, the passing years had changed him very little.

'Has Sally thought any more about what we spoke about the other day?' she asked as he held his mug out for a refill.

He nodded. 'Aye. She's right keen, Meggie.'

Knowing him as well as she did, she couldn't miss the note of regret in his voice. 'But you're not?'

He shrugged and said, 'No, it's not that,' then grinned and admitted, 'Aye. I suppose I'm not.'

'You're just old-fashioned, Ronnie, that's your trouble,' she teased, her dark eyes flashing.

'Maybe I am,' he retorted, suddenly defensive. 'But I don't understand why she wants to go out to work. It'd be too much for her, what with the weans and all and it's not as if we need the money. We manage fine.'

'Money's got nothing to do with it,' Meggie asserted firmly, beginning to sort out the papers. 'And as for it being too much for her, don't forget that Sally ran your business single-handed while you were away fighting in the war.'

'That was different.'

'Aye,' Meggie agreed readily. 'Too true it was. She worked from four in the morning until five at night, then went home

46

and looked after the weans. That was real hard work, Ronnie. Working for me won't be like that.'

He sighed. 'It's still working. The weans need her at home.'

'And that's where she'll be when they get home from the school.' She abandoned the papers and went to stand in front of him. 'Sally enjoys working, Ronnie. Lots of women do. It gets us out of the house, gives us something else to think about. I just want her to manage the other shop for me, do the paperwork, keep an eye on the staff. She can choose her own hours.'

He sighed again, put his empty mug down on the counter and smiled wryly. 'Och, I know, Meggie. I know. Truth is, I think she's finding it a bit strange, being on her own all day now the weans are all at the school. I suppose it might do her good to be able to get away from the house for a wee while.'

'Well then.'

'But I still don't like it.'

'Just let her try it, Ronnie. Give it three months. If it doesn't work out I'll find someone else. That's fair, isn't it?'

Meggie could be very persuasive when she tried and Ronnie knew when he was beaten. 'Why do I get the feeling youse're ganging up on me?' he asked, his good humour returning.

'Because we are, that's why,' she told him, grinning.

'All right. You win. I'll speak to her at lunch-time.' He glanced at his watch. 'I'd best be getting on if I don't want everyone complaining.'

'You can tell me what Sally says when you bring the evening papers,' she said, walking to the door with him.

'Och, you're an impatient woman, Meggie Laing,' he laughed, running through the rain and jumping into his van.

Meggie and Oliver ate their dinner in the sort of tense silence that had become a feature of their mealtimes. Oliver parried all her attempts at conversation with grunts or one-word replies

47

which left his wife fuming with frustration. What, she wondered, had happened to the sensitive, generous man she had married? How could they have drifted so far apart? Was it simply worry about the future of the Strathannan Mining Company? Certainly the problems facing the collieries were serious enough to explain his preoccupied withdrawal. The pits had survived the war years, when every ton of coal was desperately needed, by mining increasingly difficult seams and producing coal of a quality which would have been unacceptable at any other time. But the few good seams were petering out or disappearing along huge fault lines and the enormous sums involved in searching for new strata were beyond the company's means.

Looking back, Meggie knew there was more to her marital difficulties than could be attributed to the failure of the Strathannan Mining Company. This coldness in Oliver's manner had begun with the outbreak of the war. Stirred by patriotism, Oliver had watched his friends join up and had brooded bitterly on the loss of his right leg, a disability which would have kept him out of the action even if he hadn't had the company to run.

Although Oliver maintained that he didn't blame her for his terrible injury, Meggie couldn't help feeling responsible. After all, it had been her own brother, Matty, who had caused it in a fit of jealous anger. There was, too, the matter of her failure to conceive, a continuing disappointment that stood between them like a wall of fog, clouding every other issue in their lives.

So many problems, she thought, shoving her half-finished meal to one side. Well, this was her marriage, her life, and Oliver the only man she had ever truly loved. She would not allow things to drift on like this. She would force him to talk to her. And Sally was a safe enough starting point.

'Sally called in to see me this afternoon,' she began.

'Um.'

'I said, Sally came into the shop today.'

Oliver laid his knife and fork precisely on his plate and finally looked up at her. 'How nice.'

Meggie bit back her exasperation and went on. 'She's agreed to manage the High Street shop. On a trial basis. For three months to start with.'

'Good.'

'I'm really pleased, Oliver. Sal knows the business almost as well as I do. She'll be a great help. Don't you think so?'

Oliver ran a hand through his dark hair, which had flopped forward as he ate. It was a familiar gesture, one she knew and loved. He really was very handsome still, she thought, with his finely chiselled features, strong chin and expressive eyes. In profile he could look rather severe, but full face he seemed softer somehow. If only he would smile more. 'I suppose so,' he said now. 'But the shops are your business. None of my concern.'

'Oliver! That's not true,' she protested.

'Well.' He seemed ready to talk now but his eyes warned her that the conversation would not be a pleasant one. She wished that she had kept quiet, but it was too late for second thoughts. 'You never take any notice of anything I might have to say about the shops. And we both know you don't have to be as involved with them as you are. You shouldn't be working behind the counter. It's degrading.'

'Degrading?'

'Yes, Meggie, degrading. How do you think I feel to know my wife is working as a common shop assistant, like any miner's wife?'

'That's not the same thing, Oliver, and you know it,' she reacted angrily. 'I'm not a shop assistant, I own the shops.'

'Then leave your staff to do what you pay them for and give more attention to your home. And me.'

'But I do. You know I do.'

'Not in things that matter, Meggie,' he corrected her coldly. 'You know I'm not happy about the hours you work. Even when you just had the one shop you were spending far too long there. And though you knew I didn't approve you still went ahead and bought the High Street store.'

'They're good investments, Oliver.'

'There are more important things than making money, Meggie. Us, for instance.'

This was it: the moment of truth which, though she knew it was desperately needed, she dreaded. Getting up, she walked round the table and sat on the chair next to his, reaching out to take his hand. She felt a momentary resistance and thought he was going to draw away from her, but then he gave her fingers a light squeeze. 'It's not just the shops, is it, Oliver? Can't you tell me what's worrying you?'

'You worry me, Meggie,' he responded caustically. 'You're away from five-thirty in the morning until seven or eight o'clock at night. When you finally come home you eat your dinner then go to bed and fall straight asleep. When you do find time to talk to me it's about the shops. You are so bloody proud of yourself. You like rubbing my nose in it, don't you?' His voice was bitter. 'Always going on about how successful they are when you know fine the company's in trouble. It's as if you think you're better than me. Well, let me tell you something, running those shops is simple compared to managing the company.'

Meggie was appalled by the resentment his remarks revealed, but knew that he was at least partially justified. She was proud of all she'd achieved: Starting out with one small, run-down shop and gradually building up the business until she was able to buy a larger store, on the High Street, where she was successfully challenging Hough's, the town's biggest grocers, by offering excellent service, quality products and keen prices.

Meggie knew herself well enough to accept that personal satisfaction and raw ambition were motivating factors. But so too was her determination to provide financial security. Abandoned to the workhouse by her parents, she had experienced enough poverty as a child to have a deep fear of financial ruin. Understanding that the Strathannan Mining Company was on the point of collapse, she had worked relentlessly to secure a future, not just for herself but for Oliver too, and for the children she still hoped to have. She was hurt to realise that her own husband was too proud to acknowledge what she was trying to do, that far from appreciating her efforts, he was actually jealous of her success.

'I'll have more time now that Sally's going to run the High Street shop,' she told him, sensing they were on the edge of a dangerous precipice and biting back her own anger in an attempt to placate him.

'But you won't, Meggie. There'll always be something you think you have to deal with personally. Admit it! You'd rather be in the shops than home here, where you should be.'

Now he turned to look at her and Meggie could see the pain in his eyes. Had she misjudged him? she wondered, feeling a stab of guilt. Was it rejection he was feeling and not jealousy at all? 'I didn't think you minded,' she told him softly. 'You never said you missed me.' And that had hurt too.

'Oh, Meggie! Of course I miss you. I hardly see you these days. You're even too tired to make love.'

'I didn't think you wanted to any more.'

'I do! But how can I wake you up for that when you're always so exhausted?' His hand tightened on hers and she grasped it tightly.

'I didn't realise . . . I mean I thought . . . I thought you just didn't want me.' Her voice cracked with anguish and tears glistened in her eyes, making them unnaturally bright in the shadowy room.

'Meggie . . . of course I want you,' he murmured, his voice more gentle than it had been for many months. He lifted a hand and softly wiped away a tear which was beading at the corner of her eye. 'Don't cry, Meggie. Please don't cry.'

'This is all my fault. I'm making you miserable and I didn't even see it. I thought it was the company, or the war. Or . . .' She hesitated, still reluctant to put her deepest fear into words. Then gathering her courage, knowing that they really must clear the air now, she went on, 'Or because I've never given you a child.'

He tensed instantly. She felt it in the sudden ridigity of his fingers, the way he seemed to hold his breath. 'We both know that must be my fault,' he said coldly. 'You've already had a child. It must be me.'

Despite the warmth in the room, Meggie felt chilled. The illegitimate child she had given birth to when she was barely sixteen was a subject they never mentioned; the identity of the child's father a terrible secret which Meggie carried tight within herself. 'That was a long time ago, Oliver. I'm thirty-three now. It could easily be me.' She waited for some reaction but there was nothing. Oliver stared down at their still-linked hands, his face blank, only the muscle which twitched convulsively at the angle of his jaw betraying his inner tension. 'Does it bother you so much, us not having children?' she asked.

At last he answered her, his voice a whisper. 'I'd have liked a son, like any man. But it bothers me far more to think you don't have time for me in your life.'

'But I do!'

'No, Meggie! No you don't. You know you don't. Not with the shops to run.'

'Do you want me to sell them? I will if you think it will help.' And she meant it. Precious as this independence was to her, it meant nothing at all compared with her feelings for Oliver. Without him it would all have been for nothing.

'Would you? If I asked you to, would you really sell them, Meggie?' he asked, gazing deep into her eyes.

'Aye. I would. Tomorrow if that's what you want.'

He smiled, that wonderful lifting of his mouth which softened his whole face. She noticed tiny crow's feet at the corners of his eyes and wondered how long they had been there, unnoticed by her. 'No, I don't want you to do that,' he assured her, lifting her hand to his mouth and kissing it gently. 'But it helps to know you would. I know how much the business means to you.' He looked away again, apparently lost in thought. When he turned back to her, his smile was gone, his expression serious again. 'With the company the way it is we might be glad of the shops to fall back on,' he admitted.

'Is it that bad?'

He nodded. 'Pretty much. The seams are exhausted. There are others but they run under the river and there are too many faults to make them economically feasible. I'd say we've got another year. Maybe eighteen months at the Dene. Then we'll have to close.'

'What will you do?' She was horrified, hadn't realised it was so bad.

He shrugged. 'I'm not sure. Mining's all I know. I suppose I could look for work with one of the other mining companies. In Fife maybe. They seem to be doing all right.' He laughed briefly. 'So whatever you do, hang on to the shops, Meggie. We might need them.'

'You could always take over the books.' She knew it was the wrong thing to say, even before she had stopped speaking.

His mouth tightened into a grim line and he withdrew his hand. 'I don't think any man would be happy working for his wife.' He almost spat the words out.

'I was joking, Oliver.'

'Well, I wasn't. If you really want to do something to help, spend more time at home, with me. And take on someone else

53

for the corner shop so that at least you won't have to go there at the crack of dawn so often.'

'If that's what you want, I will. I'll put an advertisement in the paper this week. Tomorrow.'

He stared at her. 'You will?'

His obvious amazement hurt her, made her realise how much she had neglected him. 'Aye, I will. I promise. You're right, I should spend more time at home. I'd like that.' She felt his hand searching for hers again and wrapped her fingers tightly round his.

'Truly?' he asked.

'Truly,' she replied.

Very gently he placed a hand behind her head and drew her face closer to his, then kissed her, softly at first but with increasing fervour. She responded instinctively, as she always did. There had been far too few opportunities to prove her love recently.

She closed her eyes as his hand rested on her breasts, rubbing gently at a nipple which hardened instantly, feeling the familiar surge of excitement low in her belly. It was going to be all right, she told herself.

'Let's go to bed,' he whispered in her ear, sounding hoarse.

She rose slowly, bringing him with her, their mouths still locked together, their bodies straining against one another.

Gently he led her upstairs. For that evening at least, their problems were forgotten.

'That's all there is to it, Sal. And you know most of it already.'

'I've forgotten most of it,' Sal admitted with a rueful grin. 'But I'll soon pick it up again.'

'I know you will,' Meggie reassured her friend. 'What's Ronnie saying about it now? Has he got used to the idea?'

'Has he hell!' Sally responded in her usual, blunt manner. 'Not that it'll make a lot of difference to him, the hours he works. I'll still be there when he goes out in the morning and home again by the time he comes in at night. Anyway, he'll just need to put up with it.'

Despite the words, Meggie saw the smile of affection which lightened her friend's face when she spoke about Ronnie and felt a fleeting pang of envy, wishing her own marriage was in a similarly healthy state. 'At least you won't have to get up early for the papers,' she said.

'Aye. Thank goodness. I had enough of that in the war. That is, unless Mrs Snaith would be happier if we took turns, say week and week about?' She turned to the middle-aged woman who with Meggie's guidance had been managing the shop and its staff of five since it opened almost four months ago.

'Och no, hen. It suits me, getting in early. My man, he works at the Netherton mill, starts at six each morning, so I'm awake early anyway. Finishing at twelve suits me fine. Gives me a chance to tidy round a bit and get the dinner on the go before he comes home. No, lass, I'm well suited and I'd rather not change if it's all the same to you.'

'It's fine by me, Mrs Snaith,' Sally assured her happily.

'Right then.' Meggie glanced at her watch, aware of things still to be done in the old shop. 'I'll leave you to it.'

'Aye,' Sally smiled at her friend. 'And thanks, Meggie. This is just what I needed.'

Back at the corner shop, Meggie found the evening papers waiting to be sorted and Vera, who had helped her there for many years, anxious to get off home.

'Dot's husband called in to say she won't be in this afternoon,' she said, slipping into her coat. 'She's got a cold or something. Again,' she added darkly.

'Och!' Meggie couldn't hide her annoyance. 'I wanted to have the evening at home tonight.' Despite her promise to spend more time with Oliver, there always seemed to be some pressing necessity for her presence in one or other of the shops. Dot's unreliability was becoming more than just an irritation.

'I'd offer to stay on a bit but the bairns'll be wanting their tea.' Vera was apologetic. 'I could come back around five though, after Iain gets in, if you like.'

Meggie smiled. 'Thanks, Vera, but that husband of yours will be getting fed up if you spend too much time here. You go on home.'

It was after seven before Meggie wearily locked the door. By the time she had checked the cash and ration coupons, made a superficial job of sweeping the floor, dusty as always with spilt flour and sugar, then restocked the most urgent shelves, it was almost eight o'clock.

'You're late.' Oliver was waiting in the sitting-room, clearly angry.

Meggie kissed his cheek. 'Aye. I'm sorry. Dot didn't come in this afternoon. I had to stay and close up.'

She flung her coat down and hurried to serve the meal, already prepared by her daily help, Mrs Dewar. By the time she actually sat at the table she was too tired to eat. She toyed with her food then pushed the plate away.

'You'll make yourself ill if you don't eat properly,' Oliver commented.

'I'm not hungry.'

'You're exhausted!' But it was said without sympathy. 'I thought you were going to get someone else in to help in that shop?'

Oh no, she thought, not tonight. 'I am.'

'When, Meggie?' He watched her through narrowed lids.

'As soon as I can,' she snapped, regretting it instantly. 'I'm sorry, Oliver. You're right – I am tired. But I can't do everything at once. I had to get Sally started at the High Street shop first. Once she's settled in I shouldn't have to go over there so often and I'll have time to look for a manager for the corner shop. I might have to find someone to replace Dot too. She's far too unreliable. I'm going to have to ask her to leave.'

'And while you're waiting to get that sorted out I suppose you'll be coming in at this time every night?' he asked icily.

'Aye. I suppose I will. But I don't see what else I can do. I can't ask Vera to work any more hours. She's got her family to think of.'

'And what about me? What about all the promises you made to me?'

'It takes time to organise these things, Oliver.'

'Why? What's so difficult about finding someone willing to work in a shop?' he roared. 'The country's full of folk just crying out for a job. Put a notice in the window tomorrow morning and the job will be taken by the afternoon.'

'It's not that simple, Oliver. I need a manager. Someone with experience; someone who knows what they're doing; someone I can trust; someone honest and reliable. And it has to be someone I can get along with. I must like the people who work for me.'

'It seems to me that the people you work with are more important to you than I am,' he accused her angrily.

'Don't be ridiculous!'

'I am not being ridiculous! he bellowed. 'If you ask me it's a bloody good job you can't get pregnant. You'd make a lousy mother, Meggie.'

It cut into her as if he had actually attacked her with a knife. 'That's not fair,' she whispered, appalled.

'It's you. You're the one who's not being fair, Meggie. Not being fair to me. I married you, not those bloody shops. It's time you got your priorities sorted out. I'm not going to go on like this. It's your choice. Get someone in there and spend some time with me, or I warn you, the day will come when you'll find me gone.'

She could only stare after him as he went out of the room, crashing the door behind him. A minute later she heard the front door slam.

It was well after midnight before he came home. She could smell the drink from him as he got into bed.

'I'm sorry,' she said, turning towards him and putting a tentative hand on his shoulder.

He turned onto his side, away from her, refusing to speak.

Meggie rarely gave way to tears but she wept now, hot, silent tears which she simply could not hold back, though she hated to give in to self-pity. All she wanted was one small word of comfort, a loving touch, to have Oliver's arm slide around her, to feel again the closeness they had shared when they were first married. But then she became aware of his breathing, that deep, regular rhythm which indicated sleep. Her tears stopped abruptly and, furious with him now, she turned on her other side, pulling herself as far away from him as she possibly could. How could he fall sleep so easily when he knew she was upset? Surely that wasn't the action of a caring man?

Swollen-eyed and drained, Meggie struggled through the next day's morning rush, aided by an observant but wisely silent Vera. As soon as the flow of customers eased she went into Inverannan and placed an advertisement for a shop manager in the 'positions vacant' column of the local paper.

Back at the shop, when two o'clock arrived with no sign of Dot, Meggie sent Vera home. She then wrote out a card advertising Dot's job and displayed it in a prominent position in the shop window. On the stroke of five, to the astonishment of her disappointed customers, she turned the sign on the door, pulled down the blinds and went resolutely home.

Mrs Dewar had left vegetables prepared and the kitchen was fragrant with yet another stew, the only thing that could be left in the oven for indeterminate periods with any hope of being edible by the time it was wanted.

Meggie hauled the dish out and put it outside the back door to cool. Then she put the fresh chicken which she had bought while in the town into the oven to roast. It should be ready just in time for Oliver when he arrived home a little after six-thirty. That done, she went upstairs and bathed quickly, changing into her favourite dress, a marvellous creation in a petrol blue crêpe de Chine which she had treated herself to to celebrate the peace. It had a fitted bodice, the plainness broken by twenty pearl buttons which ran diagonally from waist to shoulder. The softly flared skirt fell from a tightly nipped waist, its neatness accentuated by a broad belt. Working swiftly, she powdered her face, using rouge to add the colour which had failed to revive after her sleepless night, then highlighted her lips with a soft coral lipstick. Her hair, long and with a natural wave, was soon brushed into place. That done, she examined herself critically in the mirror and was not disappointed with the results of her efforts. The smokey blue of the dress was perfect for her colouring and the design emphasized her neat figure, while the make-up, something she rarely wore, made her look less tired than she still felt. At least Oliver would see that she had made a real effort to please him tonight, she thought, running back downstairs to check on the meal.

By six-thirty the chicken was done to perfection and the potatoes had crisped up nicely alongside it. The table was properly laid with napkins and wine glasses while the wine itself chilled in a bucket of cold water at the back door. As a final touch she turned off the main light, leaving only the softer wall lights and selected a record for the gramophone.

For the next half hour she waited, assiduously basting the over-cooking chicken and potatoes. Finally, with the meal on the point of ruin, she telephoned Oliver's office. There was no reply. Assuming he was on his way home she took everything out of the oven and began to serve up, sliding the plates back to keep warm for the five minutes it would take him to get there.

Filling in the time by washing the roasting tin she managed to splash grease on her frock, the mark dark and obvious on the bodice. She rushed upstairs angrily and changed, watching all the while for Oliver's car, disappointed to be greeting him in a pretty but unexceptional dress of figured cotton.

She need not have hurried. By the time Oliver arrived it was after eight o'clock. It was obvious that he had been drinking, something he indulged in with worrying regularity. Meggie served the meal in resentful silence, offering no explanation for the dried remains which no amount of gravy could redeem.

'That was bloody awful,' Oliver remarked, having picked out the most edible bits. 'Waste of good meat. You'll have to have a word with Mrs Dewar about it.' His speech was very slightly slurred.

'I cooked it, not Mrs Dewar.'

His eyebrows shot up, disappearing under his wayward fringe. 'You cooked it?'

'Aye, I did. I shut the shop at five and came home and made you a proper meal, for the right time. And you didn't even bother to let me know you were going to be late.'

'And how the hell was I supposed to know what you were doing?' he demanded, irritated by her accusing tone. 'I can't remember the last time you were home before me in the evening. If I'd telephoned here to say I was going to be late on any other night there would have been no reply. If you'd had any sense you would have called me!'

'It was supposed to be a surprise. To make up for last night.'

'The only way you'll make up for last night is by getting someone to run the shop and by being here every night,' he told her.

'I put an advertisement in the paper today.'

'I don't want to hear any more about it until you can tell me you've actually taken someone on,' he said, walking into the hall and shoving himself back into his heavy tweed coat.

'Are you going out? But I made the effort to be home tonight,' she cried.

'And I have other plans. Goodnight, Meggie. Don't wait up.'

SIX

Oliver had been right about one thing, Meggie admitted, surveying the huge pile of post which was waiting for her when she got home – there were plenty of people looking for employment. Since the paper bearing her advertisement for a shop manager appeared, every mail delivery had brought a deluge of applications. The sooner she selected someone the better; shutting the shop at five o'clock every night so that she could be home before Oliver was bringing in complaints and losing business. But losing business was infinitely preferable to losing her husband.

She was tempted to open the envelopes there and then but there was barely enough time for her to change and finish preparing dinner before Oliver came in. Reluctantly she put them aside, slipped the steak pie prepared by Mrs Dewar into the oven, lit the gas under the vegetables and hurried upstairs.

When she heard Oliver's car in the drive, Meggie ran to open the front door for him and greeted him with a smile and a kiss, pleased to feel an answering response as his lips met hers.

'Good day?' she asked, wholeheartedly embracing her new role.

He shrugged. 'Same as any other.'

'Dinner's almost ready. Just time for you to wash and change,' she smiled, taking his coat and hanging it up.

'Right. Pour me a whisky, will you?' he answered as he went upstairs.

Meggie stifled her annoyance and poured a modest measure of neat spirit into a glass, ready for him. She hated the way he drank, ending nearly every evening in a drunken stupor, but their reconciliation was too fragile for her to tackle him about it now. Time enough for that when the shops were sorted out and he could see the very real effort she was making for him.

'No wine?' he asked, five minutes later, draining the whisky and settling at the table.

Again Meggie swallowed her irritation. 'I didn't think you'd want any. Not after the whisky,' she commented.

'Well, I do.' His voice was belligerent. Ignoring his waiting meal, he got up and limped from the room.

Meggie waited, her own meal cooling in front of her, while he made his way to the cellar where their modest stock of wine was stored.

'We're running low,' he commented, returning with a bottle of Burgundy. 'I'll call Hough's tomorrow and order some more.'

It was as if his words opened a curtain in her mind. Of course! Why hadn't she thought of it before? If she was to compete seriously with Hough's, surely her own High Street store should be licensed.

Her good intentions forgotten, Meggie ate her meal in silence, excitement bubbling inside her as she wondered which wine importer would give her the best prices, which could be trusted to offer honest advice, how to obtain the necessary licence.

So intent was she on her new idea that she looked up with a guilty start when she realised that Oliver was speaking to her. For a moment she was tempted to blurt out her plans, but stopped herself just in time. If she didn't want to upset him again, this was something she would have to look into quietly, while Oliver was at work. With a little stab of resentment Meggie realised she would have to shelve her plans, at least until she and Oliver had put their relationship back on to a more secure footing. But maybe . . . in a year or two . . .

'It's terribly sad, don't you think?' Oliver was saying now.

Meggie hadn't the faintest idea what he was talking about, but to let Oliver know she hadn't been paying attention would be to invite yet another row. She extemporised frantically. 'Aye. It is.'

'Robbie's devastated. He's very fond of Megan.'

Robbie, Oliver's older cousin, had married a Welsh girl, Megan Williams, only months after she and Oliver had been wed. It was Megan, from a wealthy, slate mining family, who had invested desperately needed capital into the Strathannan Mining Company while Robbie and his younger brother, Edwin, had gone to Wales to run the Williams's slate mines, leaving Oliver to manage affairs in Strathannan.

Meggie looked up sharply and was startled to see that her husband was distressed. What on earth had happened to upset Oliver so much? 'Megan's a lovely person,' she said, sincerely, for she was very fond of both Robbie and his warm-hearted wife.

'They say it's just a matter of time. Weeks rather than months. I had no idea she was so ill. When they were here last summer she looked perfectly healthy. She's only thirty-four you know.'

Meggie felt a leaden hand clutch at her heart. 'Weeks?' she repeated faintly.

'Aye. You never can tell with cancer, of course, but Edwin says there's no hope. She's not even able to get out of bed now. He and Gwyneth are looking after the children.'

It was so awful that Meggie could hardly speak. 'Och, poor weans.'

Oliver nodded glumly, his misery exacerbated by the quantity of alcohol he had drunk. 'Avis is twelve now, old enough to understand what's going on but wee Tommy, well, he's only six. They'll both miss their mother dreadfully.'

Meggie stared at her plate, feeling the meal congeal heavily in her stomach. 'Cancer. At that age.' It was something she associated with older folk. People of her age didn't die of horrible diseases.

'They'll let us know when ... when anything happens,' Oliver mumbled.

'But shouldn't we go and see them, Oliver? There might be something we can do.'

He shook his head. 'No. Megan's very ill. They're keeping her sedated because of the pain. Robbie just wants her last weeks to be as peaceful as possible. To tell the truth, I don't suppose he could cope with visitors right now.'

'No, I expect you're right.' Her shops forgotten, Meggie struggled with the sheer horror of such a tragedy. Robbie had been very kind to her at the time of Oliver's accident, had even delayed his own wedding plans in an unselfish effort to help Oliver recover his fitness after losing his leg. Megan, although Meggie didn't know her well, had seemed a cheerful, energetic girl with an optimistic view of the world and not a bad word to say against anyone. Overcome, Meggie wiped tears from her eyes. As she lowered her hand again she was surprised to feel it taken in a firm, warm grip.

'I'm sorry. I wouldn't have told you if I'd realised how upset you'd be,' Oliver said softly.

'Of course I'm upset. I'm very fond of Megan and Robbie. I just wish there was something we could do to help.' She gave him a watery smile.

'I don't think there is. Not at the moment. Though perhaps we could have Robbie and the children up here to stay for a while, later. You know ... afterwards. I'm sure he'll need a break. Especially if you're not out working every day. You'd be company for him. Stop him being on his own too much.'

'Aye. Of course. I know the children like coming here,' she agreed readily.

'Come on now, dry your eyes and try not to think about it too much.' Oliver helped her from her chair. 'Leave this for now. Come and sit down, listen to the radio, take your mind off it for a little while.'

She nodded. 'All right.'

The radio play was mediocre. Meggie's attention wandered and she found herself dwelling on Megan's plight until tears formed again and rolled down her cheeks. Oliver sat with his eyes closed, his head cocked slightly in the direction of the wireless set. Desperate to find something to take her mind off the tragedy, Meggie picked up the pile of applications and began leafing through them. It worked. Very soon she was engrossed, trying to decide who to interview and who to reject outright.

'What are you doing?' Oliver switched off the radio and came to look over her shoulder.

'These are the applications for the manager's job. The sooner I start the interviews, the quicker I'll have someone in the shop.'

'Tonight!' he roared, anger reddening his face. 'After what I've just told you, how could you even think about the bloody shops?'

'I was just trying to take my mind off it,' she defended herself.

He snorted his derision. 'Aye. Of course you were. How can you be so cold, Meggie? Are your shops more important than Megan and Robbie?'

'Of course not!'

'Of course not,' he mimicked cruelly. 'Och, don't let me stop you, Meggie. You go on with what you're doing. I'm going out.'

He slammed out of the house, leaving her with the unpleasant suspicion that, as far as Oliver was concerned, she could do nothing right.

Hidden in the shadows of the driveway opposite, a figure watched until Oliver was out of sight. Blowing on his hands, which had been chilled by the long wait, he crossed the road stealthily, smiling to himself. This was his chance to catch Meggie on her own – the opportunity he had been waiting for.

Only minutes after Oliver's departure the doorbell rang. Wrapped in misery, Meggie ignored it. The bell rang again, a long, determined buzz. Reluctantly she got to her feet, rubbing at her gritty eyes. Hoping to hide her tear-stained face, she deliberately failed to switch on the hall light before opening the front door.

The dark figure on her doorstep was perfectly still, unnervingly silent. His shape, silhouetted by the moonlight, threw an oddly foreshortened shadow across the black and white checkerboard pattern of the hall tiles. Feeling sudden prickles of apprehension along her spine, Meggie peered at him. 'Yes?'

Her caller laughed, a truncated grunt.

Meggie felt her heart lurch, saw the garden tilt and sway. 'Who is it?' she demanded sharply. 'What do you want?' Fear was making her sweat.

'Och, Meggie. That's some way to greet your wee brother.'

'Matty . . .?' She uttered the word on a long, disbelieving breath, though in fact she had recognised him from that first, grunting laugh. Panic made her take a step backwards, bringing the door forward as she moved, desperately trying to shut him out. His foot stopped it.

'Meggie. It's me, Matty.'

'Go away,' she cried, her voice hoarse with terror as memories of their last encounter flooded back, the details as sharp as if it had all happened yesterday.

It had been after the attack on Oliver: a brutal act of jealousy as Matty saw both his hold over Meggie and his hopes for a share in the shop threatened by her impending marriage; a cowardly assault in a dark alleyway which had left Oliver permanently crippled. Sickened by her brother's brutality,

Meggie had gone to the police and made accusations which had resulted in Matty's arrest. But there was insufficient evidence for any charge to be made and that night Matty had come back to the flat they shared over the shop, seeking his revenge. Somehow Meggie had managed to escape and had returned later, heart in mouth, to find Matty gone, the flat wrecked and her one valuable possession – a bracelet, a gift from Wallace, the father of her illegitimate daughter – missing.

It was a sharp reminder of just how dangerous Matty was. But as Meggie shoved against the door with all her might she was forced back under her brother's superior strength.

'Meggie, please. Just let me talk to you.' The door was wide open now, but though Matty could easily have walked into the house he made no attempt to do so.

'There is nothing I want to say to you, Matty,' she told him, forcing herself to stand and face him though her palms were sweating with remembered terror.

'But it's been such a long time, Meggie.'

'Not long enough for me to forget what you did to Oliver,' she hissed.

'I haven't forgotten either, Meggie. That's why I'm here. To say I'm sorry.'

'Sorry!' she yelled. 'Sorry? You crippled my husband and attacked me. What use is sorry now?'

Matty, his face still shadowed, stood perfectly still, his head lowered. When he spoke his voice was low and slightly unsteady, as though he was fighting for control of his emotions. 'I don't blame you for feeling that way, Meggie. I've had a long time to think about what I did and I'd give anything to turn the clock back. I know I was wrong but I was just a kid. I'm much older now. I've learned a lot. I've changed, Meggie. I really have.'

As children they had been inseparable. Meggie had loved her little brother so deeply that she had almost ruined her life in an effort to protect and provide for him. Now, despite all that had happened since, she felt an emotional tug, the reawakening of a bond too strong to be denied. She weakened. 'I don't know, Matty.'

Still he made no attempt to force his way in, something the old Matty would have done without thinking. 'Can't we talk?' he pleaded. 'That's all I'm asking.' Meggie hesitated and, sensing her indecision, Matty pressed his advantage. 'Please, Meggie. Just half an hour?'

'All right,' she agreed slowly, stepping back.

He took one single pace forward, then stopped, waiting.

'Come in, Matty,' she invited.

Matty stood in the darkened hallway, careful to keep a distance between himself and his sister, not wanting to frighten her, conscious that his whole future depended on what transpired between them in the next half-hour.

'Come on through and sit down.' Her heart thumping uncomfortably, Meggie led the way into the sitting-room and stood, her back to the door, staring down at the fire. Behind her the door closed. Taking a deep breath, Meggie did her best to compose herself and turned to face her brother.

She would have known him anywhere: the same dark hair, cut short now, and neatly combed, the sallow skin, the dark, heavily lidded eyes. But he had changed, she could see that now. His features had sharpened, making him look older than he actually was, and there were the beginnings of lines running down the sides of his mouth. Shorter than her by a good two inches, he was stockily built but leaner now, fitter looking, and under it all, Meggie still had that sense of something unpleasant, something dangerous. But no, she told herself, surely that was nothing more than her own overactive imagination reminding her of the past.

'Well,' he asked, smiling at her, the cheeky grin lending him the boyish look she remembered so well. 'Have I changed so much?'

Warily, still distrustful, she answered. 'No. Not really.'

'Nor you.' He stepped closer now, still smiling, judging every move.

There was a long moment of awkward silence. Everything she knew about Matty warned Meggie to be careful, to keep a barrier between them, but though she kept her expression carefully controlled, inside her emotions churned wildly and she had to resist the impulse to put out her arms to him. It was true: he had changed. His manner had lost the aggression which had been so apparent in his youth. He seemed milder, warmer, less sure of himself. Confused, she looked away and then went and sat by the fire, motioning him to the chair on the other side of the hearth. No sooner was he settled than she sprang up again. 'What am I thinking of?' she asked, laughing nervously. 'You must be frozen. Would you like a cup of tea . . . or something stronger?'

'I don't drink any more, Meggie,' he lied. 'A cup of tea later, maybe. All I really want is for you to sit down and talk to me.'

She subsided on to the chair and sat twisting her hands nervously in her lap.

He watched her intently for a minute, then got to his feet. 'I can see you're not happy having me here, Meggie. I'd better go.'

'No!'

'It wasn't fair, me just turning up like that. I should have written first.'

'No. I'm glad you've come. Really I am. It . . . it's just a bit of a shock, that's all. I thought I'd never see you again.' Had hoped and prayed that he was out of her life for ever. So why did she not want him to go? Her confusion growing by the minute, Meggie shook her head as if to clear it, then met his eyes firmly. 'Sit down, Matty. Now that you are here we should talk.'

Matty hastily concealed the thin, satisfied smile which stretched his lips. 'Sure? I could always come back another day. Or we could meet in town somewhere if you'd like that better.'

'No.' She had made her decision now. 'I want you to stay.'

Matty sat down again, perching on the edge of the seat as if he too wasn't quite at ease, his cap dangling from his hands. Again there was a difficult silence. It was Matty who broke it.

'This is a braw house,' he commented, casting an appraising eye round the spacious room.

She nodded, glad of easy ground. 'Yes.'

'Fine place for bairns,' he probed.

'We've no children, yet,' she answered softly, unable to hide the pain that admission caused her.

'You'll have been busy with the shops, I suppose?'

'Aye.'

'You've done well for yourself, Meggie. I always knew you would. Two shops now, isn't it?'

This was more like the old Matty. 'How do you know that? And how did you know where to find me?' she demanded suspiciously.

'That was easy,' he laughed. 'I just asked around. You're well known in this town, Meggie.'

'Oh,' she said, then went on quickly before a new silence had time to develop. 'Tell me about yourself. What have you been doing?'

Matty had had several weeks in which to prepare his story. 'I went down south,' he said. 'Found myself a job. In a factory. It wasn't much but it was honest. I got lodgings. A right nice room with a family. Aye, she was a braw cook was Mrs Brown. Looked after me right well, she did. Strict sort of woman, mind. Wouldn't put up with drink or noise or coming in late.'

'Have you been there all this time?'

He shook his head. 'No. Just until the war. I was in the army. A . . . a corporal by the time I got out.' He had been on the point of claiming the rank of sergeant but stopped himself just in time, sensing that this would have stretched his credibility too much.

'You were conscripted?' she asked, impressed.

'Nah . . . joined up first chance I got. Wanted to be in on it from the start.'

'But you could have been killed and I'd never have known.' The thought upset her more than she had been prepared for.

'But I wasn't. Saw plenty of action though.'

'France?' she asked.

He nodded.

'Ronnie was in France,' she told him. 'You remember Ronnie Sandys?'

'I was only there for a month or so.' Matty rapidly amended his story. 'Got moved off to North Africa.'

'The desert? What was it like?' she asked.

'Bloody hellish,' he answered sharply, knowing he was in danger of getting out of his depth. 'Look, it was terrible. I'd rather not talk about it, Meggie. I lost a lot of good mates out there.'

'Och . . . I'm sorry, Matty.' Meggie's sympathetic nature was easily aroused. 'What have you been doing since?'

'Went back to London, got my job in the factory back, but the place where I'd had lodgings . . . it had been bombed. Nothing left of it. I asked around and they'd all been killed. I was right upset. That Mrs Brown, she was like a mother to me, Meggie. Och, I couldn't stay there then so I decided to come home and look for work up here.'

Meggie felt her throat tighten. Matty's whole life had been dogged by ill luck. Was it any wonder he had acted the way he did when he was younger? But from what he said it was obvious that he had reformed and she was proud to know he

72

had played his part in the war. 'Have you had any luck?' she asked, relaxing a little.

'Not yet. I've applied for lots of jobs but there's too much competition with everyone coming back from the forces. And I've no education. Folk can pick and choose these days. I'll be lucky to get anything at all. I might have to go back to London after all.'

Meggie, thinking of the huge number of applicants for her shop manager's post, knew he was right. 'But what are you living on?' she asked, genuinely concerned. 'Do you need help, Matty? I could lend you a few pounds, if you like, just to tide you over.'

Matty stiffened his back and clenched his jaw, giving an impressive imitation of affronted dignity. 'That's not why I'm here, if that's what you're thinking. I took enough money from you before. I'll not be beholden to you again. I'll work for everything I get.'

'I didn't mean that, Matty.' Even to her own ears it sounded as if she was pleading with him. 'I just wanted to help if I could.'

'Aye, well, thanks but I've got my army pay and I saved a fair bit before the war. I'm managing just fine.'

In the months since his release from prison, Matty had indulged in a round of housebreaking and black-marketeering which had put enough cash in his wallet for him to live fairly comfortably. But his real opportunity had come with the establishment of a building site for pre-fabs near his lodgings. Staring idly out of the window of his rented room one afternoon, he had watched with interest as a lorry-load of paving slabs was deposited on the open site. That was quickly followed by a delivery of ovens and yet another of geysers. To his amazement the site was left unguarded at night and it was a simple matter for him to 'borrow' a truck and remove it all to a derelict building, from where he sold it on at a very satisfying profit.

'All right. But just remember the offer's there if you need it,' Meggie told him, convinced that her brother really had changed for the better. 'Actually,' she added thoughtfully, 'I'm looking for a manager for the old shop.' She regretted the words as soon as they were uttered, knowing she should have discussed it with Oliver first. She had grave doubts about his willingness to help the man who was responsible for his terrible injury.

'Aye, I know. I saw the advertisement in the paper. But I wouldn't want to make you feel you had to give it to me, Meggie.' Then, as if he had read her mind, 'Maybe you'd better talk it over with Oliver first? I wouldn't blame him if he didn't want you to have anything more to do with me and I wouldn't want to be the cause of trouble between youse.'

'I'll speak to him tomorrow,' she promised.

'You don't have to. That's not why I'm here either.'

'Why did you come here, Matty?' she asked.

He sighed, scratched his ear and tried to look uncomfortable. 'Och, guilty conscience I suppose. I did wrong by you, Meggie. And Oliver. I'm right ashamed of myself. I was hoping Oliver would be here tonight so I could tell him how sorry I am.'

For the first time in her life, Meggie found she was actually admiring her brother. He had done a terrible thing to Oliver, but perhaps he didn't realise how serious the injury had been. It was very brave to want to apologise in person. 'Oliver lost a leg, Matty. It might be hard for him to forgive that,' she warned.

'Aye, I know. It was in the papers. But you have to believe me, Meggie, I never meant him to be hurt so bad. I'll never forgive myself. I was a right bad lot then, Meggie. But I'm not like that now. It taught me a lesson, that did, and I've never been in trouble since.'

'It's all right, Matty. I believe you,' she said softly, moved by the remorse so obvious on his face.

They sat in silence for a moment, before Matty asked, 'What about Ma, Meggie? I wrote to her a few times but she never wrote back.'

'Ma died in 1939,' Meggie sighed. 'She had a bad heart.'

'Och . . . I didn't know.'

For a moment she thought he was going to cry. His face contorted in agony and he covered his eyes with his hands. After a few moments he looked up at her, blinking rapidly and said in a choked voice, 'I wish I'd had the chance to see her and explain.' Then he took a deep breath and added, 'Still, at least she was spared the war. Glasgow got it pretty bad in the bombing.'

'You've been to Glasgow?' She looked at him sharply.

'No!' She'd nearly caught him out there; he'd have to be more careful. 'I just heard about it. What about Perce and Bertie?' he asked, changing the subject quickly. 'Do you keep in touch with them?'

Perce and Bertie were their two brothers. They had moved to Glasgow with their parents before the war, leaving Meggie and Matty in the Inverannan workhouse.

'No. We've lost touch but I know they're both married. Perce had four bairns the last I heard and Bertie three. They work in the shipyards.'

'And what about that old wifie you were friendly with? Her that was the superintendent at the workhouse. Didn't Ma move in with her?'

'Bertha Cruickshank? Aye, that's right. When Perce and Bertie got married, Ma couldn't afford the rent on her place. She wouldn't let me help – you know how stubborn she could be. Bertha lived with her sister and when she died, Bertha was lonely so she asked Ma to move in with her. They got along just fine. Squabbling over nothing just like an old married

75

couple.' She smiled fondly at the memory. 'Bertha died in 1943. Dropped dead of a stroke in the co-operative one afternoon.'

'Shame.'

'Aye. She was a good friend to me was Bertha.'

'You'd have got the house then, you being so close to her?' he asked, trying to make it sound casual.

'No. She told me a long time ago that she didn't think Oliver and I needed the money as much as some other folk did. She left everything to children's homes in Glasgow. I think it was a lovely thing to do.'

He grunted. 'Aye, I suppose it was.'

Again there was that silence which indicated they were not quite at ease with each other yet. Meggie, aware of passing time, afraid of Oliver's reaction if he was to come home and find Matty ensconced in his sitting-room, glanced at the clock. Matty, seeing and understanding, rose quickly to his feet.

'I'd best be getting on my way then, before Oliver gets home.'

Feeling that she'd been caught out, Meggie flushed. 'You don't have to go. Stay and have a word with him if you like.' But she couldn't meet his eyes as she said it.

'Och, it's gey late. Maybe you'd be better to warn him first. But I'd really like to speak to him, Meggie, apologise, if he'll let me.'

'I'll talk to him about it tomorrow night,' she promised, leading the way to the front door.

'All right,' he agreed, shoving his cap on as he went outside. He took a couple of steps then turned back. 'About that job, Meggie . . .'

'Aye?' she encouraged him.

'Well, I do need work and I've experience of working in the shop. It'd not be like it was before. I'm honest now and I'd work hard and not expect any special treatment.'

'You'd not get it,' she told him, smiling now. 'Look, call in at the shop the day after tomorrow. We'll talk about it some more then.'

'Right you are. Good night then, Meggie.'

'Goodnight, Matty. And thanks for coming. It was good to see you again,' she called as he strode off down the drive.

His satisfied grin safely hidden by the darkness, Matty raised one arm in farewell. As he walked into town he was whistling tunelessly to himself, well pleased with the evening's events.

Meggie closed the door and walked slowly back to the sitting-room but there was no sign of the cheerful smile with which she had bidden her brother farewell. His unexpected return to Inverannan had disturbed memories which Meggie would rather have kept buried. Memories of a little boy who had loved her, had relied on her when their parents deserted them. And she had loved him back, so fiercely that she had risked everything to provide him with a home, decent clothes and nourishing food, wanting nothing more than to see her brother grow strong and healthy. A shiver started at the base of her neck and ran down her spine as she recalled the lying, thieving and ultimately violent young man he had become; a man who had blamed her for all his misfortunes, a man she had prayed never to see again.

And yet the Matty who had arrived on her doorstep tonight was changed. She would have known that even had he not told her what had happened to him in the intervening years. It was there in the way he spoke, in his manner, in everything he did, as though he were more settled . . . no, that wasn't it, she mused, trying to identify the thing which had so obviously altered her brother. And then, suddenly, she knew. Anger. That was what was missing. In the past Matty had been permanently on the edge of an argument, everything about him had been aggressive, threatening. But there had been none of that tonight. Tonight, for the first time since he had been a child, Meggie had not felt frightened of her brother.

Still she was aware of a niggle of doubt within herself, a little tongue of bitterness in her heart which would not allow her to forget the violence of those last days, the time when he had inflicted that terrible injury on Oliver, physically attacked her and done everything within his power to destroy her chance of happiness. But all that had been years ago. Meggie deliberately closed her mind to her own treacherous thoughts. Matty *had* changed, anyone could see that. Above all, he was her brother, and she the one person to whom he could turn. Surely she, of all people, should be willing to give him another chance.

'*No!* Absolutely not.' Oliver was as angry as Meggie had ever seen him.

'He's changed, Oliver,' she pleaded. 'He hasn't been in trouble since he left here and you've got to admit it took courage to come back to apologise to you.'

'He'll never change. His sort never do.'

'But he has, Oliver. When you meet him you'll see for yourself,' she insisted.

'I am not going to meet him, Meggie.' Oliver drained the bottle of wine into his glass, swallowed the half inch of liquid, flung his napkin aside and stormed through to the sitting-room.

Meggie abandoned her unfinished meal and followed him in time to see him fill a tumbler to the brim with whisky. 'That won't help,' she commented acidly.

Oliver glared at her, threw back the drink in two gulps and grimaced horribly as the neat spirit caught the back of his throat. To her dismay he then poured another.

'Oliver,' she begged. 'Won't you meet him – hear what he's got to say?'

'No.' He took a mouthful of his drink, sank into his chair and eyed her balefully.

'He has changed. He really has. He's been in the army, serving in North Africa.'

'Which is where I might have gone if it wasn't for him.'

'He's never been in any more bother. He feels guilty about what happened to you,' she persisted.

'It didn't bloody *happen* to me, Meggie,' Oliver roared. 'That little bastard did it to me.' His hair had flopped forward over his forehead and his words were indistinct, his face red. It was a frightening combination of drink and anger. Meggie, ignoring her better instincts, was determined to try and win him round. When he had had enough to drink, Oliver's mood could sometimes change with disconcerting suddenness. Perhaps, she thought, watching as he drained his glass again, if he had another whisky he would become more mellow, more amenable.

'Let me get you another drink,' she offered, taking his glass and hurriedly refilling it. 'I was thinking – ' she said.

'Hooray,' he responded bitterly.

'The sooner I get someone to manage the shop, the sooner I can be at home more.'

'And?' He stared moodily at the fire.

'Well, Matty needs a job and I thought . . .'

'And you thought you'd offer it to him. Are you out of your mind?' He shrieked the words at her. 'He's a thief, a violent criminal. He'll rob you blind just like he did before. And worse.'

'No he won't!' she yelled back at him. 'You're not being fair, Oliver. Matty's changed. I know he has.'

'Then you are a fool,' he said, coldly now, suddenly seeming perfectly sober. 'I won't have him in this house, Meggie. Do you understand? I don't want to see him. I will not talk to him.'

'What if I give him the job?' she asked, knowing she was pushing him to his limit.

Oliver surged to his feet, his eyes blazing with fury. For a moment he stood, tension almost palpable in his body. Then in one swift movement he drained his glass and threw the tumbler into the grate where it shattered, sending dangerous shards over the hearth rug. 'Do what you bloody well like, Meggie. You always do. Never mind about me.'

'Oliver . . .' But whatever she was going to say was lost as he stomped from the room, his limp more pronounced than ever. The sound of the front door slamming was so loud that it rattled the glass in the windows.

The argument with Oliver heavy on her mind, Meggie got little sleep that night. She was glad to rise at five o'clock and busy herself in the corner shop. It wasn't as if she was disturbing Oliver. When he eventually came home last night, he had shut himself in the spare bedroom.

'Och, Meggie, that's one hell of a face you've on you the morn,' Ronnie commented as he hauled the papers into the shop.

She shrugged. 'I'm tired.'

He dumped the last bundle on the counter and waited, tapping his foot on the floor. At last she looked up. 'Och, the tea! I forgot.'

'Aye. So I see.'

'It'll not be a minute. I'll just away and put the kettle on,' she said, hurrying through to the rear storeroom. 'There. Five minutes, that's all. I'm sorry, Ronnie.'

'I'll not wait, Meggie. Once I get behind I never catch up. But you sit yourself down and have a nice cup. You look as if you need it.'

She smiled ruefully. 'I'll have a good strong cup waiting for you this afternoon,' she promised.

'Aye. You do that. Look, tell me to mind my own business if you like, but is everything all right?' he asked, concerned by her pallor.

She sighed. 'Och, just a row with Oliver. A big one.'

'Is that all?' he laughed. 'Sal and me row all the time. You'll soon get over it,' he assured her, heading for the door.

'I'm not so sure,' she murmured. 'I'm not so sure.'

'Hello, Sal. Everything all right here?' Meggie asked, walking into the High Street shop. Sally looked up with a cheerful grin. 'Aye. Everything's just fine,' she said. 'Och, I'm really enjoying working again, Meggie. This job's perfect. Just what I needed to get me out of the house.'

Sally, plump, pretty, irrepressibly cheerful and outspoken, was Meggie's best friend. There were no secrets between them and Sal was one of the very few people who knew the shocking truth about Meggie's past, including the true identity of Meggie's ex-lover. It was a terrible secret, the only one which she had kept from Oliver; one he must never know because the truth was so awful that it would destroy them both. Knowing Meggie as well as she did, Sally quickly sensed that all was not well with her friend. Leaving her colleagues to serve the steady trickle of customers, she led the way into the back room, piled high with cartons and crates.

Meggie peeled off her gloves and sat down with a small sigh, grateful to have a friend to confide in but, acutely aware that Sal had every reason to detest Matty, not knowing where to start.

'Come on then, out with it. I can see there's something bothering you,' Sal said in her usual straightforward manner. 'Ronnie said you'd had a row with Oliver?'

Meggie smiled ruefully. 'Aye. We seem to be doing a lot of arguing these days.'

'Don't we all?' Sally responded easily. 'Ronnie and I spend half our lives arguing. And the other half making up.' She giggled shamelessly and added, 'In the bedroom.'

Meggie had to laugh back. 'I wish it was that easy.'

Sal perched on the edge of the table she used to do the

accounts and watched her friend closely. 'Things will be easier when you've got a new manager for the other shop. Oliver is right, you know. You don't spend enough time at home.'

'And what would I do at home all day long?' Meggie demanded. 'Even you couldn't wait to get out of the house and you've got three bairns to look after.'

Sally nodded. 'Aye, I know. But Ronnie doesn't like it. Thinks folk will say he doesn't make enough money to keep his family. Pride, that's what it is. And your Oliver's just the same. It's worse for him, isn't it?' she went on. 'The Mining Company's on its last legs, despite all the hard work he's put into it, while your shops are thriving. No wonder he feels a bit jealous.'

'I suppose so,' Meggie mumbled.

'And he never really got over the war, did he? Oliver resented not being able to join in the fighting. Though goodness knows why anyone in their right mind would want to volunteer to get killed. Still, you can see how he must feel.'

Meggie was no longer surprised by her friend's keen powers of perception, but even so it was slightly disconcerting to have her problems so accurately pinpointed. 'All the more reason for me to keep the shops,' she retorted. 'If the Mining Company has to close we'll be glad of them.'

'Aye, I know that. But you don't have to get rid of them, Meggie, just spend less time in them.'

'I'm already doing that. I've advertised for a manager for the old shop and until I get someone I'm closing up at five o'clock every night, just to be sure I'm home before Oliver.'

'Have you had many applicants?' Sal asked.

Meggie nodded. 'One too many.'

Sally raised one plucked and pencilled eyebrow. 'One too many? How?'

'Matty.'

Sally's expression froze in a mask of appalled astonishment. 'Matty! *Your* Matty?'

'Aye.' Meggie gave a brief account of their reunion.

'You're not actually thinking about offering him the job, Meggie? Not after what he did?' Sally couldn't keep the note of disbelief out of her voice.

'He's my brother. The only one of my family who wants anything to do with me.'

'He may be your brother but he's a lot of other things as well.' Sally saw the way Meggie's colour heightened but ignored it and went on. 'He's the one who crippled Oliver! He would have injured you too if you hadn't managed to get away from him that night, and you damn well know it.'

'And he came all the way back here to say he was sorry.'

'To see what he could get from you, more like.'

'No! I offered to give him money but he wouldn't take it.'

Sally was dismissive. 'Even Matty's not that stupid.'

Meggie was really angry now. 'You're as bad as Oliver! That's all in the past. I think he deserves the opportunity to prove himself.' Stubborn determination had always been one of Meggie's strongest traits; now, with every word uttered against her brother, her resolve to give him another chance hardened.

'Another opportunity to do what? To steal from you? To ruin your marriage?' Sally sighed her exasperation. 'Och, Meggie. People like Matty don't change. He's jealous, twisted, dangerous, can't you see that?'

But it was too late for Meggie to go back on her words now. She would prove them all wrong. Her jaw took on the set lines that Sally recognised so well. 'I am going to offer him the job.'

'Then you are a fool, Meggie Laing.'

'And you are being unfair,' Meggie shot back furiously.

'Well, you must have known what I'd say,' Sally challenged her. 'If you didn't want me to tell you the truth you shouldn't have come here.' For a moment the two women faced each other, eyes blazing. Then Sal, who found it impossible to remain angry for long, said softly, 'That's what friends are for, Meggie. To tell each other the truth, to help one another.'

Meggie let out a long sigh and sagged, as if exhausted. 'I know,' she admitted. 'Let's not fall out about it, Sal?'

Sally smiled. 'No, we'll not fall out but perhaps you should think this over for a bit longer. Discuss it with Oliver.'

'I have. He said almost the same things as you did.'

'You can't blame him for that.'

'No.'

'But you're still going to give Matty the job?'

Meggie nodded. 'Aye.' Briskly now she got to her feet, pulled her gloves back on and turned to go. 'I'll pop in later in the week.'

'All right.'

Sally went to the shop doorway with Meggie and watched as her friend walked quickly away. Under the cheerful smile and wave she gave as Meggie turned the corner, Sally was truly worried. If Matty McPherson was back in Inverannan there would be serious trouble. Nothing in the world was more certain than that.

SEVEN

'Braw.' Davey Brebner shoved his empty plate aside, mopped his perspiring face with the corner of the tablecloth, patted his stomach and belched hugely. Rising from his seat at the head of the kitchen table, he strode across the room, his boots thumping dully on the flagged floor.

Dorothy frowned at the trail of mud he was creating, opened her mouth as if to say something, then seemed to change her mind. Kate scowled, knowing full well that she would be the one who would have to sweep up after him. She watched as he helped himself to a glass of beer from the keg which was stationed by the door, fascinated, despite her distaste, by his ability to swallow a full pint in one long gulp, and that after a gargantuan meal.

Davey Brebner, running the farm until such time as Edward could take over, was a slightly less obese version of his father, from whom he had obviously inherited his bullying manner. Kate loathed him as she had never loathed anyone in her life and knew that he viewed her with equal antipathy. Bombastic, coarse and loud-mouthed, he had taken over as if the place was his by right. Only Dorothy accepted his intrusion with any degree of ease, an attitude which was helped by the upturn in profits which had already become apparent.

Dragging the back of his hand across his mouth, Davey turned to Duncan, who was still working his way through a mound of apple pie and custard. 'Get a bloody move on! That big field's to be cleared by the night so's we can start on the other one the morn.'

Duncan scowled, shovelled the last two spoonfuls into his mouth and got to his feet, still chewing.

Kate groaned. Tattie picking was surely the worst job of the season; back-breaking manual labour which left everyone filthy and exhausted. And this year, clearing the big field, a job which usually took a full seven days, even with the help of three or four casual labourers, would be finished in eight with just the three of them and old Tam Henty from the village, working from dawn until it was too dark to see. Even Edward and Victoria were pressed into service after school, a strategy which kept them out of mischief and left them too exhausted to protest when they were finally packed off to bed. Davey Brebner, Kate decided, was nothing short of a slave-driver.

The sun had long disappeared over the horizon by the time Kate and Duncan, side by side, trailed wearily back to the farmhouse for a late supper that Sunday evening. Henry's death had done much to repair the relationship between the two youngsters, who were united in their hatred of Davey Brebner. Preoccupied by grief, with no one else to turn to, Kate forced the earlier incident to the back of her mind and was grateful to know she had an ally in her childhood friend.

Duncan, as had become his habit, disposed of his meal in the shortest possible time and escaped gratefully to his own home. Davey, prematurely middle-aged at thirty, washed down his meal with another glass of beer, then finally kicked off his boots and retired to the fireside chair which had been Henry Brebner's. There he lit his pipe and sat in silent contemplation, hidden behind clouds of noxious smoke. It was a routine which was already a set pattern, varying only on Saturday nights when he took himself off to the local public house from where he returned, at precisely eleven o'clock, red-faced and clumsy, to waken the whole household.

But for Kate the day's work didn't end when she came in

from the fields. There were the dishes to be washed, the kitchen to be tidied, the floor to be swept, the range to be raked out and the table to be set for tomorrow's breakfast.

'When you've finished the dishes the twins need their clothes ironing ready for school the morn,' Dorothy added to the list of chores.

Tiredness making her unusually bad-tempered, Kate protested. 'Mum, I've been working since half-past five this morning! Could you not have done the ironing for once?'

Dorothy flushed, took a deep breath which seemed to have the effect of inflating her already impressive bosom, and snapped, 'And I've been doing nothing I suppose? Do you think breakfast and two huge three-course meals for youse lot get to the table all by themselves, eh? And then there's all the cleaning and the weans to run around after.'

Kate sighed. It was true that Dorothy worked harder now than she had done for many years. Determined to make this farm more profitable and so prove his worth to his hypercritical father, Davey had deemed the woman who came in to help about the house for three hours each weekday morning a waste of money, seeing no reason why his aunt, a fine strong woman, should not undertake her own domestic chores. By way of compromise he had agreed to let Kate take every Monday morning 'off' to see to the laundry.

'All right, all right.' Kate knew it was simpler and less exhausting to capitulate.

Dorothy nodded, satisfied, and took herself off to join her nephew beside the fire.

'All done?' she asked when Kate joined them in the overheated sitting-room an hour and a half later.

'Almost. There's still the sheets and pillowcases.' Kate was so tired she could barely stand.

'Och . . .' Dorothy's irritation was plain. 'Could you not have finished the job properly for once?'

'I'm tired, Mum.' Kate sank wearily onto a chair.

Davey looked up with a grunt. 'Tired? Tired! A young lass like you? By, and you don't know what hard work is. You've had it too easy, that's your trouble. You don't know when you're well off. You should count yourself lucky. There's many a one like you who hasn't got a warm bed and good food. Aye,' he went on pompously. 'All the years of kindness you've had here and all you can do is moan when my aunt asks you for a wee bit help about the place. Bloody ungrateful, that's what you are. That's no way to thank folk who took you in and looked after you all these years, just from the goodness of their hearts. And you not even family.'

Kate gaped at him, anger buzzing round her skull like a trapped wasp. 'That's not fair!' she responded furiously. 'I do more than my share of work round here. And I don't get paid.'

The warm room seemed to freeze. The silence was so intense that even the fire ceased to crackle. Davey regarded her from a face set in granite, his expression so sour that even Kate's brave spirit quailed, but only momentarily.

'You don't get paid?' he snarled. 'Don't get paid! You get a couple of bob to yourself each week. And how much do you think it costs to keep you? Eh? How much money do you think you've cost this family over the years?'

The buzzing in Kate's head exploded, blowing away the last shreds of caution, laying bare the resentment that had been accumulating since her father's death. 'I work harder than anyone round here but I never get any thanks for it. A slave, that's what I am. Well, it's wrong. You can't treat me like this.' She faced Davey without fear, oblivious to the rage building in him. 'It was never like this before Dad died,' she ended.

There was a long, tense silence. 'But he wasn't your Dad, was he?'

★

The memory of that conversation was still with Kate the following evening. Although it was pitch black, the farmyard thrown into even deeper shadow by the buildings which surrounded it, she found her way with sure-footed familiarity. Outside the door of the heather loft she located the long-handled spade which Davey had left there for her to clean and put away. She grabbed it and thumped it viciously against the yard setts, dislodging the lumpy soil, then repeated the exercise, less harshly, with her own implement. Holding them both in one hand, she unlatched the wooden door and stepped into the draughty interior.

It was the oldest building on the farm, a relic from the past which had been allowed to fall in to semi-dereliction. The wonder, she thought, was that it had lasted this long. Standing on the east side of the farmyard, where it was open to the full assault of the gales which howled down the Forth estuary, it should have collapsed long ago. As it was there were holes in the roof and gaps in the wood-shingled walls which on nights like this let the wind whistle in, stirring the heather and hay which littered the floor and making it drift down in dusty clouds from the loft above. But there was, she thought, setting the tools against a supporting pillar, something peaceful and comforting about this place.

As a child she had loved to nurse the weak and orphaned lambs which were brought here to recover in snug nests of springy heather or, better still, scramble up the rickety ladder and wriggle down with the cats among the hay. On sunny days, shafts of dusty sunlight streamed through the gaping walls, making her feel safe, cocooned by warmth, and even on windy days there was an unexpected sense of security in the creaking and shifting of the timber. When it rained, as it was doing now, the sound was amplified by the roof which, amazingly, was still sound enough to keep out all but the heaviest downpour. It had been her refuge: a place to hide from trouble, a haven in which to relish her small successes, a place to mull over injustices and to dream of her future. Now, tired from fifteen hours in the fields, she felt a sudden urge to return to the safe world of childhood, to escape from the unhappiness which had dogged her since her father's death. Even though she knew supper would be ready and that any delay would bring yet more criticism from Davey, she scaled the ladder, carefully avoiding the rotten rungs, then flung herself, stomach down, on the broken hay bales which littered the floor. From this position it was possible to peer through the warped wooden boards, across the farmyard to the house itself. Through the damp night air the kitchen lights glowed, throwing a golden reflection on to the glistening setts. She glimpsed Dorothy, busy at the range, and watched as Davey pulled out a chair and took his place at the table.

Simply looking at him was enough to spark the fuse of resentment Kate carried within herself these days. It wasn't just that Davey made them all work so hard, denying them even one day of leisure a week. The very house itself had seemed to change with his arrival, becoming greyer, colder, emptier, less welcoming than before. Even the twins had been affected by the cheerless atmosphere, becoming unnaturally subdued and spending an unhealthy amount of time in their rooms, where loneliness and boredom were a small price to pay to avoid attracting their cousin's critical attention.

But it was his manner towards her that really hurt Kate; an attitude echoed in the way her mother treated her. On the day of Davey's arrival Kate had come in from the fields to find she had been ousted from her comfortable bedroom to make way for him. She now slept in a tiny attic room, cold, draughty and barely furnished. Nor was she made to feel welcome in the sitting-room but, after her chores were completed, was expected to take herself off to bed like the lowliest servant. With her father's death, and the revelations that had brought,

Kate had lost not only his gruff affection but her place in the family. She was bereft. The very foundations of her life had been undermined, taking even her identity away from her.

Lost in miserable thought, she did not hear the groaning of the barn door, nor recognise the creak of the ladder behind her. Duncan, whose eyes rarely left Kate, had seen her enter the heather loft, and waited in the yard, eager as ever for the chance of a few private words with her. When five minutes passed and there was no sign of her, he had followed her inside.

He too had spent many happy hours in here as a child. When he couldn't see Kate among the general muddle of heather, hay bales, old tools, half-empty sacks and rusting machinery which littered the ground floor, he knew instinctively where to find her. He moved quickly, any noise he made lost in the general shifting and stirring caused by the wind. He saw her as soon as his head rose over the boarded loft, her rounded buttocks clearly silhouetted against the lighter hay. He froze, feeling his pulse quicken, enjoying the rush of heat to his groin. The passing months had done nothing to lessen his desire for her but instead had aggravated his frustration to the point where he could hardly bear to let her out of his sight, making his nights an unbearable ordeal of hot, unsatisfying self-release. He was relieved to know she had forgiven him for his earlier lapse. He knew, of course, that she was fond of him – that much was obvious from the way she confided in him – but he had kept his distance, giving her time to come to terms with Henry's death, sensing that she was not yet ready for what he had to offer. But it had been six months now and six months was long enough to wait.

'Kate.' His voice emerged as a throaty croak.

Kate jumped and swung round, knuckling tears from her eyes. 'What? What do you want?' she demanded sharply, resenting his intrusion.

'Are you all right?' He moved towards her, peering into the darkness, trying to see her more clearly in the gloom.

'Aye.' But her voice quavered.

'You'll miss your supper.' He heard the misery in her voice, longed to reach out and comfort her.

She shrugged. 'I'm not hungry,' she said, her voice thick with tears.

Duncan sat down in the hay beside her, the movement raising clouds of invisible dust. 'They'll be wondering where you are.'

'No they won't.' Her misery was too deep, had been contained for far too long to be denied release now. The last word ended on a stifled sob.

'Och, Kate. What's wrong? Please don't cry.'

'I'm not crying,' she sobbed, feeling tears run freely down her face.

'What's this then?' Duncan put a finger to her cheek and dabbed the moisture on the tip of her nose.

'Nothing. It's . . . it's the dust.' But then she was overwhelmed, the anguish of the last months finally overcoming her self-imposed discipline. Her shoulders heaved, her whole body trembled and she buried her face in her hands and sobbed without restraint.

'Och . . .' Duncan edged closer and put an arm round the trembling shoulders, half expecting her to push him away. Instead she allowed her head to fall against his chest.

He waited, cradling her tenderly until the tears began to ease, his hand gently stroking her face.

She raised a hand and rubbed at her eyes. 'I'm sorry,' she mumbled, feeling ashamed of herself now.

'What for?' he asked.

'Making a fool of myself.'

'What is it?' he asked now. 'Who's upset you? Davey?'

She shook her head, then nodded it. 'Aye. No. Och,

everything.' She took a deep breath, glad to feel his comforting arm around her. Duncan, her childhood playmate, the one person who was unchanged by all that had happened. 'I feel so lonely,' she said simply.

He let his face fall against her hair, nuzzling against the silky softness, breathing in the faint, earthy smell of her. In his groin fierce heat burned. He tightened his hold, slipping a hand off her shoulder and down, under her arms, his fingers reaching along the hard line of her ribs towards the first, yielding smoothness of her breasts. 'You're not alone,' he told her. 'You've got me.'

'Aye, I know,' she murmured, unaware of his rapid breathing, feeling nothing but reassurance in the tightness of his grip. 'But everything's changed. Nothing's the same.'

'I'm the same,' he rasped. 'I'm still here, Kate.' He inched his fingers further on until his palm was filled with ripeness. Still she made no move to reject him. Encouraged, he dropped a kiss on her head.

Kate shifted, raised her head and looked at him. 'Thanks,' she whispered. 'You've made me feel better already.'

When he kissed her it seemed absolutely innocent, the natural response of her oldest friend. And there was nothing in that first tentative brushing of lips to alarm her. Even when he brought his face on to hers for the second time she did not draw away immediately. It was only when his arms tightened round her again, forcing her down while his body rolled on top of hers that she realised her terrible mistake.

'No,' she yelled, but his face was back on hers, choking the sound, his tongue forcing its way into her mouth.

'Yes,' he muttered, knowing she wanted him. He was drowning in her. The taste of her mouth, the feel of her body under his as she thrashed beneath him heightened his arousal until he was past control. His hands tore roughly at her shirt, exposing her breasts. It was his fantasy come true. Every night he had dreamed of this moment. Only, in his dreams, her breasts were not so warm, had not this tantalising combination of firmness and softness that was inflaming him beyond everything but his own frantic need. Ignoring her frenzied struggle, he drove a hand up between her legs, then tore at the fastening on her trousers. He succeeded in ripping them open and half dragging them over her hips before fumbling with his own buttons and releasing himself.

'No!' she gasped, fighting for breath, jerking her legs together.

'Och, Kate, Kate,' he mumbled, drawing back, forcing her legs apart with his knees.

'No!' She screamed to no avail as her body tore.

'Where the hell are they?' Davey demanded, peering impatiently from the steamy kitchen window. 'The food'll be ruined.'

'Och, just start without them,' Dorothy suggested, eager to appease. 'If their meal gets cold they've only themselves to blame.'

Across the yard the door of the heather loft, caught by the wind, crashed back against the wall. Davey watched for a minute more, a suspicion forming in his mind. Then, turning abruptly, he slammed out of the kitchen and ran across the puddled yard.

Inside the barn he paused, his head cocked on one side, listening. Even above the wind and rain the sounds were quite clear. The noise of bodies thrashing together, groans, moans, cries of excitement. Moving stealthily, he climbed the ladder.

In front of him, Duncan, senseless with lust, thrust into Kate. Davey stilled, a willing voyeur, his breathing sharp and fast, relishing his own arousal as Duncan cried aloud, shuddered, then collapsed over the now still and silent Kate. Davey waited a moment to allow his own hammering pulse to calm, then with a realistic roar of outrage, threw himself into the loft.

Kate, who had endured the final moments of violation with her eyes closed against the horror of Duncan's distorted face, was aware of the weight being lifted from her. There was a sharp crack as Davey's fist connected with Duncan's jaw and she opened her eyes to see Duncan sailing through the air. She lost sight of him in the confused shadows of collapsing bales and flying heather.

'Get up.' She felt herself dragged upright and fumbled to haul her ripped trousers over her exposed belly and gather the edges of her shirt together across her breasts. She was barely decent when he shoved her down the ladder so roughly that she lost her footing and fell the last three feet, collecting more bruises as she crashed to the earthen floor. Before she had time to gather her senses, Davey pulled her to her feet and propelled her roughly through the open door into the farmyard. She slithered and stumbled across the yard and was sent into the kitchen by a single shove in the small of her back. She landed on her knees at Dorothy's feet.

'What in the name . . .?' Dorothy stared at her dishevelled daughter in open-mouthed astonishment.

David, his face working in a paroxysm of disgust, slapped Kate's hands away as she tried to pin her shirt together.

'Look,' he snarled. 'See what she's been doing. I warned you about them. I told you they were not to be trusted.' His hand lashed out again, dragging at her fingers, revealing the loosened trousers. 'In the heather loft they were, and her like a bitch on heat.'

'*No!*' Kate found her voice at last. 'It was Duncan. He ra—'

'*Kate!*' Her protests were drowned out by Dorothy's shocked exclamation.

'I didn't . . . it's not like that.' Kate saw too clearly that she had already been judged and found guilty. 'It was Duncan.

95

He . . . he attacked me,' she sobbed, shivering with shock, her legs barely supporting her, Dull, throbbing pain radiated from the place of defilement.

'Lying wee bitch. I saw youse. You were enjoying it!' Davey's eyes burned with excitement and dropped briefly to her half-exposed breasts as he remembered what he had seen.

'Duncan raped me.' Kate heard her own expressionless voice as if from a great distance. She wanted only to curl up in some forgotten corner and sleep, never to wake up. She took a lurching step away from them.

Davey stopped her, grabbing her arm and swinging her round to face Dorothy with a force that almost wrenched her shoulder from its socket. 'Stay there. Don't you bloody move.' He shook a fist in her face and slammed out of the house, back to the heather loft.

'Mum . . .' Kate appealed desperately to her mother. 'I didn't . . . I wouldn't . . . It was Duncan. Please . . .' Her voice died away in despair as Dorothy stepped away from her, as if frightened of contamination.

'How could you?' She looked at the girl in front of her as if she barely recognised her, then surging forward suddenly, she slapped Kate's face so hard that she left an imprint of her fingers on the girl's cheek.

The unexpected pain penetrated Kate's shocked, almost apathetic state, leaving her trembling with rage. She had done nothing wrong. She must make them understand that she had nothing to be ashamed of. 'It wasn't me. It was Duncan. He . . . he . . .' She choked on the words then, forcing herself to calm down, and repeated in a low but firm voice, 'He raped me.'

There was something about Kate's manner which made Dorothy bite back the bitter, accusatory words which had been on her tongue, but what she said next hurt Kate almost as much. 'You must have been leading him on.'

'No!'

'You were in the heather loft with him! Any lass who goes to a place like that with a lad is asking for trouble.'

'It wasn't like that! I went there on my own. He followed me.'

At that moment the kitchen door burst open again and Davey came in, dragging a pale and disorientated Duncan after him. 'Like a pair of bloody animals,' he roared. 'At it in the hay not caring who might see them.'

'That's not true'! Kate yelled it. 'He raped me.' She couldn't even bring herself to look at Duncan as she said it.

'I did not!' Duncan seemed suddenly to collect his fuddled wits. 'You wanted to. You know you did.'

'Aye. That's what it looked like to me,' Davey growled. 'And if you weren't willing why were you not yelling and struggling, eh? I saw you laying there with your legs wide apart. Enjoying it.' He licked his lips and rubbed a hand over the sweat beading on his brow.

Dorothy flushed and looked away, mortified.

'Please. Listen to me!' Kate pleaded.

'It doesn't matter what you say. I know the truth of it. I saw youse with my own eyes.' Davey ogled her gaping shirt for another glimpse of those firm, pert breasts.

'You saw him raping me. He pretended to comfort me and then he attacked me.'

'Is that right, Duncan?' Dorothy asked.

'No! She let me kiss her and everything and she never even said to stop.' It was the truth as he knew it. 'Honest. And I wouldn't . . . not to Kate. Not if she didn't want to.'

'I told you to stop. You didn't want to hear,' she accused him bitterly. 'Just like the last time.'

Davey and Dorothy looked quickly at one another. Dorothy opened her mouth to speak but Davey silenced her with a frown. 'Aye,' he said. 'I always knew there was something going on atween youse two.'

'There is nothing going on,' Kate screamed, sounding almost hysterical now.

'Aye there is,' Duncan argued. 'You know fine the way I feel about you, Kate.'

'And I told you I wasn't interested.' She glared at him now, her eyes dark with undisguised hatred. 'I was in the heather loft, just to have five minutes on my own before supper,' she told Dorothy, making a great effort to stay calm. 'I was upset . . . missing Dad.' She fought back tears and went on. 'I didn't even know Duncan was there until he spoke to me. He . . . he put his arm around me until I stopped crying. I thought he was just being kind. And then he kissed me.'

'Aye, and you didn't stop me,' he accused her.

'No,' she agreed. 'Not the first time. But then you started to . . .' It was too much, the horror still too raw in her mind. She stopped, turned away from them and stared blindly out of the window.

'We all know what happened then,' Davey said coldly. 'I saw it for myself and you were leading him on like a common little tramp.'

'No,' she moaned. 'No.'

'Well, there's only one thing for it,' Davey went on, ignoring her. 'Youse'll have to be wed. I'll not risk a wean on the way and youse not married.'

Dorothy breathed a sigh of relief.

Kate's sigh was more sudden, an inward jerk of terror as the possible outcome of the night's events suddenly became all too real. But to marry Duncan, after what he had done, even if there was a child on the way? '*No!* Never.' Kate rounded on him, her back stiff, her head high. 'You can't make me.'

'Kate, lass,' Dorothy took her daughter's icy hands. 'It's for the best. You know it is. Go on like this and you'll end up in trouble like Mary Soutar. Och, Duncan's a fine young lad. Marry him before you get yourself in real trouble.'

'I hate him! How could you want me to marry him after what he's done?' She would face the consequences, whatever they were, alone, because alone was better than being tied to the monster that was Duncan Auld.

Insensitive to the terrible injustice she was condoning, Dorothy spoke with devastating callousness. 'You knew fine the way Duncan felt about you. You should never have led him on like that. The lad's not to blame for thinking what he did. Not that I'm saying he was right mind. I don't agree with that sort of carry-on. Not afore marriage. But I do know what men are like and this is your fault, Kate, not Duncan's.'

'I will not marry him.' Kate's face was deathly white and her whole body shook but her voice, though low, was absolutely firm. 'I've done nothing wrong. I've got nothing to be ashamed of.'

'Right. Then if you won't marry him, get out.'

'David!' Too late Dorothy protested.

'Let me deal with this, Aunt Dorothy.' He turned to Duncan. 'Are you willing, lad?'

Duncan nodded stupidly, still dazed and unable to assimilate all that was going on. Five minutes ago he had thought he was going to be beaten, arrested, thrown out on the streets. Now his dream was coming true.

'I will not marry Duncan.' Kate's voice was still steady.

'Then pack your bags.' Davey was sure he was calling her bluff. The girl had nowhere to go – no money, little education, few friends. She would see sense in the end, and then everyone would be happy and the farm would have a source of cheap labour for decades ahead. 'You've got until the morning to change your mind.' he told her smugly.

'I won't change my mind.'

Kate looked at the cardboard suitcase with a feeling of desolating sadness. So little to show for seventeen years. From her empty bedside cupboard she took her post office savings book.

She slumped on the bed, almost overcome by hopelessness. Where was she to go? Where would she live? How long would her fifty pounds last? They were questions to which she had no answers. The only thing she was sure of was that she couldn't stay here.

Slowly she picked up the suitcase and, not even bothering to take one last look at the cheerless attic room, started down the stairs.

In the kitchen, Dorothy stationed herself by the range and refused to look up as Kate came into the room.

'Goodbye, Mum.' Kate waited by the back door, hoping, even now, for some small sign of affection. There was nothing. Even the twins, watching with round-eyed confusion from their places at the table, had been warned into silence. To Kate, Dorothy's attitude was the ultimate betrayal, wounding her as much as the physical violation she had suffered from Duncan. She knew then that, no matter how uncertain the future, she was doing the right thing. There was no comfort here, no help for her in this family that had never truly been hers. Tears threatened to spill down Kate's face but she fought them back bravely, determined not to let them see how much they had hurt her. She smiled valiantly at the twins and opened the back door.

On the doorstep she hesitated, casting one last imploring look at her mother, but Dorothy's back was implacably turned. Kate stepped outside and walked across the farmyard for the last time.

EIGHT

Inverannan, a determinedly old-fashioned burgh containing, among other things, fourteen places of religious worship, twenty-seven public houses, a magnificent public park and two brothels, nestled comfortably on the rise of land which climbed up from the Forth Valley. A small town built on a grand scale, it boasted an architecturally superb but poorly stocked library, an imposing town hall, a beautiful abbey and a masonic lodge of proportions envied throughout Scotland. As if trying to live up to the image of these greying sandstone edifices, Inverannan made much of its historical significance, as demonstrated by the now ruined castle, but attempted to ignore the importance of the clutch of linen mills and clothing factories, all conveniently tucked out of sight at the 'bottom end', to which it owed its continuing prosperity.

Kate arrived in this proud, class-conscious town a little after ten o'clock on Monday morning. Weary after the long walk from the farm, she set her case on the pavement outside the offices of the Strathannan Friendly Society and gazed towards the High Street, a frown of worry creasing her brow as she wondered where to go and what to do next. So unhappy had she been, so desperate to get away from the scene of her humiliation, that she had thought no further than simply packing her bags and leaving. Now here she was, alone in a town which, beyond the limits of the High Street, bus stance and public park, was as alien to her as Edinburgh or Glasgow might have been. Somewhere in this town of strangers she had to find a job and, even more urgently, somewhere to sleep, at least for tonight. With an uncomfortable tightening of her chest, she realised she hadn't the faintest idea of how to go about finding either. And what would happen if her worst nightmare became true and she really was pregnant with Duncan Auld's child? The enormity of her plight finally overcame the anger and sense of injustice which had propelled her this far. Panic anchored her to the ground, rendering her brain incapable of logical thought and making her head spin so much that she did not see the officious-looking man leave his station just inside the office doorway and strut over to her.

'Have you business here?' he demanded curtly.

Kate looked up blankly. 'What?' she stammered.

The man straightened his braided cap, rocked back on his heels and gave her his most disapproving stare. 'Do you have business with the Strathannan Friendly Society?' he asked, making sure he spoke loudly enough to attract the attention of passers-by.

'No.'

'Well, move along then. You're blocking the doorway.'

'I am not!' Kate retorted, angered by his inimical manner. 'My case is heavy. I was just resting for a wee minute.'

'Aye. Well, do it somewhere else. Not outside this building. We've our reputation to think about.' He gave her case a light kick with his shiny boot.

'Don't do that!' Kate glared at him.

By now they had a small audience, watching with goggle-eyed curiosity, anxious for any snippet of gossip with which to enliven their humdrum days.

'Wee hussy,' one woman commented, her voice carrying clearly.

The carelessly offered insult reminded Kate again of all that had happened to bring her here in the first place. Mortification brought a fiery flush to her cheeks and for a moment she wanted nothing more than to melt away, to disappear from under the derisive smiles, sneering eyes and hostile faces of these folk who knew nothing about her, and had no right to judge. But, she reminded herself firmly, she was doing nothing wrong. She had as much right to be on this particular piece of public pavement as anyone else. Mustering the small amount of dignity at her disposal, Kate retrieved her case, straightened her back, and turned to face the uniformed doorman who now blocked her way.

'Excuse me,' she said coldly, making no attempt to push past but waiting, her eyes fixed unwaveringly on his face until, losing his nerve, he moved aside. 'Thank you.' Her tone was icily polite but though she sounded calm she had to fight the impulse to run. It was with great difficulty that she confined herself to a steady walking pace until at last she was swallowed up by the throng of housewives who were crowding the pavements.

She didn't stop again until she was half-way down the High Street and this time, wary of being moved on again, she held on to her case and turned, pretending interest in the window of the shop behind her. But she saw nothing of the goods displayed there. Instead she found herself peering at her own reflection, clear in the sparkling glass, and what she saw dismayed her. Her hair had escaped from its restraining ribbon and hung over her face in untidy, wispy straggles. The weight of her case dragged at her shoulder, distorting the collar of the overly large, navy blue coat which hung lopsidedly round her legs, drawing attention to her dusty-covered shoes. She might easily be mistaken, she realised with a sense of shock, for one of the tinkers who came to the area at this time of year, looking for casual work. And if that was the impression she was giving there was no hope of finding either a job or a decent place to live.

The thought horrified her so much that she was galvanized

into action. Her mind seemed to pull itself out of the sad lethargy which had brought her automatically to this thriving little town and all at once she began to think rationally.

First, before she did anything else at all, it was obvious that she badly needed to tidy herself up. The only facilities available to her were those at the public conveniences.

Kate tightened her grip on her case and strode off with a marked sense of purpose, crossing the setted road and climbing the steep side wynd which brought her out opposite the town's main post office.

The neighbouring public conveniences were guarded by a stumpy woman, wrapped in an old-fashioned shawl, who watched impassively as Kate delved desperately in her pockets for the farthing coin which would give her access to the facilities.

Once inside, Kate washed her hands and face, then tidied her hair, carefully drawing it back and securing it more firmly in the slippery ribbon. Taking her coat off, she went over it with her dampened handkerchief, dripping water on the worn seams so that they didn't look so shiny. Still using her handkerchief she rubbed at her shoes until the original shine began to reappear. Then, realising there was nothing she could do to redeem her white ankle socks, she undid her case and ferreted around for her only pair of stockings and suspender belt, locking herself into a cubicle while she changed. She emerged in an altogether more confident mood, the stockings making her feel more grown up, even if they were strangely uncomfortable and looked a bit odd with her newly cleaned shoes. A further foray into her case produced her only pair of dressy shoes, which she hurriedly substituted for the sturdy, everyday ones in which she had walked from the farm. Then, in a moment of lucky inspiration, she drew out the silk scarf which had been a present last Christmas, and wound it round her throat. The effect was immediate, the soft pinks and mauves breaking the rather dreary effect of the navy blue coat and giving extra colour to her cheeks. Kate smiled at her own reflection and picked up her case, ready now to meet any challenge.

'My, lass, that was a farthing well spent, eh? You look a treat, so you do.' The fat woman beamed her approval, revealing horrifically perfect pink and white dentures, then motioned Kate through.

Her first priority, Kate realised, was to get herself some money, and the post office just across the road was the only place she could do that. With her savings account book in her hand she went inside and joined the queue. When her turn came she stepped forward nervously, half expecting her request to be denied.

'Yes, madam?' The clerk looked up at her with an expectant smile, clearly seeing nothing unusual in the attractive young woman facing him.

Kate's spirits took another upward bound and she handed her book across calmly. 'I'd like ten pounds from this account please.'

The clerk nodded, scribbled on a form, stamped it and passed it back to Kate. 'Just sign there, please, Madam.'

Kate signed her name self-consciously and accepted the ten single pound notes gratefully before thanking him and moving away.

Well, she thought, at least I won't starve for the next day or so. But her fifty pounds was already seriously breached and the thing she needed more than anything else was a job. How on earth did people find work? The newspaper, she decided quickly.

Happier now that she had some idea of what to do next, she picked up her case again and went back to the High Street in search of a paper shop. Newspaper in hand, she decided to make for the town park where she would be able to look through the positions vacant in peace. While she was there she might as well use the time to have something to eat. The long walk had made her hungry.

Across the road was Hough's, the town's largest grocery store. From past experience, Kate knew they sold the biggest, tastiest bridies in the town and one of those delectable parcels of flaky pastry, filled with tender steak, would be enough to keep her going until tomorrow if necessary. She dodged through the traffic and looked in the window, tempted by the cakes on display in the bakery department, wondering whether to treat herself. But the thrifty habits learned at the farm warned her that she shouldn't spend a single ha'penny more than she needed to. While she stood there, still undecided, a gentleman opened a door in the back of the window display and, as she watched, fastened a notice to the glass.

Kate could hardly believe her eyes. '*General Assistant Wanted. Apply Within.*' That would suit her down to the ground, she thought happily. Just as soon as she had found herself somewhere to stay, she would come back and ask to be considered.

She had already picked up her case, ready to move on, when a pair of girls, arms linked, came to stand beside her.

'Look at this,' one of them said, pointing to the card. 'I wouldn't mind working for Hough's.'

'Nor me,' her friend replied. 'And our Trish is looking for a job. As soon as I get home I'm going to tell her to get up here and see about it.'

'Best tell her to come today then. That job'll be taken before tonight,' the first girl added as they walked away.

Kate stared after them in consternation. The girl was right, of course. Hough's was the smartest shop in Inverannan and most folk would be proud to work for them. If she didn't go in and apply for the position now, someone else would take it. Drawing a huge breath, her heart thumping with nervous apprehension, Kate pushed open the door and walked boldly up to the gentleman as he strode through the shop.

'Excuse me, sir,' she said, fixing him with her brightest smile.

'Aye, lass, what can I do for you?' The gentleman, immaculately dressed in a black jacket and grey striped trousers, regarded her sternly over the top of half-moon glasses, but his voice and expression were friendly.

'I would like to apply for the job, please,' she said, keeping her head up.

'My,' he smiled, 'that was quick.'

'I was standing outside when you put the card in the window,' she admitted.

'Well, lass, come with me and we'll have a wee chat,' he said, starting to walk away.

Still clutching her case, Kate followed him through the bakery, past the counter selling cheese and dairy products, and finally behind the dry goods counter. The assistants all said, 'Good morning, Mr Wemyss,' and Kate noticed that he greeted them all by name, smiling as he did so. Though it was obvious that the shop was strictly run, the shelves and counters all spotless, the assistants neatly dressed in black with long white aprons to protect their clothes, there was a pleasant atmosphere and customers and staff alike smiled as they went about their tasks. How wonderful it would be, she thought, hurrying to keep up with Mr Wemyss's long stride, to actually get a position here on her very first morning in town. She hardly dared to hope she could be so lucky.

At last they reached a door at the back of the shop. They went through it, walked down a short corridor and came, finally, to his office. A brass plate on the door informed her that he was Mr G. Wemyss, Manager.

'Right lass, sit yourself down.' He indicated a chair and took his own place on the other side of a highly polished desk.

Kate settled herself, trying to put her case unobtrusively to one side, then waited for him to ask the inevitable questions. To her discomfort he merely sat and looked at her for what seemed to be a very long time, though in fact it could hardly have been more than a minute. It was a minute which saw all Kate's newly acquired confidence wither and die, leaving her flushed and uncomfortable in the hard wooden chair.

Mr Wemyss noted her lowered eyes and the gentle bloom of discomfort on her cheeks and smiled, pleased to see that she wasn't quite the over-confident young thing he had first taken her to be. 'So, lass, you've worked in a shop before, have you?'

Kate's head jerked up, the dismay plain in her guileless face. 'No, sir,' she admitted, knowing it had been too much to hope for.

'Where have you been working?' he asked, watching her closely.

'On the family farm, sir.'

'A farm!' His eyebrows shot skyward.

Kate felt ashamed. 'Yes, sir,' she mumbled.

'Then you've no experience?' He was disappointed. Bright young things like this lass were just what the shop needed.

'No, sir.' Then she sat up straighter and looked across the desk, meeting his pale grey eyes with her intense brown ones as she insisted, 'But I can learn, sir. I'm good at arithmetic and I'm used to hard work.'

'We have very high standards here, Miss . . . Miss—?'

'Brebner, sir. Kate Brebner.'

'Brebner?' He looked surprised. 'You're no relation to the Brebners out at Nether Appin farm are you?'

'Their daughter, sir.'

'Ah. I was sorry to hear about your father, lass. He was a fine man and Hough's have bought produce from Nether Appin for as long as I can recall. A great loss. A great loss indeed.'

'Aye.' Kate felt suddenly choked with grief.

'Well, well, and what brings you here looking for work then, lass? Do they not need you at the farm now then?'

'Not really, sir, and I always wanted a proper job.' She tried hard to keep within the bounds of truth.

'And how were you at school, Kate? Did you do well?'

'Aye, sir.' Smiling again now, she delved into her case. 'See,' she said pulling out a dog-eared envelope, glad she had remembered to retrieve her papers from the sideboard in the front room, 'There's my school certificate and . . . and all my reports. They were aye . . . always good.'

He took them and leafed through them. 'Aye,' he agreed, 'so they were.' He handed them back. 'We expect the best of our staff here at Hough's, Kate. You would need to work hard, to be punctual, always polite and respectful, and above everything else never be anything less than perfectly clean and tidy.'

'Yes, sir.'

'Hold out your hands, lass.'

Kate felt her fists clench into tight balls, well aware that the rough, reddened appearance of her hands would impress no-one. Slowly she raised them on to the desk top and extended her fingers so that the ragged nails were almost under his nose.

He held them lightly, turning them over twice before letting go. Kate had cause to be very grateful for the fact that last night's bath had soaked the ingrained soil from beneath her nails.

'Do you bite your nails, Kate? It's a bad habit and not one I'd want to see in this shop.'

'No, sir! It's working on the farm. My nails just break all the time. That's why my skin's so red too, sir. I have to scrub it so hard to get it clean.'

'Well, no one could say your hands are not clean, Kate. But they are very rough-looking.' He looked up, ready to smile at her, but met only the top of her head as she tried to hide her disappointment. 'Still – ' he stood up, causing Kate to scramble to her own feet. 'Not to worry. We'll start you off in the stock room, filling shelves, weighing out sugar, things like that. You can have a month's trial. If you work hard, and if your hands are fit to be seen by the customers at the end of that period, well, then I think you might have a job. Tomorrow morning, seven o'clock sharp.'

Kate merely gaped, then realising how silly he must think her, smiled, lighting her whole face up. 'Thank you, sir.' She managed to blurt the words out at last.

Back outside, Kate knew she was still grinning. In her wildest dreams she would never have imagined that getting a real job would be so easy. Even when she realised that she hadn't asked how much she would be earning, or what hours she would be working, she still smiled.

With one of her two big problems solved, Kate felt fully justified in treating herself to a large steak bridie and a mouth-watering cream slice which she carried to the park to enjoy, sharing the crumbs with the seagulls who waited impatiently within inches of her feet.

'That's all,' she said, scattering the last flakes of pastry over the ground beside her seat and laughing as the ill-tempered birds fought over the smallest morsel.

Now, comfortably full and secure in the knowledge that she would at least be earning a living, no matter how modest, Kate gave her attention to her remaining problem, that of finding somewhere to stay. Her copy of the local paper was still in her case so she took it out, battling against the breeze which licked at the broadsheet pages, threatening to tear them out of her hands and send them scattering across the parkland.

In this late-morning, autumn sunshine, Inverannan's public park was a very attractive place. Great swards of grassland sloped gently towards the River Annan, which wound its way down towards the wider Forth, visible as a great shining ribbon below.

Dotted over the parkland were mature trees and flower beds, while in the distance thicker woodland marked the place where the picturesque glen, the feature for which this particular park was famed throughout the county, was hidden. Kate, who had frequently come here as a child, knew that there were many pretty paths to follow and hothouses and aviaries to explore, as well as a small museum and a tea room, and wished she could spend the afternoon simply enjoying herself in leisurely exploration. Later, she promised herself. When she had found somewhere to live.

In the distance the town clock struck twelve. Kate straightened the paper and ran her eye down the column advertising accommodation to let, disappointed to see many whole houses but few rooms for rent and horrified at the prices asked.

Her ebullient mood somewhat dulled, she brushed a few stray crumbs from her coat, tightened the ribbon in her hair and picked up her case again, flinching slightly as the handle rubbed against the blister which had formed on her palm.

Armed with the addresses of the only two rooms which had been advertised in the paper, she left the park.

Following the directions given by a friendly shopper, Kate easily found the first of the two houses. It was a stone-built terraced house, not more than five minute's walk from the High Street. Kate opened the gate and walked up the narrow path, then knocked on the door, which was quickly opened by a woman whose colouring and expression matched the house's weathered stonework.

'Well?'

'I've come about the room advertised in the paper,' Kate said.

Again there was the rapid appraisal – her integrity, personality and ability to pay the rent all judged on the tidiness of her hair, the cleanliness of her shoes and the condition of her old suitcase.

'I don't rent to single women. Working men only.' Already the door was closing.

Kate shrugged philosophically, knowing she wouldn't have been happy there anyway, and aware that the day was creeping by, quickly set off for the other side of town and the second lodging house.

'Och, this is not the sort of place for a bonny lass like you. It's working men I take in and a right rough lot they can be too.' The second landlady stood on her doorstep and shook her head.

'Oh, I see. Well, thanks anyway.' Kate picked up her case, then hesitated, not sure which way to go. Was it her imagination or had the case trebled its weight in the last five minutes?

'Wait a wee minute, lass.' The woman called her back. 'If you're interested I could give you the address of a friend of mine who might just be able to help you out.'

'Could you?' Kate's face lit up with a hopeful smile.

'You go down to Netherton. That's over yonder, see, behind that mill?'

Kate nodded. 'Now, it's nothing special down there, mind. But Mrs Traynor's as kind-hearted a soul as you'll find anywhere. Just tell her Dorry Duncan sent you.'

If Mrs Traynor was the kind-hearted soul of Mrs Duncan's description, Kate couldn't see much evidence of it in the grim, too-thin face which stared down at her from the front door step of Netherton Place.

'Well, I don't know what Dorry Duncan's thinking of, sending you here. I don't just take in anyone off the street, you know.'

'I'm not just anyone,' Kate retorted hotly.

Despite herself Mrs Traynor smiled. 'Well then, suppose you tell me who you are, lass.'

'Kate Brebner.'

'And how do you propose to pay me, Kate Brebner? I'd want a week in advance before you put a foot over my doorstep.'

'I have enough for that.' Kate counted out five pound notes and held them out.

Mrs Traynor had learned the hard way that money waved under her nose as an incentive was all too often spent by the time the rent was due. 'Aye, and what about next week?'

'I have a job. I start at Hough's tomorrow,' Kate told her wearily, resenting this need to establish her reliability. Surely she didn't look so disreputable as to warrant this sort of cross-examination.

'Oh you do, do you? Well, Hough's is a good enough place to be working. They're strict there though. You'll need to tidy yourself up a bit before then.' Mrs Traynor's eyes were sparkling now though her mouth was still set in the same discouraging line with which she had answered the impatient rattle on her front door. She liked this girl: there was something sparky and defiant about her which reminded her of herself forty long years ago, before marriage and six children drained her of everything except the grim determination to put enough food on the table to feed them all.

Kate's hand flew to her hair, realising too late that it had once again worked itself loose from the ribbon which had almost slipped off the end of her ponytail. 'Och no!' she exclaimed in exasperation, wishing she had thought to check her appearance before coming here. 'I'm sorry if I look a mess, but I've been trailing round the town all day looking for a job and a place to stay. I just washed my hair last night and it's too soft for the ribbon to hold it properly. And it is quite windy.'

'Aye, so it is,' the other woman agreed, trying hard not to laugh aloud.

'Well, it's almost four o'clock. If you can't let me have a room just say so and I'll go and try somewhere else.' Though goodness knows where, she thought.

'Och, you can have the room,' Mrs Traynor conceded at last.

'Fine. Here's the advance rent you asked for.'

'Don't you even want to look at it first?' Mrs Traynor accepted the money, then stood back and allowed the girl to cross her well-scrubbed threshold.

'No. I'll just be grateful for a bed to sleep in,' Kate retorted brusquely, instantly regretting her tone when she looked up and realised that her new landlady was laughing at her.

'All right, lass. Keep your breeks on. No need to lose the rag with me. This is my home after all and I can't be letting just anyone in here, can I?'

With a smile on her face, Mrs Traynor was a lot less forbidding. Tall and thin, she had the lined face, shadowed eyes, salt and pepper hair and sallow complexion that spoke of a lifetime of hard work and poor food. Now that she had decided to accept Kate into her home, her manner had thawed a little and the twinkling eyes were matched by an unforced smile which Kate couldn't help responding to. 'No, of course you can't. I'm sorry,' she apologised readily.

'Och, that's all right, lass. I can see you're tired out. Now then, I expect you could do with a nice cup of tea?'

There was nothing Kate wanted more. 'That is exactly what I'd like. Thank you.'

'Right, I'll get the kettle on. You sit yourself there. I'll not be a minute.'

She bustled off to her kitchen, leaving Kate to cast her eyes round her new home. Typical of the terraced houses which had originally been built to house the mill workers, the front door opened straight into the living room which, in turn, led to the kitchen and scullery. Upstairs Kate would later discover two fair-sized bedrooms. For now all she could see was the room in which she was seated. A fire burned in the grate, giving the room a cosy feel, and grouped round it were a sofa and two armchairs, all with a well-used but comfortable appearance. The mantelpiece and windowsill were covered with small ornaments and the shelves which lined the recesses on each side of the fireplace were crammed full of framed photographs. On the floor was a square of patterned carpet, edged by plain brown lino. Despite the fire which crackled in the grate and the proximity of the mill chimney, there was not a speck of dust visible anywhere and the brass window catches shone almost as much as the windowpanes themselves. It was, Kate decided, very like the farm – a well-cared-for but comfortable home. Despite the grimness of the surrounding streets, Kate knew she could be happy here.

'Here we are then. Help yourself to sugar and milk.' Mrs Traynor returned, handed Kate a plain white cup and saucer, then sat opposite her, watching her closely.

Kate, feeling the older woman's eyes on her, coloured slightly.

'I can see I'm making you uncomfortable,' Mrs Traynor said with a frankness which Kate would come to appreciate. 'But I was just thinking that you're gey young to be leaving home. I hope you're not in trouble, lass. Not run away from home, have you?'

Very carefully, using the time to compose herself, to put her greatest fear to the back of her mind, Kate put her cup back on the saucer and faced her inquisitor. 'No, I haven't run away and I'm not in any trouble.'

Mrs Traynor watched her closely. The last thing she wanted was a teenage mother in her spare room and in her wide experience, pregnancy was the reason for most unmarried girls finding themselves ejected from the family nest. But there was something in the girl's eyes which discouraged further questions and, on the whole, she was inclined to believe she was telling the truth. The one thing she was sure of was that there was some mystery about Kate Brebner's past, some deep unhappiness which had driven her away from home. Well, time and a sympathetic ear had a way of sorting everything out, and with her husband dead these last seven years and her family all off her hands, those were both things she had plenty of. A bit of female company would be just the thing for the coming winter evenings.

'Right, lass. Yours is the door at the top of the stairs. You look as if you could do with a good sleep. Away up to your room and get yourself settled in. I'll give you a shout about six the morn.'

Kate smiled and got to her feet, glad to have someone else making the decisions, just for tonight.

NINE

'I think we should take the offer and get out while we can,' Robbie Laing spoke from the depths of an armchair in Meggie and Oliver's sitting-room.

'Perhaps.' Meggie thought she heard a note of doubt in Oliver's reply and watched him closely as he went on. 'But I don't think you should be making such important decisions yet, Robbie. You're supposed to be on holiday.'

Robbie shrugged. 'Some decisions can't be delayed. If we don't give an answer soon the offer will be withdrawn and I can tell you this, Oliver, we won't get another one like it.' He seemed to take a deep breath, then, speaking for the first time about the tragedy that had engulfed him, added, 'And you're wrong. The last thing I need is a holiday . . . all that time to think, to go over what's happened again and again. If you want to know the truth I'm glad this has come to a head now. I need something like this to occupy my mind.'

Though Megan's death, six weeks previously, had been expected, Robbie had been devastated by the loss of his wife. At Meggie's urging he and his young son and daughter had come to spend a few weeks in Inverannan with the specific purpose of giving them time to come to terms with the tragedy. Meggie had been dismayed by the change in him. The bright, humorous man who had been such a support to her at the time of Oliver's accident had aged ten years since she had last seen him. He rarely smiled now and even with his children seemed detached and unresponsive. Fond as she was of Robbie, Meggie longed to help him but knew that there was nothing she or Oliver could do which would begin to compensate for Megan's death. But perhaps the Strathannan Mining Company could provide the distraction he so badly needed. Catching his eye, Meggie gave him an encouraging smile and was relieved to have it returned.

'If the Strathannan Mining Company goes I'll be without a job,' Oliver reminded his cousin coldly.

'Do you not think I'm aware of that?' Robbie retorted sharply.

Oliver shrugged. 'I don't suppose it makes any difference. We all know it's going under. One way or another I'll end up on the rubbish heap.'

'Oliver, of course you won't,' Meggie tried to reassure her husband, flinching when he turned his bitterness on her.

'Oh, of course, I forgot! You'll know about these things, won't you, Meggie, you being such an important business woman yourself.'

Meggie forced herself to ignore the deliberate sarcasm. 'I thought you were considering standing for a seat on the local council? Won't that take up a lot of your time?' It was his pet subject, an ambition he had never had the opportunity to pursue.

'I am,' he snapped. 'But that will not bring any money into the house, Meggie. Even if I am fortunate enough to be accepted as a candidate, I will still need to earn my living.'

'But surely you won't have any trouble finding a good position, Oliver? There must be plenty of businesses which would welcome someone with your experience.'

'Och aye, they'll be standing in line just waiting to offer a job to a man with one leg; a man whose last company went to the wall. That's right, Meggie, don't you worry your head about me. I'll find something else. And let's be honest, it'll not really matter what I do, will it? There are always your shops to fall back on. Maybe you could arrange a job for me. I know!

I'll work as an assistant in the shop that brother of yours manages so well for you, eh? That'd be braw and cosy, wouldn't it?'

Oliver's face had flushed puce with anger and he leaned across the table, thrusting his face aggressively at his wife who turned red with mortification and looked away. 'Still,' he added, delivering a final, poisonous thrust. 'At least we've not got a family to worry about. No school fees to be paid. I should be grateful for that at least.'

Meggie cringed, loathing this bitter side of her husband; a side which increasingly dominated and tainted their relationship, despite her honest attempts to devote more time to him.

Witnessing this unpleasant interchange, Robbie was appalled to realise that the obvious tension between Meggie and Oliver stemmed from something much deeper than the impending failure of the Strathannan Mining Company. Oliver's words, fuelled no doubt by the huge amount of alcohol he had drunk, had been revealing, and worse, deliberately calculated to wound Meggie, whose humiliation was obvious in her flaming face and bowed head. Robbie felt a flash of anger on her behalf. After all Meggie had endured she surely deserved better than this, especially from her own husband who, as far as he could judge, was wallowing in self-pity. Uncomfortable to be a party to such rancour between husband and wife, he hastened to intervene.

'I don't think it will come to that,' he murmured.

'Oh you don't, don't you? Well, perhaps you've got some suggestions? Maybe you can tell me where I'm going to find a decent job?' Oliver rounded on his cousin belligerently. 'And don't bother offering to take me on in your slate mines if that's what you have in mind. I'm a Scot and Scotland is where I'll stay. I'm not going to bury myself in some ugly little Welsh valley.'

Even Robbie's temper was beginning to fray. For Meggie's

sake he controlled the angry retort and merely commented, 'Actually, North Wales is very beautiful. But,' he hurried on before Oliver could interrupt, 'that is not what I had in mind.'

'Good,' was Oliver's ungracious response.

Robbie felt rather than saw the exasperated look that Meggie bestowed on her husband. 'Go on, Robbie,' she said.

'I've seen a business I think you might be interested in. With the money we should realise from the mines we'll be able to buy it outright.'

Despite himself, Oliver was interested. He said nothing but raised an eyebrow quizzically.

'It's a quarry. Just off the coast road. It's a bit run down but there's plenty of potential there.'

'A quarry!' Oliver was openly derisive. 'A bloody quarry?'

Again Robbie bit back his anger. 'You know about quarrying, do you Oliver?' he asked coldly.

'Enough to know it's Douglas's you're talking about. That place hasn't made a profit since before the war.'

'And do you know why?'

'Badly managed,' Oliver answered at once.

'Aye. Badly managed. Not that it's old Jock Douglas's fault, mind you,' Robbie went on, his enthusiasm overcoming his anger. 'It's a family business. Jock and his two sons ran it. Like you say, Oliver, it's not made a profit since before the war. Then, of course, the sons went off to fight and old Jock struggled along on his own with just half a dozen old men to help him. That wouldn't have mattered. All they had to do was wait until the boys came home to take over. Jock could have retired then and left the business to his sons.'

'But?' Meggie asked.

'But they didn't come back. Both killed. One in North Africa, the other in the Far East.'

'But that's terrible.' Meggie was easily moved by the tragedy of others.

'Jock Douglas lost heart. And he's an old man now. All he wants is enough cash to see him through his retirement. He's prepared to sell at a reasonable price.'

Despite his bitterness, Oliver was as astute a businessman as his cousin. 'But a gravel quarry, Robbie? Is there anything to be made in gravel?'

'Of course there is! Just think about it, Oliver. With all the building work going on, the country's crying out for gravel. There will always be a call for it.'

Oliver was thoughtful. 'Aye, you're right! Can't say I've ever given it much thought before but it's obvious really, isn't it?' The truculence disappeared as he responded to Robbie's obvious enthusiasm and his mind turned instantly to the practicalities. 'It's a small quarry, though. There'll not be much profit from a place that size.'

'Enough,' Robbie reassured him, 'to start with. We'd need to get the place up to scratch quickly though, invest in some new plant. Then we can begin to expand.'

'Douglas has the mineral rights, does he?'

'Better than that. He owns the land too. The whole of that hillside and more. Enough to satisfy even you, Oliver,' he said, a note of triumph in his voice.

'You've gone into this pretty thoroughly, then?'

Robbie nodded. 'I was glad of something to get my teeth into. I've got maps and all the figures with me. We'll look at them later if you think it might be a sound proposition. Are you starting to fancy yourself as a quarryman now, then?'

Oliver actually smiled. 'I think I could live with it, if it's as good an investment as you seem to think.' The cousins grinned at each other, hostility forgotten.

Meggie watched, relieved at the lessening of tension and pleased to see Robbie looking more like his old self. Even Oliver's habitually sour expression was lightened by the prospect of a new challenge. It was, she knew, precisely what he needed;

something to distract him from the bitter disappointments that overshadowed his life. Even though the collapse of the Strathannan Mining Company was in no way his fault, she understood that he saw it as a personal failure. But if the company was in such a perilous state, who would consider buying it? 'I don't understand,' she said hesitantly, reluctant to dampen their enthusiasm. 'Surely no one in their right mind would buy the company?'

'The Fife Coal Company would,' Robbie smiled.

'But why? There's no coal left to mine.'

'Ah, but that's where you're wrong,' Oliver told her. 'There's plenty of coal there. It's just all either under the sea bed or in new seams. Either way, we can't afford to open them up.'

'And the Fife Coal Company can?' she asked disbelievingly.

'Well – ' Robbie pulled a wry face – 'enough to keep the place going for a year or so, which is more than we can hope to do, more's the pity.'

'Och, surely not! I know the Fife Coal Company is prospering but even they wouldn't buy into something just to keep it limping along for another year. They couldn't hope to cover their costs. It doesn't make any sense.'

'It does if the mines are nationalised,' Oliver chuckled, instantly understanding.

'The government will buy them out. Or that's what they're banking on,' Robbie added.

Meggie knew that nationalisation of the coal fields was almost inevitable. 'I see . . .' She smiled now. 'So the Fife Coal Company are taking a calculated risk.'

'Aye. But to my mind it's more a bit of shrewd investment,' Oliver commented.

'In that case surely it's better for us to hold on until nationalisation?'

'If we could, yes, of course. But it's too late. We can't afford to carry on, not even for another year. We'd have to close long before the government moves in. They won't take over a mine that's no longer operational. No, if we delay we'll lose everything. I say we make the deal now.' Robbie looked at Oliver for confirmation.

'And the price?' Oliver asked.

'Enough to buy out Douglas, to re-equip and invest a little. After that we'll have to work bloody hard to make a go of it, but there is no doubt at all in my mind that it'll be a success.' He stood up, charged with energy, his eyes bright and eager. 'Come on, Oliver. I'll show you the figures.'

The train drew to a steamy halt, covering the waiting passengers in sooty smuts. Robbie and Oliver hurried to find an empty carriage and get the cases inside.

'Goodbye, Aunty Meggie.' Avis, a lamentably plain girl whose bright personality was in shocking contrast to her mousey hair and chubby, bespectacled face, hugged Meggie tightly.

Meggie, who was extremely fond of her niece and nephew and had enjoyed having them stay with her, returned the hug fiercely and dropped a kiss on the girl's head. 'Goodbye, Avis. I'll miss you,' she mumbled, feeling very close to tears.

'Me too,' Avis sniffed noisily, then drew away, rubbing at her eyes.

Meggie smiled and, not wanting to upset her any more, resisted the temptation to draw the child back into her arms. Avis had suffered terribly watching her mother's agonising death but had coped with a maturity far beyond her twelve years, doing her best to comfort her brother, Tommy, and making few demands on her distraught father. It had, of course, taken its toll on her. The naturally exuberant child had arrived in Inverannan pale, listless and withdrawn. Her heart breaking for them, Meggie had abandoned her shops and, for the last four weeks, while the men were wholly immersed in business matters, had concentrated on the children. Sensitive to Avis's needs, Meggie had gently encouraged her niece to talk about her mother and to cry, but had also given her privacy when she needed it. Then, determined to inject some pleasure into their young lives, she had filled the days with activity. The three had shared many pleasant outings, sometimes visiting the wonderful beaches on the Strathannan coast, sometimes going further north into the hills and even indulging in extravagant shopping expeditions to Edinburgh and Glasgow. There had been trips to the pictures, a visit to the summer fairground, an outing to the zoo and many days spent in the freedom of Inverannan's wonderful park with its paddling pool, swings and slides. Meggie had thoroughly enjoyed indulging them and had been immensely relieved to see Avis's natural high spirits gradually re-emerge. As the family prepared to go back to Wales, she knew she would miss them all terribly. If only, she thought, reaching out to give young Tommy a huge hug, she had children of her own.

'Ready then?' Robbie asked.

'Do we have to go?' Avis said, her Welsh accent heavy with tears. 'Why can't we stay here?'

'And miss your first day at your new school?' he asked gently.

'But I want to stay with Aunty Meggie,' she insisted.

'I'd like that too,' Meggie told her. 'But it would be selfish of me to keep you here, wouldn't it? You have to start at the senior school with all your friends. If you don't you'll feel like the odd one out later on. Anyway,' she added briskly, 'I know you're looking forward to it. You're going into the A class aren't you, with all the other clever girls?'

Avis nodded, causing her wire-framed glasses to slip forward on her freckled nose. 'So's Mona, she's my best friend. But Betty's to be in the B class.'

Robbie caught Meggie's eye and smiled, admiring her skill with his children.

'Well, you see it wouldn't be fair to Mona, would it, if you stayed here? She'll not want to go to a new school without her best friend.'

Avis grinned. 'We're going to sit together. And we're going to learn French and Latin and Chemistry and . . . and' – she screwed her face up in concentration – ' . . . lots of other things they don't do in the primary school. Dad's going to help me with my maths,' she ended, smiling up at her father, who took the opportunity to draw her away from Meggie.

'I'm going to a new class too,' Tommy reported solemnly.

'I know. And next time you come to see me you can read me a bedtime story instead of me reading one to you,' Maggie laughed, picking him up and handing him into the carriage.

'Got a kiss for me too?' Oliver helped Avis on to the train and got a more restrained kiss on his cheek from both children, who were more than just a little in awe of him.

Further down the platform the guard was slamming doors, ready for the train to leave. Meggie felt her throat tighten and had to look away from the children who sat with their noses pressed against the window.

'Thank you, Meggie. I'm extremely grateful for all you've done with the children. Avis is much more like her old self now. I was getting really worried about her,' Robbie said, coming to stand in front of her.

'She's a lovely bairn. They both are. And I've enjoyed having them here. Just be sure and bring them back soon,' she told him.

'Aye.' He turned as the guard came and stood by their still open door.

'Time to be leaving, sir.'

'Right.' Robbie stooped suddenly and caught Meggie to him, giving her a soft, lingering kiss before breaking away abruptly, shaking Oliver's hand and climbing aboard the train. 'I'll be back in a fortnight, just as soon as the children are settled with Edwin and Gwyneth,' he called as the train began to pull out. 'With any luck we should be able to sign the papers for Douglas's then.'

Oliver nodded and raised a hand in farewell. 'Take care,' he called.

'Bye bye, Aunty Meggie.'

To Avis's intense disappointment, Meggie did not look up. As the train rumbled out of the station, Meggie was aware only of the feeling of warmth on her lips where Robbie had kissed her.

'My, my! And here I was thinking you'd gone into retirement,' Matty teased as Meggie came into the corner shop for the first time in over a month.

'You only had to lift the phone if you needed my help,' Meggie told him, laughing. 'Och, I knew you'd manage fine without me. No problems, were there?'

'No, not really.'

Meggie looked at him sharply, recognising the guarded tone of his voice. 'But?' she asked.

'Och, nothing much. Just that Mrs Coulthart's left.' He busied himself at the shelves behind the counter, not meeting her eyes as he spoke.

'Oh no!' Meggie sighed. 'We don't seem to be having much luck finding someone to work here do we? She's the third one in three months.' And that wasn't counting Vera. Meggie bitterly regretted the loss of a friend who had worked for her for many years. But Vera, who had worked with Matty in the past and, like Sally, could say nothing good about him, had handed her notice in within ten minutes of learning of his return. Nothing Meggie could say would induce her to change her mind. Feeling betrayed, she had even refused an offer of a job at the High Street shop with Sally.

'Aye, I know.'

'What went wrong this time?' she asked, irritated.

'Says her husband doesn't like her working.'

'Och, for goodness sake! Mary couldn't add up and Agnes Rutter said standing up all day was making her legs bad.' She sighed. 'I suppose we'll need to put another card in the window and start someone else. Let's hope we have better luck this time.'

Matty finally turned round. 'I've already put one in. It's been right busy here, Meggie, with just me and Mrs McManus. We'll need to take someone else on as soon as we can.'

She nodded, frowning. 'Maybe I should interview them this time,' she suggested.

Matty bristled at once. 'It's not my fault. They all seemed right enough when I interviewed them. How was I to know Agnes had bad legs or Mr Coulthart didn't want his wife to work?'

'But you should have made sure Mary could add up. You can't work in a shop like this if you can't do simple arithmetic,' she responded sharply.

'Och, Mary could add up all right. It's just that she kept short-changing folk.'

'You mean she was stealing?' Meggie was horrified. Mary Robertson had seemed an honest, straightforward sort of woman.

Matty shrugged. 'I can't prove it. She said she just made a lot of mistakes, but the customers were starting to complain.'

Meggie couldn't help remembering a time, years ago, when Matty himself had been guilty of exactly the same thing. In the days when she had first taken over this shop he had helped himself to cash from the till and cigarettes from the stock-room. Still, she reminded herself quickly, he really had reformed and there had been no discrepancies in the time he had been manager here.

'I didn't realise she'd been doing that! Why didn't you tell me?' she asked him.

Matty's dark eyes were hooded, giving nothing away, but his voice was hostile. 'I'm the manager here, aren't I? I'm the one who is supposed to be in charge, aren't I?'

'Aye,' she agreed, 'You know you are.'

'Then it was up to me to sort it out. And I did. I sacked her. All right?'

'All right.'

'There's no point in you querying everything I do, Meggie. Either you trust me to manage the shop and leave me to get on with the job you pay me to do or you can come back and take over for yourself.' And that was the last thing he wanted.

Twelve years ago Meggie would have been intimidated by his manner, but he had let her down badly once and she had learned a lot from the experience. 'This is my shop, Matty. You might be the manager but you are still accountable to me. For everything. Just like Sal is. Now.' She went on briskly, giving him no chance to argue. 'Let me see the books for the past six weeks so I can see how we've been doing.'

Matty scowled, then quickly forced a smile to his thin lips. 'They're under the counter. But there's no need to worry, everything's up to date.'

'Just the same,' she insisted.

Meggie sat at the end of the counter, looking up from the books every now and then to greet old customers as they came into the shop. This was something she really enjoyed, this contact with folk she had known since she was just a young lass, catching up on the gossip, passing the time of day with people who had become her friends.

But as she worked her way through the pages of figures in Matty's untidy hand, her smile became a frown.

'The takings are well down,' she commented when there was a brief lull in trade.

Matty looked shifty and made a show of tidying the papers and magazines which were spread over the counter top. 'It's summer. A lot of folk are on their holidays.'

'Aye. The fair fortnight is always slack, but business should have picked up over the last four weeks. In fact we usually take as much in the first week after the fair fortnight as we do just before Christmas.'

Matty shrugged. 'We've been right quiet.'

'But I thought you said you'd been busy. That's why you're in a hurry to get someone to replace Mrs Coulthart.'

'Aye, I am. Even when it's quiet there's too much work for just two of us, what with the orders to be got ready and everything.'

'I suppose so.' Feeling the first stirrings of unease, Meggie stared at him. He didn't look up. Surely he wasn't up to his old tricks after all?

As if he read her mind, Matty suddenly glared at her. 'Och, I know fine what you're thinking, Meggie. I stole money from the till when I was just a kid so if the takings are down you think I must be doing it again. Once a thief always a thief, eh? Well, if you can't trust me you'd better find yourself another manager.' He started to undo the white apron which covered his clothes, his face dark with fury.

Meggie flushed with guilt. He was right – she had thought that and she was wrong. Matty was a reformed character. He worked hard, never took a day off and kept the shop scrupulously clean and tidy. There had to be another explanation. He had too much to lose by pilfering from the till.

'Matty! For goodness sake, don't be so touchy. But there must be some reason for it. Maybe we're charging more than the other shops. The women round here have a keen eye for a bargain. They'd rather walk all the way into town than pay an extra penny for a pound of best butter. If I come in and look after the shop tomorrow morning, maybe you could have a look round and check our prices against what Mr Brown on Laidlaw Street is charging, and look at Wishart's down in Campbell Drive too. They're the closest shops and they change their prices every week to try and get customers from us.'

'All right,' he agreed gruffly, keeping up the pretence of outrage, careful not to let her see how relieved he was. It had been too tempting, too easy to fall into his old ways when Meggie wasn't there to check up on him. He would have to be more circumspect in future. If he wanted to persuade Meggie to cut him in on a share in the business he couldn't afford to arouse her suspicions.

'Meggie!' Sal Sandys ran from behind the counter and hugged her friend.

Meggie laughed. 'You'd think I'd been away for months.'

'It feels like it,' Sally laughed.

'How's business?'

'That's my best friend! Business first.'

'Sorry. How are you, Sal?'

'I'm fine, the bairns are fine and Ronnie's fine. How are you?'

'Fine.' They both giggled. 'Actually,' Meggie admitted, 'I loved having Avis and Tommy. Once they'd settled in we had a wonderful time, doing the sort of things you can only really do with bairns.'

Sally, who knew Meggie so well, understood exactly why the wistful expression had come over her face. 'You'll have a family of your own one day,' she assured her softly.

Meggie sighed and looked quickly towards the door as a customer hurried in. 'Not much chance of that the way things are between Oliver and me,' she admitted sadly before stepping aside to leave Sally to serve the woman who was now standing at the counter.

'Things are no better then?' Sally dispatched the woman and resumed the conversation as if there had been no interruption.

'No.' Meggie couldn't quite overcome the feeling that she was being disloyal, but she badly needed someone to confide in. 'He's so bitter, Sal. About his leg, about Matty, about the company. He's out every evening and when he does come in he's always so drunk that he just collapses into bed and falls straight to sleep. When he does . . . you know . . . I hate it. I don't want him near me when he's like that. Then he gets angry, says I'm cold, not natural . . . all sorts of names he calls me . . . says it's my fault that we haven't had children. Oh Sal, I wish I could do something to put things right, but I can't. I've done everything he asked me to do. I look after the house, I go and visit his mother, I keep myself nice for him, I take an interest in his work and I don't spend half as much time at the shops as I used to do. I'm always there when he comes in at night, but even that doesn't please him. When he is at home he buries himself in the newspapers. He won't let me talk about the shops and he won't talk to me about anything that interests him. And now he says I'm boring.'

'Was he like that even when Robbie and the children were staying?' Sal asked.

Meggie nodded. 'Aye. Och, he put on a good front for them, most of the time, but as soon as we were on our own he was as bad as ever. I'm sure Robbie knows there's something wrong.'

'He felt pretty bad about not being able to do anything for the war effort, didn't he?'

'Aye. That's when all this started.'

'It must be hard for him, knowing the company's in trouble. What with that and Matty turning up again he must be feeling nothing's going right for him. And I do think you were asking a lot of him, expecting him to let Matty come back as if nothing had happened.' As always, Sal spoke her mind. 'I warned you there might be trouble there.'

'I know. But Oliver and Matty never meet. Oliver won't let him come to the house and – '

'You can't blame him for that!' Sally exclaimed.

'No, I suppose not,' Meggie sighed. 'Still, with any luck the company will be sold and Oliver will soon be running a quarry.'

Sal broke off again to serve two more customers, then turned back to Meggie. 'He's selling up? But I thought the mines were unworkable.'

'They are.' Meggie smiled and explained the plan to Sally. 'So you see,' she ended. 'With any luck at all everyone will be happy.'

'Aye. And if you ask me, that's exactly what Oliver needs. You'll see, Meggie. If this all works out Oliver will be his old self again.'

'I hope you're right,' Meggie said heavily. 'Because I don't know how much longer I can put up with things the way they are.'

Sally looked at her for a long moment, then said, 'Be careful, Meggie. Don't do anything you'll regret. Oliver's been going through a tough time. He's had a lot of bad luck and he needs your support.'

'He's got it!' Meggie snapped. 'The trouble is he's too proud to take it.'

'Aye well, talking about trouble, how is that brother of yours?'

Meggie groaned. 'Do you know he's given that new girl the sack?'

'But she's only been there a month or so.'

'That's right, and she's the third one since Vera left. Apparently her husband didn't like her working.'

'Aye, Ronnie could tell you all about that,' Sally said with feeling. 'Not that he's going to get me out of here,' she added quickly.

'Thank goodness for that. Anyway, another one had bad legs.'

Sally giggled. 'Oh no.'

'And another had her hand in the till!'

'Matty should have spotted that easily enough. He is an expert.'

'Sal!'

Sally held her hands up. 'Sorry. I know. He's reformed.'

'I certainly hope so.'

Sally looked up sharply, sensing a certain reservation in her friend's voice. 'Has something happened?'

'No. Probably not. It's too easy to think the worst of Matty and it's not fair to blame him every time something goes wrong.'

'Come on, Meggie. Tell me about it. You know it won't go any further than me and Ronnie.'

'It's just that Matty was down about sixty per cent over the fair fortnight.'

'I think we were too. That's normal, isn't it?'

'Aye. But even now he's still almost twenty-five per cent down on the same weeks last year.'

For once Sally could find nothing helpful to say. 'Oh.'

'Och, it's likely just because I've not been around to keep an eye on the prices; we'll have lost some customers to the other shops. But Matty thought I was accusing him of stealing. He's still in the huff.'

'And are you quite sure that it's not Matty?' Sally stared hard at Meggie, waiting in silence until her friend finally met her steely gaze.

Meggie flushed and when she spoke she sounded angry. 'No, I'm not sure. But I feel awful about it, Sal. I should be able to trust my own brother.'

'Aye. You should. But the truth, if you would only open your eyes and see it, is you can't trust Matty.'

'You don't like him!' Meggie accused.

'No. I don't and there's no point pretending I do. You know me better than that.'

'I know.' Suddenly Meggie felt weary.

'Look, Meggie, there's no point in me saying anything about Matty. We'll only fall out about him and frankly I'm not going to risk our friendship for him, he's not worth it. But for goodness sake be careful and remember what happened last time.'

'I will.' Meggie smiled wryly. 'One thing about you, Sal, you always tell me the truth whether you think I'll like it or not.'

Sal laughed. 'Come on, I'll put the kettle on and you can look at the books.'

'Good idea.' Meggie followed her through to the back room thinking, not for the first time, how lucky she was to have a friend like Sally Sandys.

TEN

Kate had the day marked on her calendar. It was the first thing she thought about when she woke that morning. Lying in bed in her dark room, she concentrated on that area in the very pit of her stomach; the place which every month ached with the bleeding she had always seen as a messy inconvenience but which she would now welcome as a blessing.

Raised as she had been, on a farm, Kate was more aware than most girls of her age of the mechanics of reproduction. Her arrival in Inverannan was overshadowed by the mind-numbing fear that she might be pregnant; that as a result of the rape she might be carrying Duncan Auld's child. The thought terrified her, sending icy shivers of fear down her spine and into her stomach until she felt physically ill.

This morning, twenty-eight days since her last curse, there wasn't even the faintest twinge. Even as she lay there, Kate felt her heart quicken with the onset of panic. She closed her eyes again, concentrating on her body, but there was nothing, not even the faintest physical clue to her condition, nothing to tell her whether she was facing the ultimate disgrace. A disgrace, she suddenly realised, that her own mother must have felt. And what would she do if faced with a similar situation, Kate wondered, imagining the hardship, the disadvantages that the child would suffer should she try to raise it herself. Quite apart from the practical problems of raising a child single-handedly, there was a terrible stigma attached to illegitimacy. How much worse it must have been when she herself had been born. Now, for the first time, she could begin to accept the possibility that her own mother's decision to part with her might have been an act of unselfish sacrifice. Perhaps it had been the only way of giving her illegitimate daughter a chance to overcome the ignominious circumstances of her birth. Faced with the possibility of having to make the same decision, Kate found herself thinking of her natural mother in a new, more sympathetic light. But, she told herself, there was no point in taking such a black view yet. Even if nothing happened today, it would be another full month before she could be sure.

Slowly, with no real enthusiasm, Kate dragged herself from bed. Then, hearing Mrs Traynor bustling about in the kitchen, she deliberately took her time, leaving it until the last possible moment before going downstairs, unable to face her landlady on this terrible morning.

'Och, lass, you're as white as a sheet. Are you not well?' Mrs Traynor asked as soon as Kate appeared.

'I've a thumping headache,' Kate answered, realising as she spoke that it was the truth. She had been so overwhelmed with fear that she hadn't even noticed.

'Here, have this. It'll help.' Mrs Traynor emptied an Askit powder into a glass of water and stirred it vigorously.

'I'm going to be late,' Kate protested, anxious only to be out in the fresh air on her own, to think and think.

'Take it, Kate. You've only been in that job for a couple of weeks. You can't afford to be ill already.' Mrs Traynor shoved the glass against Kate's chest and held it there.

'All right.' Unequal to the fight, Kate took the glass and swallowed the contents in three long gulps, retching as the fluid hit her troubled stomach. 'Thanks,' she managed at last, wiping a film of sweat from her upper lip. 'I'd better hurry.'

Mrs Traynor had reached her own conclusions about the cause of such early morning fragility. She felt angry to have had her initial judgement proved wrong and turned away with a shrug as she started to clear Kate's untouched breakfast from the table. 'Suit yourself.' But there would be words spoken with that young lassie tonight, she promised herself as she let Kate out.

Kate's headache seemed stubbornly resistant to the powers of Askit powders. By lunch-time it was thumping away so violently that she could hardly think straight. By contrast her lower stomach was distressingly pain-free. Kate toiled through her allotted tasks wondering how long she would be permitted to go on working at Hough's, how long she could hope to disguise her condition, how long she would be allowed to stay in Netherton Place. But every time she tried to imagine what would happen to her then, her mind went blank, as if, she thought miserably, there was no future at all. Was this, she wondered in a moment of total despair, how her natural mother had felt when she discovered she was carrying her?

By six o'clock she was exhausted and the fifteen minute walk back to Netherton took her twice as long as usual.

'You're late the night, lass.' Mrs Traynor's greeting was deliberately cheerful. Time enough to be firm when she had got the girl to admit to her condition, though she was more disappointed than angry now. Plenty of girls got themselves into trouble. The war had produced a crop of fatherless bairns and even in Inverannan, attitudes were softening. It was the deception she objected to, the feeling that Kate had used her, was hoping to take advantage of her good nature.

Kate looked surprised. 'Am I?'

'A good fifteen minutes. Your dinner's in the oven. Wash your hands and come to the table before it dries up altogether.'

Kate, sensing her landlady was not in the best of moods, hurriedly sluiced her hands under the scullery tap and sat at the table.

'Head better now, is it?' Mrs Traynor asked pointedly.

'Aye.' Kate moved it cautiously from side to side and realised that her head had at last cleared. 'It is. Mind you, it thumped away all day. I don't mind of the last time I had a headache like that.'

'Upset stomach if you ask me. I saw the way you were heaving this morning.'

'No, that was the Askit powder. They always do that to me,' Kate admitted.

'Och, lass! I wasn't born yesterday. I know fine what's bothering you.'

She would have gone on but for the fact that Kate leaped suddenly to her feet and ran for the stairs.

Five minutes later Mrs Traynor shoved her empty plate aside and, somewhat reluctantly, slid Kate's into the oven to keep warm. Though why she should bother was a mystery.

On the way back from the kitchen she stopped for a minute at the bottom of the stairs and listened. To her consternation, she heard the sound of muffled tears. Well, the lass had enough to cry about, that was certain, but, she thought, her soft nature getting the better of her, Kate was only young and would likely think the world was at an end. Maybe she would just go upstairs and have a wee talk with her. Better to have it out in the open before the lass got even more upset.

'Kate.' She knocked softly on the bedroom door. 'Are you all right?'

There was a sudden silence, a shuffling noise and then the door was thrown open and Kate, her face tear-stained but radiant with joy, was smiling at her. 'Och, my dinner's still on the table! I forgot all about it.'

'Aye, well, I daresay you've more on your mind than your dinner.'

'I'm sorry, Mrs Traynor, I . . . I . . .' She trailed off into new tears, real heart-wrenching sobs which seemed to drive straight into her landlady's heart.

'Och, Kate. Whatever's the matter, hen?' Mrs Traynor put an arm around Kate and led her to the bed. 'Is there something you'd like to tell me, lass?' she asked, her anger replaced by sympathy now. When Kate failed to reply she went on, 'Och, you're not the first lass to be caught out, Kate. It happens all the time. The important thing is to be sure. There's no point in getting yourself into a state over a false alarm. Now, just tell me when you last came on.'

To her amazement, Kate gave a soft laugh. 'Today.'

'Today? Och, and I thought . . .' She trailed off in confusion, appalled to have made such a bad misjudgement.

'You guessed,' Kate said. 'But how?'

'But you're not? I mean . . .' Mrs Traynor sighed, shook her head in confusion, then opted for honesty. 'Kate, I feel right mean when I say this but I have to admit I was thinking the worst of you. What with you turning up on my doorstep like that. And then you'd sit there night after night just staring at the fire, your bonny young face all screwed up in a frown. And then, when you weren't well this morning, well, I jumped to the wrong conclusion. I'm sorry, it's not a nice thing to think about a decent lass like yourself, but I was sure you were in the family way.'

Kate sat quite still for a moment. When she finally looked up, Mrs Traynor saw that her eyes were again flooded with tears. 'What is wrong, Kate?' she asked again. 'Can you not let me help you, whatever it is?'

Kate's wounded heart opened up to this generous woman who had made her feel so welcome in her small home. 'You were right about me,' she admitted, unable to hold back the truth any longer, desperately needing someone to confide in. 'I thought I was pregnant. Until just now,' she whispered.

'But you're not?' Somehow Mrs Traynor kept her voice steady.

'No.' Kate shook her head and teardrops splashed over the counterpane.

'You're quite sure, Kate?'

Kate nodded.

'But how late were you, lass?'

'I wasn't late at all. I was due today,' Kate sobbed. 'I was just so frightened. I thought I was going to have a baby. His baby. I hate him. But it wouldn't have been the baby's fault, would it? And how would I have cared for it?' She broke off to dab at her eyes and take a long, sobbing breath. 'I would have had to give it up for adoption, just like my real mother gave me away.'

It was obvious that Kate was too overwrought to make any sense yet. 'Dry your eyes, Kate, and wash your face. I'll go and make us a nice cup of tea and then you are going to tell me everything.' Mrs Traynor was on her feet and out of the door before Kate could object.

Over the next hour Kate allowed Mrs Traynor to draw her story from her. The older woman had long since passed the stage when she was easily affected by the tragedy of others, but Kate's story brought a lump to her throat and a mist to her faded grey eyes.

'But that's terrible, Kate,' she murmured. 'I don't understand how she could do it. Your own mother, willing to see you married off to someone who raped you.'

'She wasn't my mother, and they said I led him on.'

'But you didn't, Kate. And don't you ever let yourself think otherwise. To my mind that lad should be locked up. They should have called the police in and had him taken away. But there he is, still working on the farm, while you've been put out of your own home. Och, it makes my blood boil, so it does, just to think about it.' She reached over and took Kate's cold hand and squeezed it gently. 'You've been very brave, Kate. And I'm sorry for thinking what I did about you.'

Kate gave her a watery smile. 'Thanks for listening to me. I feel a lot better just for talking about it.'

'Aye, lass, most troubles don't seem half as bad when they're shared. Still, you can put yours behind you now, can't you? You've a good job, somewhere to live and your whole life in front of you, just waiting for you to enjoy it.'

'I suppose I'm lucky compared to a lot of folk,' Kate said, sighing as though she didn't really believe it.

'Indeed you are,' Mrs Traynor told her firmly. 'And just because your real mother had you adopted, it doesn't mean she didn't care about you. More likely the very opposite. It was nearly impossible for unmarried mothers then. I expect she thought she was doing her best by you. Now then,' she went on briskly, 'I don't know about you but I'm fair tired out. Och, but you've had nothing to eat and you must be hungry after all those tears. I daresay your dinner will be past saving but I could make you a piece and bacon.'

'No.' Kate smiled at her with real affection. 'You go on to bed. I'll do it.'

'All right, lass. Sleep well.'

'I'll do that all right,' Kate laughed, feeling as though she was human again.

When the door had closed behind her landlady, Kate sat back on her bed immersed in thought. Facing the possibility of pregnancy had at least given her a new perspective on her own position. No longer would she let herself believe that she had been abandoned. Now she could tell herself that she had been given for adoption for the best of reasons; that it was concern for the welfare of her baby that had motivated her natural mother and not just a selfish unwillingness to raise an unwanted child. Was it possible that somewhere there was a woman who sometimes wondered what had become of her daughter? Who was she, and where was she now? Kate's eyes narrowed, then opened suddenly as she reached into her bedside drawer for the envelope of papers she had brought with her from the farm.

Slowly she drew out her birth certificate and smoothing it carefully, laid it on the bed. For many minutes she stared at it, wondering why she had not thought to look at it before, for there it was in rusty ink, the one link between herself and her true identity. Her mother's name.

ELEVEN

'What you are really saying is that you don't trust me to run the quarry! The Mining Company finally failed while I was in charge so you think it was my fault.' Oliver's voice lashed across the dining table.

Robbie's expression tightened and he closed his eyes, desperately trying to hold on to his temper. When he did speak his voice was terse with the effort of control. 'You know that's not the case, Oliver. Look.' He sighed, put down his knife and fork and met his cousin's hostile stare with his own steady gaze. 'We've been over and over this. You know as well as I do that there's too much work for you on your own. If we're going to make a success of this we need to work together.'

'Aye.' The other man's voice was scornful. 'As long as you're in charge.'

'We have different talents. I have no more interest in the engineering side of it than your mother has. I don't know one piece of machinery from the other. I don't have your ability to go out there and see, instantly, what needs to be done on the site. I'm just a glorified clerk, Oliver, nothing more, but until this place is on a secure footing I intend to be financial director because that's what I'm good at and I know damn well that you haven't got the time to do it all.'

For a moment the two men stared at each other and Meggie was struck again by how alike and yet how totally dissimilar they were. Both of the same height and build, both dark-haired and brown-eyed, a verbal description would have failed to highlight the differences between them. Of the two, Robbie, three years the elder, looked the younger. His mouth was wider, fuller and more inclined to smile, his eyebrows were finely shaped, almost feminine, and arched high above his eyes, opening them out and softening his whole appearance, whereas Oliver's more bushy brows almost met over the bridge of his nose and gave his face a permanently lowering expression. It was, Meggie realised, the expression rather than facial features which distinguished the two men, making them appear so different that unless you looked at them both closely, it was hard to see the family likeness at all, even though it was there in the prominent Laing nose, high cheekbones and firm jaw line.

Oliver's slurred, angry voice reclaimed her wandering attention. 'I did it all at the Mining Company.'

'This is different. We're going to be expanding, we need to sell our product, to go out and look for business. I'll bring the buyers in and make sure we operate within our financial limits. You see to the management of the site itself, find first-rate men to work it, make sure we meet our deadlines, keep an eye on the plant and equipment, ensure the quality of the end product. You won't have a minute to call your own, Oliver, and if everything goes as we've planned it, neither will I.'

'And while you're so busy up here, what is happening to the slate mines in Wales? Or are you telling me that something ten times as big as our poxy little quarry can be managed by Edwin on his own?' Oliver refilled his glass with red wine, drained it and topped it up again. 'Cheers,' he offered sarcastically, aware of Robbie's critical observation.

Robbie eyed the two empty bottles with pointed distaste. 'Edwin has a whole team of people working for him. The slate mines run like clockwork and it's not as if I'm backing out altogether. I'm still on the board, and available for any major decisions. In any case, Edwin is more than capable of managing without me.'

'And I'm not.'

Robbie's face flushed a brilliant red. Meggie, an unhappy witness to all this, saw the way his fist curled around the fragile stem of his empty wine glass and felt the momentary urge to slap her husband, to give full vent to the anger which had been building inside her for the last six months. As if sensing her eyes upon him, Robbie looked up, and for a moment their eyes locked. Meggie, unable to turn away, felt the now familiar melting sensation start in her stomach, knew her face and neck were burning. In the space of five seconds Robbie communicated more to her in one silent but intense look than Oliver had stirred himself to do in the last year. She felt the longing to reach out, to touch him, to feel his skin against hers, to feel his breath on her face. Horrified, she finally dropped her gaze, only to feel her eyes lifting again, of their own accord.

It was always the same. Whenever she and Robbie were in the same room they were drawn to each other, as if by some biological magnet, a force which attracted and repelled in equal proportions, lacing their every small contact with danger. How, Meggie wondered, her eyes still locked on to Robbie, could she feel like this when she was married to Oliver, the only man she had ever truly loved? But did she still love him?

Now she managed to pull her eyes away from Robbie and look at the drunken, belligerent, self-pitying man who lounged lopsidedly at the head of the dining table. Was he really the same man who had taught her to trust again, who had loved her enough to overlook the dreadful details of her past, who, despite her vast experience, had awakened her body to physical pleasures she had not dreamed were possible? What had happened to the Oliver she had loved so much that she would willingly have died for him? Was it really just the terrible disappointments of his life which had soured him, or was it her? Could it be that she was the root cause of all this? Would things have been any better between them if she had managed to give him the one thing he truly yearned for – a son? Watching him now, Meggie felt not the faintest stirring of desire for her husband who, in the drunken state in which he habitually arrived in their bedroom, revolted her so much that her physical reaction to his fumbling attempts at love-making made penetration an ordeal of hot, dry pain, something to be dreaded and then endured. How different it would be if only he would come to her sober, his hands soft and tender, concerned as much with her pleasure as with his own. But looking at him now she could feel no spark of passion, no tiny seed of longing; only anger, a feeling of rejection and a deep emptiness, the yearning of a warm-blooded woman for a full, satisfying sexual relationship.

Unbidden, her eyes slid back to Robbie. What was it about the Laing men which made them so attractive, she wondered, feeling the shiver of pleasure which always went through her when she allowed herself to watch him. It had been a Laing man who had first awakened her, taken the first tiny notch of her heart; and then Oliver. How she had fought for him, battling her own conscience, denying the knowledge that any relationship with Oliver would be based on a lie, that even though he thought he knew the worst about her there was still one last terrible secret that must always stand between them. So absolute in her certainty that he was the only man for her, that she would always love him, that he would always love her, she had never envisaged a time when she would feel so cold towards him. And now Robbie, a recent widower, still mourning his wife; another Laing man who set her pulses racing like a schoolgirl's just by looking at her; a man who felt the chemistry between them as much as she did. And who knew that she felt it too. So much at risk did they both feel that they went to extraordinary lengths to avoid being alone together, so much so that Oliver actually believed that his wife and his cousin had conceived a dislike for one another.

Meggie's attention was reclaimed once again by Robbie's furious voice. 'No, Oliver, if you want to know the truth, you are not capable of managing without me. And you bloody well know it. You're just too damn proud to admit it. No one could run that place alone! And if you were to try you would soon run into serious trouble. Like it or not, Oliver, you need me right now.'

'I need you?' Oliver's voice rose to a shriek. 'From where I'm standing it looks more like you need me. Whose house are you and your family staying in, eh? Whose wife is being a mother to your poor bloody kids? Face it, Robbie, you've fallen to bits since Megan died. You can't live down there without her. You were looking for an excuse to get back up here and now you've found it. Well, that's fine by me, but don't you bloody dare use me as an excuse for your own weakness.'

'Oliver!' Meggie stared at her husband, outraged that he could refer to Megan's death so callously. 'Robbie.' She turned to him, trying to reassure him. 'Oliver didn't mean that. He's just . . .' Drunk, she thought, horribly, disgustingly drunk. 'Worried,' she ended, lamely.

'You damn well stay out of this,' Oliver rounded on her bitterly. 'But I'm right, aren't I, Robbie? You are running away.'

To Meggie's astonishment, Robbie's anger seemed to melt away. Instead of the enraged retort she was expecting he gave the wry half-smile she had come to recognise and admitted, 'Not running away, Oliver, but you're right, I don't want to stay in Wales. There's nothing there for me now. I suppose you could say this new venture has come at the right time, given me the excuse I needed to come back to Scotland. But even if Megan was still alive I'd have come back now. Whether you like to admit it or not, Oliver, you need me here.'

Anxious to forestall another explosion from her husband,

Meggie asked, 'But what about the children, Robbie? It will be very hard for them to be taken away from all their friends.'

'We've talked about it and decided that they should stay with Edwin and Gwyneth.' Robbie kept his eyes lowered as he spoke. 'Och, it's for the best, though I would have liked it better if they'd wanted to come here with me. They've been staying with their aunt and uncle since before Megan died. I can't look after them, Meggie, I work such long hours. Gwyneth offered to have them stay on and it seemed kinder than letting them live in that big empty house with some sort of paid housekeeper to look after them when I wasn't there, or else sending them away to school. And they are happy with Edwin and Gwyneth. Avis never wanted to come home after her mother died. Too many memories, I think.'

'They could have come here,' Meggie offered. 'I'd love to have them.'

'Aye. I know you would, Meggie, and they will come to Inverannan in the holidays, but they're better staying where they are. They've had enough upset without making them change schools, taking them away from their friends.'

'Aye. I think you're right about that anyway,' Oliver conceded. 'And I suppose I'll need to put up with you at the quarry. You're obviously set on coming, no matter what I bloody well say.' He flung his napkin down and lurched to his feet, scraping the chair back across the newly polished parquet flooring.

'Aye, I am.' Robbie's voice was uncompromising. In that moment Meggie thought she saw positive dislike in the way Robbie regarded his cousin's unsteady progress towards the door.

'Suit yourself,' Oliver flung back. 'Anyway, with you there I suppose it will give me time to concentrate on the council. You do know I'm running at the next local election?'

Robbie cast a quick, puzzled glance at his cousin. 'What?' he exclaimed in exasperation.

'I told you about this months ago,' Oliver insisted, standing with his back to the door and looking ready for another argument.

'You mentioned you were interested in local politics, yes. But you didn't tell me you were planning to stand for election so soon!' Robbie's temper came close to exploding. 'How do you think you are going to have time for that? We've got a new business to set up!'

'Because, Robbie, *you* are actually going to be running the place, aren't you? *I* am to be nothing more than a site manager. Well, if that's all you need me for, so be it. That suits me just fine. I can do it with my eyes closed and with plenty of time left over for other things.'

Robbie gave a huge sigh of frustration. 'We need to work together on this, Oliver, if we're going to make a success of it.'

'Don't worry, Robbie. I'll pull my weight. I've never been afraid of hard work. I just hope you can say the same.'

'You bastard, Oliver!' Robbie finally lost his temper.

Oliver ignored the angry outburst from his cousin. 'I'm away out. I'd ask you to join me but I feel like some pleasant company for a change.'

Meggie watched him go, then rose wearily and began to clear the table. She felt infinitely depressed, tired of the constant bickering, the lack of warmth between them, and embarrassed too to realise that Robbie must understand just how little affection Oliver had for her. She went about her task with her head lowered, aware as always of his proximity. She sensed rather than saw him come round the table to stand beside her.

'Is it me, Meggie? Am I making him like this? Would it be better if I stayed somewhere else?' He took the pile of plates from her hands as he spoke and placed them firmly on the table.

'No!' She knew she had spoken too sharply. 'No, Robbie. It's not you. He's always like this. I think it's my fault.'

'How could it be your fault? You didn't cause the Strathannan Mining Company to fail, and neither did Oliver, though he's determined to think I hold him personally responsible.' He slipped an arm round her shoulders as he spoke. Meggie tensed but did not move away.

'It's more than just the company, Robbie. It's everything. His leg. The shops. The fact that we've no children. And all these things are my fault.'

'I give up!' Robbie took his arm away and scowled in exasperation. 'What is it with you two? Why are you so determined to blame yourselves for everything that goes wrong? I might as well say it was my fault that Megan died, that I should have made her see the doctor before she did. Maybe it's my fault that you two are so unhappy. After all, it was me who helped Oliver to walk again. You know he wouldn't have married you if he hadn't got the hang of that artificial leg, don't you? He wouldn't have wanted you to be tied to a cripple. Maybe I should have just left him to get on with it and married you myself instead?'

'Robbie,' she pleaded, her voice a quavering whisper. 'Don't, please don't.'

'I loved you even then, you know, Meggie, but I couldn't say anything. You were only interested in Oliver. You hardly knew I existed.'

Meggie could only look at him, meeting his dark eyes with her own, seeing nothing but the truth there. They were absolutely still, not touching, but she knew he was going to kiss her, knew she couldn't let him and managed to move away, breaking the spell, just in time. 'No,' she whispered. 'I can't.'

His hand reached up and touched the side of her face so gently that it was as if a feather had brushed against her skin. He smiled softly then leaned forward and just touched her cheek with his lips. 'I know,' he whispered. 'I know. But remember I've always loved you. Always.'

'But Megan . . .' she said.

'I knew you loved Oliver. There was no hope for me then, and Megan was a good woman. I was very fond of her, Meggie. I wish I had learned to love her and I hope she never knew I didn't.'

Meggie's eyes flooded with tears. 'Robbie, I . . . I don't know what to say. It's so sad . . .'

'It's not too late, Meggie. You don't love Oliver, any fool can see that.'

'Oliver is my husband, Robbie,' she reminded him gently, though her body burned for his faintest touch.

He smiled again, then took a step backwards, away from her. 'You're right,' he said sadly. 'And I'm wrong to even put you in this position. I'm sorry, Meggie. Forgive me?'

She nodded, seeing him as a blur through tears of regret. 'There's nothing to forgive, Robbie. Nothing at all.'

He stayed perfectly still, looking down on her but making no move towards her for many seconds, then, a rueful smile on his lips, said, 'I'll get my things together and move out. I'll get a room at the City Hotel until I can find somewhere permanent. It'll be easier for all of us.'

'No!' Meggie couldn't help herself. 'No, Robbie . . .'

He lifted a hand and gently drew it over the softness of her cheek. 'It's for the best, Meggie, you know it is.'

She caught his hand and held it against her face for a brief moment, then, sighing, her eyes glistening with unshed tears, she nodded. 'Yes, I know.' Turning away from him, she moved to the window, staring blindly out into the night. He was right, she knew he was right, but that knowledge did nothing to ease the pain in her heart, the overwhelming sense of loss which had enveloped her, filling her mind with darkness.

She was still there when she heard the front door close

behind him twenty minutes later, then the roar of his car as he slammed his foot on the accelerator and sped down the drive.

With a single cry of despair she learned forward and rested her hot head against the cold glass of the window, the tears falling unheeded now.

Meggie, who seldom cried, gave herself up to misery for a full half-hour, weeping for Robbie, for Oliver, for the children she wanted so badly, for everything that was wrong in her life. When the tears would come no more she stared out into the blackness for a few more minutes, then, stiff with cold, drew herself up and turned to face the room, meaning to take her unhappiness off to bed.

The unexpected brightness startled her and she stared around her for a moment, as if seeing the room for the first time. She was struck by the cheerfulness of the fire burning heartily in the grate, the atmosphere of warmth emphasised by the soft lighting and comfortable furniture. With a swift, decisive move-ment she turned back to the window and drew the curtains across, banishing the darkness. This was her home, the place she and Oliver had worked so hard for, the house in which she still hoped to raise a family. She closed her eyes briefly as if to gather her senses, then took a deep, shuddering breath as she contemplated how close she had come to throwing it all away. She had made her choice all those years ago when she married Oliver. He had been the one to show forgiveness and under-standing then. Now, now that he was the one who needed help, she had almost been tempted to betray him. If things had gone wrong between them, then she was at least as much to blame as he was. She sighed softly, recalling how much they had loved one another. Surely, she told herself, there must be something left, some small spark of affection between them which could be kindled afresh.

The clock on the mantelpiece struck ten, breaking into her

thoughts, and suddenly she knew what she must do. Soon Oliver would be home and when he came in he would find his wife waiting to welcome him, to take the first steps towards mending their marriage. Though she felt drained by the turbulent emotion of the evening, she went quickly upstairs and set about repairing the damage done by the tears.

She heard his key in the lock and when he came into the sitting-room she turned to greet him, a smile brightening her face.

'Would you like some supper?' she asked, going to kiss his cheek.

'Supper?' He stared at her as though she had lost her senses. 'Of course I don't want any bloody supper. If you want to do something useful get me a drink.'

The smile stiffening on her face, Meggie poured a modest amount of amber fluid into a glass and handed it to him. 'Come and sit by the fire, Oliver, your hands are freezing.'

He scowled at the drink in his hands, tossed it back in one go and went to refill the glass before finally sitting down.

'I was thinking, Oliver,' she continued doggedly, refusing to be discouraged by his continuing truculence. 'Why don't we take a wee holiday? Maybe we could have a week away somewhere, go up to the Highlands. I've never seen the mountains properly.'

He laughed, an unpleasant snort of derision. 'Why the hell do you think I need to go on holiday?'

'Well, you haven't had a break for ages. And neither have I. A rest would do us both good.'

He glowered at her then, and draining his glass again, crashed it on to the table. 'Are you completely out of your mind?' he demanded, roaring at her.

'Oliver! You don't need to yell at me. It was only a suggestion.'

'A bloody stupid one! How can I take a holiday when there's all this work to be done with the quarry and a local election coming up?'

'I just thought we might take a few days off before you really get involved.' She went on, careful to keep her voice light and reasonable. 'Once things get started goodness knows when you'll be able to get away. Can't Robbie look after things for a few days?'

'Oh that's it is it? He's put you up to this, has he? Wants to get me out of the way so he can be in control?.'

'Don't be ridiculous!' She snapped the words at him angrily.

Oliver surged to his feet, stumbling against the table as the whisky hit him. 'Where is he?' he thundered. 'Trying to get me out of the way. I'll bloody fix him.' He blundered towards the door but Meggie got there before him.

'Oliver, it's not like that,' she pleaded. 'It was my idea. Nothing to do with Robbie.'

But Oliver shoved her aside. Opening the door, he roared, 'Robbie. Robbie, get yourself down here!'

Meggie could have cried again in sheer frustration as she watched her good intentions dissolve in Oliver's drunken anger. 'He's not up there, Oliver. He's moved out.'

He gaped at her. 'Moved out? What the hell for?'

She stammered, unable to tell him the truth. 'I . . . I . . . I think he felt it would be better . . . that it was time he found a place of his own.'

'So, where's he gone?' he yelled.

'I think he's gone to the City Hotel for tonight.'

'The City Hotel! When my mother's got that big bloody empty house to rattle around in? If this place isn't good enough for him why didn't he go there?'

Meggie knew this wasn't the time to remind him that Mrs Laing senior was hardly the most welcoming hostess. Even the few close friends who could bear an hour or two of her caustic tongue were required to sit wrapped in coats, scarves and gloves while they drank their afternoon tea because the elderly lady could not bring herself to part with the money to pay for coal in any room but her own small bedroom. Nor had she ever bothered to disguise her rancour towards her late husband's nephews who had, in her opinion, robbed her of her own just inheritance.

'I expect he just wants some time on his own, Oliver. And you know he doesn't really hit it off with your mother,' Meggie suggested, tactfully.

'And that's Mother's fault, I suppose?' he demanded angrily, pouring another glass of whisky and tossing it back.

Meggie felt the thin ice crack its warning under her feet. 'No, Oliver, of course it's not your mother's fault. This is nothing to do with her.'

Looking at her more closely now, he brought his face down so that she could smell the whisky on his breath as he yelled, 'It's you, isn't it?'

Meggie's heart missed a beat.

'It's you. I know you didn't like having him here. You said something to him, didn't you? You made him go.'

She stepped back, away from the fury she saw building in him. 'No!'

'Of course you did. Och, I know you better than you think, Meggie. You were jealous.'

'Jealous?' She repeated the word incredulously, unable to keep up with this twisted reasoning.

'Aye. Jealous because I have finally got the opportunity to make something of myself. You can't bear the thought that I might do better than you so you're trying to make trouble between Robbie and me.'

Meggie bit back the furious retort that hovered on her tongue and merely pushed past him.

'Where are you going?' He stopped her at the door, grabbing her upper arm.

'To bed,' she replied coldly. 'There's no point in talking to you when you're like this.'

'Like what! Like bloody what?' His grip tightened, hurting her, the pain finally overriding her resolution to stay calm.

'Drunk! Drunk, drunk, drunk, Oliver,' she cried. 'Go to bed and sober up and we'll talk in the morning – if you're not too hung-over, that is.'

The blow took her by surprise, so unexpected that for a moment she didn't even realise what had happened. Then before she had time to move away he hit her again, on the same side of the face. Shocked, she raised a hand to her lip and brought it away wet with blood.

'Bitch,' he hissed at her, pushing past and storming out of the room, slamming the door behind him.

TWELVE

Meggie, rising stiffly from the sofa where she had spent the night, examined her face in the mirror and experienced a faint shock to realise that the damage, although visible, was less than the gnawing pain had led her to expect. Her eyes were still puffy from weeping, and on the right side of her face a bruise showed red and purple along the line of her cheekbone. Her upper lip too was swollen but the cut which had bled so much last night was hidden inside her mouth.

Despite a sick headache and a deep craving for the warmth and comfort of her own bed, Meggie's desire to avoid Oliver, who was still shut in the spare bedroom, outweighed all other considerations. After twenty minutes with cream, powder, rouge and mascara she felt able to face the outside world and slipped quietly from the house.

But the cosmetics, though they disguised the external damage, did nothing to ease the pain she felt inside and it was a very unhappy woman who went about the early morning tasks in the corner shop.

'Didn't expect to see you here this morning,' Matty remarked, coming down from his upstairs flat on the dot of six o'clock.

Meggie shrugged and busied herself with the kettle. 'I woke up early,' was all she said.

The bell over the door rang, sounding incongruously cheerful to Meggie, and Ronnie hurried in, his arms full of bundled newspapers.

'Braw! You've got the kettle on,' he laughed. 'I'm ready for a cuppa this morning.' He rubbed his hands together and waited expectantly. To his surprise Meggie, rather than joining him as she usually did when she was in the shop, took her own cup to the counter and got on with sorting out the papers, leaving him with Matty, a situation neither man relished. Sensing that something was wrong, but assuming Meggie and Matty had fallen out, Ronnie drained his cup as quickly as he could.

'See you this evening then,' he called to Meggie.

A toneless 'Aye' was her only response and with a puzzled look in her direction he left to get on with his round.

Alerted by his sister's unusually brusque manner, Matty watched her carefully for a moment, then went quietly about his own duties.

For the rest of the day Meggie busied herself checking the books, orders and invoices, rarely looking up and not once venturing into the shop itself, not even when a queue of customers had built up. When Ronnie returned with the evening's papers she ignored him completely.

'Well, that's it for the day,' Matty said a little after seven o'clock when the shop had finally closed, taking off his apron and hanging it on the back of the door.

Meggie sighed, shut the ledger and reached reluctantly for her coat, knowing that she couldn't delay going home any longer.

To her surprise she felt her coat being lifted from her and strong hands pushing her firmly back into her seat.

'Now then, you are going to tell me how this happened,' Matty said, sounding uncharacteristically concerned for her.

'How what happened?' Meggie feigned surprise but could not look at him.

'This, Meggie.' Matty passed a finger over her bruised cheek, which was throbbing uncomfortably.

'Och, that! It's nothing.' She tried to laugh.

'Nasty looking nothing,' he commented, frowning down at her. 'How did it happen, then?'

'What's all the fuss about, Matty?' she snapped. 'It's just a wee bruise. I can't even remember how I got it.'

'Och, Meggie, don't lie to me,' Matty sounded impatient now.

'I'm not –'

'Don't bother saying any more, Meggie. Just come and have a look at yourself.' Matty pulled her from the chair and led her to the mirror above the store-room sink. 'Look,' he ordered when she refused to raise her eyes to her own reflection.

Reluctantly Meggie lifted her head and was horrified by what she saw. Over the course of the day the coating of powder and rouge had worn off and the bruise on her cheek had darkened, standing out vividly against her blanched face. Her eyes were underlined by violet shadows and her top lip was noticeably swollen. 'Oh no.' Meggie closed her eyes and looked away, not wanting to have to identify herself with the pathetic creature who had stared back at her.

'Did Oliver do this?' Matty disliked Oliver intensely, but even he could hardly believe that his brother-in-law would hit Meggie.

'He didn't mean to. It was an accident.' She knew this wasn't true, but felt too humiliated to admit that the attack had been deliberate.

'He hit you accidentally? Twice?' Matty put his forefinger against her cheek then stabbed it at her lip.

Meggie jerked her head away and still refused to meet his eyes.

'I'll bloody kill him!' Matty, his face suffused with rage, marched towards the door. 'You wait here.'

Appalled, Meggie leapt to her feet. 'No. Matty, please. *No*.'

Something in her anguished appeal stopped him at the door. 'It's what he deserves,' he growled, his voice full of menace.

Meggie couldn't stop herself from slipping back in time, to a night when that menace had been aimed at her. She shivered.

'You'll only make things worse for me,' she told him, her voice sounding hoarse.

Matty hovered at the door for a moment longer, still undecided, then, with obvious reluctance, came and sat down opposite her. 'All right. But you are going to tell me what happened.'

'It was a stupid argument.' Briefly, and without giving him any hint of her feelings for Robbie, she explained. 'He was drunk,' she ended.

'Aye and I've heard he gets himself into that state every night.' Not a lot escaped Matty.

'Where did you hear that?' she demanded, anxious to know what folk were saying about her husband.

'Och, Meggie, this is a small town and Oliver's well known. When someone like him gets himself stottin' drunk every night of the week folk are bound to notice.' Matty exaggerated. Oliver was a proud man and far too careful of his reputation to risk appearing drunk in public. But Matty's hatred of Oliver, the thing which had driven him to make a frenzied attack on the other man all those years ago, had never waned. Oliver had taken his sister from him and in so doing had deprived him of his rightful share in Meggie's business, a share he was determined to get back. And this could be the opportunity he had been looking for, a chance to break them up, one where no blame could possibly be attributed to him. It was almost too easy.

Meggie groaned and sank her aching face into her hands. 'I think he hates me, Matty. I can't do anything right. All I did was suggest a holiday. Things have been . . . well, difficult between us. Oliver's been under a lot of strain lately. I thought a break would do us good.'

'Meggie, has he done anything like this before?' Matty asked.

'No! Of course not.'

Matty stood up and went to wrap an arm around his sister. 'Look, I know what you must think of me, Meggie, after what I did to Oliver, but you know I'm not like that now, don't you?'

She nodded.

'You have to believe me, Meggie. I'm not proud of what I did then,' he lied. His only regret was that he hadn't killed Oliver when he had had the chance. 'But I would never hurt you and I won't let anyone else hurt you either. You do believe me, don't you, Meggie?'

She smiled, touched by his earnestness. 'I know, Matty. That was all a long time ago.'

'Aye, but I can't forget it. I wish there was some way I could make it up to you but I can't, I know that. But one thing I will do is look after you. If you need me I'll always be here.'

'Och, Matty.' Meggie felt tears sting her eyes and buried her head in his muscled shoulder.

'I think you should come and stay with me, Meggie. You're not safe with him.'

Meggie sighed. 'I can't.'

'A man that's hit his wife once will do it again, especially if he drinks.'

'He won't. I know he won't.' But in her heart she wasn't sure.

Matty knew when he had said enough. 'Well, he is your husband. But if anything like this happens again all you've got to do is phone me. I'll come and get you. You've always got a place with me. Haven't I always told you we belong together?'

The words made Meggie's stomach lurch. They were the ones he had used to her many years ago and she knew they had no place in the relationship between brother and sister. But Matty had been young, hurt and confused then, and in the year since he had returned to Strathannan she had had no reason to believe he still thought of her in those terms.

'Yes,' she said.

'I wish you'd stay here, Meggie, at least for tonight.'

'Thanks, Matty, but I have to go home. Oliver and I . . . well we've got to talk. I don't even think he knew what he was doing.'

'No, I don't suppose he did. And that's why he's so dangerous'. He added deliberately to her fear. 'Still, you know what's best.'

'Aye,' she sighed standing and retrieving her coat. 'Best get on with it, hadn't I?'

'You don't have to.'

Impulsively, she leaned over and kissed him. 'It helps knowing you're here if I need you,' she told him.

Meggie steered her car into the driveway, her heart thumping with apprehension. Without opening the garage there was no way of telling whether Oliver was already home or not. So nervous was she that she dropped her keys and then fumbled with the front door lock. But as soon as she stepped inside she sensed he wasn't there. Relief swamped her.

As the evening wore on with no sign of Oliver, relief turned to apprehension as she waited, not knowing what to expect when he did finally come home. She switched on the radio but turned it off again minutes later, unable to concentrate on the evening play, then made herself a sandwich only to toss it in the bin untasted. By ten o'clock she was in such a state of dread that she could no longer even sit still. The phone, when it rang, almost made her leap out of her chair in shock.

Thinking it would be Oliver, she hesitated to answer it, but when the ringing persisted, eventually lifted the receiver, pressing it against her ear but saying nothing.

'Meggie! Meggie, is that you?'

'Sal.' Meggie's voice was a mixture of relief and disappointment.

Sal, as perceptive as ever, knew instantly that Ronnie had been right. Something was far wrong with Meggie. 'Meggie, is everything all right?'

Even to her best friend, Meggie couldn't admit that her husband had hit her. 'Yes. Why shouldn't it be?' she asked harshly.

'How did you get the bruised face?' Blunt as ever, Sal wasn't prepared to let Meggie lie to her.

'Oh, that.' Meggie attempted to laugh but to Sal listening it sounded much more like a sob.

'Aye that. Do you think Ronnie's blind, Meggie? I always told you having Matty back was a mistake.'

Meggie's denial was out before she could stop it. 'It wasn't Matty!'

There was a long silence from the other end of the line as Sal digested this unexpected piece of information. 'Surely . . . surely it can't have been Oliver?' But who else could it possibly have been? Sal knew better than most just how bad things were between her best friend and her husband. 'Oh, Meggie, I'm sorry . . . I never thought . . .' Sensing how distressed her friend must be, Sal knew that now was not the time to press Meggie with questions, and simply said, 'I'll be there in ten minutes.'

'No!' Meggie knew she had shouted. 'No, Sal. I'm all right. Really.'

'Is he there?'

'No, but he could come in at any minute.'

'When did this happen, Meggie?'

'Last night.'

'And have you seen him since?'

'No.'

'Then you shouldn't be there on your own. You don't know what sort of mood he could be in when he comes home.'

Meggie sighed. 'He might not come home at all.' And that, she realised as she spoke the words, was what she feared more than anything. 'If he does, then we've got to talk, Sal.'

'Won't you at least let me be there?'

'It'll make things worse if he thinks I've told anyone what happened.'

'Then promise to call me if you need me for anything. I can be there in ten minutes, Ronnie too.'

'I promise. But I'll be all right, honestly.'

Sally sighed, feeling helpless but knowing Meggie had the right to sort her problems out in her own way. 'I'll talk to you tomorrow then.'

'All right. Thanks for calling, Sal.'

'Just remember, I'm at the end of the phone if you need me, no matter what time of the day or night.'

Meggie replaced the receiver, then, knowing there was no point in sitting waiting for someone who was unlikely to come in, took herself up to bed.

She slipped between the sheets, sure she would still be awake in the early hours, but lack of sleep the previous night had drained her more than she realised. Within half an hour she had drifted into a restless sleep.

She woke with a start and knew at once that she was no longer alone in the room. Hardly daring to breathe, she let her eyes open just a fraction. There, sitting on the edge of the bed, his head in his hands, was Oliver. Believing that he would be more than a little inebriated, she closed her eyes again quickly and tried to feign sleep. But she must have given herself away because Oliver sat up and looked round at her still form.

'Meggie,' he whispered, his voice perfectly steady, with no trace of the slurring she had come to expect at this hour of the night. 'Are you awake?'

She opened her eyes but didn't move.

He looked away and rubbed his hands over his face. 'I didn't think you'd be here,' he said, his voice hardly above a whisper. When she still didn't respond he went on. 'Do you want me to go?'

For a moment Meggie recalled all the arguments and all the hurt she had endured from him and was tempted to say 'Yes', to ask him to leave, to finish it now. To leave herself free for . . . Even as the image of Robbie's face formed in her head she deliberately closed her mind to it, the enormity of the step she would need to take scaring her. But if Oliver ever hit her again there was no doubt in her mind that she would leave, even if she did not go to Robbie.

At last she answered Oliver. 'No. I don't want you to go. At least not until we've talked.' Deliberately she reached out and switched on the bedside lamp. Then she lay quite still, knowing the harsh light was shining directly on her damaged face.

Oliver stared at her, his mouth open in horror. Tentatively he reached out a hand towards her bruised cheek, but she drew her head back sharply and turned her face away from him.

'Did I do that?' he asked, his expression one of stunned disbelief.

'What do you think, Oliver?' she asked coldly.

'I didn't realise . . . I didn't know . . .'

'Aye, you did,' she retorted furiously. 'You knew what you were doing, Oliver. You knew you were hurting me.'

He just shook his head and stared at her, as if still unable to believe that he could have been the cause of such damage. Then, quite suddenly, his face seemed to crumple and Meggie saw tears sliding down his cheeks.

'You bastard,' she hissed. 'I'm the one that's hurt, Oliver, but you're sitting there, weeping like a lassie, expecting me to comfort you!'

'No,' he choked, rubbing the back of his hand across his face. 'I'm sorry, Meggie . . . I'm sorry.'

'Sorry for yourself! What about me? What about *us*, Oliver?'

'I'm just so ashamed, Meggie. I never meant to hurt you.' He glanced up and for a moment their eyes locked.

Determined not to weaken, Meggie looked away again. 'Don't lie to me! You might be sorry now but at the time you meant to hurt me, Oliver.'

'It was the drink, Meggie. You know I'd never do anything like that if I hadn't been drinking.'

'And that's supposed to excuse you, is it?'

'No, of course not,' he mumbled.

'Because if that's the way it's going to be,' she went on as if he hadn't spoken, 'you'd better pack your things and go. Now.'

'Meggie, please, listen to me,' he begged.

She shrugged, then waited in silence for him to go on.

'I'll never do it again, Meggie. I don't know what got into me, honestly I don't.'

'You were right,' she said, her voice so coldly contemptuous that he shivered. 'It is the drink, but no one forces it down your throat, Oliver.'

'I know,' he agreed sadly. 'But I'll stop. I promise I will.'

Meggie sat up suddenly, leaning close to him to say, 'You'd better, Oliver, because if you don't I will leave you. And that's a promise too.'

For a moment they stared at one another, but this time it was Oliver who looked away first. 'I don't know what I'd do if you left me, Meggie,' he croaked. 'I couldn't bear it without you.' He looked up at her angry face again and added, 'I know I can't expect you to believe me but I do love you.'

'Do you, Oliver?' she asked.

'Aye. I do. I always have.'

Meggie sighed, the anger dying away to leave her feeling confused and depressed. 'Och, Oliver . . . it's not just what happened last night. It's everything – the way you speak to me, the way you look at me . . .'

'I'm sorry,' he said again. 'I'll do anything to put things right, Meggie. Anything.'

'You'll never hit me again, Oliver.' It was warning, not a question.

'No! Of course I won't.'

'And you'll cut down on the drink?'

'Aye. I promise. I promise.' He looked at her and smiled wryly. 'I don't deserve you,' he said.

Meggie closed her eyes for a second, telling herself that everything was going to be all right. 'No more coming to bed drunk,' she insisted.

'I'm not drunk now,' he replied, reaching for her.

Meggie felt his hand on her breast, his lips on her neck, and laid her forehead on his shoulder as he pushed her gently back against the pillows. He took her fiercely, with a passion he hadn't shown since the early days of their marriage. Meggie did her best to respond, but inside she felt cold, detached. As he shuddered over her, sending his seed deep inside her, she turned her head away to hide the tears which slid silently over her bruised cheek. She knew then that last night, with those two blows, Oliver had killed what little was left of their marriage.

THIRTEEN

Kate stood in line with the other assistants as Mr Wemyss and Mrs Donald, his deputy, worked their way towards her.

'Billy Brown!' Mrs Donald's voice was shrill with outrage. 'Have you never heard of soap and water?'

The unfortunate Billy lowered his head and mumbled something at his feet.

'Speak up, lad, I can't hear a word you're saying,' Mr Wemyss barked at him.

'Mr Wemyss . . . sir. That's oil under my finger-nails, not dirt. It was my bicycle chain, it came off, sir . . . on my way here this morning. I didn't have time to wash my hands properly, sir, or I'd have been late.'

Mr Wemyss took the offending hand and examined it closely. 'That might be so, young Billy, but the customers won't know that, will they? They'll just think you haven't bothered to wash. Now lad, off you go and get busy with soap and hot water. You'll not serve any of Hough's customers until Mrs Donald is satisfied that those finger-nails are baby pink.'

Billy scuttled off to the big sink in the stock room and the morning ritual continued. Kate gave her own hands a furtive glance, knowing that to fail this inspection meant not only embarrassment and the teasing of the other young people who worked here, but a loss of wages. No one who came to work with grubby hands, a dirty apron or untidy hair was allowed into the shop that day, and no work meant no pay. Not that this dire fate had befallen anyone in the time she had been here. Hough's staff were proud of their high standards and any lapses had generally been accompanied by a plausible explanation and treated in a stern but fair manner.

The manager and his deputy were standing in front of Kate now and she coloured faintly, as she did every morning, while Mrs Donald's keen eyes made their sharp assessment. There had been occasions when her hair wasn't pulled back tightly enough, or her apron was tied unevenly. And although Kate's farm-roughened hands were never dirty, there had seldom been a day when they hadn't attracted comment. She held them out now with the familiar feeling of trepidation.

Mrs Donald took them and turned them over gently. 'Well, lass, I'm right pleased with you, so I am.' She glanced up and laughed aloud at the expression of astonishment on the girl's face. 'You've worked wonders with these hands, Kate. Och, when I think what they were like when you first came here . . . I never thought you'd be fit to be seen in the shop. And just look at them now. You've hands to be proud of, Kate. Well done.'

Kate blushed almost as brightly as Billy had minutes before, then stifled a giggle as her friend, Betty, standing next in line, nudged her sharply in the ribs. 'Thank you, Mrs Donald.' She collected herself quickly and relaxed as the older woman moved on down the line.

Since Kate had been at Hough's there had been so much to learn and so many things to remember that the time had simply flown by. At first she had been confined to the stock rooms measuring out endless supplies of flour, sugar, tea, cheese and butter, which were wrapped into tidy packages then stacked on the shelves behind the shop counter, all under the critical gaze of Mrs Donald. When she had proved that she was a neat and industrious worker she had been moved to the delivery department, where she spent the day assembling orders for those customers who wanted their messages delivered to their homes, and woe betide her if so much as a single item was wrong. Then, at last, Mrs Donald had decided that Kate's hands were 'just presentable'. She had stepped out into the shop itself, wearing the stiff blue apron of a trainee, and had shadowed one of the other girls for a full two weeks before she had been allowed to change into whites and attend to her first customer.

Kate knew that if her mother could see her serving behind a shop counter, even a shop as good as Hough's, she would be affronted. With the prejudice typical of her generation, Dorothy Brebner had considered all female shop workers to be common. But Kate cared nothing for what other people might think of her. She loved every minute of it and nothing in her life had been quite as satisfying as getting her first pay-packet and knowing that she had given a fair week's work in exchange for a fair amount of money. When the others grumbled about their wages at the end of the week, Kate merely smiled to herself and remembered the long hours she had worked on the farm for no pay at all. She might not have a lot to spare after she had paid Mrs Traynor, but at least what was left was hers and she no longer had to beg every time she needed to buy even the most personal of things for herself.

'Good morning, Kate. How are you today?' As Kate took her place behind the counter, Tom Herriot, the young accounts manager, handed her one of the receipt pads, with its loose leaf of carbon paper, which were handed out to each assistant every morning. On the pages of these pads were recorded details of the orders and the amount of money proffered, together with the change expected. The page was then folded, with the money carefully enclosed, and placed in a metal canister which hissed and clanged its way through a series of echoing pipes to the accounts desk, where the figures were checked and the change inserted before being launched on the return journey. Mistakes were rectified in red ink, which made the error plain to the customer as well as attracting a comment from Tom Herriot the following morning. Apart from being an obvious check on the accuracy of the assistants, when totalled at the end of the day these little slips gave an easy guide as to who was working hard and who wasn't.

'Good morning, Mr Herriot,' Kate answered, blushing for the third time that morning as she felt his eyes on her. She wasn't the only girl who felt colour rising to her cheeks when Tom Herriot was around. He was easily the best-looking young man in the shop, and possibly, Kate thought, in the whole of Strathannan, and female eyes – those of the customers too – followed him longingly wherever he went. He was not too tall, not too thin, with hair unusually fair for a man. And as for those eyes, such a deep blue that it was hard to look away from them . . .

'I told you he likes you!' Betty whispered when she had taken her own pad and they stood watching Tom Herriot make his way to the glass-walled office from which he controlled his small empire.

Almost as if he knew they were talking about him, Tom Herriot looked up and caught Kate still staring at him, then held her gaze for a second before settling down at his desk. Kate's cheeks flamed afresh.

She turned away and busied herself at the shelves behind her, feeling foolish. Pleasant though he was, a man in Tom Herriot's position would hardly lower himself to take anything more than a passing note of the girls who worked in his uncle's shop. It was a waste of time to imagine there might be anything more to the friendly greeting he gave her each morning.

'Are you all ready?' Mr Wemyss asked his customary question, flashed his staff a broad smile, then opened the door with a flourish, greeting the first customers as they crossed the threshold, most in search of fresh bread and milk.

Kate was used to flutterings of nerves during this early morning routine. Usually, as soon as the shop was open and the business of the day began, she settled down. But today, despite the healthy plateful of porridge with which Mrs Traynor insisted she start the day, Kate's stomach gurgled as if empty and her heart beat fast with apprehension.

Somehow she managed to greet her first customer with a smile and then did her best to put her nervousness to one side, at least until lunch-time.

By the time Mr Wemyss ushered the last customer of the morning outside, then bolted the doors and drew down the blinds to signify lunch-time, Kate was seething with impatience. But she would have to contain herself for a little while yet.

Mr Wemyss was a strict but kind man and when the shop closed for lunch at twelve-thirty every day, the assistants were all expected to file upstairs and take their places at the long wooden table where plates loaded with bridies, pies, rolls and scones awaited them. Although they were encouraged to take a healthy stroll in the fresh air before the shop re-opened, no one was allowed to leave until he or she had eaten a filling meal and washed it down with a cup of strong tea. Normally Kate was more than ready for something to eat and appreciated this gesture of generosity in an era when some employers simply closed the premises and banished staff and customers alike to the pavements for an hour every lunch-time. Some office workers were allowed to remain at their desks to eat sandwiches they had brought from home, but many others thronged the town's cafés, spending their hard-earned wages on a place in which to take the weight off their feet, in readiness for the afternoon. Kate had quickly realised how fortunate she was to work for Hough's, who still kept to the old-fashioned ways.

Today, though, she was too excited to eat more than a single buttered roll. She waited impatiently for Mr Wemyss to give the slow nod of his head which indicated they were free to leave.

'Fancy a walk down to the glen gates and back? There's a braw dress I want to show you in the Co-operative window.' Betty had also risen and was following Kate down the long room.

'Och . . . I can't, not today, Betty.'

'Why? Where are you going? Och, never mind, we'll see it the morn. I'll come with you.'

'You can't.' Kate realised from her friend's startled expression that she had almost snapped the words at her and sought desperately for a plausible reason to go off on her own. 'Look,' she said, pulling Betty aside, 'I've to go to the chemist . . . you know. And the only one open at lunch-time is Souters, way down the bottom end.'

Betty nodded quickly. 'Oh. Aye, so it is. I'll stay here then. No point in us both trailing away down there.'

Kate sighed with relief and, flashing her friend a grateful smile, hurried out of the building. Despite the fact that since the war women had had more freedom than ever before, the monthly ordeal of going to a chemist's shop and buying a bulky packet of sanitary pads was something they all secretly dreaded. Girls had been known to waste an entire morning waiting until a shop was empty before sneaking in, scarlet-faced, to make their purchase. Some, despite good intentions every month, were simply overcome with embarrassment and never found the courage to buy anything more than a packet of Askit powders, finding themselves still relying on the messy monthly rags which had been their mothers' only option. To venture into Souters, an old-fashioned place run by an elderly, deaf gentleman, was something they resorted to only in absolute desperation and Kate had rightly guessed that Betty would not want to accompany her there.

As she hurried along the High Street she felt a small pang

of guilt at the deception. Betty had been the first to offer friendship in the lonely days when Kate had started work at Hough's and when she learned a little of Kate's background had been quick to defend her from the determined prying of some of the other girls. But this was something Kate felt she couldn't share with anyone. Not yet.

There was a sharp breeze whistling up the High Street and by the time Kate reached the council offices her cheeks were stinging with the cold. The Town Hall was the burgh's most ostentatious landmark, famous throughout the county. Set back off the High Street behind a large, neatly manicured lawn the building itself was suitably imposing, with its pillared doorway rising from a grand sweep of double steps. But the thing which had proved to be the most contentious issue of the decade was the set of permanently closed gates which guarded the formal approach. These gates – functional, black painted ironwork – had been one of the very first things to be donated to the war effort, leaving a gaping void through which the citizens of Inverannan had begun to wander in order to take advantage of the well-kept gardens; gardens which, for reasons best known to the council itself, had never been a part of the 'dig for victory' campaign which had despoiled so many other areas of public greenery.

The council, who had not appreciated the inquisitive faces of the townsfolk peering eagerly through their windows, had made it a priority to re-erect the gates just as soon as they decently could. But the barrier which had now appeared was as remote from its modest predecessor as it was possible to imagine. On each of the two ten-foot-high gates, great swirls of intricate wrought iron surrounded a vast embossed impression of the burgh's coat of arms. Atop this, rows of vicious spikes deterred all but the utterly foolhardy from attempting to climb over into the neat gardens. And just to be quite sure that the importance of this edifice was plain to even the most transitory visitor, the ironwork had been painted in shining gold leaf, the town shield picked out in the most garish of primary colours.

Kate found herself in front of these glaring gates and looked in vain for some way in, eventually discovering the public entrance down a scruffy side path overhung with shrubs and dotted with litter which brought her, at last, to the back of the building.

'Yes?' A woman rose from behind the public counter and regarded Kate with the dazed stupor of total boredom.

'I've come to speak with Mr Carlyle,' Kate announced, trying to sound businesslike.

'You'll have to wait. He'll only just be back from his lunch.' The girl sank back on to her chair.

'But he's expecting me and I have to be back at work in half an hour,' Kate insisted, thinking that the girl could do with an hour or two with Mr Wemyss. He would surely show her the correct way to deal with enquiries from members of the public, like herself.

The girl shrugged but turned and disappeared through the door behind her. Kate waited, uneasily aware of the minutes ticking relentlessly away on the big wall clock.

Using the few details on her birth certificate, she had gone first to the old workhouse where she had been born. To her dismay she found it had closed long ago and the building was now occupied by the county surveyor and his staff. She had discovered that all the workhouse records had been moved to the Town Hall, where the former workhouse superintendent, a Mr Carlyle, was in charge of them.

'Well?' The door opened and an ageing, dour-faced man limped through and stood facing her across the counter. 'I am Mr Carlyle. State your business. I'm a busy man. No time to waste,' he growled, considerably overstating his situation.

In a voice trembling with nerves, Kate made her request.

Carlyle shook his head. 'But these are personal details. I can't just go giving out information like that to anyone who cares to walk in here.'

'But I have to know,' Kate pleaded desperately. 'Please, Mr Carlyle, it's very important.'

Carlyle eyed her speculatively. 'And then there's the charge. It all costs money, getting out the records and looking them up. All takes time. Time I could be spending on more important matters.'

'I don't mind paying,' Kate offered, quickly making a mental tally of what she had in her purse.

'Ten shillings,' he said quickly, looking round to make sure he wasn't overheard. 'Just to look in the books, mind, nothing else.'

Kate stifled a gasp, then rummaged through her purse and pushed the precious note across the counter at him. A knotted, veined hand shot across the counter top, grasped the money and shoved it into a jacket pocket.

'Wait,' he told her, disappearing through the door.

By the time he came back Kate was hopping from foot to foot in impatience. She knew she was going to be late back to work.

'Right then.' Carlyle dropped a pile of books and files on the counter top. 'What name are we looking for?' Kate stepped back from the sour, cigarette-tainted breath that enveloped her.

'McPherson. Margaret McPherson.' She showed him the birth certificate with the name and year clearly printed on it.

'McPherson.' Carlyle's eyes showed a spark of real interest. Of all the people who had passed through the workhouse the McPhersons were the only ones who had impressed themselves forever on his memory: trouble from the day they arrived and the reason why he, judged to have been remiss in his duty, had ended up in this poorly paid job in the council back rooms when others had found themselves promoted into positions of influence and authority. All thanks to two little urchins from the poorest, roughest village around, abandoned by their parents for the town to support. Oh yes, he had good reason to remember the McPhersons. Ended up in prison, the boy had, and no better place for him to be. But the girl . . . Aye, there had been something very odd about what happened to the girl, one minute giving birth to a bastard in the workhouse and the next all set up in a shop of her own and married to a toff. Aye, he'd kept a bitter eye on Meggie McPherson all these years. But now she was going to get her come-uppance. You didn't need to be a genius to work out who this pretty little piece was.

'Well.' He raised yellowing eyes to Kate and smiled. 'Maybe I can help you, lass. Aye, maybe I can help.'

'I'm sorry, Mr Wemyss.' Red-faced and breathless, Kate took up her place behind the counter, a full ten minutes later than she should have done.

'I am disappointed in you, Kate. I will not tolerate bad time-keeping.' Mr Wemyss frowned at her, his displeasure plain. 'Now, go and tidy your hair and wash your hands before you begin work.'

'Yes, Mr Wemyss.' Kate's embarrassment was exacerbated by the fact that this was a very public admonishment. Several customers were watching her disgrace with open interest.

'But before you do that report to Mr Herriot and ask him to deduct half an hour's pay from your wages.'

'Yes, Mr Wemyss.' Mustering as much dignity as she could, Kate straightened her back, held her head up, walked through the small crowd of customers and knocked on the door of Tom Herriot's glass-walled office. 'I was late back from lunch so I've to lose half an hour's pay,' she told him without preamble.

He greeted her with a wry smile then shook his head in

mock severity. 'Och, Kate, this'll not do. Next time you'll need to do your shopping on your half day off.'

'I wasn't shopping!' Kate defended herself sharply. Then, seeing the laughter crinkling the skin round his eyes and realising that he had only been teasing, she blushed furiously and lowered her head in an agony of embarrassment.

Tom Herriot was intrigued. 'Then it was something important?' he asked gently.

Kate nodded, feeling her heart thumping unevenly in her chest.

'Why did you not ask for an extra half an hour? Mr Wemyss is not an ogre, Kate. If there was a good reason he would have let you have the time off. Would you like me to have a wee word with him for you?' he offered, dearly wanting to do something to make her think well of him.

'No! I mean, no thank you, Mr Herriot.' The thought of having to explain her disgraceful start in life to Mr Wemyss, or worse, to Tom Herriot, filled her with horror.

He looked at her for a moment, wondering what had happened to upset her, for she clearly was very upset, but knew instinctively that she wouldn't thank him for prying. 'All right, Kate. Back to work now. But next time, please ask if you need extra time.'

'Yes, Mr Herriot.' Kate turned gratefully for the door, eager to escape the humiliation of being told off by the one person she wanted to have a good opinion of her.

'Oh, Kate.' She turned back and found him smiling at her.

'Yes, Mr Herriot?'

'Your receipt book?' He held his hand out.

Another mistake and again she flushed scarlet, this time with shame. Every lunch-time before they left the floor the assistants handed their books to Tom Herriot. He merely scrawled his initials in the corner, then repeated the exercise when they went back to the shop floor after lunch. Betty said it was to check they weren't 'working any fast ones' and Kate had been shocked to realise that they weren't entirely trusted.

She delved into the pocket of her apron and drew the book out quickly, bringing with it a shower of other bits and pieces.

'Kate!' Tom shouted with laughter and sprang from his seat to help her. 'You're not having a very good day, are you?' He smiled, picking up a folded sheet of thick paper which had landed under his desk.

Kate felt her mortification was complete. She kept her head down as she collected the slip of paper with the precious name and address given to her by Mr Carlyle and tucked it back inside her pocket.

Tom glanced at the paper in his hand and saw at once that it was a birth certificate. 'Is this yours?' he asked, scanning the details, his eyebrows arching with interest at what he read there.

Kate's mortification deepened, then transformed itself into anger as she realised that the worst possible thing had happened. Tom Herriot had seen and understood the shameful details of her birth. Her head snapped up and, eyes blazing, she reached over and snatched it from his hands. 'Yes it is mine,' she told him fiercely. 'And it's private, Mr Herriot. You had no business reading it.'

Now it was Tom's turn to flush. 'I'm sorry . . . I didn't mean . . .'

But Kate was already at the door. He stopped her there a second time. 'The receipt book!' He scrawled his initials across the top of the page and held it out to her.

Kate was forced to walk back across the room to retrieve it. When she went to take it from him he tightened his grasp and kept her there for a moment. 'Kate, I apologise. I didn't mean to upset you, truly I didn't.' How he wished he could put the clock back five minutes.

To Kate's dismay, tears flooded her eyes. All she could do

was grab the book and run from the room, leaving Tom Herriot staring thoughtfully at the open door.

Sitting on the edge of her bed that evening, Kate stared at the piece of paper in her hands, not at all sure that she was ready for this. Perhaps it had all been just a bit too easy. She had been expecting a long and difficult search, time to grow accustomed to the probability of rejection, to consider the faint chance of acceptance. Perhaps a tiny part of her mind had been hoping that it would all prove impossible, that her real mother would have disappeared, that the intervening years would have covered all trace of her with the flotsam and jetsam of passing time. But a larger part of her yearned to meet this unknown woman, to see where she herself had come from. Now, barely ten days after beginning her search, she had an address where she could contact the woman who had given birth to her, a woman who, it seemed, owned a shop here in Inverannan. Unexpectedly, the prospect filled her with fear.

Putting the envelope carefully into the drawer of her bedside table, Kate slipped into bed and lay trying to sort out the mass of confusion in her mind. Some time, some day in the future, she knew she would try and make contact with her natural mother. But not yet. Not until she had made herself face the possibility of rejection. For now it was enough to know that the choice was hers, that she could make the final step at any time of her choosing.

FOURTEEN

The change in Oliver was so dramatic that Meggie couldn't doubt that he had been as shocked by his violent behaviour as she had been. Though he still spent little time at home, when they were together he was unfailingly pleasant and sometimes openly affectionate. If he couldn't resist a bottle of wine with his dinner and a couple of whiskies later in the evening, then at least he stopped while he was still simply tipsy rather than carrying on until he was too drunk to stand up straight.

So why, Meggie asked herself, did she still feel so unhappy? Was it the knowledge that he seemed unable to stop drinking completely; a lurking fear that all the time he drank there was still a chance that he would hit her again? Or did her feelings stem from something deeper?

Try as she might, Meggie failed to respond to Oliver. In bed he was as amorous as he had been in the early years of their marriage. Confusingly, though she hated to see him drinking, Meggie was sometimes glad to know he had drunk too much to realise that her response was less than enthusiastic. Or was it the very fact that the alcohol made him more selfish, less attuned to her needs, that was making her feel like this? Sometimes she looked into his face as he sweated over her and wondered if he was ever aware of her as anything other than a means of attaining his own sexual relief.

Oliver, trying desperately to make amends for his shameful behaviour, was determined to give his wife the attention she deserved. Looking at her anew with sober eyes, he realised that he had much to be grateful for and was frightened by how close he had come to losing her. His burgeoning political career would come to an abrupt and premature end if any hint of scandal touched him or his family. And in terms of building his new career, Meggie was a very definite asset. Unlike some other married women, she had kept her trim, girlish figure and her face was still smooth, fresh and unlined. She was the perfect hostess, making him the envy of his colleagues. He knew too that under the sophisticated facade she had worked so hard to acquire, there lurked a passionate, sexually demanding woman. Remembering this, sex, something long lost in the nightly alcoholic haze, was suddenly something he yearned for with an almost adolescent lust. His frustration when he sensed Meggie's inability to respond to him was intense, adding to his sense of failure and firing in him a determination to rouse her again, to restore the ardent lover he recalled with increasing longing. Night after night he took her, closing his eyes against the distaste he read on her face, always hoping for that generous, uninhibited response; always disappointed. And, inevitably, disappointment led to nights of humiliatingly obvious failure, nights when, feeling the softness of him, she turned silently away, leaving him shamed and lonely on his own side of the big bed. It wasn't long before fear of failure led him back to the whisky bottle. But by then the seed which would change their lives for ever had already germinated.

'Well, I'm glad things are going better for you two,' Sally advised when Meggie confided in her. 'You can't have everything, you know. Och, Meggie, at least he's not drinking like he used to and you don't argue any more, do you?'

'I suppose not,' Meggie agreed, her beaming smile belying her recently expressed doubts. 'Oliver's too busy to have time to waste arguing with me. Especially now that he's got a seat on the town council. Between that and the quarry he doesn't have a lot of free time.'

'I'm surprised he's got time to get involved in local politics. I shouldn't think Robbie's too happy about that, is he? Aren't they supposed to be partners in the quarry?'

Meggie shrugged. 'I think Oliver has always had political ambitions, but all the time he was tied up with the Mining Company he didn't have the chance to do anything about it. Anyway, to tell you the truth, I'm sure Robbie prefers it this way. He even did some canvassing for Oliver. Mind you,' she added with a wry laugh, 'that could have been because they don't get on very well these days. I think Robbie saw it as a way of getting Oliver off his back. And Oliver is spending quite a bit of time at the quarry. Nobody could say he isn't pulling his weight.'

'Seems to me that between Oliver's ambitions and your shops you've both got your hands full. Anyway,' Sal laughed, 'there's more to marriage than sex. And what do you expect after all this time? You're not newly-weds any more. There's times,' she confided in a whisper, 'when Ronnie and me don't do it for a week or more. Mind you,' she added with a giggle, 'when we do get round to it, it's certainly worth the effort.'

And that, thought Meggie with a pang of envy for her friend, was the difference. Still, they seemed to have weathered the crisis and now the one thing which was sure to put the seal on their future had finally happened. She smiled to herself, feeling happiness bubble up inside her.

'Och, Meggie, it's good to see you looking yourself again. You've been that miserable lately.'

'Aye, well, I've got something to be really happy about,' Meggie beamed, hugging herself.

Sal looked up sharply. She knew Meggie well enough to understand there was more to Meggie's obvious delight than could be attributed to Oliver's changed behaviour. 'Is there something you haven't told me?' she teased.

'Can't you guess?'

'You're not ... Och you are, aren't you!' There was no mistaking the joy in Sal's voice. 'You're pregnant, aren't you?'

Meggie nodded, suddenly too overcome by happiness to speak.

'How far along are you?'

'Doctor Tranter says I'm about twelve weeks.'

Sal flew from her chair and clasped her friend in a tight hug, her own eyes filling with tears. 'I'm that happy for you, Meggie,' she sniffed.

They clung together for a moment longer, then Meggie laughed. 'I was starting to think it would never happen.' Then, becoming serious, she asked, 'You don't think I'm too old, do you, Sal?'

'Old! You? Of course not, Meggie. My mam was forty-five when she had our Jeannie and she'd still be having bairns yet if she was able.' She chuckled, then said, 'Oliver must be right pleased.'

Meggie looked down at her hands, feeling a flash of guilt, then admitted, 'He doesn't know. You're the very first person I've told.' Seeing the look of astonishment cross her friend's face, she hurried on. 'I wanted to be sure, Sal. It would have been cruel to raise his hopes for a false alarm. I'm going to tell him tonight. I've got a special meal planned, all his favourite foods. Och, Sal, this is just what we need. A baby! We'll be a real family at last. Everything will be all right now, Sal, I know it will.' If there was a slight note of desperation in her voice, Meggie wasn't aware of it, so convinced was she that the coming child would heal her ailing marriage. And if Sally was less sure, she cared too much for her friend to say so now.

'Och, Meggie,' Sally whispered to herself as she said goodbye and hurried off down the road, wanting to be home in time for her own children coming in from school. 'I just hope you're right.'

'Well, at least you'll have to give up working now,' was Oliver's immediate reaction to Meggie's news.

Meggie froze, her bubbly, excited mood dying abruptly. Slowly she lowered the glass she had raised ready to propose a toast to their child, their future. 'Is that all you can say?' she asked, her voice flat with disappointment. 'Aren't you pleased?'

Oliver, realising he had said the wrong thing, rapidly tried to recoup the situation. 'Of course I'm pleased.' He grinned at her and drained the rest of the wine in his glass to give him time to think.

'You don't sound it!'

'I was just thinking of you,' he assured her, reaching across the table to take her hand. 'I don't want you working too hard. You have to take care of yourself, and the baby.'

'I will, of course I will,' she said, steering away from an argument, though she had no intention of sitting around in idleness for the next six months.

Oliver squeezed her hand, then raised her fingers to his lips and kissed them gently. 'I am pleased, Meggie. More than pleased, and if I said the wrong thing I'm sorry. It's just that after so long I'd given up hoping for a child. It's come as a bit of a shock, that's all.'

She smiled at him, ready to forgive, grasping at this chance to mend their marriage. 'It was a shock for me too. A nice one though. Just think, Oliver,' she went on, her happy mood restored, 'in six month's time we'll have our own wee bairn. We'll be a proper family.'

'A wee boy,' Oliver laughed, 'I'll have to make sure the quarry's a success now that I'm going to have a son to pass my share on to, won't I?'

'And what if it's a girl?' Meggie asked quietly.

'Then she'll be her daddy's little angel and if she's anything like her mother she'll be more than capable of taking over from me at the quarry.'

'You won't mind if it's a girl?'

'I'll be happy whatever it is, Meggie. Just so long as you and the baby are both healthy. Shall we drink to that?' he asked, filling her glass then topping up his own.

'Aye.' She raised her glass until it was touching his.

'To us, Meggie, to us and the baby. Our family.'

'To us,' she echoed. 'To us.'

'I don't think we should, Oliver. Not now. I don't want to hurt the baby.' Meggie felt a moment of shame at using her unborn child as an excuse to avoid Oliver's attentions.

'I suppose you're right,' he mumbled, the words a drunken slur. Relieved, he turned on his side and turned off the bedside light.

Meggie too turned away and they slept, their backs to one another, no part of them touching.

'Well, that's a turn-up for the books,' Matty said, looking pointedly at the small, rounded mound of Meggie's stomach.

'You'll be an uncle,' she teased him. 'Uncle Matty.'

'Aye,' he agreed. 'So I will.'

She smiled at him, her face radiant. 'I'm so happy, Matty. I was starting to think Oliver and I would never have weans of our own.'

Matty turned away quickly to hide the scowl on his dark face. 'Well, you'll have to be careful,' he advised. 'You're gey old to be starting a family.'

Meggie laughed, refusing to let him upset her. 'I'm not old, Matty. Anyway, the doctor says I'm fit and healthy so there's nothing to worry about.'

'Aye, but maybe you should rest up a bit, Meggie. There's

no need for you to spend so much time in the shops and you've got the baby to think of now.'

Meggie laughed. 'You're as bad as Oliver! I'm not ill, Matty. Pregnancy is a perfectly natural condition.'

'Aye, I know that fine, but there's no point in taking chances, is there? If anything happened you might not be able to get pregnant again. Just think how long it's taken you to fall for this one. Now just you sit there and I'll fetch you a cup of tea. Then you can get away home and I'll close up.'

'I'd like a cup of tea right enough but then I've got to call in at the other shop.'

'Fair enough, but when you're there you can tell them that I'll be looking after things from now on.' And that, he thought, would put Sally Sandys in her place once and for all.

'You will not! For goodness sake, Matty, keeping a check on the shops is hardly going to wear me out, is it?'

Matty made no immediate reply but busied himself making tea. Eventually he placed a cup in front of her, shoved the door between the store room and the outer shop shut and slid into a chair opposite her. 'Muriel can manage on her own for a wee while. We're not busy just now.'

'She's settling in all right, is she?' Meggie asked anxiously. Every other woman who had worked with Matty had been unsuitable for one reason or another.

'Och aye, Muriel's a right wee grafter, Meggie.' With three illegitimate children, all to different fathers, and with her latest partner serving nine months for assault, Muriel was desperate enough to work for the pittance Matty was paying her, though according to the books she was receiving the full wage. Nor was she bright enough to discover any of the other little swindles Matty employed. All in all, as far as Matty was concerned, Muriel was perfect.

Matty took a sip of his tea then went on. 'I'm serious,

Meggie. Leave the shops to me to look after, at least until after the baby's born.'

'Matty, I enjoy being in the shops and it gives me something to do.'

'You don't trust me. That's what you really mean, isn't it? You'll always hold the past against me, won't you, Meggie?'

'Och, Matty, don't start that again!' Though the profits were not quite as healthy as they had been, the books were always immaculate, correct to the last penny. There was absolutely nothing to substantiate her lingering doubts about his honesty and over the last year he had worked very hard, given her every reason to believe he was the reformed character he claimed to be. He was right she decided. She wasn't being at all fair. 'Look, it's not that I don't trust you. It's just that I don't want to sit at home doing nothing for the next six months.'

'Aye, but it's not what you want that's important now, Meggie. It's what's good for the baby that counts. You can't afford to take any chances. Not at your age.' He waited a moment, then added craftily, 'If anything happens to that baby, Oliver will never forgive you.'

Meggie knew she was beaten. 'All right,' she conceded with a sigh. 'You win. You can look after the business for me.'

He grinned, seeing endless possibilities for siphoning more cash into his own pockets. 'Right.'

'But not yet. Wait a month or so. When I start getting tired, then you can take over for a couple of months.'

He could see he wasn't going to get any more from her and agreed quickly. 'Aye, that's the best plan.'

Meggie, feeling a surge of affection for her younger brother, kissed him on the cheek as she left. 'I'm glad you came back to Strathannan, Matty,' she told him.

'Me too.' He stood at the door and watched as she got into her car, smiling and waving as she drove past him. But when he went back into the shop his face was a mask of fury. A baby! Just when he had been sure that Meggie's marriage to Oliver was over; just when it looked as if he was going to get his rightful share in the business after all. Matty lit a cigarette, then in a sudden fit of rage picked up Meggie's half-empty cup and hurled it at the wall. Already he thought of the unborn child as his rival, the person to whom Meggie would naturally leave everything she had. And as soon as the child was born, he knew what would happen. Meggie would concentrate all her love on it and forget about him, just as she had done when she met Oliver. Letting him, her own brother, down. Just like before.

He sank slowly back on to the chair and sat at the table, deep in bitter thought. His eyes, deep pits of darkness, held no spark of light and his mouth was twisted almost into a snarl. Had Meggie been able to see her brother at that moment she would have been truly afraid.

FIFTEEN

Well aware of the fact that she was late, Meggie was already shrugging her coat off as she hurried through the front door. Pausing in front of the hall mirror, she quickly tidied her hair and pinched some colour back into her pale cheeks before stepping into the sitting-room. Her smile of greeting died as soon as she saw her husband's grim face.

'You're late.' Oliver delivered his words with a coldness that clutched at Meggie's stomach.

Aware of Robbie, who was watching the scene in silence, Meggie turned to him and managed to smile. 'Sorry I'm late, Robbie.'

'You knew fine that we're having dinner with Robbie tonight. Could you not have had enough manners to get home on time, just for once?'

'No harm done. And I've only just got here myself,' Robbie did his best to smooth things over. 'The table's booked for nine so there's plenty of time.'

Oliver made a grunting noise and turned away to pour himself a drink. Robbie walked across the room and stood looking down into Meggie's eyes. 'You're looking very well, Meggie. Pregnancy suits you.'

She was aware of a warm flush creeping up her neck and over her face. There was something about Robbie that made her feel like the most desirable woman on earth, even with the now noticeable bulge of pregnancy distorting her normally trim figure. Though they were three feet apart it was almost as if he was touching her and the urge to step closer to him was nearly irresistible as the tension crackled between them. Behind them Oliver cursed loudly as he splashed whisky over the table top, breaking the spell.

'I'll have to go and get tidied up if we're going out,' she mumbled, backing away from Robbie and almost running from the room.

She was sitting at her dressing table, wearing only her slip, when Oliver came into the room behind her. 'Aren't you ready yet?' he snarled.

'Almost,' she answered tonelessly, coiling her hair round her fingers and pinning it atop her head so that soft tendrils escaped to frame her face.

She knew Oliver was standing behind her, watching her, but she refused to look up and meet his eyes in the mirror. When she felt his hands on her shoulders she stiffened and stilled.

But his tone when he spoke was gentle. 'Meggie,' he said, crouching down so he was on a level with her. 'Don't you know why I'm angry with you?'

'Because I was late.' She moved her head away from the whisky fumes on his breath.

'No. I'm angry because I don't think you're taking enough care. You're pregnant, Meggie, and you should be resting, but for the last week you've been at that shop from six in the morning until seven at night. If you want to hurt the baby you're going the right way about it.'

Meggie sighed, too weary for an argument now. Instead she allowed her head to lean against his shoulder. 'What else can I do, Oliver? Matty's hurt his back. He's laid up in bed. Someone has to look after the shop. Muriel's a nice lassie but she's not capable of running the place on her own.'

'Can't Sally help?'

'She's got her hands full with the children. They've all been poorly, one after the other. I don't know how she's managed to get into work as it is.'

'Then you'll just have to close the place down until Matty's better.'

'I can't do that! People rely on that shop.'

'I give up!' Oliver bellowed. 'But if anything happens to this baby, Meggie, I will never forgive you.'

'Nothing is going to happen to the baby, Oliver.' She shouted the words at him, then suddenly remembering that Robbie was downstairs, lowered her voice and said placatingly, 'You know how much I want a child, Oliver. Do you really think I'd do anything that might harm it?'

He took a deep breath and pulled a wry face. 'No, not deliberately. But you are working too hard, Meggie.'

'I'm as strong as a horse, Oliver. I've never felt better. Look at me – don't I look well to you?' She stood up and span round lightly to prove her point.

Oliver did look, drinking in the more rounded curves of her figure. 'Okay', he conceded, 'but please, promise me you'll take care of my son.'

'Our son or our daughter,' she corrected him, irritated by his constant assumption that the child would be a boy. Despite his assurances, she suspected that he would be deeply disappointed if she failed to present him with a son.

He laughed. 'Our daughter then.' Moving with great agility, despite the handicap of an artificial leg, he caught her as she tried to move away from him and placing a hand on her swelling breasts, kissed her deeply. 'If you are so fit and well then you can spare a little time for your husband,' he rasped, his intentions clear in his heavy breathing and the way his hands raked over her body. He pressed her to him and she felt him hard and ready through the silk of her slip.

'No!' She managed to break away and stood facing him, her hands held defensively over her chest.

'Why the hell not?' he roared, furious at this fresh rebuff.

'Because we're supposed to be going out for dinner and we're already late,' she said, smiling in an attempt to soften the blow.

'Then another ten minutes won't make any difference,' he insisted, coming towards her again.

'But Robbie's downstairs. What will he think?' she pleaded desperately.

'Why are you worried about Robbie?' he asked. 'Do you think he will be jealous, Meggie?'

Meggie's heart missed a beat. What did he mean? Had he realised how they felt about one another? But no, she told herself. How could he? She and Robbie seldom met and when they did they were very careful not to be alone together. She felt the heat rush to her face and knew there was no way she could refuse Oliver now without precipitating the kind of argument she most dreaded, an argument which Robbie, waiting downstairs, could not fail to overhear. And to submit to Oliver was preferable to risking Robbie hearing the sort of vile insults which Oliver was liable to bawl at her if she continued to refuse him.

'No! No, of course not.' Fixing a smile to her face, she opened her arms to him.

Fifteen minutes later, she slipped off the bed and went to the bathroom. When she came back into the room Oliver was sitting on the edge of the bed. He looked up at her without smiling. 'Thank you, Meggie,' he said coldly.

'What?' She looked at him in surprise.

'Thank you for putting up with my animal lusts.'

'Oliver!'

'Well, that's what you think I am, isn't it? An animal?'

'Of course not.'

'But that's what you make me feel like, Meggie. Lying there with your eyes screwed shut and your fists clenched.'

'It's not that, Oliver.'

'Then what is it, Meggie?' he asked, his face frighteningly cold.

'It's the baby, Oliver. We had to wait so long before I became pregnant and I know what the doctor said but I'm just so scared of hurting him.'

Oliver stared at her for what seemed like a very long time, 'I hope you're not using the child as an excuse, Meggie.'

'No.' She denied it hotly, though she knew it was the truth.

'I'll stay away from you until after the child's born, Meggie,' he went on, ignoring her, 'because I wouldn't want you to hold me responsible if anything goes wrong. But you will only have yourself to blame if I look elsewhere for what you are so unwilling to give me.'

He looked at her again, a long, cold appraisal which seemed to see inside her very soul. Then, silently, he turned and walked from the room.

At a little after five-thirty the next morning, Meggie parked her car outside the corner shop. This shop, half-way up a hill lined with terraces of small, grey, stone-built houses, was her favourite. She had first come here when she was sixteen years old and with guidance from her friend, Bertha Cruickshank, had worked hard to build it from a corner shop selling little more than sweeties and papers into the thriving store it had become. Even now she still got a glow of pleasure to unlock the door and go inside, looking round with pride at the spruce interior. In the early days, before she and Oliver had married, she had lived in the flat above the shop where Matty lived now, and over the years she had made many good friends among the local women. Very much aware that they relied on her, she tried never to let them down. It was her loyalty to her customers which had brought her here again today, in direct contravention of her husband's wishes.

Shivering in the keen, early morning air, Meggie unlocked the doors then stretched into the windows, raising the blinds and letting the sunshine flood in. She stood for a moment, casting a critical eye around the place, seeing at once what needed to be done and glad of something to take her mind off her problems at home.

The floor first, she decided, so it would have time to dry before folk started to call in on their way to work. Hurrying through to the store room, she set the kettle to boil while she filled the pail from the sink, then crossed to the door which guarded the stairs to Matty's flat. Opening it quietly she listened carefully, but there was no sound from above. Obviously Matty still wasn't well enough to come back to work. All the more reason to get on with the chores before the customers began arriving.

She made quick work of the floor, noting with disapproval that the corners looked as if they hadn't been thoroughly scrubbed for several weeks and resolving to have words with Muriel about that later. The girl had to understand how important it was to keep the standard high, even in places the customers couldn't see. As she worked, Meggie hummed to herself. It was almost like the old days, when she had had just the one shop and did everything herself, loving every moment of it.

'Well, and I hope you're not going to shout at me for walking over your nice clean floor,' Ronnie, laden with newspapers, laughed as he picked his way across the wet tiles.

Meggie straightened with a grimace. 'Ouch! It's easy seeing it's been a while since I last scrubbed a floor,' she said rubbing the small of her back but smiling cheerfully at him.

'Matty's still poorly then?' Ronnie asked, on his way back for a second load.

'No sound from him but I'll take him up a cup of tea later and see how he is.'

'Let him make his own tea. You've enough on your plate,' was Ronnie's advice. 'And if he's no better the day make him see the doctor. You can't have him lying up there doing nothing while you're working yourself to the bone down here. Not in your condition.' Ronnie was far from convinced that Matty was as ill as he claimed to be.

Meggie simply smiled and handed Ronnie his mug of tea before getting on with sorting the papers.

'You just mind and take care, Meggie,' he called five minutes later as he left to finish his round.

Meggie bent and grabbed the last parcel of papers by the string which was holding them and hauled it on to the counter. The wave of dizziness which hit her took her by surprise and she sat down quickly, feeling sweat beading her upper lip. The feeling passed, but knowing her body was giving her a warning, she remained seated on the high counter stool while she finished bundling papers for the delivery boys.

She had just finished when the first of them sauntered into the shop. There followed five minutes of laughter and cheerful banter as half a dozen lads slung their bags over their shoulders and set off on their rounds.

No sooner had they gone than the first customer of the day came in and the next half hour was busy as folk called in for their daily supply of papers and cigarettes on their way to work.

'My and it's nice to see a smiling face first thing in the morning,' Tam Hendrie grinned, handing over his money. 'That brother of yours is a dour-faced so and so at this time o' the day.'

'Aye,' another of the men agreed. 'It's good to see you back behind the counter, Meggie lass.'

Much cheered by their comments, Meggie worked on, kept constantly on the go, first by the menfolk, then later by children wanting a penny's-worth of sweeties on their way to school, and finally by the first of the local women buying the day's messages.

'Morning, Mrs Laing.' Muriel, ten minutes late, hurried through the shop door. Taking her coat off, she hooked it on to the back of the store-room door and immediately took her place behind the counter. 'Sorry I'm a wee bit late,' she offered. 'The weans just wouldn't get out of their beds. I've had to run all the way to the school and back.'

'So long as you're on time the morn,' Meggie said, frowning at her. 'And I hope you're going to wash your hands before you start serving.'

Muriel looked at her hands in some surprise. 'They're clean enough.'

'Not for my shop!' Meggie snapped at the younger woman.

The look Muriel directed at Meggie suggested that the other woman was not quite sane. Deciding to take offence, she huffed, 'I hope you're not saying I'm a dirty person, Mrs Laing!'

Meggie sighed. 'I am saying that when you are working with food, touching it with your bare hands, you have to be extra specially careful. Now, please go and wash your hands.'

The girl flounced off to the store room.

'She's a funny lassie that one.'

'Mrs Haddow!' Meggie looked up with a huge smile of welcome. Mrs Haddow was one of her oldest customers and one who had become a friend.

'Well, Meggie, you're looking a treat, so you are. And are you keeping well, lass?'

'Apart from a wee bit indigestion, I'm fine,' Meggie told her.

'It'll be a lassie then,' another voice joined in. 'I had terrible indigestion wi' both my lassies but not a bit of it with the laddie.'

'Well, I'll be happy whatever it is, boy or girl, Mrs

McElwain,' Meggie told the thin woman who was wrapped up in a winter coat and head scarf despite the warm sunshine.

'Aye, and that's the best way to be, seeing as you can't choose what you get,' Mrs Haddow nodded sagely.

'Och, I had a terrible time wi' all of mine.' Mrs McElwain leaned against the counter, looking forward to a long conversation about health, her favourite subject. 'And I was that bothered wi' piles. You've no got them then?'

Meggie smothered a laugh. 'No. Thank goodness!'

'Just awful they are. The pain! Well I can tell you the doctor said he'd never seen the likes of it. Thirty-six hours I was in labour with my first. Agony it was.' Her face contorted at the memory.

'Och, wheesht will you?' Mrs Haddow spoke sharply but winked at Meggie. 'You'll scare the lassie half to death. 'Don't you worry, Meggie. You're a fine strong lassie. You'll have nae bother, nae bother at all.'

'Aye but the first one's aye the worst. I was torn frae front to – '

Meggie flushed, remembering all too clearly the birth of her first child, the daughter she had held in her arms only once. These kind-hearted, church-going women would be outraged if they ever discovered the truth about her past.

'I'll just take a quarter of tea, please, Meggie. Och, and some of your strong cheese.' Mrs Haddow raised her voice and easily drowned out her neighbour's gruesome account of childbirth. 'Your Matty still in his bed, is he?' she asked, determined to change the subject.

'Aye. His back's right sore. He can hardly walk,' Meggie replied quickly.

'Funny that,' Mrs Haddow mused. 'For Mr Haddow was sure he saw him in the Glen Tavern last night. Och, if your Matty's that poorly still, he must've been mistaken. Mind you,' she went on, glancing up to watch Meggie's reaction, 'it's not like George to make a mistake like that and he was sure it was your Matty – he was that surprised to see him out and about, see.'

'Well, Matty could hardly get out of his bed yesterday afternoon so I don't think it can have been him,' Meggie insisted.

'Aye, lass. Like I said, George likely made a mistake.'

It was after ten o'clock before the shop became a little quieter and Meggie felt able to leave Muriel to serve while she went up to see Matty.

'Matty,' she called, knocking on the door at the top of the stairs. 'Are you up?'

Getting no reply, she took her key from her pocket and let herself in. She looked around the sitting-room in dismay. Used cups and plates littered the floor beside Matty's favourite chair, along with half a dozen empty beer bottles. A couple of newspapers had been tossed carelessly down in a crumpled heap and the small room smelt airless and stale. Quickly she threw back the curtains and hauled the window up, letting a soft breeze into the room.

It took her ten minutes to set the room right then she went through to the kitchen to wash the dirty dishes and make a cup of tea. Her stomach heaved as she emptied the congealing dregs out of a teacup and found a soggy cigarette butt in the bottom of it. Still, she told herself as she poured her brother a cup of weak, milky tea, if he was able to get up and sit drinking beer last night he must be feeling better. And where, she wondered, had he got the beer from? The unpleasant suspicion that George Haddow had not been mistaken after all sent her marching into her brother's room with a furrow of anger marring her brow.

'Wake up, Matty,' she called, depositing the teacup on his bedside table and pulling back the curtains.

'Bloody hell,' he swore bad-temperedly, covering his eyes with his arm. 'Shut the curtains. The light's hurting my eyes.' He rolled over in bed and dragged the blankets up round his ears.

Meggie pulled them away with a sharp jerk. 'It's after ten o'clock, Matty. Time you were awake.'

'Why?' he demanded grumpily.

'Because I've brought you a cup of tea and it'll be getting cold if you don't hurry up and drink it.'

Relishing the idea of a nice sweet cup of tea to freshen his mouth, which tasted like an old sock, Matty hoisted himself up in bed and rubbed at his bleary eyes. 'Thanks, Meggie,' he said.

'I'm glad you're feeling better, Matty. You're moving about much more easily this morning, aren't you?'

Matty took a gulp of his tea. 'Aye, it's not just as bad as it was, but then it always feels a bit better in the mornings,' he said, adopting a whining tone.

'Well, you'll not help yourself by staying in bed all day again. From the state of your sitting-room you were up and about last night and judging from the way you sat up in bed just then it obviously didn't do you any harm.'

'Aye . . . if you say so,' he said, swinging his legs out of bed and groaning loudly.

'If you were well enough to go out for beer last night there can't be that much wrong with you. You were in the Glen Tavern last night, weren't you?'

'Who told you that?' he demanded, instantly defensive.

'One of the customers,' she answered calmly.

'Well it wasn't me,' he lied. 'It was . . . Davey . . . Davey Donald. Aye, Davey brought the beer round last night. Came to see how I was. I never left the house.'

Meggie turned away to hide the grim smile that came to her lips. 'I'll wait for you in the sitting-room.'

Ten minutes later Matty, bent almost double, hobbled into

the room and lowered himself on to an upright chair, accompanying every movement with a low gasp of pain.

'Don't bother sitting down,' she told him briskly. 'Get your shoes and coat on. If we hurry we'll just catch the end of the morning surgery.'

'Och, I'm not needing to see the doctor,' he assured her.

'Matty, you've been like this for a fortnight. You should have been getting better by now. If you're not bad enough to see the doctor then you must be fit to go back to work.'

'I'm not ready for work yet, Meggie.'

'Get your shoes on then!' she ordered, flinging them at his feet.

'I don't know what you're making all the fuss about,' he complained, slipping his feet into his shoes and bending easily to tie the laces. 'Folk are hurting their backs all the time. It'll get better on its own without any help from the doctor.'

'Hurry up,' she snapped.

They drove the short distance up the hill to the surgery in silence, then waited with half a dozen other patients to take their turn to see the doctor.

When his turn came it took Matty less than two minutes to convince the elderly GP that his back was genuinely painful.

'I'm sorry, Meggie,' he informed his waiting sister. The Doc says it could be a long job. I've to take it easy and rest up for at least a month yet. If I don't I could do myself some serious damage.'

Meggie gasped in dismay, then wondered who was the most stupid, herself or the doctor. 'Are you sure that's what he said, Matty? You don't look that bad to me.'

'You think I'm putting it on, don't you?' he challenged, his face twisting in an angry scowl. 'You don't trust me, not even when I'm ill. You always think the worst of me.'

'Well, you seemed all right when I woke you up,' she retorted. 'But, if that's what the doctor said I suppose you'd better go home and rest. And hurry up. Muriel will be wondering where I've got to. I don't like leaving her on her own for too long.'

Matty got himself into the car quite nimbly, then seeing Meggie watching him, said, 'It comes and goes, Meggie, but like I said, it's better in the mornings. By this afternoon I'll be in agony again.'

'If you say so, Matty, but I want you back in the shop just as soon as you're fit.'

'I can't help it if my back's bad! And don't forget I hurt it in the shop. Lifting bags of flour, that's what did it.' He scowled at her. 'You can do yourself a lot of damage hauling heavy things about.'

'I know,' she retorted hotly. 'Especially if you're pregnant, Matty.'

An accomplished actor, Matty contrived to look contrite. 'I can't help it, Meggie, but I'm sorry, I really am.'

She sighed and rammed the car into gear.

Matty left Meggie in the shop and hobbled upstairs, a hand pressed against the small of his back. In the safety of his room he flopped down in his chair, an unpleasant grin on his dark face. If all the heavy work Meggie was having to do didn't take care of the child then he would have to think again, but somehow he didn't think that would be necessary.

It was after midnight before Oliver came stumbling up the stairs. Meggie, who had been sound asleep, was immediately awake. In the darkened room he appeared as a deep, shambling shadow. With the exaggerated caution of the very drunk he crept into the room, closing the door slowly, then groped his way to his own side of the bed where he collapsed with a grunt. Still fully dressed, he hauled his legs on to the bed and sighing, appeared to fall instantly asleep. Underlying the ever-present smell of whisky, Meggie caught the drift of expensive perfume.

Tense and resentful, Meggie lay in rigid, miserable silence. What, she asked herself, had become of her resolution to heal the rift between them; her hope that the coming child would mend their ailing marriage? Deep in her heart she knew that at least some of the blame could be attributed to her complete inability to respond to Oliver. But things would have been so different if only he didn't drink. It had changed him. The strong, determined man she had married, a man who had fought so bravely to overcome a terrible handicap, had disappeared, drowned in alcohol. In his place was a bitter, bad-tempered drunkard who resented his wife's success and seemed incapable of making the effort needed to save his marriage. Now, like his father before him, Oliver had found another woman. Turning her face into her pillow, Meggie wept.

'I'm sorry, Meggie. Ronnie thinks I shouldn't say anything to you but folk are talking. You were bound to find out sooner or later. I thought it was better coming from me.'

Sally looked so utterly miserable that Meggie's heart went out to her. 'Thanks, Sal. You're right, I'd rather hear it from you than someone else.'

'I'm sorry, Meggie,' Sal twisted her hands in her lap and fought tears, deeply distressed to have been the bearer of such unpleasant news.

'Och, Sal, please don't be upset. It's not your fault.' Meggie sat beside her friend on the sofa and hugged her briefly.

Sal gave a lopsided grin. 'It's me who should be comforting you.' Then she rubbed a hand over her eyes and made a determined effort to compose herself. 'I thought you'd be broken-hearted,' she sniffed, looking at her best friend more closely now. 'You knew! You already knew, didn't you, Meggie?' Her voice was shrill with astonishment.

Meggie nodded slowly. 'Well, I had a good idea anyway. I've thought there was something going on for about a month now,' she admitted sadly.

'Did someone tell you?'

'There was no need. Och, it was just wee things – him coming in late, strange phone calls, spending ages getting ready to go out even when he said he was just going to the local pub. And he's supposed to go to his mother's once a week but when I saw her the other day she was complaining that she hadn't seen him for more than a month. But the smell of perfume he brings home with him every night would have given him away in any case.' She laughed, a short staccato sound. 'He's not being very clever about it really.' Or was it, she wondered, just that he cared so little about her that he was indifferent to the pain he was causing her?

Sally wasn't fooled by Meggie's false cheerfulness. 'He's being a real bastard.'

'Tell me about it, Sally.' Seeing her friend's obvious reluctance, she added, 'I want to know what folk are saying about us, Sal. If Ronnie knows you can bet a lot of other people do too. If you were me you'd want to know, wouldn't you?'

'Aye, I suppose I would, but Ronnie wouldn't – ' She stopped abruptly, wishing she had been more tactful.

Meggie smiled wistfully. 'You've got a man in a million with Ronnie, Sal.'

'I know.' Sally sighed then went on. 'Oliver's been seeing someone else for three or four months now.'

'So long?' Meggie breathed.

'Are you sure you want to hear this?' Sally asked gently, looking at her friend's bleached face then squeezing her hand, shocked to find it so very cold.

'I have to know the truth, Sal. Who is it? Who is Oliver seeing?'

'Morag McNab.'

Meggie felt her stomach lurch. The McNabs were business acquaintances. Meggie and Oliver had had dinner with them on half a dozen occasions and Meggie had marvelled at how mismatched the other couple seemed. Young, attractive and vivacious, Morag McNab appeared to have little in common with her dour husband who was at least twenty years her senior. But far from giving the impression that he admired Morag, Oliver had commented that she was childish and vain. Certainly Meggie had never for one moment suspected that she might be the other woman in her husband's life. 'I wouldn't have thought she was his type,' she said, striving to stay calm.

'Well, she obviously is.' Sally made no attempt to disguise her antipathy towards the other woman. 'Brazen she is. Flaunting herself all over the place with another woman's husband. And her married with two weans!'

'That's what really upsets me,' Meggie whispered. 'Them being seen all over Inverannan, not caring that folk must be laughing at me.'

'Well,' Sally admitted, 'maybe not all over Inverannan. Oliver's not that stupid. But someone Ronnie knows lives further up county and he's seen them a couple of times in his local hotel – you know, one of those smart country places. Oliver must think he won't be recognised up there and I suppose it's only pure chance that he was seen with her. I wouldn't worry too much, I don't think it's common knowledge. Yet.'

'What am I going to do, Sal?' Meggie asked, sounding utterly defeated.

'You know you can always come and stay with Ronnie and me,' Sally offered at once.

Meggie seemed to consider this for a moment, but when she spoke there was a new note of determination in her voice. 'Thanks, Sal, but I'm not leaving my home.'

'You're going to make him move out? Quite right too.' Sal

nodded her approval. 'After all, you've done nothing wrong.'
Sally looked at her friend, recognised the stubborn expression
on her face and gasped. 'You're never going to stay with him,
Meggie, not after this?'

'I've got the baby to think about, Sal. This is only because
I'm pregnant. Everything will be all right once the baby's born.
I know it will.'

As she drove home an hour later, Meggie kept repeating
those same words over and over to herself. Once the baby was
born, everything would be all right again. After all, Oliver
wasn't the first man to stray while his wife was pregnant and
the truth was she had to take her share of the blame for driving
him away. She was a married woman and marriage was a
commitment for life, something to be worked at, the difficulties
overcome just as the good times were there to be enjoyed. And
now she had the child to consider, a child who would need a
father, the security of a loving home, something she herself
had missed so much. But deep inside herself, Meggie's heart
bled.

Meggie let herself into the empty house and collapsed in a
chair, not even bothering to switch the light on. The house
was chill, the fire dead, but she had no energy left to do
anything about it. Her back ached, her head throbbed and all
she wanted to do was sleep.

The sharp ring of the doorbell roused her from an uneasy
doze half an hour later. Startled, momentarily confused, she sat
up with a jerk and felt the baby kick in protest. The bell
sounded again. She levered her cumbersome bulk from the
chair and made her way to the door.

'Robbie.' She greeted him in obvious surprise. She rarely
saw him and he never came to the house without first letting
her know.

'Meggie!' He peered at her through the gloom, his astonishment even greater than hers. 'What on earth are you doing stumbling about in the dark?' Taking her arm, he stepped into the house and led her up the hallway, switching on the lights as he went.

'I'm sorry Robbie, I was sound asleep.' She smiled wryly.

'You look exhausted, Meggie. Don't tell me you're still working?' To Robbie, who hadn't seen her for two months, the change was dramatic. Gone was the bloom of early pregnancy: she looked too fragile to support the burden of her growing child, her skin so drawn and pale that it seemed translucent in the cruel artificial light. Truly concerned for her, he steered her gently back into her chair and then knelt to light the fire.

'There,' he said, standing up and wiping his hands on a crisp, white handkerchief. 'That should get some warmth into you. You look perished.'

'If I'd had any sense I'd have lit the fire before I sat down,' she smiled wryly.

'I'd have thought Oliver would have lit the fires ready for you coming home,' he said. 'Where is he? I need to have a word with him.'

Meggie shrugged. 'I don't know.'

Robbie looked at her for a moment, his expression eloquently conveying his opinion of his cousin.

To her shame, Meggie felt tears flood her eyes. Try though she might to contain them they overflowed and slid silently down her ashen cheeks.

'Oh, Meggie. Don't cry. Please don't cry.' Robbie was on his knees at her side instantly. Very gently he put an arm round her shoulders and drew her to him.

At his touch something inside Meggie broke, releasing all the misery she had been refusing to face.

Robbie simply listened, his face taut with anger at what she was telling him, then held her until she had cried herself out.

When the rivers of tears had finally dried and the only sound she made was the occasional dry sob he stroked her hair gently and said, his voice just above a whisper, 'I am so sorry, Meggie.'

Meggie pulled her swollen face away from the warmth of his shoulder, feeling suddenly ashamed. 'No, I'm the one who should be sorry, Robbie,' she muttered, her voice hoarse. 'I shouldn't have told you all this. I feel a proper idiot.' She kept her head bent, unwilling to raise her face to his, not wanting to see the pity that must be there.

Gently he stroked the damp hair away from her face, then, putting a hand under her chin, tipped her head up, forcing her to look at him. 'Not an idiot,' he told her, his dark eyes drawing hers so that she could not look away. 'You have got every reason to be upset.' A muscle twitched at the angle of his jaw and his lips were drawn in a tight, angry line.

Watching him, sensing the anger inside him, she felt a frisson of excitement which sent tingling fingers down her spine.

Robbie, looking down on a face which was tear-stained and swollen, thought her the most beautiful creature in the world and felt nothing but hatred for a man who could reduce her to such deep unhappiness. Every fibre of his being longed to protect her, to give her what his cousin clearly could not, to offer the love and security she deserved. Very slowly he lowered his head to hers. Had she made any move away from him he would have stopped. But, instead, she held herself perfectly still, her eyes never wavering from his, her lips slightly parted.

When he kissed her Meggie closed her eyes and sighed, then gave herself up to a brief moment of sweetness. Then, very slowly, though her whole body ached to be still closer to his, to lose herself completely in him, she turned her face away.

'I love you, Meggie,' he whispered, burying his face in her hair. 'Come home with me. Let me look after you. And the baby.'

'Robbie . . .' The word emerged on a long, wistful sigh. 'I wish . . .' Then, gathering herself, she pulled right away from him and shook her head. 'I can't. You know I can't.'

'Are you telling me you still love Oliver?' he asked softly.

He watched her closely, seeing the conflicting emotions in the agonised expression on her face. 'I don't know!' she cried. 'I don't know what I feel any more.'

'Do you love me, Meggie?' he challenged her. When she tried to turn away, he caught her and held her face firmly, making her look at him again. 'Tell me, Meggie.'

'Yes!' She shouted it at him. 'Yes! There! Now you know the truth. But I can't do anything about it, Robbie. I am married to Oliver and I am having his child. We will be a family.'

'Meggie,' he pleaded with her in despair. 'He's seeing another woman, he's hit you, he's a drunk. What future do you and the child have with him?'

'I put my hand on the Bible, Robbie, and promised to stay with Oliver through good and bad. I can't walk away from that.'

He looked at her with new respect in his eyes. 'Even though you love me?'

She nodded sadly. 'Even though I love you,' she choked.

Robbie closed his eyes against the bleak emptiness which was engulfing his soul.

Meggie pulled herself away from him. 'We can never be together, Robbie,' she told him, in control of her emotions now but with a slight tremor in her voice. 'When the baby is born things will be better for me and Oliver. I owe him so much, Robbie, and I am going to try my very best to make our marriage work.'

There was nothing Robbie could do to hide the raw pain her words had inflicted.

'I'm sorry, Robbie. I didn't mean to hurt you,' she whispered.

'I know.' He gave her a rueful smile, sat for a moment longer, his shoulders bent, then, gathering himself, stood up. 'I'd better go.'

'Aye,' she nodded and stood in the sitting-room doorway, watching as he walked up the hall.

At the front door he turned briefly. 'Goodbye, Meggie, and good luck,' he said, his voice soft and sad.

'Goodbye, Robbie,' She choked on the words, then ran down the hall towards him. But he was already gone, lost in the shadows of the night.

SIXTEEN

Meggie tossed a handful of coins into the till, brushed a stray strand of hair from her face and turned wearily to her next customer, wondering if the queue of folk waiting to be served was ever going to die down.

'Five pounds o' tatties, Meggie, please.' The woman made her request cheerfully. 'You're run off your feet the morn, lass.'

'Aye.' Meggie turned round and frowned in annoyance to find the potato sack empty. 'Matty,' she called, then tutted in irritation when he didn't respond. 'I just need to fetch a new sack from the storeroom, I'll not be a minute,' Meggie told the woman before hurrying through the door behind the counter.

She found her brother seated at the small table, the local paper open in front of him, a cup of tea in one hand, a cigarette in the other. 'Did you not hear me calling you?' she demanded irritably.

'I'm having my tea break,' he retorted, not bothering to look up.

'There's half a dozen folk waiting to be served out there,' she hissed. Her temper finally snapping she grabbed the paper and flung it to the floor. 'And there's no tatties left in the front shop.'

Banging his mug down, Matty stood up, his fury matching hers. 'And what do you expect me to do about it?'

'I expect you to bring another sack through for me,' she insisted, facing him with her hands on her hips.

'You'll have to wait until Muriel comes in,' he growled.

'She's not due in until two o'clock!'

'Then you'll just have to come through here and fetch the tatties as you need them 'cos I'm not shifting them.'

'Matty, I'm eight months pregnant. I can't lift that sort of weight.'

'And neither can I. You know what the doctor said about my back.'

'There's nothing wrong with your back now!' she almost screamed, it at him.

'That's how I hurt it in the first place,' he insisted, 'shifting great sacks of tatties about. If I damage it again the doctor reckons I could do myself some permanent harm.'

'Huh!'

'Is that what you want, Meggie, to see me crippled?'

'Now you're being ridiculous!'

'And you're being selfish,' he threw the accusation at her with a smirk on his face.

'Selfish! Matty, I have an unborn child to think about.' She gaped at him, hardly able to believe he could be so callous.

'Well, youse two are certainly giving the customers something to talk about,' said Sally breezing into the storeroom. Grabbing a sack of potatoes with one hand, she dragged it over Matty's toes as she hauled it into the shop.

'Cow!' he hissed, glowering at her back.

'You can call me all the names you want, Matthew McPherson, just so long as you get off your lazy rear end and get these customers served.' Sally stuck her head round the door and spoke with deceptive sweetness. 'And you.' She turned her attention to her open-mouthed friend. 'Sit down and have a rest, Meggie.'

Knowing he had met his match in an enraged Sally, Matty scuttled through to the shop like a chastened schoolboy and was mortified to be met with smothered laughter as the customers took maximum enjoyment from the little drama.

'Right then, it's quieter now so you can manage out here

on your own until Muriel arrives,' Sally told him fifteen minutes later.

'I'm supposed to be taking it easy,' he whined. 'I've got a bad back.'

'It's not just your back that's bad, Matty. You're a bloody bad lot through and through. Rotten to your nasty little core, so you are. Meggie's baby's due in less than a month and here she is working herself to a standstill because you're nothing more than an idle, lying little tyke.'

'You've no right to talk to me like that. I'm Meggie's brother and I'm the manager of this shop.'

'Then act like it!' she retorted. 'And if you can't do that then at least show your sister some consideration. The way you're behaving, anyone would think you want her to lose that baby.'

Matty's already dark face became even darker as the blood infused his cheeks. Scowling, he busied himself at the shelves behind him, refusing to meet Sally's eyes.

Giving him a look of pure hatred, Sally went back to the store room.

'Thanks, Sally.' Meggie smiled up at her friend.

Sally shrugged. 'Good job I happened to turn up when I did. I brought the monthly accounts up for you to check. Thought I'd save you the trouble of coming down for them. I think you'll find everything's right.'

'Your books are always just fine, Sal, but thanks for bringing them up here.'

'No trouble.' Sal sank into the chair on the other side of the small table from Meggie. 'Isn't it about time you put your feet up, Meggie? Surely Matty can manage on his own now?'

'I am going to. From next week I'm going to be a lady of leisure. Muriel has agreed to work extra hours until Matty's back is properly better.'

'For ever then?' Sally commented caustically. 'Honestly,

Meggie, I don't know why you let him get away with it. You and I both know there's nothing wrong with his back.'

Meggie sighed. 'The doctor says there is and I can't argue with that, can I? Anyway,' she went on quickly not giving her friend time to reply, 'I don't mind working. Time drags when I'm at home. I feel as if I've been pregnant for ever.'

'Only four weeks to go. I'd make the most of it if I were you. Once the baby arrives you won't have a minute to call your own.'

Meggie laughed softly. 'I can't wait. I feel like an elephant, Sal. I've forgotten what my feet look like and I hate these smocks. I might as well wear a potato sack, it wouldn't look any worse.' Then, her smile fading, 'No wonder men turn to other women when their wives are pregnant.'

'Are things any better between you and Oliver?' Meggie rarely spoke about her personal problems these days and Sal eagerly seized the chance to find out if her friend's situation had improved.

Meggie looked uncomfortable and fiddled with the pencil she still held in her hands.

'I'm sorry, Meggie.' Sal offered her apology quickly. 'It's none of my business.'

'Och, it's all right, Sal,' Meggie sighed. 'It's a relief to be able to talk to someone who knows the truth. To be honest, I don't see very much of Oliver these days. He hardly ever comes home until late and he sleeps in the spare room in case he disturbs me. Still,' she added, making an effort to sound cheerful, 'when we are at home together he's really considerate. And I know he's just as excited about the baby as I am. He wants to call the baby Iain. Don't you think that's a lovely name?'

'And what if it's a girl?' Sally asked, pinpointing Meggie's anxiety with unnerving accuracy.

'Och, what do men know about girl's names?' Meggie dismissed Oliver's all too obvious refusal to consider the possibility that the child might be female. 'If I left it up to Oliver he'd probably call her Elsie, after his mother! We've agreed that I can choose. If it's a girl.'

'Ah . . . I see . . .'

And Meggie knew that Sally did indeed see.

With five minutes to go before closing, Matty slipped furtively from behind the counter. Checking quickly behind him to make sure that the door to the store room, where Meggie was working, was still shut he flicked the sign on the shop door to 'closed' and slipped the catch across. What he didn't want was for some last-minute customer to come rushing into the shop and fall, breaking a leg or arm on the premises. Seeming to suffer no discomfort from his back, he sank on to his hands and knees just inside the doorway, produced a slab of butter from his apron pocket and spread it liberally over the floor, leaving a greasy sheen on the smooth tiles. That done, he levered himself carefully to his feet and surveyed his handiwork with satisfaction.

Meggie, who had spent most of the afternoon on the relatively undemanding task of checking the books, leaving the shop to the combined efforts of Matty and Muriel, looked up as he came into the store room, a smile on his face, their earlier disagreement obviously forgotten. Meggie smiled back. Even after all these years, she still found Matty almost impossible to read and had known him to sulk for days over very minor issues. Today, much to her relief, it was as if he was actually trying to make amends for his unhelpfulness.

'We've been quiet for the last half hour so everything's tidy, ready for the morn. Come on, you've done enough for today. I'll let you out of the shop door, save you walking all the way round to get to your car.'

'Thanks, Matty.' Meggie closed the books and slid them to

the edge of the desk, realising that she was tired, ready for home, a hot bath and an early night. The child kicked restlessly as if it too was eager to go home. She smiled and placed a hand on her abdomen, still enthralled by the ever stronger movements which were visible even through the generous folds of her maternity smock.

Carefully avoiding the greasy area, Matty preceded her to the door and held it open while Meggie, as he had known she would, stood for a moment behind the counter, casting a critical eye around the shop, already making a mental note of tomorrow's early morning chores.

'Come on, Meggie, hurry up,' he chivvied her, careful to make it sound like a joke. 'If I hold this door open for much longer someone's bound to come in and want to buy something and the till's all locked up for the night.'

'All right,' Laughing, she walked quickly towards him, her hand rummaging inside her handbag for her keys, and for a moment he thought his desperate plan had failed. Then, even before he was aware that she had lost her footing, he saw her eyes widen in alarm, her mouth open in shock as, quite abruptly, she plunged to the floor, landing with a hard thud on her right hip.

'Meggie!' He delayed for a vital second before making a pretence of grabbing for her.

Meggie moved gingerly, felt her head spin wildly and fought rising nausea.

'Meggie, are you all right?' Matty hooked an arm under her shoulder and attempted to pull her to her feet.

Dazed and shocked, Meggie hauled herself upright and leaned heavily against her brother. 'Come on, sit down for a wee minute. You went down with one hell of a bang,' he told her, dragging her towards the hard seat on which some of the older customers liked to rest while being served. 'There, just rest there for a minute or two.' He looked at her, satisfied to see her face had drained of all colour. 'Maybe I should call the doctor?'

'No.' At last she managed to speak. 'No. I'll be all right. I just gave myself a bit of a fright, that's all.'

'Are you hurt?'

She concentrated, almost frightened of what she might feel, then closed her eyes thankfully. 'No, I think everything's fine.'

'I'll call Oliver, tell him what's happened, then I'll drive you home. You shouldn't really be on your own after a nasty fall like that, Meggie.'

'*No!* Even in her shocked condition, Meggie could imagine exactly what Oliver would say if he knew she had fallen in the shop.

'Well, I'll drive you home then.'

She nodded. 'Thanks.' Then, looking towards the door with a bemused expression, 'I don't know what happened. My feet just seemed to slide from under me. Something must have made the floor slippery.'

Matty hurried to the spot and made a performance of examining the floor. 'It looks all right to me,' he assured her. 'But I'll run the mop over it just to be sure. We can't have you falling over again, can we? You might not be so lucky next time. You just sit there. I won't be a minute.'

He fetched the mop and a bucket of hot water and took great care to remove every last trace of butter from the floor. 'There. I don't think there was anything there, but better to be sure, eh?' He turned and grinned at his sister, whose face was, if anything, even whiter than before.

'Could you take me home now please, Matty?' she asked, sounding exhausted.

'Right then, lean on me and take your time.' He tugged insistently on her arm and pulled her roughly to her feet, feeling her weight sag against him.

Meggie took a single step, then stopped, unable to do

anything to prevent her knees buckling under the sudden vicious assault of pain which cut through her abdomen. At the same time she was aware of a gush of liquid from between her legs.

'The baby!' she gasped, gritting her teeth against a fresh onslaught of agony. 'Help me, Matty.'

Meggie, fully rested, sat up in bed and cradled her baby daughter in her arms. One finger softly stroked the infant's downy cheek while her face, showing no trace of the agony she had so recently endured, was radiating happiness.

Oliver, standing unnoticed in the doorway, felt his throat constrict with emotion at the tableau before him.

'Meggie,' he said, his voice emerging as a strangled croak.

Meggie looked up, her eyes shining, the resentment she had felt that he could not be contacted last night, that it had been ten-thirty this morning when he finally walked into his office and discovered that his baby daughter was already twelve hours old, dissipating in her eagerness to show him the small miracle they had created between them. 'Isn't she beautiful?' she asked, raising her arms and offering the child to its father.

The little girl, as if sensing a momentous occasion in her young life, obligingly opened her eyes but, as if the effort was all too much for her, quickly closed them again. Meggie watched, entranced. Such a good baby, so placid and contented, one who seemed to want nothing more than to sleep, who even had to be woken up to feed. So different from Sally's babies, who had been loudly demanding from the very first moments of their lives. Meggie felt her heart might actually burst with love for this tiny, helpless creature.

Oliver, intimidated by such a tiny scrap of humanity, actually took a step backwards and peered awkwardly into the nest of covers. What he saw excited not even the slightest stirring of love. Instead he was aware of a shock of revulsion and an almost overwhelming sense of disappointment. A baby, certainly, but an incredibly unattractive one with her strangely shaped head, slanting eyes and disconcertingly old-young face. She was, he thought, like a badly modelled doll, almost human in appearance, but not quite. Perhaps if she had been beautiful, a delicate, feminine child, there might have been some compensation for the fact that he had been denied the son he wanted so badly. But this bland-faced, waxy looking infant repelled him. As he stared, fighting to disguise his feelings from Meggie who was still expecting him to take the child from her, the baby's eyes flickered open and Oliver had the strange sense of looking at nothing. Shaking his head, he straightened and moved away slightly. Meggie lowered her arms, cradling the child back close against her.

'She's so small,' he muttered, feeling the need to excuse his behaviour.

Meggie smiled, thinking she understood. She had felt similarly helpless when confronted with Sally's new-born infants. 'You'll soon get used to her,' she said, her attention again riveted on the child.

Already, as he stood looking at his wife and child, Oliver knew what was going to happen. Since he had entered the room, Meggie had looked at him just twice, sparing him two brief glances before returning her gaze to the baby. Far from getting his wife back now that the pregnancy was over, he believed that he had lost her to a rival against whom he could not hope to compete. Oliver's mind, blunted by the effects of too much alcohol over too many years, stubbornly failed to admit that he was to blame for his wife's withdrawal and was incapable of recognising that she had offered him the child as a gesture of reconciliation, her hope for a new start, as a family.

Wishing there was some way he could escape from the claustrophobic little room he sank on to the bedside chair and avoided looking at the baby.

'And you, Meggie, are you all right?' he asked.

She looked at him again and nodded. 'I'm fine.' In fact the birth had been relatively easy.

'You were lucky. I told you you shouldn't have been working in that bloody shop.' Disappointment made him spiteful. 'If anything had happened to her it would have been your fault.'

Meggie felt the familiar sinking feeling in her stomach. 'She's fine, Oliver.'

'How did you come to fall anyway? What were you doing? Something that brother of yours should have been doing for you, I bet.'

Meggie felt a chill creep up her spine. Why was he being so aggressive when they had such a lot to be grateful for? Suddenly angry she challenged him. 'What's wrong, Oliver? Aren't you glad that your daughter and your wife are both safe and well? Why are you trying to pick an argument with me today of all days?' Then, confusingly, she felt her eyes fill with tears and angrily scrubbed at them, furious with herself and with him. 'If that's all you've got to say to me then you'd better go.' Hugging the child to her breast, she turned away from him.

'If that's the way you feel . . .' He got up, glad of the excuse to escape, to go home and try to adjust to the disappointment, to ponder on their future – if they had a future.

'Ah, Mr Laing?' The ward sister came into the room just as Oliver turned to leave. 'Before you go would you just pop into the office for a wee minute? Mr Simmons would like a word with you.' She took him to the corridor and pointed. 'Down there, fourth door on the right.'

'Now then, Mrs Laing, what's all this about?' she asked briskly, removing the baby from Meggie's arms and depositing her firmly in the bedside cot. 'Not crying, are we?'

Meggie sniffed but remained silent.

The sister, well used to the emotional vagaries of new mothers, settled herself on the edge of the bed and took

Meggie's hand in hers. 'It's quite normal, you know, to feel a wee bit tearful after you've given birth. It'll soon pass, lass, you'll see.'

When Meggie failed to respond, she went on doggedly. 'And what are you going to name the wean? Has Mr Laing chosen the name or is he leaving it up to you?'

'My husband wanted a boy.' Meggie choked on the words. 'He wouldn't hold her. He hardly even looked at her.'

'Och, lass, men are feart of wee babies. Especially first-time fathers. It's not that he doesn't care for her. He'd have been the same even if it had been a boy. Once you and the baby are home he'll soon get used to handling her, you'll see. Now try and get some rest before baby needs her next feed.' She patted Meggie's hand, then, aware of other patients requiring her attention, walked smartly away.

Meggie turned on her side, her back to the door, and wept.

'Mr Laing? Do come in.' Mr Simmons, the consultant paediatrician, offered Oliver his hand. Oliver, who had had little time to wonder what this was about, asked, 'My wife is all right, isn't she?'

'Yes, Mr Laing, your wife is fine.'

'The fall didn't cause any permanent damage?'

Simmons tried to ignore the patronising arrogance of the younger man's tone. 'There is nothing to worry about there, Mr Laing. It was a straightforward birth, I believe, though that is not my area of expertise, you understand.'

Then we will be able to have more children?'

'Yes, of course. There is no reason why not.'

'Then, if everything is all right . . .' Oliver got up, ready to leave.

'Not quite, Mr Laing. Please, if you would sit down I will explain.' Simmons tried hard to keep the note of impatience out of his voice. There was something unlikeable about Oliver

Laing but that did not make the task before him any easier. Oliver sat down again and waited expectantly.

'You have seen your daughter, Mr Laing?'

'Just now.'

'And what did you think of her?' Simmons asked, wondering if the man had noticed anything amiss. It was always easier to break this sort of news if the parents were already suspicious that all was not well.

Oliver disappointed him. He shrugged. 'I've not had much to do with babies.'

'No. Well, then, I am sorry to have to tell you that your little daughter is not as well as we would like her to be.' The doctor folded his arms on the table and regarded the younger man with a solemn expression.

Oliver felt a sickening lurch in his stomach. 'She's ill?'

Simmons cleared his throat. 'The child is not responding as she should. Some of the reflexes we would expect to see in a normal new-born infant are not present.'

Oliver stared, his mind swirling with horror. 'I . . . I don't understand.'

'Your daughter is damaged, Mr Laing. The indications are that her brain is not functioning as it should. It's early days yet, of course. We will know more in a few months, but preliminary examinations indicate that she will need a great deal of care and attention. I am deeply sorry.'

'She's retarded?' Oliver was so overwhelmed with shame that he could hardly say the word.

'That would seem to be the case, yes, though as I say, it is too early to give a precise prognosis.'

Oliver sat in tense silence, fighting the anger which was coursing through his veins, unable to trust himself to speak.

To give him time to recover his composure, the doctor tidied his papers, then waited patiently. When Oliver finally spoke, the physician was startled by the bitterness in his voice.

'It was that fall, wasn't it? She damaged the baby when she fell.'

Simmons looked at his hands. 'It is possible, I suppose, but we are seldom able to discover the precise reasons for such tragic events.' He cleared his throat. 'Have you or your wife any family history of mental disorders? Are there any family members who are perhaps a little backward?'

'No!' Oliver was outraged by the suggestion. 'My family have all been perfectly healthy.'

Simmons was used to this reaction. 'And Mrs Laing's family?'

'There is nothing like this in either of our families, Mr Simmons.' Though with Meggie's background, he thought bitterly, there was no way of being sure.

'Then we can assume that the damage occurred in the womb.'

'So it might have been the fall?' Oliver persisted.

Simmons frowned. 'I would not like to say, Mr Laing. It is more likely that the damage occurred in the very early stages of pregnancy. Was your wife unwell at any time?'

'Not that I know of.'

'Was she in contact with anyone, a child perhaps, who had German measles? Unfortunately, contact with German measles during the first months of pregnancy can cause quite serious problems for the child.'

'No. No there was nothing like that.' Oliver felt as though someone was sitting on his chest. The room was unbearably warm; perspiration soaked his shirt.

'Your wife will have to be told, Mr Laing. There is no easy way to do this, but I believe that sad news of this kind would be better coming from you than from someone she hardly knows.'

Oliver looked up and met the other man's eyes squarely for the first time. 'I will tell my wife, Mr Simmons,' he said, getting to his feet. 'Thank you for your time.'

Oliver got up and left the room, leaving the consultant with the strong but ridiculous impression that he was relishing the opportunity to give his wife the tragic news.

Back in the corridor, Oliver hardly paused before retracing his steps to the side ward where Meggie, in anticipation of this moment, had been given a room to herself. He waited outside the door for a moment, standing stiffly, his arms rigid at his side, clenching and unclenching his fists as he fought desperately to regain control of his emotions. Finally, taking a deep breath, he went inside.

Meggie was lying with her back to the door. He was glad to see that the baby was asleep in a wheeled cot.

Moving silently, he sat in the hard chair at the side of the bed and considered what he was going to say to her. Then, shaking her quite roughly by the shoulder, he said, 'I want to talk to you, Meggie.'

Meggie turned round, instantly alert, startled to see Oliver at her bedside again. 'What do you want?' she asked softly, hoping he had come to apologise.

'Sit up.' The words were not encouraging but she did as he asked, very conscious of the fact that she looked far from attractive. Beside her the baby whimpered and Meggie turned instantly, leaning towards the cot, ready to lift the child if she woke.

'Leave it.'

Meggie gaped at him, shocked by the harshness in his voice.

'I've been to see Mr Simmons,' he said, his eyes fixed on her face, unnerving her.

'I know.'

'You don't know what he told me though, do you?'

Meggie felt the first prickling intimation of disaster. 'What? What did he tell you?'

'She's damaged. Retarded. Not normal.' The words were deliberately cruel, delivered with such anger that Meggie almost expected him to reach across the bed and strike her. Paralysed with horror, she could have done nothing to defend herself if he had.

'Damaged . . .' The word swirled in her mind.

'Aye, Meggie. Damaged. Brain-damaged.'

'*No!*' The word emerged as an agonised scream as Meggie's world collapsed around her.

'Yes.' He spat the word at her.

'She can't be. It's not true,' she cried, but even as she spoke the words she knew that what she had taken for a placid nature had a far more ominous cause. 'No . . .'

'Yes. And you know why, Meggie, don't you?'

She looked at him, shaking her head, wide-eyed and dumb with horror.

'You caused it when you fell.'

Meggie found her voice in time to defend herself. 'No! They said I hadn't done any damage.'

'Well, they were wrong. And if it wasn't that then it must be something in you, something from your side of the family.'

But Meggie was already past hearing his insults. Her mind and eyes focused solely on the child sleeping so peacefully by her bed. Tenderly Meggie leaned over the crib and picked up her daughter, cradling her protectively against her aching breasts. 'Will she get better?' she asked. 'Is there something they can do for her? How bad is she, Oliver?'

Oliver felt rage boiling inside him and knew he had to get out of the room, away from Meggie and the thing in her arms. He got up so suddenly that the chair fell, crashing to the floor. The noise brought the sister running, but Oliver barged past her, leaving his wife to face her own private hell.

SEVENTEEN

Kate stood in the back doorway of Houghs, battling to put up her umbrella against the blustering March wind. No sooner did she raise it than the wind ripped into it, bending the spokes and tearing the fabric. Disgruntled because it was brand new, she bundled it into a dustbin and, head tucked into her shoulders, her collar clutched round her face, started off down the rain-lashed road.

Crossing the High Street she was aware of a car horn hooting furiously, but having no reason to believe anyone with a car could be trying to attract her attention, she ignored it. Keeping in close to the partial shelter of the shop fronts she hurried along the darkened street, anxious only to get back to Mrs Traynor's warm fireside. So intent was she in trying to keep the worst of the rain off her face that she didn't notice the car which had slowed to match her pace.

'*Kate!*'

Hearing her own name at last through the keening of the wind, she looked up.

'Come on.' Tom Herriot leaned across and opened the passenger door for her. 'Get in,' he gestured frantically.

Kate, with freezing rain already soaking through to her skin and running down her neck, needed no second bidding.

'I was starting to think you were deliberately ignoring me,' Tom said, sliding the car into gear and moving off.

'I didn't realise it was you,' she answered, wiping water from her face, so preoccupied that she forgot to be shy of him. 'Thanks for stopping. I was near drowning out there.'

'I could see that,' he quipped.

She smiled back at him. 'You'll maybe regret this later. I'm dripping all over your seat.'

He laughed, then concentrated on peering through the teeming rain. 'Netherton, isn't it?'

She nodded. 'I'm in lodgings there,' she told him, in case he might think her family came from the area, which was the poorest in Inverannan. But as soon as the words were out of her mouth she felt ashamed. Poor it might be, but the people were friendly and her landlady was the kindest person she had ever known.

'Aye, I know. You're from Brebner's farm, aren't you?'

'You seem to know a lot about me!' The sharply delivered words disguised a spasm of pleasure. Though the other girls teased her, saying Tom often watched her, and though she longed with all her heart for it to be true, he had never given her any real reason to think he was any more interested in her than he was in Betty. After the first six months she had given up hoping.

His delighted grin was hidden by the darkness. How different Kate was now to the quiet, too-anxious-to-please teenager she had been when she first started work at Houghs, eighteen months ago. Even then she had been a beauty, but still immature, little more than a child in both years and manner. A year and a half of independence had revealed a poised, confident and capable young woman who was surely the most beautiful in the county. And as Kate's looks and personality had ripened, so too had Tom's feelings for her, so slowly that at first he had hardly been aware of them. She intrigued him more and more with each passing day. Her self-possession, her total lack of vanity, her freshness slowly entranced him so that by the time he understood what was happening he was totally and absolutely besotted with her. He was always aware of her, found himself thinking about her when he should have been keeping his account books in order, and frequently contrived to find a seat at the lunch table close to where she was sitting so that he could talk to her. For the past month he had been searching for an opportunity to ask her out, not an easy thing to do under the alert eyes of Hough's staff. Tonight's rain had been heaven-sent.

But unless he did something soon it would be an opportunity lost. Already they were splashing through the water under the railway bridge which spanned the only road into Netherton. Why, he wondered, searching his brain for the right way to ask her out, was he finding this so difficult? He had never had this problem with the other girls he dated.

'Where now?' He drew the car to a halt against a kerb.

To his dismay she opened the door and started to get out into the rain which was, if anything, coming down even harder. 'This'll do.'

He lunged across her and grabbed the door, pulling it shut. She jerked back, startled.

'Sorry!' He cursed himself for his clumsiness. What on earth was the matter with him? 'I've brought you this far, so I might as well deliver you to your front door.'

'There's no need, really,' she said, amusement making her eyes shine.

'In this weather there is. Just tell me which way to go,' he insisted.

'Over there.' She laughed aloud now and pointed to a house no more than ten yards up the road.

Tom laughed and drove very slowly until he was outside the front door.

'Thanks for the lift. I would have got soaked through if I'd had to walk all the way.'

'My pleasure,' he murmured and there was something in his voice that told her it was nothing less than the truth.

Though she tried to appear calm, Kate's blood was singing

with excitement as she let herself hope that he was actually going to ask her to go out with him. Yet though she moved as slowly as she could, pulling her collar up and fiddling with her bag, giving him plenty of time to speak, it seemed that she had misread his intentions. Utterly dejected now and feeling rather foolish for having entertained such ridiculous thoughts, she opened the door and had one foot in the rain-filled gutter before he finally spoke.

'I was wondering if I could take you out one night? For a meal, or to the pictures? Anywhere you like, really.' He knew he was waffling and again wondered why this nineteen-year-old girl had the power to reduce him to the babbling equivalent of an adolescent on his first date.

The fact that her feet were planted in a puddle no longer mattered. 'If you like,' she replied, striving to sound cool and sophisticated.

'Tomorrow?' That was better, now that she had not turned him down he felt more in control. 'I'll book a table at the City Hotel, they have a dinner dance there. Eight-thirty all right?'

'Yes, fine.' She hopped through the puddle and went indoors, resisting the temptation to look back at him, afraid to let him see the beam of pure joy which was spreading across her face.

For only the second time since she had started working at Hough's, Kate slipped out in the lunch-time. This time she was intent on spending some of her precious savings on a dress and shoes which would not disgrace her when she went out with Tom.

'Och, Kate.' The admiration in Mrs Traynor's voice was enough to tell her that she had made the right choice. 'You look . . .' Words failed her. 'Well, it's just beautiful lass. You look a treat, so you do.'

The silky, midnight-blue material flared from a fitted bodice into a full skirt that rustled when she walked. The colour was echoed in the sheen of her dark hair, the whole seeming to emphasise the exotic slant to her eyes, the definition of her cheekbones.

Kate gave a delighted twirl, too excited to stand still. 'I've never had a dress like this,' she admitted, running a finger over the fabric, marvelling in the luxury of it, closing her mind to the cost.

'He must be very special,' Mrs Traynor observed softly, glad to see the girl so happy. In all the time she had lived here, Kate had been the model lodger, keeping herself and her room neat and clean, paying her rent on time and rarely going out. But surely that was unnatural for such a pretty lass? Of course she knew the real reason for Kate's reluctance to get involved with lads, but all Kate needed was the right man, someone who could show her how precious it was to be loved. Nor had she ever known Kate to spend money on anything so extravagant. She kept herself tidy, that was true, but her wardrobe was limited to functional clothing, with none of the fripperies the young lassies of today seemed to spend their money on. Aye, this lad, whoever he was, must be very special, very special indeed.

Her reverie was broken by the sound of a car drawing up outside, an unusual enough sound to attract attention in a street where no one owned such a thing.

Practically dancing with excitement, Kate grabbed her handbag and checked her hair in the mirror above the fire for one last time. 'Do I look all right?' she asked as the doorbell rang.

'You look wonderful, lass. Now off you go. Don't keep that young man waiting.'

Aware of curtains twitching all along Netherton Place, Kate felt like a princess as Tom opened the car door for her and settled her in the passenger seat before closing the door and hurrying round to slip behind the steering-wheel.

They drove the half mile to the town centre in electric silence, feeling tongue-tied and shy with one another. Kate, whose heart was thumping with nervous excitement, was relieved when they parked the car outside the town's most prestigious hotel.

The epitome of good manners, Tom helped her from the car, then led her into the hotel dining-room, standing back and holding the door open for her to precede him into the room.

Never having been inside such a smart establishment before and with no idea of what to expect, she hesitated for a moment, feeling self-conscious in her new dress, wishing he would go in first so that she could shelter behind him. But then, as if sensing her insecurity, he took her arm and they made an entrance together.

Kate was glad Tom was at her side. Every pair of eyes in the room seemed to turn on them as they waited just inside the door of the magnificent dining-room. She flushed, not much liking the sensation of being on display, but when she looked at Tom she saw that he too looked ill at ease and was running a finger round his stiff, white collar, almost as if it was choking him. Somehow, knowing that he too was uncomfortable in these opulent surroundings made her feel less nervous. She smiled at him and he grinned back, giving her arm a light squeeze as a waiter, complete with a white cloth draped over one arm, hurried towards them.

'I am sorry, we are fully booked,' the man said in artificially haughty tones, designed to intimidate. He was almost smirking at them as he shook his head.

'Then it's a good thing I reserved a table for eight-thirty, isn't it?' Tom said coolly. 'Herriot.'

'Er . . . yes, sir. Follow me, please, sir', the waiter gabbled, reverting to his native, broad Strathannan accent. Recovering his composure, he led them to a table near the wall. By the time he had taken their coats, settled them fussily in their seats, fiddled with the place settings, adjusted the lamp that burned in the centre of the table, given them a brace of menus and finally left them to make their selections, Kate was feeling totally overwhelmed by all the attention. She quickly glanced over the top of her menu to see Tom's reaction. To her astonishment, he was chuckling.

His amusement was contagious. In another moment Kate too was giggling like a schoolgirl and the ice was broken.

'Look around you,' Tom said in a loud whisper. 'No wonder that waiter thought we didn't belong here. We're the youngest by about half a century.'

Kate glanced round the luxurious room, realising that most of the other patrons were middle-aged. 'So we are,' she agreed merrily.

'I'm sorry, Kate,' Tom offered, afraid that he had made a terrible blunder. 'I didn't realise it would be like this. I just wanted to bring you to the best place in Inverannan. Would you like to go somewhere else?'

'Certainly not! This *is* the best place in Inverannan and I've never been here before, so I mean to make the most of it,' she told him.

Tom breathed a sigh of relief and they smiled at one another across the table. 'So, Kate Brebner,' he said. 'Tell me all about yourself.'

She pulled a face. 'There's not much to tell.'

But by the time they had finished their puddings, Tom had managed to get most of her story from her. What he heard only increased his admiration.

'Your uncle and cousins sound like dreadful people. But I can't understand why your mother let you leave home like that. She must be worried about you. Hasn't she ever tried to contact you? Didn't you write and let her know you were all right?'

Kate flushed and studied the table-cloth. 'No.'

Tom was aware that he had managed to upset her and wished he had been more tactful, but the truth was he was greedy to know everything about her. Leaning across the table, he took one of her hands in his. 'I'm sorry,' he said. 'I shouldn't be prying, I know, but . . .' She looked up at him then and he flushed, keenly aware that he was in danger of making a mess of the whole evening. 'It's just that . . . well, I like you a lot, Kate, and I hate to think someone's been unkind to you.'

Her hand was tingling where his fingers were interlacing with hers, but confusingly, she felt very near to tears. Already she knew that she could become very fond of Tom Herriot, but what would he think of her if he knew the real story behind her flight from the farm? Always truthful, hating any kind of deception, she nevertheless could not bring herself even to think of confessing what had happened to her to this wonderfully attractive man who was still almost a stranger. She looked down at the table again, unable to offer any sort of explanation.

In one corner a quartet played modern tunes and several couples were already dancing. The general atmosphere, helped no doubt by the generous amounts of wine being served at most tables, had thawed to one of friendly enjoyment. Tom, looking frantically for some way of recouping the situation, jumped quickly to his feet.

'Come on,' he said. 'Let's dance.'

She rose quickly, as eager as he to get away from the thorny topic of her past.

On the dance floor, surrounded by middle-aged couples, they stood for a moment, as if wondering what to do.

'I'm not much of a dancer,' he confided.

'Good, because neither am I,' she said, smiling up at him again, then stepping easily into his open arms and letting him lead her round the floor.

They danced in silence for a minute or two, each concentrating on their footwork, anxious not to make a spectacle of themselves. Then, as they grew accustomed to the movements, they relaxed a little. Kate felt Tom's arms tighten round her and shivered slightly as his mouth brushed her ear. 'Am I forgiven?' he whispered.

She nodded, then let her head fall against his shoulder, giving herself up to the sensation of being held by the most attractive man she had ever known.

'Thank you, Tom. I've had a lovely evening.' Kate sat in the warmth of the little car, reluctant to get out and bring this magical night to a close.

'Me too.' He smiled at her, his features blurred by the darkness. 'Can we see each other again?'

'I'd like that.'

'Saturday?'

'All right,' she agreed, already counting the hours. She sat on, not knowing what to do, wondering whether he would kiss her, afraid that he might not. Finally, when he made no move towards her, she grappled with the door handle.

Tom hurried out of the car and ran round to her side to open the door for her. He extended a hand to help her out then, very gently, pulled her towards him. His lips brushed hers, lingering for just a second before moving on to kiss her gently on the neck, just below her ear, which startled to tingle.

'Goodnight, Kate,' he whispered, struggling to resist the urge to pull her into his arms and kiss her properly. Then he was back in the car and already pulling away from the kerb. Kate felt the childish impulse to scream with joy and stood for a moment, composing herself.

Hearing the car draw up outside the little house, Mrs Traynor checked the clock and smiled. Eleven o'clock. A reasonable time, early enough to make the lad go up a notch in her estimation. Hurriedly she took up her knitting, not wanting

Kate to think she had been sitting waiting for her, though in truth she could hardly have been more anxious had she been the girl's mother.

One look at Kate's radiant face was enough to tell her that the evening had been a success.

A month later, well wrapped up against the winter chill, Kate and Tom wandered hand in hand through the Glen, Inverannan's famous park, named for the picturesque ravine that twisted through it.

'Are you cold?' he asked, slipping an arm round her.

'Not now,' she responded, nestling against the breadth of his shoulder.

The park was quiet now, most folk having gone home in search of warm hearths and hearty dinners. Only a few other courting couples shared the huge expanse of parkland with them, all intent on privacy. They walked on, content just to be together, not needing to talk, until they found a sheltered spot in the cover of a clump of evergreens.

Placing her gently with her back to a tree he ran a finger down her face then kissed her, a soft exquisite touching of lips that made her yearn for more.

Raising her arms and twining them round his neck she pulled him to her, shivering as his hands ran down her back. This time it was her mouth that sought his, her lips that pressed against his until she felt his arms tightening round her, pressing their thickly clothed bodies together as their mouths opened to one another. They kissed until forced to stop by the need to breathe.

Kate dropped her head on to his shoulder, marvelling at how fast everything was happening. It was as if she had known him for ever, as if he was her best friend.

Above all, she trusted him. Even as he kissed her and she felt his body hardening, she knew he would not attack her in the way Duncan had. Never for one moment did she doubt his ability to control himself until the time was right for them both.

Was it possible, she wondered, to fall so completely in love in so little time? For, much as she would have scoffed at the idea before, she had fallen in love with Tom that very first night, somewhere between soup and coffee at the City Hotel. She laughed softly, feeling happiness overwhelm her.

'What are you giggling at?' He smiled down at her, tangling his fingers in her hair to make her look up at him.

'I'm just happy,' she told him, the simple truth of that statement shining out of her eyes.

'Me too.' They gazed at each other, recognising a moment of infinite importance. 'I love you, Kate,' he said, putting it into words for the first time.

She didn't take her eyes away from his as she answered, 'And I love you too. I can't imagine a time when I didn't love you.'

They kissed, a gentle, searching kiss, then he whispered, 'I can't believe we have only been seeing each other for a month.'

They kissed again, a more urgent, more demanding thing, their bodies, hampered by their clothing, pressing against one another. 'I want you, Kate.'

'I want you too,' she admitted.

'We'd better not wait too long before getting married,' he said.

Kate thought her heart had stopped, but then, with a tremendous, juddering thud, it resumed a racing beat. 'Married?' she repeated, as if she wasn't sure she had heard him properly.

'Aye. Married.' He was laughing at her now. 'Isn't that what folk usually do when they love one another?'

But to his astonishment, Kate's face was a picture of dismay.

'Kate?' he said when she remained silent. 'Don't you want to get married?'

But Kate turned and began to walk away from him, forcing

him to run to catch up with her. She had known from that very first evening together that she and Tom would fall in love; had known too that she would have to be honest with him, to tell him the truth about why she had been driven from her home. But everything had happened so quickly. Too quickly.

'Kate.' He pulled roughly at her arm, forcing her to stop. 'Will you just please tell me what's wrong?' he cried, the pain of rejection making him sound angry.

Kate stood with her hands shoved into her pockets, her shoulders hunched. She should have known it would never work, she thought, angry with herself now. Tom was exactly what he appeared to be: a decent, well brought up young man who respected her – or what he thought was her. Though they had both felt an urgent physical desire which left them shaking with frustration, he clearly expected to save the final intimate act for their wedding night. Tom wanted to make her his own, to be the first and only man to make love to her. And if she accepted his proposal, she would be deceiving him. Their whole marriage would be built on a lie. And how could she tell him what had happened? How could she disappoint him so badly? How could she ever describe to him the sordid events which had led her to this heart-breaking impasse? And how could she ever bear to know that he would always wonder whether she truly had been raped? After all, even her mother had doubted her.

'Kate,' he said again, shouting the word at her. 'Will you tell me what I've done?'

She choked back a sob. Better to end it now, as kindly as she could. To let him think she was simply not ready for marriage. Anything rather than having to live with the knowledge that he despised her. So distraught was she that she never even considered any other possibility.

'I can't,' she said, her voice husky with strain.

'Can't what?' he demanded.

'I can't get married.' Not to anyone, she thought miserably. Because no man would want her if he knew the truth. But she didn't want any other man. Only Tom. And only then did she truly realise how deeply she loved him.

'Why not?' he asked, bewildered by this sudden change in her.

She took a deep breath, desperate to get away from him, to run home to the miserable solitude of her own room. But first she had to finish it. To make him see that it was hopeless. 'Tom,' she said, fighting to control the tremor in her voice, to hurt him as little as possible. 'I'm sorry. I should never have let things get this far.'

'I don't understand, Kate,' he said, shaking his head, totally perplexed.

'You're my first proper boyfriend, Tom, and I've only known you for a month. It's too soon. I'm too young. I . . . I want to meet other people . . . other boys . . . before I settle down.'

'But I thought you loved me,' he mumbled as the bottom fell out of his world.

The pain in his face was too much. 'I'm sorry,' she cried. 'I never meant to hurt you.' And she turned away and began to run from him.

He stood, unable to move, watching the woman he loved more than anything in the whole world disappear from sight.

EIGHTEEN

The job that had given Kate so much pleasure was now the source of intense pain, for every minute she spent at Hough's was a minute when she might see or hear Tom. So deep was her shame, so guilty did she feel about hurting him so badly, that every time he came anywhere near her she looked away, unable to bear the sight of his wretched face. She went about her tasks in silence, her head permanently bowed, her heart so wrapped in misery that she was afraid to speak in case she cried.

Tom, who sat in his glass-walled office, spending much of his time simply watching her, was more confused than ever. If Kate had truly meant what she said, if she genuinely wanted to stop seeing him so that she could have the chance to meet other young men, then why was she so unhappy? Several times he tried to talk to her, but each time he got near her she moved away, turning her back to him, refusing even to look at him. Defeated, he retreated to his own office and immersed himself in his work.

Kate, glimpsing his bent form as he toiled over the account books, felt a surge of love so strong that she actually thought her legs might give way beneath her. She knew then that, much as she loved her job, she would have to look for something else. She simply could not bear to have to see Tom every day, to go on loving him, knowing what she had lost.

Watching her as she served another customer, Tom was thinking the same thing.

'You look terrible,' Betty commented at the end of the week

as they were putting their coats on ready to go home. 'Are you coming down with something?'

'I'm fine,' was Kate's dismissive reply.

Betty was persistent. 'Tom Herriot looks as if he's sickening for the same thing, then.'

'Does he?' Kate was careful to keep her face averted from her friend, who was watching her very closely. 'Look, I'm in a hurry tonight. I'll see you on Monday,' she said, picking up her bag and hurrying from the shop.

Betty sighed and followed more slowly. Obviously Kate wasn't going to confide in her although that was no surprise: the other girl was very self-contained. But it looked very much as though the romance was off. And that, she thought, making her way home, was a great shame, because if two people were ever made for one another, those two people were Tom Herriot and Kate Brebner. Still, Kate was attractive and would soon find another boyfriend. Who knows, maybe now that Tom was unattached again, he might be on the look-out for someone else. She would wash her hair and set it in pin-curls on Sunday night, just in case.

'Hello, lass.' Mrs Traynor turned from the stove and greeted her young lodger with a smile. 'Your tea's just ready.'

'I'm not hungry,' Kate said listlessly. 'I think I'll just go on upstairs and have an early night.'

Mrs Traynor looked at her more closely, remembering the swollen eyes and miserable face the girl had brought to the breakfast table with her that morning. She had eaten nothing then either. 'You need some good food inside you, Kate, especially in this weather.'

'I couldn't eat anything,' Kate insisted, starting to go upstairs.

'All right, lass. Not to worry. It's only a lamb stew. It'll keep until the morn.'

But the next day Kate still had no appetite.

'This won't do, Kate,' Mrs Traynor told her sternly, worried by the girl's pallor. 'A lassie of your age needs to keep her strength up. You'll be fading away to nothing. Now, try to eat something, before Tom gets here.' Mrs Traynor was expecting Tom to call for Kate as he had done every Saturday evening for the last five weeks.

'He's not coming.'

Ah, and those three words explained everything, Mrs Traynor thought, sitting down opposite Kate and tucking in to her own meal while the girl played with the food on her plate. 'There are plenty folk in this street who would be grateful to sit down to a plateful of good meat and vegetables like that, Kate. Food's o'er expensive to waste, so unless you are really ill, you'd best get it eaten else you and I will be falling out.'

Reluctantly, Kate placed a forkful of succulent beef in her mouth, then chewed and swallowed. She tasted nothing.

Mrs Traynor sighed, recalling similar traumas when her own daughters were courting. 'You and young Tom falling out is one thing, lass, but just tell me how you are going to make things better by making yourself ill over a lovers' spat?'

'It's not a lovers' spat,' Kate retorted.

'More serious is it?' Mrs Traynor asked, glad to have got the girl talking about it.

Kate nodded. 'It's all over.'

'Aye well, these things happen. He can't have been the right one for you, Kate. You'll find someone else, you'll see.'

'I don't want anyone else.' There were no tears in Kate's eyes now, just a total hopeless bleakness that touched Mrs Traynor's heart.

'Then why . . .? Och, I see! It was Tom who finished with you, was it?' And that was a blow to the pride as much as anything else.

But Kate was shaking her head. 'No. It was the other way round.'

Now Mrs Traynor was truly puzzled. 'Then why are you so upset about it?'

Kate put her knife and fork down and shoved her plate aside. 'Because I love him,' she whispered.

'Then go and tell *him* that. Everyone argues, Kate. If it was your fault and you said things you didn't mean, then apologise and make up. If he cares for you he's likely just as upset as you are.'

'You don't understand.' Kate got up and started to clear the table.

'Then why don't you explain it to me,' Mrs Traynor suggested, removing the plates from Kate's cold hands and taking them through to the scullery.

While the older woman washed the dishes and Kate dried them, Kate told Mrs Traynor about Tom's proposal and her own reaction to it. 'So you see, I had no choice,' she ended sadly. She waited, expecting sympathy from her warm-hearted landlady, and was startled to see the other woman scowling at her.

'And do you not think,' the older woman asked coldly, 'that Tom at least deserved the truth from you?'

'I couldn't!' Kate was horrified.

'So you lied to him.'

'No!'

'Aye, you did! You were too much of a coward to tell him the truth so you lied.'

Kate had gone even paler than she had been before. 'But what would he have thought of me?'

'Well, Kate, you will never know, will you, because you didn't give him the chance to think about it. If you want the truth, I think you've been selfish and unfair to that poor lad. Just think how he must feel! He asked you to marry him and you threw it back in his face, as if he meant nothing at all to you.'

'But that's not true. I did what I did because I didn't want to hurt him.'

'No, Kate. You did not.'

Kate gawped at the older woman, hardly able to believe what she was hearing.

Mrs Traynor was merciless. 'It wasn't Tom's feelings you were worried about, Kate. It was your own. You couldn't bear to think that Tom might look down on you for what happened. For all you know, he might have understood. But, like I say, you'll never know, will you?'

Kate stood, completely immobile, reeling from the older woman's attack. Her skin was ashen, her expression one of total despair. Seeing her, Mrs Traynor wondered whether she had gone too far, but it would be terrible to see a loving relationship wasted, all for the sake of a pinch of pride and a measure of common sense. Sighing, she went across to Kate and put an arm round the tense shoulders.

'I didn't mean to be cruel, Kate. I can understand why you should think the way you do and, well, maybe you are right; maybe he won't be able to come to terms with what happened to you. But you can't possibly know that. And you should never make someone else's decisions for them. You do see that, don't you?'

Kate nodded. She did see, all too clearly, that she had made a horrible, unforgiveable error. But it was too late to do anything about it now. Even if she went to Tom and tried to explain, she had hurt him so badly that he probably wouldn't even want to listen to her. She paused. I'm doing it again, she thought. Trying to read his mind. Making Tom's decisions for him.

To her landlady's astonishment, Kate turned and kissed her on the cheek. 'Thank you,' she said.

Mrs Traynor beamed and hugged her back. 'Talk to him, Kate.'

'Perhaps. But now I think I'll go to bed. I've a lot to think about.'

A decision reached, some nourishing meals and two nights of sound sleep did much to restore Kate. When she set out for work on the Monday morning she was apprehensive but determined to see Tom and tell him the absolute truth.

As always, the shop was busy on Monday morning. There was the usual steady stream of customers for Hough's fresh bread, but the shelves also had to be restocked after the Saturday rush so there was little time to spare. At breaktime Tom sat with Mr Wemyss, and in any case the staff room was not an appropriate venue for what Kate had to say to him. The same applied to the lunch-break. By the end of the day, Kate had found no single opportunity to speak to Tom alone. Resorting to desperate measures, she was deliberately slow in getting her coat on, lingering upstairs long after the other assistants had gone, then going back to the shop, hoping he would be working late, as he frequently did. But there was no sign of him and his overcoat was missing from the coat stand just inside his office. She made her way sadly to the back door.

Mr Wemyss was standing just inside it with the keys, ready to lock up and go home. 'Och, Kate, I thought you'd long gone. You nearly got yourself locked in for the night, lass,' he laughed.

She heard the key turn and the heavy bolts drawn across, then the lights went out one by one as the manager worked his way to the front of the shop. His final duty was always to pull down the window blinds and let himself out of the main door, locking it securely behind him.

She stood for a moment, watching as the building sank into darkness, wondering whether she would like her next job as much as she liked this one. She would look through last Friday's local paper and apply for anything that looked even remotely suitable. The sooner she was away from Tom, the better it would be for both of them. Unless he could forgive her . . . But no. She turned and started to walk towards the High Street. She couldn't let herself begin to hope.

A little more than an hour later Tom laid down his knife and fork, pushed aside his half-eaten meal and addressed his parents. 'There's something I've got to tell you.'

Mrs and Mrs Herriot exchanged a brief glance, then both fastened their attention on their only son.

'I have decided to leave Hough's,' he said firmly.

A look of utter dismay passed between his parents, but when his father spoke all he said was, 'Why, Tom?'

Tom had prepared for this question, but even so he couldn't quite bring himself to look his father in the eye as he answered: 'I've decided I would like to make my career in accountancy. I think I would like to work for one of the big banks or insurance companies in Edinburgh.'

'But why go and work for some big organisation where no one knows who you are when you are all set to inherit your uncle's business?' his mother asked, as he had known she would.

He tried to appear nonchalant and shrugged lightly. 'Uncle is likely to go on running Hough's for another twenty years yet. Until I take over I'll be exactly what I am now. I want to try something else, get some more experience.'

'Well, I suppose it's natural enough for a lad of your age to want to spread his wings a bit,' his father said. 'But you have a very good future ahead of you, Tom. Don't throw it away without giving this a great deal of serious thought. I'm not at all convinced that your uncle will leave you the business if you go off and work for someone else.'

'Are you unhappy at Hough's, Tom?' his mother asked.

'You've always seemed quite settled there,' his father added.

'A lot of young men would be very grateful for the opportunity your uncle is offering you. I know I would have been.'

'I am grateful,' he assured them. 'But I don't want to spend my whole life living and working in Inverannan.'

'And what's wrong with Inverannan? If you ask me, I think you're being stupid,' his father said, his voice rising in line with his temper. 'Why would anyone in their right mind want to throw away an opportunity like that? No one knows what the future might bring, but you will always have a job and a steady income from that shop. Personal service, high quality goods, that's what people want. No matter what else happens, folk will always need to eat and there will always be a need for a shop like Hough's.' Having had his say, Mr Herriot left the table in high dudgeon.

Mrs Herriot lingered long enough to say, 'Tom, promise me you won't do anything drastic before we've talked about this some more?' Then she followed her husband.

Tom was in his office a couple of days later when there was a knock on the door. He looked round then got to his feet and ushered in Hough's solicitor with a smile.

'Mr Porteous! What brings you here?' he said, shaking the other man's hand and offering him a chair.

The older man sat down and looked around him, admiring the shop. 'Looks like you're very nicely set up here,' he commented. 'My wife does all her shopping at Hough's. Says you're the best.'

'We like to think so,' Tom agreed, feeling proud to be a part of such a respected institution. Then, remembering that he was about to sever that connection, perhaps for good, he asked, 'Is this a business matter or is there something I can get you?'

'It's neither really. You see I've a vacancy for a junior clerk in my office. You know the sort of thing. Someone bright and presentable.'

Tom nodded, wondering where he fitted in to all this.

'Well, I placed a small advertisement in the *Courier* last week and one of your lassies has applied for the post. She's got the right qualifications and writes with a neat hand. I'm tempted to give her a chance but I thought I'd have a wee word with you first – off the record you understand – just to see what the girl's like. I make a point of having a word with former employers before I take anyone on. More reliable than a written reference, I always think.'

Tom laughed. 'Aye. But if she's a good worker I might be tempted to say something a wee bit negative, just to put you off. I can't say I like the idea of helping you to steal our staff.'

'I've known you since you were a babe in arms, Tom Herriot, and your father and I sat next to one another at Pittenlaw school. I know you'll give me a fair picture of the lass, even though you might just end up losing her. To my mind, once the staff get unsettled you're as well helping them on their way. If someone's not suited in their job they never work as well as they could.'

'All right. Who is it?'

'A girl by the name of Brebner. Kate Brebner.'

'Kate!' The exclamation was out before Tom could stop it.

'You weren't expecting her to leave then?'

'Well, no.'

'And is she a good worker?'

'Aye, Mr Porteous, she is. A very good worker. She's bright and accurate and punctual and neat and tidy. She's helpful and polite and she's quick to learn too. And – '

Porteous stopped him with a laugh. 'Enough! It sounds like I'll be taking your best assistant away from you then. The way you were praising her there, Tom, anyone would think you were sweet on the lass.' He got to his feet and offered his hand in farewell. 'Thanks, Tom, I appreciate your help. Expect young Kate to be handing in her notice at the end of the week.'

Kate had almost given up hope of getting a moment alone with Tom to explain her reasons for turning him down. It was obvious that he was avoiding her and the more time that passed, the harder it was going to be. She had considered going to his house and asking to speak to him but was daunted by the prospect of having to explain any part of this to his parents, who probably didn't even know of her existence. Yet that was precisely what she was going to have to do if she failed to catch him alone today.

When the shop closed for the day she again lingered for a few minutes after the other assistants, but she wasn't surprised to discover that Tom had left before her. Determined to go straight to his home and demand to speak to him there, she hurried out of the back door, anxious to get out of the shop before Mr Wemyss should discover her again and begin to wonder why she was always last out of the shop at night. As she walked out into the back lane she was already rehearsing what she might say if Tom's mother answered the door.

'Kate.'

'Tom!' Her heart leaped and she span round to greet him. They stood facing each other in the back wynd, the wind whipping round them, neither knowing what to say. It was Kate who finally broke the silence.

'I've been wanting to speak to you . . .'

'I've got something to tell you.'

'Tom, I'm sorry for what happened. I want to ex – '

He cut her short. 'There's no need to explain, Kate . . . I understand . . . you've applied for a job at Porteous and Cain because you can't even bear to go on working in the same shop as me . . . but I know you like working at Hough's . . . well, *I* have decided to go and work in Edinburgh, so you see, you don't need to leave.' It emerged as one long sentence, so anxious was he to get the words out.

She stared at him, trying to make sense of the gabbled words, then, understanding at last, cried, 'But it's *you* who can't stand to be near *me*! All week I've been trying to talk to you and you won't even look at me and now you're telling me you're going to Edinburgh to work. To get away from me!'

'No! I mean . . . well, yes, but not because I can't stand to be near you . . . well, not the way you mean.' Why had he said that, he wondered, when he had been so determined to conduct himself with dignity, to hide his pain from her? His next words were bitter with the anger which had welled inside him. 'Anyway, you were the one who turned me down. It's you who doesn't care for me, Kate, not the other way round.'

'That's not true!' she protested, taking an agitated step towards him.

'You want to go out with other men!' He almost spat the words at her.

'No, I do not.'

'You do, Kate. You told me so yourself.' He stood perfectly still and Kate could feel his pain as though she had been stabbed by it herself.

'I lied to you, Tom,' she admitted quietly. 'I thought I was doing the right thing, but I was wrong.' She shivered as a blast of icy wind whipped along the road.

'You lied! How could you lie about something like that?' he yelled, too proud to want her to see just how much he hurt, though he longed to take her in his arms, to shield her from the wind that was turning his body to ice.

She didn't answer, but stood there, her arms wrapped defensively around her body, visibly shivering.

'And I suppose you lied when you said you loved me?' he demanded.

'No.' she whispered it and the word was lost in the howling wind.

'What did you say?' he roared.

'I said *no*. I didn't lie. I love you, Tom.'

They stood looking at each other, one too proud, the other too ashamed to make the first move. But when Tom mutely shook his head and turned as if to move away, Kate shouted, 'No, Tom! Don't go. Please.'

He hesitated, then looked back at her.

'I'm so sorry, Tom,' she sobbed. 'I love you so much. Please, don't go.'

He wasn't aware of moving towards her, nor she to him, but somehow they were together.

After a moment they moved apart and he took her hands in his. 'You're frozen.'

'You too.' But she couldn't smile at him, couldn't bear to look into his eyes.

'Do you want to talk?' he asked.

'We've got to, Tom. There's something I've got to tell you: something I should have told you weeks ago.'

'I meant to tell you. I knew I should but ... but it was so awful. I knew you would be shocked. But I would have told you, Tom, honestly I would. It's just ... well, everything happened so much faster than I thought it would.' She had told him it all, everything, and now babbled on, afraid to stop, afraid to face his reaction. But suddenly, in an odd jerky movement, he raised one hand, silencing her immediately.

They were in his car, in the same back wynd behind the shop, the wind still whistling around them.

She watched him, her whole body rigid with tension, saw with dismay the way he leaned his head forward on to the steering wheel and knew he could not accept that she had

250

been with another man before him, that he would not be the first.

'I'd better go,' she said, struggling desperately with the door handle, not wanting to see the expression in his eyes when he was finally able to bring himself to look at her – if he ever could.

'No!' He leaned over and knocked her hand away from the door, then lifted it up and kissed her fingers. 'Did you really think I could hate you for what someone else did to you, Kate?' he asked, pulling her close and looking down into her eyes, which shone back at him in the darkness.

'I thought it would be important to you,' she croaked, her throat so tight that she could barely talk.

'Of course it's important to me! Of course I care that someone hurt you!' He raised a hand and put it gently behind her neck. 'But, one day . . . one day very soon, Kate, I will show you the way it should be between two people who really love one another. Then, whatever happened to you before won't matter any more. I promise.'

With that he lowered his face to hers and they kissed, and with that kiss all the pain and anguish of the last two weeks disappeared as though it had never been.

'Has Tom said any more to you about that hare-brained scheme of his to take himself off to Edinburgh to work?' Mr Herriot asked his wife about two weeks later.

She smiled across the table at him. 'Hasn't said a word.'

'Thank goodness for that. Young idiot!'

'Now, didn't I tell you that if we didn't make a fuss he would forget the idea?'

'Yes, my dear. Right again.' But he smiled fondly at her.

'Anyway,' she confided. 'I think he's found himself a young woman. And it's serious.'

'Oh?' His eyebrows shot up. 'What makes you think that?'

'Well,' she said, eyeing her son's empty seat. 'I can't think of anything else that would induce Tom to miss his Sunday dinner. Can you?'

NINETEEN

'A toast.' Edward Murcheson, Provost of Inverannan, raised his glass in Oliver's direction. 'To Inverannan's next Member of Parliament, Oliver Laing.'

The dozen guests assembled round Meggie's dining table scrambled to their feet and chorused their congratulations.

Meggie too raised her glass and sipped at the champagne specially purchased for just this moment, wondering where all this would lead them. It seemed like only yesterday that Oliver had decided to emulate his father by following him into local politics. Many folk who recalled with affection Wallace Laing's days as provost were only too willing to support his son's bid for power and Oliver had won his seat with surprising ease. Since then he had surprised Meggie with his flair and enthusiasm for politics. Oliver took his new responsibilities seriously, thriving on Town Hall intrigues and quickly establishing himself as a force to be reckoned with. Rarely a week went by without Oliver Laing's face featuring prominently in the local press. Within six months of winning his first local election, Oliver had announced his ambition to stand for Parliament. A bare three months later, he had been adopted as Conservative candidate to replace the current Member who would be standing down at the next election because of ill health.

Meggie, witnessing the transformation of her husband with considerable astonishment, was nevertheless awed by the single-mindedness with which he fostered his public image. Despite his private resentment, he even contrived to turn her success as a businesswoman to his own advantage by publicly praising her in an interview with the *Courier*. The resulting article described her as 'one of a new breed of women'. But any pleasure she might have gained from those words rapidly vanished when she read the next paragraph, which seemed to ascribe her success solely to her husband's generous support.

Still, Meggie mused as the local party chairman began to add his felicitations in a rather long-winded speech, Oliver's preoccupation with matters political left him little time in which to concern himself with her activities. Unchallenged by him, she had expanded further, buying a third shop and, in a direct challenge to Hough's, adding a wine and spirits department to her existing High Street store.

Glancing round her table, Meggie realised that although she knew the names of all her guests, and had met them all at various official functions, they were little better than strangers to her. The irony of her situation brought an unhappy tightness to her throat and she took a hasty gulp of champagne. Did any of them, she wondered, realise that the picture that Oliver was so careful to present of a dedicated family man was nothing more than a charade? True, Oliver was no longer involved with other women – or if he was, he was extremely discreet – but their marriage was dead, his interest in her and their child non-existent, and her role in his life nothing more than that of hostess.

Feeling the familiar spear of resentment burn her stomach, she sipped again at her drink, then looked at her husband as he rose to make his reply. Surrounded by and at ease with the Burgh's most prominent citizens, Oliver was in his element. It was as if she were seeing him properly for the first time in many years. Almost unnoticed his hair had started to turn grey at the temples, lending him the same aura of distinction that had marked his father. In profile his face had always seemed severe, but now a few added pounds had softened his jawline slightly and the deep lines which radiated out from his eyes and down the side of his mouth only added character to his undeniably handsome appearance. Listening to him as he thanked those who had helped him and went on to give a brief outline of his political ideals and aspirations, Meggie realised that he was a skilled speechmaker too. To almost everyone here tonight, she realised with a slight tremor of apprehension, he was an ideal candidate. What would they think of him, she wondered, fixing the obligatory smile to her lips, if they knew that he drunk himself into a stupor every night; that in private he treated his wife with a cold civility which had destroyed her last hopes of reconciliation; that he had a year-old daughter he refused to talk to? What would they think of him if they knew that the smiling and supportive wife regarded her husband with contempt, and longed to be free of this sham of a marriage?

As if of their own volition, Meggie's eyes travelled down the opposite side of the table to where Robbie sat. He wore a faintly glazed expression as he listened to his cousin's speech, but sensing Meggie's gaze upon him, he looked up at her. Their eyes met briefly and a flash of understanding passed between them before Meggie looked away, aware as always of how vital it was to hide her feelings for this infinitely desirable man.

Robbie, the only other person at that table who knew the private face of Oliver Laing, allowed himself a wry smile. But no matter what he might think about the way Oliver handled his marriage, he had a sneaking admiration for the manner in which he had orchestrated this new career. Many of Oliver's most useful supporters were business acquaintances, but that sort of relationship worked both ways and Robbie had to concede that, despite putting in no more than a dozen hours a week at the quarry, Oliver had brought in more new business than he had himself. It was a situation that had necessitated the hiring of an experienced site manager to oversee the day-to-day running of the quarry, but though Robbie was sometimes irritated by his cousin's lack of commitment to the more mundane side of the business, profits were healthier than he had dared to hope for. He had very weak grounds for complaint. If he was truthful he would have to admit that when the two of them were forced to spend too much time together their relationship became extremely strained, and that it was perhaps fortunate for them all that Oliver had other interests. Looking across at Meggie, who was again playing her role as devoted wife, Robbie was aware of a lump of anger and resentment. Meggie surely deserved better than Oliver. He was more than willing to give her the love and security she so richly deserved. But it was hopeless. Meggie would never leave Oliver, especially not now that they had the child to consider. He didn't know why he went on torturing himself like this when every minute spent in her company just added to the sense of miserable frustration which continually dogged him.

Meggie herself had told him to find someone else. There were plenty of eligible young women who would be keen enough to marry him, if only for the comfortable life he could provide; nor was there any shortage of females offering the sort of physical relief he had needed like a drug for the first year or so after Megan's death. But not any more. Now he was almost resigned to living out his life without a partner, to bringing up his children alone, because if he couldn't have Meggie he wanted no one. But always, buried in his heart, was that tiny germ of hope: that one day, somehow, she would be free.

Oliver sat down to generous applause and the conversation round the table became more general. Meggie made small-talk with the local party chairman's wife, then suggested that they all move into the drawing-room.

While the men congregated around the fireplace, the women arranged themselves comfortably on the sofas and chairs and the talk immediately became less formal.

Meggie, making sure her guests were comfortable and well supplied with liquid refreshment, turned with a smile when the door opened to reveal Jessica, the nanny, with a child wrapped in her arms.

'I've brought Ellen to say goodnight, Mrs Laing,' she said, crossing the room with the wide-eyed infant.

Meggie smiled and opened her arms in welcome. 'Come on then,' she laughed.

The little girl stared round, momentarily confused by the sea of strange faces, then, spotting her mother, gave a throaty cry and an open-mouthed grin that released a stream of dribble over her chin.

Oblivious to the guests who were watching in uncomfortable silence, Meggie swept the child up, laughing as Ellen grabbed her face between two pudgy hands, and delivered a brace of soggy, smacking kisses, accompanying the action with loud grunts of affection.

'All right.' Meggie laughed again and extricated herself, with difficulty, from her daughter's wet embrace. Drawing a handkerchief from up her sleeve she dabbed at the saliva-soaked chin before standing up with her daughter in her arms and carrying her to where Oliver had been engrossed in conversation with a senior party member. 'Now say goodnight to Daddy,' she said. Normally Oliver took no part in the night-time routine, but to allow the child to leave the room without bidding her father goodnight would surely invite comment.

Oliver glowered at his daughter, his face almost purple with fury. Ellen, suspended in mid-air between her mother and father, held out her arms trustingly towards him. Getting no reaction, she clenched her little fists, screwed up her face and started to complain in a series of discordant grunts and shrieks. Oliver, his face taut with humiliation, turned pointedly away. Meggie, rendered momentarily immobile by her husband's callous and very public rejection of his daughter, was slow to react. Ellen, desperately frightened now, broke into a loud howl which changed to a delighted gurgle as familiar hands fastened firmly round her waist and whisked her out of her mother's arms and high into the air.

'Unc!' she grunted, dribbling delight as she rewarded Robbie with a particularly wet kiss.

'Ellen!' he chortled, throwing her up again and blowing a raspberry on the child's soft neck, his pleasure in her gurgling, giggling response obvious to everyone watching. 'Come on then, it's past your bedtime. Be a good lass and kiss your daddy and I'll tuck you up in bed.'

The little girl, at ease with her favourite person in all the world after her mother, clapped her hands and then reached out for her father, who had no option but to face her. Aware that the whole room was watching, Oliver allowed Robbie to place the wriggling infant into his rigid arms. Ellen, hypersensitive to her father's moods, tensed and Oliver, worried that she would compound his earlier mistake by trying to escape from him, quickly dropped a kiss on her head and shoved her back into Robbie's waiting arms, aware as his did so of the look of utter disgust which his cousin levelled at him.

'Thank you, Robbie,' Oliver blustered, trying desperately to make the best of a bad situation. 'It's easy to see you're the favourite uncle, isn't it?' He smiled expansively round the room, noting with dismay that no one would meet his eye.

'Yes, isn't it?' Robbie hissed, hugging the child, who, suddenly tired, dropped a head on his shoulder and put her thumb in her mouth.

'It's all right, Robbie. I'll take her up,' Meggie offered, recovering.

Ellen shook her head violently and tightened her grip on Robbie's neck, determined not to be denied this special treat.

'No, let me, please, Meggie.' Robbie had resolved to show everyone that he at least was proud of his niece. In truth it was a pleasure to put the child to bed, to watch as she slipped into peaceful, innocent sleep.

The door closed behind him and the silence in the room was absolute. Then Oliver laughed, a forced, over-loud noise. 'Spoiled, that's what they are, children today. Can twist her mother round her little finger that one can, and her uncle too.'

Muted laughter greeted this and gradually the tense atmosphere eased as conversation resumed. But everyone in the room had witnessed the scene and Oliver knew there was no longer any way of hiding the shameful secret of his daughter's condition.

'Are you deliberately trying to ruin my chances of becoming an MP?' Oliver walked into his wife's room, slammed the door and roared at her. From the driveway below came the sound of a car engine sparking to life as the last of their guests finally left.

Meggie carefully finished wiping make-up from her face and dropped the soiled cotton-wool ball into the raffia basket beside her dressing table before turning to face him. Those people who were familiar with the cheerful, beautiful and successful young businesswoman would hardly have recognised her at that moment. Anger and contempt had drained her face of all colour and set it in a stiff, ugly mask. When she spoke her lips barely moved but her voice, though low, was pregnant with loathing. 'How could you turn your back on your own daughter? You disowned her, Oliver. In front of all those people.'

'You realise, don't you, that no one will vote for me once this gets out? No one will want to vote for a man who has fathered an imbecile.'

'Ellen is not an imbecile. She is a loving, affectionate child, as you would know if you had ever bothered to spend some time with her.' Though Meggie's chest ached with the effort it was taking her to control her fury, her defence of her daughter was made in the same low tone.

'She's an imbecile! Face facts, Meggie. She can't talk and she never will. She can barely crawl. She slobbers. She has no control of her bodily functions. She will never progress.' Oliver paced the room in agitation, trying to find the way to say what had to be said, the only solution to the constant threat this child would be.

'Do you think I don't know all that, Oliver?' Meggie asked coldly. 'And I love her just the same.'

Oliver took a deep breath, fighting to keep his temper, wishing he had thought to pour himself a whisky before coming up here. As on all public occasions, he had drunk little this evening, his liking for alcohol as closely guarded a secret as this monster he had sired, but now he badly needed a drink. But if he was to get Meggie to agree to his suggestion then he would need a clear head.

'Meggie,' Deliberately he softened his voice. 'I know you are very attached to the child –'

'Ellen,' she interrupted him angrily. 'Your daughter's name is Ellen.'

'I know you are very attached to Ellen, but she is still little more than a baby. How will you cope when she is ten? When she is fifteen? When she is thirty? Because she will always need someone to care for her, Meggie, and the older she gets, the harder that job will be.'

'What are you trying to say, Oliver?' So rarely did they have any sort of conversation, especially at this time of night when he would normally be too inebriated to string more than two coherent words together that she knew he had some ulterior purpose in mind.

'I am only thinking of you, Meggie,' he assured her with the false sincerity of the politician.

'Then don't,' she retorted bitterly. 'Ellen and I have managed very well without any support or help from you until now and there is no reason why we can't go on as we are.'

'I have been making enquiries, Meggie. There is a very pleasant little home for cases like this. Big airy rooms, lots of fresh air, plenty of staff . . .'

Now Meggie was on her feet, the aura of calm anger replaced by blazing fury. 'You want me to put our daughter in a home?'

'She will be well looked after and we can afford it.'

'We can afford it?' she shrieked. 'You won't take any responsibility for her while she lives here, you make no contribution towards the nanny, but you are willing to pay to have her put away so you can pretend she doesn't exist?'

Oliver still tried to reason with her, knowing his future career could well depend on what happened tonight. 'But she has no hope of a normal life, Meggie . . .'

'And that is a good reason to lock her away, is it? Just because she is not the same as you or me? Because she is different from other people?'

'I think it's for the best, yes.'

'She is happy, Oliver. Isn't that what really matters?'

'Happy!' His voice was laced with scorn. 'How can she be happy? She has no future, she will never marry, will never have any of the things a girl like her should grow up to expect.'

'She has love, Oliver, from me, and from Robbie and his children. And that's what really matters, being loved.' She walked across the room until she was facing him, her eyes almost on a level with his. 'I will never let you take her away from me, Oliver. Never!'

He stared at her for a moment, then looked away, defeated by the absolute determination he read in her blazing eyes. Already he could see his embryonic career in ruins, could hear the pitying whispers, the innuendo, the doubts about his own mental stability.'

'If you are so determined to be rid of Ellen then you will

have to get rid of me too,' she told him, still watching his averted face.

He looked up again then, wondering if he had misunderstood.

'I want a divorce, Oliver.'

His face, which had been flushed with anger, blanched with shock. '*No!*'

'It would be for the best, Oliver,' she said, sadness welling in her chest. It was defeat, she thought miserably: the final acknowledgement that the marriage she had tried so hard to salvage was beyond saving. 'We are making one another miserable. We can't go on like this.'

'Never!' he roared. 'Think of the scandal. It would ruin me – and you too. No, I will never divorce you, Meggie, and you cannot divorce me. You have no grounds. Nothing,' he added grimly, 'that you can prove.'

Now it was her turn to look away, knowing he was right, understanding that her life, her happiness, their daughter's future were all as nothing compared to his precious political career. But Meggie wasn't beaten yet. She might be tied to an unhappy marriage, but she would stay on her own terms.

'Are you sure, Oliver?' she asked. 'Are you quite certain that you have been as careful as you should have been?' She saw the momentary flash of doubt on his face and knew she had struck a tender nerve. Now that she had him on the defensive she couldn't resist adding to his discomfort, needing desperately to pay him back, however pettily, for the pain he had caused her. She gave a short laugh. 'Och, you didn't think for one moment that I don't know about you and your "lady" friends. No, Oliver, even you are not that clever. And think what a scandal that would cause among your Tory cronies if it ever became public knowledge.'

'Are you trying to blackmail me, Meggie?' he asked, a dangerous snarl on his face.

She appeared to consider this calmly, though she could feel herself trembling. 'Blackmail, no, I wouldn't stoop so low, Oliver.' And anyway, she knew she could never prove anything, not without exposing herself to public humiliation. 'But perhaps we could make a bargain?'

'A bargain!' he exclaimed, sneering at her now, his confidence returning. 'What have you got to bargain with?'

'You said it yourself, Oliver. Your career. Your chance of being an MP. You give me your promise that you will never try to send Ellen away and I will promise you that I will not start divorce proceedings, naming Morag McNab as the other woman.'

'That was over more than a year ago,' he said, clearly flustered again.

'Aye, but think of the gossip, Oliver, think of the damage I could do just by naming her.'

'You bitch,' he hissed, turning and slamming out of the room.

Meggie stood for a moment staring at the door, feeling her legs tremble until she was forced to sit down for fear of collapsing. Far from relishing her victory, her overwhelming emotions were of shame and dismay. Shame for the unscrupulous way in which she had manipulated him and dismay to know that she was permanently trapped in this sham of a marriage. But, she told herself, she would do the same again, and worse, to protect Ellen.

Oliver, shutting himself in his own room with a bottle of whisky, was already applying his mind to the situation. If he was to have any hope of winning a seat in the next election he must avoid any possible whiff of scandal. Extra-marital affairs, though common enough among his peers, were only tolerated if conducted with the utmost discretion. To find himself embroiled in a messy divorce case as the guilty party would end his political career before it had even begun.

Meggie's terms for avoiding any unpleasant disclosures had been quite clear. That left the child. Already people would be talking, wondering why he had never mentioned her, speculating too about his obvious reluctance to kiss his own child goodnight. That, he admitted, draining his first glassful of whisky in one go, had been a stupid mistake, and one which he would never repeat. And thinking about it, that unfortunate scene also ensured that he couldn't pack the child off to some home. Now that the secret was out, folk would wonder what had become of her, would accuse him of callousness.

The only way, he saw it clearly now, was to bring the whole shameful thing out into the open, to brazen it out, to turn it . . . yes to turn it to his advantage. A grim smile tightened his lips. From now on he would make sure he was seen in public with his family. He would parade the child, making sure everyone could see how very brave he was, how well he was dealing with a tragic situation. Far from trying to hide shame, he would flaunt it. And very soon folk would be openly admiring him.

TWENTY

Sally hurried across the Glen Pavilion Tea Room with a wide smile on her face. 'Och, Meggie, congratulations. I'm right pleased for you.' Sal hugged her friend tightly.

'Thanks, Sal, but it's Oliver you should be congratulating, not me.'

'You too. You did a lot of hard work campaigning for Oliver.'

Meggie dismissed this with a slightly bitter laugh. 'I didn't have a lot of choice. It's expected.'

They waited in silence while the waitress set the silver teapot, water-pot and milk jug on the table alongside the sandwiches and the tiered stand crammed with a variety of mouth-watering cakes.

Sal helped herself to a crustless sandwich and examined it critically. 'Considering what they charge for these, you'd think they'd leave the crusts on, wouldn't you? You only get half a sandwich.'

Meggie erupted into a gust of laughter. Two women at a neighbouring table glared at her, their eyebrows raised in disapproval. 'Och, Sal . . .' Already Meggie's spirits were rising as they always did when she was with Sal.

'I remember coming to play in the park when I was a wean. I used to wish I could come in here for my tea. It was o'er expensive but I used to stand, with my sister, our noses pressed up against the glass, staring at the folk inside, making faces at them.'

'You would!'

'We'd make a game of it. See how long we could stand there afore one of the waitresses was sent out to chase us away. We got caught by a park keeper once though. He made us give our names and addresses and then took us home to complain. Ma apologised to him and walloped us both for misbehaving. When Pa found out about it he walloped us again for being stupid enough to get caught.'

'I can imagine your Pa doing that.'

'Imagine what he'd think if he could see me sitting here now. He'd say I was getting above myself.'

'Aye. My Ma and Pa were like that too. Everyone in his or her place. My Pa would have had a fit if he'd known his son-in-law would end up as a Conservative MP. He was a strong union man, my dad. Lost his job because of the role he played in the miners' strike in 1926.'

'And that's when you and Matty were put into the workhouse?'

Meggie nodded. 'They couldn't afford to keep us. I thought they didn't want us. I was wrong but I was just a bairn then. I didn't understand how hard it was for them.'

'It was hard for my ma and pa too, Meggie, but ma would have died before she'd let any of us go.'

'But at least you always had a home, Sal. When my pa lost his job, he lost his house too. They had to go and live with Pa's brother and his family, through by Glasgow, and there wasn't room for all of us.'

Sal, with the benefit of a loving, if rough family behind her, simply couldn't comprehend how Meggie's parents could have abandoned her, but didn't pursue the subject for fear of hurting her friend. 'Remember when we first met, Meggie? Kept women we were, both of us.'

Meggie nodded, recalling the days when she and Sally had been neighbours, both living in little upstairs flats, paid for by their respective lovers. 'We neither of us had a very promising start, did we, Sal?'

'Still,' Sally laughed. 'We've not done so badly, have we? There's me and Ronnie with our own business and I'm your senior manageress, in charge of the smartest shop on the High Street. As for you ... Och, Meggie, you must be feeling right proud. Imagine my best friend being the wife of a Member of Parliament.'

'Imagine,' Meggie echoed softly. 'That's the trouble, Sal. Everyone will think of me as an MP's wife now. I own three shops but Oliver still treats my business as if it's some little hobby. Goodness only knows how I'll find the time to keep an eye on things now.'

'But you don't need to spend so much time in the shops these days, Meggie. You've even got an accountant to take care of the books. You can afford to sit back and let other folk run the business for you.'

'But I don't want to do that, Sal! I love being involved in the shops. Trouble is I just don't have the time any more. It was bad enough when Oliver was on the council – folk calling at the house at all hours, the phone always ringing. Now he's an MP it'll be even worse.'

'I suppose you'll be spending a lot of time in London.' Sal couldn't disguise the sad note to her voice. She would miss Meggie.

'I'm not going to London, Sal.'

'But I thought ... Don't you want to be with Oliver?'

Meggie almost shrugged, but stopped herself just in time. Her pride wouldn't let her admit how unhappy her marriage was, even to her best friend. In public she and Oliver played their parts: he as a committed family man, a brave and caring father to his unfortunate daughter, Meggie as a devoted, supportive wife. But beyond that there was nothing. Living in the same house, they barely communicated. But the thing Meggie could never forgive Oliver for was his attitude to Ellen, which was so hostile that the child was terrified of him. In the first months after Ellen's birth, Meggie, with the support of a nanny and housekeeper, had managed to spend several hours each day with her daughter while still taking an active role in the shops, relishing the combination of motherhood and business. But as Oliver's career blossomed, she found herself being dragged further and further into the role of politician's wife. She had lost count of the number of functions she had been obliged to accompany him to, functions where she was expected to echo, reinforce and regurgitate her husband's views, no matter what her own opinion might be. As Oliver's popularity grew so too did the demands of his electorate, with the result that Meggie's time with Ellen was frequently disrupted by people who, finding their councillor wasn't at home, brought their problems to his wife. Time, always a precious commodity, simply wouldn't stretch to accommodate all of Meggie's responsibilities. Determined not to sacrifice any of the time she spent with Ellen, Meggie had no choice but to lessen her involvement in the day-to-day running of her three thriving stores.

'I'm happy here, Sal, and so is Ellen. I wouldn't want to start dragging her up and down to London, it wouldn't be fair.'

'No,' Sal agreed. 'She's made a lot of progress lately. Taking her somewhere strange would only upset her.'

The two women sat on, talking as only very close friends can, totally at ease with each other. Gradually the cake-stand emptied of all but the plainest scones. Sally, wiping traces of cream from her mouth with a linen napkin, laughed. 'It's easy seeing I don't do this very often, isn't it? I'd have been shamed if my kids had come in here and made pigs of themselves like I have.'

Meggie looked ruefully into the empty teapot. 'I don't think I dare ask for another pot.'

'I've got to go anyway. The weans'll be home from the school and I promised Ma I'd take them down to see her today.'

'Aye, and I want to call in and see Matty before I go home.'

They argued briefly about the bill, finally agreeing to split it equally, then left, walking out into the spring sunshine, two elegantly dressed women, past the first flush of youth but both attractive enough to draw admiring glances as they made their way, arm in arm, through the town.

'Hello, stranger.' Still buoyant after her afternoon with Sally, Meggie greeted her brother cheerfully.

'I hope you haven't come expecting me to congratulate you,' he said, leading the way into the back room, leaving the shop in the care of two assistants.

'No. I know better than that,' she laughed. Matty voted Labour and abhorred everything the Conservative Party stood for. 'I just came to see if everything was all right.'

'Why shouldn't it be?' he demanded.

'For goodness sake, Matty, don't be so touchy.'

'You don't need to come checking up on me, Meggie. The books are finished and are with the accountant, the stock's been checked and the order list has been made up and sent down to the High Street shop.' It was a serious bone of contention with Matty that an accountant had been engaged to check the books and reconcile the stock in all the shops. Nor did he like the new ordering system where the two smaller shops sent their requirements through Sally, the High Street store manager, who then ordered on behalf of the others, saving money by buying in bulk.

Meggie smiled to herself, well aware that Matty resented having to send his books to be checked each week.

'You'll be off to live in England, then?' he asked, echoing Sally.

Meggie didn't miss the hopeful note in his voice. 'You'd like that, wouldn't you, Matty?' she teased.

'No. I just thought you'd have to go with Oliver, that's all.'

'Sorry to disappoint you, but I'm staying in Inverannan,' she told him, smiling sweetly.

Confusingly he seemed cheered by the news. 'Everything all right between you and Oliver?' he asked. 'I mean, I know you weren't getting along too well and this won't help, will it, him being in London and you being stuck up here? I don't know why you don't leave him, Meggie. He doesn't treat you right and you know it.'

'Mind your own business, Matty,' she retorted sharply.

'Och, Meggie. Don't be like that. I'm your brother, I can tell when things are not going right.' And it was true. Matty had an uncanny instinct for trouble of all sorts.

'Oliver and I have had our share of troubles, just like any married couple. But we're fine. It just doesn't make any sense for me to go trailing off to London with him. After all, I have got a business to run here.'

'I could take over for you,' he offered quickly. 'I am your brother, Meggie, you can trust me to look after things for you.'

'There's no need, Matty. I'm not going anywhere.'

He sighed. How much longer did she expect him to go on working for her without giving him a share in the business? It was nothing more than he deserved after all they'd been through together. A full half-share, that's what Matty wanted, was what he thought she owed him. And once he'd got that, well, there was no knowing what might happen. Even he knew he had no hope of getting his hands on any of the profits all the time she was tied to Oliver, not after what had happened between the two men in the past. But if she and Oliver were to part? Who would she turn to then for advice and support but her brother?

'Do you mind what you told me, Meggie?' he asked,

adopting a wistful tone. 'Years ago when you first started in this shop, do you remember what you said?'

She looked at him, puzzled, but said nothing, waiting for him to go on.

'You said you'd always look after me.'

'Aye,' she agreed softly. 'So I did and so I will, Matty.'

'I know . . . och, I don't like saying this, Meggie.'

'Matty! Stop blethering and tell me what's on your mind,' she teased.

'Well . . . it's just . . . well, I thought if I worked hard you'd see me right, Meggie.'

'I do, Matty. You've got the flat, rent-free, I pay you more than anyone else who works for me – '

'Aye. That's just it. Don't you see? I'm your brother, Meggie. I shouldn't be your employee. What if something happened to you? I'd be left with nothing.'

'Nothing's going to happen to me, Matty,' she told him firmly.

'Aye, I hope not, but you never know.'

'What are you trying to say, Matty?' she asked, encouragingly, pleased to have her normally taciturn and secretive brother talking so openly.

'I want you to think about letting me have a share of the business,' he said, risking everything.

'A share of the profit, you mean?' she asked astutely.

To her surprise, he admitted it. 'Aye. Why not?'

'Well . . .' She hesitated, unable to find the words to explain her desire to keep this business as hers, to control it, guard it as an investment for Ellen; her daughter's future security.

'You don't trust me. Och, don't bother to deny it, Meggie. And I know I asked for it, behaving the way I did. But that's all years ago, before the war. I don't even have a packet of fags without paying for them now and that's the truth,' he lied

271

easily. 'Trouble is, Meggie, you think I haven't changed, you'll never see any good in me.'

'Matty! That's not true.'

'Then why don't you prove it? You know the business is too big for you to handle all on your own. Especially now that Oliver's an MP. You won't have time to keep an eye on things the way you should. Things will go downhill, you know they will. Folk get slack if they think the boss isn't around to see what they're up to. If you brought me in with you, officially, I could help you. We could manage it between us! You know it makes sense, Meggie. Why rely on strangers when you've got your own brother to help you? And don't you think you owe it to me, Meggie? Look at how long I've worked here for you when I could have gone and got myself another job. Do you think I want to be the manager of a corner shop for the rest of my life? Och, don't get me wrong, I was right glad to work here after the war but I always thought you'd make sure I got on, Meggie. To tell the truth I'd have left before now, but I didn't want to let you down. But I'm not a young lad any more, Meggie, I need to be earning enough to be able to think about settling down and getting a proper house of my own.'

Meggie flopped down on the nearest chair, overcome with guilt, still burdened by her sense of responsibility for him, the legacy of their traumatic childhood. She had never known him to make such a long speech. And he was right. She couldn't expect him to stay in this little shop for ever. 'I never realised,' she murmured. 'Why didn't you say something before?'

'I didn't think I'd have to, Meggie.'

'You make me sound so selfish.'

'No.' He sat beside her and patted her hand. 'But you've had a lot on your mind what with Oliver and then wee Ellen being the way she is.'

'I don't know what to say, Matty.'

'Well, why not think about it, eh? And that's another thing. I maybe shouldn't say this, but I know the way Oliver is with Ellen. If anything happened to you, what would become of her? At least if you made me a partner in the business, I'd be able to look after things for her, make sure she was all right.'

Meggie looked at her brother with new affection. That was one aspect of him that she couldn't doubt. Matty treated his niece as if she was as normal as any other child. His affection for Ellen was natural, unfeigned and totally reciprocated and Meggie frequently brought her daughter to the shop just for the pleasure of seeing the little girl's face light up when she saw her uncle.

In fact, Ellen had revealed a side to Matty's character which Meggie would never have guessed existed under the aggressive manner and hooded eyes with which he guarded his private thoughts. The little girl seemed to bring out the very best in Matty, who gleefully jumped at any chance to entertain his niece, frequently leaving the shop in Meggie's care so that he could take the child to the park. Meggie had been amazed to realise that, where Ellen was concerned, Matty had inexhaustible patience. Not only was he happy to spend hours amusing her, but he, more than anyone, seemed to understand her grunting efforts to communicate, gently encouraging her, repeating the same word over and over again, until she understood and repeated it.

'I know you would do your best for Ellen, Matty,' she said, squeezing his hand.

'But you won't bring me into the business.' It wasn't a question, just a cold statement of fact.

Meggie felt that the least she could do was to be as open with Matty as he had been with her. 'I didn't say that.'

'But you're not saying yes either, are you?'

'It's not that easy, Matty. I can't make you a partner without discussing it with Oliver.'

'He'll never agree! He hates me.'

'Yes,' she nodded. In the years since Matty had arrived back in Inverannan, Oliver had refused to meet him, would not even allow him inside the house. For her to suggest bringing Matty into the business would spark a terrible argument.

'Do you have to tell him? After all the business is yours, not his.'

'I don't know.' Meggie hated the thought of deception; her life had had too much of that already. But, she wondered, weren't the shops hers? The fruits of her hard labour, often in the face of Oliver's outright opposition? Wasn't she entitled to do what she wanted with them, especially if it was a case of securing Ellen's future? And wasn't Matty right? Didn't he deserve some sort of reward, some guarantee of his future security? 'I'll have to think about it,' she told her brother.

Matty knew when to back away. He had made a lot of progress today; no point in throwing it all away for the want of a little patience. 'That's all I wanted to hear, Meggie. I didn't expect you to say aye right away, you know,' he laughed. 'Just so long as you're going to have a think about it.'

'Yes. I will. I promise,' she assured him.

Matty stood in the shop doorway and waved as Meggie drove away up the hill, but the smile he had worn while talking to her had completely disappeared.

TWENTY-ONE

'Right, Muriel, you might as well get on home, now. I'll stay and help Matty lock up.'

Muriel gave Meggie a look that suggested she couldn't quite believe what she had heard. 'But I've another half-hour to work, Mrs Laing.'

'That's all right.' Meggie tried to smile pleasantly at a young woman she didn't really care for. Muriel's sloppy ways and over-familiarity with the customers did not convey the sort of impression that Meggie was anxious to promote in her shops. Still, the girl seemed to work well with Matty and he certainly had no complaints about her.

'Well, as long as I get paid for the full day.' Muriel still lingered.

'Of course you will!' Meggie was irritated that the woman could think her so tight-fisted.

'Right!' Muriel beamed and shoved her coat on, on top of her apron. 'See youse the morn,' she called, rushing out of the shop before Meggie could change her mind.

'I'd have made her stay,' Matty commented, joining Meggie behind the counter. 'She was fifteen minutes late again this morning.'

'I don't know why you don't get rid of her, Matty. I'm sure you would easily find someone more suitable. Would you like me to have a word with her?'

'No!' Matty protested, alarmed. If the complacent Muriel was to be replaced by someone more conscientious then he would feel the effects in his own pocket.

'For goodness sake! Why not, Matty? There's hardly been a full week when she's been on time for work each day.'

Matty shrugged. 'Aye, I know that fine. But she's a hard worker, Meggie and, well, if you must know, I feel sorry for her.'

Meggie raised her eyebrows in silent but eloquent disbelief.

'She's got a lot on her plate, Meggie. That man of hers is a right bad lot. In and out of trouble all his life. More time in the jail than out of it. And she's left with three weans to raise on her own. She has a tough time of it. Leave her be, Meggie, she does her best.'

Meggie smiled at him, pleased to have more evidence of Matty's caring side, an aspect of his personality that she had never suspected existed until Ellen was born. 'All right. It's your shop. You do what you think is best.'

'Why did you send her home?' he asked, wondering uneasily if she could possibly have discovered one of his little money-making schemes.

'I've some good news for you,' she told him happily.

'Oh aye?' He was alert now, aware that she had an air of suppressed excitement about her.

'Close up first, then we'll go upstairs and talk,' she laughed.

'Well?' he demanded as soon as they were in his little flat.

'Aren't you going to offer me a cup of tea, Matty?' she teased, thoroughly enjoying herself.

He scowled, then, seeing the fleeting frown that creased her forehead, rapidly grinned at her. 'After you've told me what this is all about,' he retorted.

'All right. You win. But at least let me sit down.'

She took her time disposing of her coat and handbag, then settled herself as comfortably as she could in the old armchair that had been in the flat when she herself had first moved in, back in the late twenties. It seemed like a lifetime ago.

'I think you're going to like what I have to tell you,' she said as he sat opposite her, his impatience barely contained.

'For goodness sake, Meggie, just get on with it!'

Meggie gave a gust of laughter, then announced, 'I have arranged for you to have twenty per cent of the business, Matty.' She looked at him expectantly, her face glowing with pleasure.

'Twenty per cent?' he echoed, caught between surprise and disappointment.

Misinterpreting his stunned expression for one of shocked pleasure, she went on. 'You see, I do take notice of what you say to me, Matty.' When he failed to reply she added, 'You are pleased, aren't you? It is what you wanted?'

Realising that he had to say something, he answered, 'Aye, of course I am,' in a far from convincing way.

Meggie felt the pleasure drain from her and stared at him, feeling completely perplexed. 'You look as if I'd just given you the sack,' she snapped.

Matty collected himself just in time. 'No! But I'm just so surprised. I never expected this, Meggie,' he told her with a convincing display of stunned gratitude. 'I mean, it was only the other day that I spoke to you about it. I didn't expect you to do anything so quickly.' It was her turn to be shocked when he leaned over and kissed her on the mouth. 'Thank you, Meggie. Thank you!'

Meggie relaxed again. 'I'm glad you're pleased, Matty. There are some papers to be signed so you'll have to call in to my solicitor. After that it'll all be legal.'

'I'll do that tomorrow,' he promised, grinning at her in feigned delight now that his initial disappointment was under control. What he had really wanted was a full half-share. Twenty per cent might put more money legally in his pocket than he had now, but would give him no real say in the running of the business.

'I might as well tell you the rest,' she said.

'The rest?' He was alert again, concentrating on what she was saying rather than on his own black thoughts.

'Well, while I was seeing the solicitor I thought I might as well put everything on a proper footing, in case . . . well, you said it yourself, in case anything happens to me.'

'Don't say that! Nothing's going to happen to you, Meggie,' he objected loudly.

'I hope not too. But I have to think about Ellen. You made me think very seriously about her future, Matty.'

'Aye, we do need to think about what might happen to her,' he agreed, wondering what was coming next.

Meggie hesitated, disturbed by the possibility that she might have to leave Ellen in someone else's care. 'If anything happens to me, you will get another twenty per cent of the business. Ellen will inherit the rest. I know you love her, Matty, and I want you to promise me that you will do everything you can to make sure that her share of the profit is used to make her life comfortable, to give her the best possible care.'

'Do I really need to promise you that, Meggie?' he asked, a note of mild rebuke in his voice.

'Just make sure she is well looked after, Matty.'

'You know I will. I love that bairn as if she was my own.' Meggie could not doubt his words, uttered as they were in an unsteady voice, a bright sheen in his dark eyes.

'Now.' She stood up sharply, wanting to shake the melancholy mood which had suddenly engulfed her with the bitter truth that she could not depend on Oliver for Ellen's future well-being. 'I'd best be getting home or she will be in bed.'

Matty walked downstairs with her. At the door he held her back and, surprising her again, folded her in a hug. 'Thank you, Meggie,' he whispered into her hair. 'Thank you.'

Choked with emotion, she simply squeezed his arm and hurried to her car.

Matty watched as she drove up the hill, then carefully locked the door and made his way back upstairs, where he retrieved a bottle of whisky from the kitchen cabinet and took a huge slug straight from the bottle. Wiping his mouth with the back of his hand, he took the bottle with him into his sitting-room and sank into a chair, deep in thought.

A mean twenty per cent wasn't anywhere near what he wanted from Meggie. She owed him more than that; much more than that. Even the promise of a forty per cent share, should she die before him, was worthless.

The more he brooded on it, the more angry and resentful he became. With half a bottle of cheap whisky inside him, Matty knew there was only one way he would ever get control of the business and get his hands on the money it represented. And as for Ellen: well, there were places for people like her.

Meggie drove home unable to shake the unsettling feeling of apprehension which had swamped her so suddenly. It was, she knew, the result of knowing that she still couldn't quite bring herself to trust her brother sufficiently to risk him ever gaining full control of the business, and even worse, of her final acceptance that Oliver could never be relied upon to care for his own daughter. But, she told herself, she was doing the right thing. Matty deserved his share of the business, and making her will now had been a necessary step to safeguard Ellen's future. Should the worst happen then Ellen's share of the business would be administered jointly by Matty, Robbie, Sal and the solicitor, all of whom would have her welfare at heart. Not that she had told Matty the full terms of her will. Meggie was uncomfortably aware of the unpalatable fact that she had deliberately kept the full truth from her brother. But, she consoled herself, there was no reason to think that he would discover what she had done for very many years yet, if ever.

'Are you crazy?' Sally demanded, staring open-mouthed at her best friend.

'Twenty per cent doesn't give him any real power, Sally. The business is still mine.'

Sally shook her head, unable for once to find words to express her distress.

'It won't make any practical difference, Sal. He won't have any control over you.'

Sal hadn't yet thought of the implications for her own position. She looked up sharply. 'I should damn well hope not, Meggie. If Matty thinks he can throw his weight around with me, he's in for a shock. And so are you, because I couldn't go on working for you if that happened.'

'It won't,' Meggie said shortly.

'Does he know that?'

'I've discussed it with Matty, and he will have nothing more to do with you than he does now. The only thing that will change is the amount of money Matty will get from the business.'

Sal seemed to relax a little, although she was clearly still unhappy with the situation. 'I just hope you know what you are doing,' she said.

Meggie sighed. She had known Sally would react badly, but hadn't been prepared for quite the degree of anger with which she greeted the news. Robbie's reaction had been equally vehement. Meggie was heartily sick of other people trying to tell her how to organise her affairs. 'It's done, Sal, so nothing you can say will make me change my mind. Now, can we please talk about something else?'

'She's done what?' Ronnie was horrified.

'I told her she was crazy,' Sal said, snuggled warmly in bed against her husband's comforting bulk. 'The last thing she should have done is give Matty any share of the profits. He doesn't deserve it, but she can't see that. After all that's happened she still won't hear a word against him. I don't understand her.'

'Matty's her brother,' Ronnie pointed out unnecessarily. 'They went through a lot together when they were kids and she still feels responsible for him.'

'He's old enough to be responsible for himself!' she retorted hotly. 'He'll ruin her.'

'He might do worse than that,' Ronnie muttered darkly.

'Why?' She pulled herself up to rest on an elbow and looked down at him, her hair falling forward over his bare chest.

He put a hand up to stroke the hair away from her face. 'Think about it, Sal! Matty thinks the only thing that stands between him and the business is his sister. What do you think his evil little mind will make of that?'

Sal's face blanched in horror. 'You can't mean . . . ?'

'Oh, but I do,' he assured her grimly. 'There is nothing I wouldn't put past Matty McPherson.'

'But hurting Meggie?' she whispered, sliding down into bed and cuddling close to him again, feeling an overwhelming need for the security of his arms around her.

They cuddled together in preoccupied silence. It was a long time before either one of them drifted into sleep.

TWENTY-TWO

'Miss Brebner, a word if you please.' Mr Wemyss beckoned with his forefinger.

Kate flushed, aware of her colleagues' speculating eyes upon her, mortified to have been singled out in front of the whole shop. A summons from Mr Wemyss invariably presaged serious trouble; lesser offences being dealt with by Mrs Donald. Kate would have been the first to admit that she was as capable of making an honest mistake as anyone, but pride in her work ensured that these errors were few and far between. Except for that one occasion when she had been late back from lunch, she had never attracted serious criticism. Perplexed and just a little apprehensive, she followed him to his office.

'Come on in, lass.' Mr Wemyss, always the perfect gentleman, held the door open and ushered her in.

Kate's heart missed a beat when she saw Mrs Donald and Tom already there, seated one on either side of the big desk, obviously waiting for her. Though they both acknowledged her arrival, there was no clue for Kate in their expressions, which were carefully blank.

It seemed that she stood there for a long time while Mr Wemyss closed the door and walked slowly to the other side of his desk, settling himself in his chair and shuffling some papers before finally looking up at her. Then, to her consternation, he chuckled.

'Och, lass, don't look so worried. We're not going to eat you.'

'But if . . . if I've done something wrong . . .' she stammered, appalled to realise that whatever it was, Tom would witness her disgrace.

'Wrong?' Mr Wemyss laughed again and Kate had the sudden feeling that he was enjoying himself. 'No, Kate, you've done nothing wrong,' he went on, quickly deciding to put the girl out of her misery. 'Quite the reverse.' He beamed at her now, his expression mirrored by Tom and Mrs Donald, and Kate exhaled sharply with relief.

'Are you happy here, Kate?' Mrs Donald's question took her by surprise.

'Aye, Mrs Donald, very happy.' There was no hesitation in her reply. She loved the contact with people that was such an important part of her job. More than that, she was interested in what went on behind the scenes – the ordering, the stock-taking, the cashing-up, and revelled in any opportunity to learn more.

'Then what would you say to taking over from Miss Laidlaw when she leaves us to get married?' Mrs Donald, who had watched as Kate matured from a green newcomer to an experienced and responsible assistant to whom the others frequently looked for help, smiled as she asked the question.

'Me . . .?' Surely she was too young? There were others who had been here much longer than she, who would expect to be considered for the senior assistant's post. But then, feeling three pairs of eyes boring into her, she raised her chin and answered firmly, hoping they had not noticed her momentary hesitation, 'I would say thank you very much, Mr Wemyss.'

Yes, he thought, watching her, seeing the pleasure light up her eyes: Kate Brebner was a good choice. Despite her youth, she had the assurance to carry the responsibility. Once she had recovered from the shock of his offer, she had not had the slightest qualm about accepting. She would be an asset to the business, someone to be relied upon.

'Good. That is exactly what I expected you to say,' he told her.

'Congratulations, Kate.' Tom and Mrs Donald spoke in unison.

'It's a good job, Kate, and a rise in pay for you too,' Mrs Donald went on. 'I just hope you're not planning on leaving us?'

For a moment Kate felt a pang of unease as she wondered whether Tom would object to his wife working. Many men did and it was still the accepted thing for young women to leave their employment when they married. But not her, Kate decided. She liked her job and though she loved Tom dearly, she had no intention of giving it up and becoming totally dependent on him. 'No, Mrs Donald,' she said firmly. 'I'm not planning to leave Hough's.'

Even as she spoke she couldn't help darting a quick glance at Tom. To her relief, he simply smiled his support. She couldn't help smiling back, wondering what her colleagues would have to say when they found out about them. They had agreed to keep their relationship private, at least until they had set a date and bought an engagement ring, and they couldn't do that until Tom's family had been told. Even over her pleasure at the unexpected promotion, she felt a tremor of nervousness as she wondered whether Tom's family would like her. But at least she would be a step up from an ordinary shop assistant . . .

'Then this is for you.' Smiling, Mr Wemyss broke her train of thought and handed over two neatly folded white aprons with the black edging that denoted the senior assistant's rank. 'All you have to do is be yourself, Kate, and I'm sure you will justify my faith in you. It's time for lunch now, but Mrs Donald will have a word with you about your new duties this afternoon.'

'Well done, Kate.' Jeanette Laidlaw was the first to offer her congratulations after Mrs Donald's lunch-time announcement.

'Aye, well done.' The others filed past on their way back to the shop floor and already Kate was aware of a change in their manner towards her.

Eadie Crichton, a girl with a viciously spiteful tongue, stopped and looked Kate up and down. 'I've been here longer than you. I should have been offered that job first,' she hissed. 'But we all know why it was given to you, Kate Brebner.'

Kate simply waited, knowing she wasn't going to like what would come next.

'Aye. We all know about you and Tom Herriot. Well, I'd rather not have a job at all if that was what I had to do to get one.' With that she flounced away, leaving Kate staring after her from the top of the stairs.

'Och, take no notice of her. She's only jealous. And we all know she's not good enough for that job.' Betty touched her friend's arm gently. 'Anyway, I'm right pleased for you, Kate.'

'Does everyone know?' she asked, appalled by Eadie's accusation.

Betty looked at her friend for a moment, then said with an affectionate chuckle, 'Of course we do. Och, Kate, Inverannan's just a wee town. You couldn't buy a new coat without someone seeing you. And when a lad as good-looking as Tom Herriot starts walking in the park with a lassie, well, word gets round. Don't let the likes of Eadie Crichton worry you. She's never got a good word to say about anybody.'

'But what about Mrs Donald and Mr Wemyss? Do you think they know?'

'Mrs Donald doesn't miss much.'

'Oh no, whatever will she think of me?'

Betty guffawed. 'Och, Kate, will you stop worrying. Anyone

would think you were doing something to be ashamed of.' She paused for a moment, looking at her friend impishly, and added, 'You're not, are you?'

Kate gaped at her, blushing furiously. 'No! Of course not.' Then, realising her friend had been teasing, she managed to laugh.

'Well then, stop worrying about what folk think. Tom Herriot's a good catch, Kate. If it was me that was walking out with him I'd be making sure he paraded me up and down the High Street so everyone knew he was mine. I'd be right proud, so I would.'

'Thanks, Betty,' Kate murmured, though the joy she had felt at her promotion had vanished, replaced by a terrible gnawing suspicion.

Betty, sensing that Kate was seriously upset, said briskly, 'Come on then. We'll be late back if we don't hurry up. You don't want them to take that fancy apron away before you've even had a chance to try it on.' She ran out of the door and down the stairs, her feet clattering on the bare wood.

Kate followed more slowly, her mind reeling. For a moment she hesitated, unwilling to go back into the shop now that she knew what her colleagues were thinking, but then she smiled grimly to herself. Betty was right. It was only jealousy and her conscience was clear so there was nothing to be worried about. If she couldn't cope with a little envy from her colleagues then she shouldn't have accepted the job in the first place. And she had won her promotion on her own talents alone. Hadn't she?

The little worm of suspicion refused to go away.

'Well done, Kate.' Tom was waiting for her in his car when she finished work that night. Leaning over, he tried to kiss her.

Kate pulled away. 'Anyone might see!'

He frowned at her for a moment but then started the car.

When she hadn't said anything else by the time they reached Netherton, he pulled into the side of the road, switched the engine off and waited, watching her but saying nothing.

Kate sat, staring at her hands until she could bear the silence no longer. 'What's the matter?' she demanded. 'Why have you stopped?'

'Nothing's the matter with me, Kate.' His voice was soft, exasperated but not yet angry. He waited again, staring at the blank wall of the mill which flanked the road. After five minutes of continued silence – minutes during which Kate several times appeared to be about to speak, only to change her mind and return to the endless contemplation of her hands – he tried again. 'Are you going to tell me what's the matter?' Still she didn't respond and when he spoke next he was clearly struggling to keep his temper. 'For goodness sake! If you've got something to say, say it. You've been promoted. You should be over the moon, not sitting there with a face long enough to trip over.' Patience exhausted, he started the engine.

'It was you, wasn't it?' Knowing that if she didn't say it now she would be throwing her chance of happiness away, Kate finally blurted her accusation.

The engine died with a noisy splutter. 'It was me what?' He looked at her in utter bewilderment. 'What am I supposed to have done?'

'You got me the promotion. Your uncle owns the place! Mr Wemyss would have to take notice of you if you said you wanted your girlfriend to have the job.'

He grunted. 'So that's it!'

'It's true, isn't it?' she demanded.

He counted to five, took a deep breath and said coldly, 'For your information, if I tried to do anything like that I'd soon find myself looking for a new job.'

'Don't be ridiculous!' she sneered. 'Of course you wouldn't.

287

What could be more natural than trying to pull strings to help your girlfriend get a better job?'

'That would be favouritism,' he raged. 'I would never do that. It wouldn't be fair.'

'Then how come you're the accounts manager in your uncle's shop, Tom? Isn't that favouritism?' She was too angry to mind her words now.

'No it is not!' he retorted furiously. 'I got that job because I'm bloody good at it! I might be in line to inherit the place one day but I started out on the shop floor, just like you. I don't get any favours and I wouldn't dare ask for them for myself, never mind anyone else. My uncle believes in working for what you get and if I don't come up to the mark, *his* mark, then he's quite capable of turfing me out and selling the place.'

'Oh.' She felt humbled.

'Aye! Oh!' For a moment he glared at her, then slowly his face relaxed. 'Did someone say something to you?'

She sighed and nodded. 'Aye. Och, it was just a spiteful comment but then I got to thinking and I wondered why it was me and not one of the others. Some of them have been there for years, Tom.'

'And that's where they'll stay. Shop assistants for ever. You got the job because you're better than them. And that's the truth.' He reached across and took one of her hands, lifted it to his lips and kissed it, never able to stay angry with her for long.

But Kate hadn't finished yet. 'Maybe Mr Wemyss, if he knew about you and me, maybe he was trying to curry favour. After all he must know you're going to own the shop one day.'

To her amazement he dissolved into laughter. 'Kate!' he gasped at last. 'Come here.' Still laughing, he pulled her into his arms.

'What's so funny?' she asked, struggling against him.

'You are.' He kissed her cheek. 'It's the idea of Mr Wemyss

currying favour! I doubt he even knows the meaning of the word.' Then he was serious. 'He's a good manager, the best, and that shop is his pride and joy. He'd never do anything that wasn't good for the business. And that, Kate, is why he chose you.'

'He doesn't know about us, then?' She had stopped fighting him now.

'Aye, he knows about us.' He silenced her with a finger on her lips. 'But only because I told him. He asked me what I thought about you last week. I had to tell him. Surely you can see that? How would it have looked if I'd said I thought you were perfect for the job and then he'd found out?'

'I suppose so . . .'

'You know so. You got the job because you deserve it, Kate.'

'Really?'

'How many times do I have to tell you?'

'I just wondered – '

'Well, don't.' He silenced her in the most effective way, ignoring the amused glances of the mill workers who were starting to throng the street.

Fifteen minutes later they drew up outside Mrs Traynor's neat little house.

'By the way. Mother has invited you to have dinner with us on Saturday evening,' he said as she started to get out of the car.

She grimaced. 'That's nice of her.'

'You've got to meet them some time. And I don't know what you're worried about. They don't bite. Well, not often anyway.'

'I'm sure they're not expecting you to want to marry a shop girl.'

'Why not? I'm just a shop boy, after all.'

She laughed, feeling better now, her usual confidence returning. 'If you put it like that . . .'

'And then we'll have to break the news to your family. It's only right.'

She leaned in the car for one last kiss, then stood and watched him drive away. If all he said about his family was true she probably had nothing to worry about; they sounded like kind-hearted people. But what about her family? Well, she thought, going into the house, that was easy. She didn't have one. And what would Tom's parents make of that?

TWENTY-THREE

'I never thought I'd see the day when this county elected a *Conservative* M.P. Inverannan doesn't need the likes of Oliver Laing at Westminster. An independent Scotland, that's what we want. This country will never get what it deserves all the time it's governed from London.' Tom's father fixed his son with a fierce glare.

'Don't be ridiculous! Scotland hasn't got the resources to stand on her own.' Tom's reply was equally passionate. 'I think Oliver Laing's a good man. I'm not ashamed to admit I voted for him.'

Kate watched, startled by the ferocity of the argument. Glancing across the table, she found Mrs Herriot watching her, her face wreathed in smiles.

'Don't worry, Kate. This is a nightly event in this household. These two would argue that night was day, just for the fun of it.' She got up and beckoned to Kate to follow her. 'We'll leave them to it, shall we?'

She led the way to the sitting-room and settled in a chair, apparently perfectly relaxed.

'I suppose this has all been a bit of an ordeal for you, hasn't it?' she asked, sipping at her coffee. 'It's never easy, meeting the prospective in-laws for the first time. Are we as bad as you thought we would be?'

Kate had to laugh. 'I was nervous about meeting you,' she admitted, liking this woman more with each passing minute.

'No more nervous than I was about meeting you,' Mrs Herriot confided. 'You know, Kate, Tom loves you very much.

It would have been terrible if I didn't like you. Because I love him too I was prepared to make a big effort, but thank goodness I haven't had to. I think you and I will be friends, don't you?'

Kate was glad to be able to answer honestly. 'I know we will be.'

When Tom had picked her up that evening she had been so nervous at the prospect of meeting his parents that she had felt sick. But her apprehension had vanished almost as soon as she stepped out of Tom's car. It was as if the very house itself had lit up in welcome as the front door opened and his parents, together with two boisterous retrievers, hurried down the steps to greet them. Kate hung back momentarily while Tom made a brief introduction but there was no time for awkwardness as Mr Herriot took her hand in a firm handshake which drew her forward into the family group. Tall and lean, Tom's father wore horn-rimmed glasses which failed to disguise the twinkle of merriment in his grey eyes as he winked at Kate and then introduced her to his wife. Mrs Herriot, almost as tall as her husband, her hair still blonde and arranged in soft, enviably natural-looking waves, had kissed Kate's cheek and tucked her arm through hers as she led them into the house. Kate's initial shyness had quickly evaporated under the genuine warmth of her welcome and it wasn't long before she was joining in the conversation round the dinner table, feeling much more at ease than she had expected.

'Tom tells me you want to get married as soon as you can?' Mrs Herriot placed her cup and saucer back on the tray and swivelled to face Kate directly.

'We need to find somewhere to live but after that I can't see any reason to wait,' she said, fully expecting to be advised the opposite.

Mrs Herriot surprised her again. 'Quite right. If you are both absolutely sure then there's absolutely nothing to be gained by waiting. What do your parents say about it?'

For the first time that evening, Kate felt truly uncomfortable. Perhaps there was some way she could avoid the issue. But no, she dismissed that idea almost before it had formed in her mind; that would be both dishonest and cowardly. And anyway, Tom's parents would have to be told about her background at some point. Why not get it over with now? She opted for the truth. 'They don't know.'

Now it was Mrs Herriot's turn to look disconcerted. 'They don't know? But surely you've told them about Tom?'

'I never see them.' Kate twisted her hands in her lap.

'Oh, Kate! But that's terribly sad.'

Kate risked looking up and saw nothing but compassion in the older woman's eyes. 'They weren't my real parents. I was adopted.'

'But to have lost contact with them . . .' Mrs Herriot shook her head sadly. 'Why, Kate? What happened?'

Kate looked away again, not knowing where to begin, and Mrs Herriot gave a little gasp of dismay.

'What on earth must you think of me! I'm sorry, Kate, I had no right to ask such a personal question. Forget I even mentioned it.'

'No! I mean, it's all right, I don't mind you asking. Hasn't Tom said something to you already?'

'Only that he had met the girl he wanted to marry.' Mrs Herriot smiled.

'Everything changed after my father – my adoptive father – died . . .'

'You don't have to tell me, Kate. Not if it makes you uncomfortable.'

But suddenly Kate did want to confide in this sympathetic woman. 'After Dad died his nephew came to take over the farm. He resented me because I was adopted. It was as if I wasn't part of the family any more.' She sighed, still hurt by the memories, then went on in a deliberately matter-of-fact tone. 'He just saw me as a cheap labourer . . .' Slowly she related her story, leaving out only the harrowing details of Duncan's attack, unable to admit to anyone other than Tom the true horror that lurked in her past. Then, not wanting to be pitied by anyone, least of all her mother-in-law-to-be, she looked up with a bright smile. 'It all worked out for the best really. I never did want to work on the farm. I always wanted a proper job. And it was very lonely out there in the middle of the countryside – I lost touch with all my friends once I left school. It's much better living in the town.' She realised with a small shock that she had spoken the truth. She was far more contented now than she ever had been on the farm.

'It must have taken a lot of courage to leave home at that age. I think you were very brave,' Mrs Herriot commented softly.

'It didn't feel brave at the time.'

'No, I don't suppose it did,' Mrs Herriot agreed, sensing there was more to this story than Kate was able to tell her, half-guessing what it might be. 'Thank you for telling me, Kate.' She reached over and squeezed the girl's hand briefly, then making a determined effort to change the subject, said, 'It's going to be so exciting, isn't it, planning the wedding?'

'I don't know where to start,' Kate admitted frankly.

'Then that's where I can help. If you'll let me,' Mrs Herriot offered enthusiastically.

For the next ten minutes they talked avidly about weddings until Kate held up her hands and pleaded. 'Stop! I never realised there was so much to be done. I think we'd better just run away to Gretna Green and save everyone a lot of trouble.'

'Indeed you will not. A lass as beautiful as you should have a wonderful wedding, white dress, bridesmaids, everything.'

'I think, if you don't mind, that I'd prefer something smaller,' Kate insisted in a quiet voice.

Mrs Herriot opened her mouth to protest but closed it again

quickly when she saw the grim expression on her guest's face. 'Kate,' she said thoughtfully. 'I know what you're thinking, and you've not to concern yourself about money. Tom's our only child and we'll do anything we can to make this a very special day – for both of you.'

But Kate had realised that she lacked more than just money. 'Thank you. But I would prefer to have a private ceremony.' Even to her own ears it sounded awkward and ungracious.

Mrs Herriot was nonplussed by the cold rebuff and puzzled by the change in the girl's manner, which was suddenly stiff and withdrawn – almost as if something had been said to offend her. She frowned, wondering if she had misjudged her son's fiancée. Kate had seemed a likeable, unspoiled girl, but now it sounded very much as if she was going to let pride ruin the wedding for everyone. Attempting, but failing, to keep her tone of voice neutral, she said, 'Well, of course the decision will be for you and Tom to make together. You must talk it over with him. Let me know what you decide, Kate, but my offer of help still stands.'

Realising, too late that she had managed to upset Tom's mother, Kate stared at her in horrified dismay. 'Oh no! I didn't mean . . . that is, I do want . . .' She gave up, sighed and raised her eyes heaven-ward. 'I'm sorry,' she offered eventually. 'I'm not trying to be difficult, it's just . . .'

'Just what, Kate?' Mrs Herriot asked, seeing real consternation in the girl's worried eyes.

Kate sighed. 'Who will give me away?' she asked, her voice little more than a whisper.

'Have you no one at all, Kate?' Mrs Herriot asked, a note of disbelief in her voice.

'No. No one.' Kate's reply was whispered and she felt shamed by the admission.

'No uncles or cousins?' The girl must have someone.

'No one,' Kate repeated miserably.

'Oh, Kate. It's me who should be sorry. I didn't even think . . .'

Kate shrugged. 'It doesn't matter. But you do understand why I wouldn't want a big wedding? It would look a bit odd, wouldn't it, with all the guests on your side of the church and no one on mine?'

'Now you are being over-dramatic, Kate.' Mrs Herriot said firmly. 'I'm sure you have plenty of friends. Why don't we compromise and say fifty guests, twenty-five on each side? Does that sound reasonable?'

But Kate still sounded doubtful. 'I don't know.'

Now Mrs Herriot laughed. 'What about all the people from Hough's? I'm sure you've made lots of friends there. And you must want some of your old schoolfriends to see you married. Surely you haven't lost touch with all of them?'

'No,' Kate agreed. 'There are a couple of lassies from my class at school who work in the town now. I see them quite often.'

Mrs Herriot beamed, well pleased with herself. 'There, I knew everything would be all right.'

Kate's eyes were beginning to sparkle again. 'My best friend, Betty, would love to be my bridesmaid, I know she would,' she enthused. But suddenly her face lost its animation again. 'But I still can't think of anyone who could give me away,' she repeated quietly.

Mrs Herriot frowned and applied her mind to the problem. 'Well, you've no relatives, so the best thing is to ask some older gentleman. I'm sure you have someone, Kate but if not, Mr Herriot would be honoured.'

'That would be nice, but it might look a bit strange – the groom's father giving the bride away. Folk would just think I couldn't find anyone else.' And they would be right, she thought.

'Wait! I know just the person,' Mrs Herriot announced triumphantly.

'Who?'

'Mr Hough, of course.'

'*The* Mr Hough?' Kate gasped.

'Actually,' Mrs Herriot laughed, 'He's my older brother, William.'

'That would be lovely,' Kate smiled. 'But I don't know him.'

'Ah . . . yes. I suppose you wouldn't feel quite comfortable with him, would you?'

'But I know who I could ask,' she beamed excitedly as the solution occurred to her.

'Who?'

'Mr Wemyss.'

'Of course!' Mrs Herriot clapped her hands in approval. 'Now why didn't I think of that?'

'You don't think he'd mind?'

'Mind? Of course not. He'll be proud to be asked, Kate. He'll be perfect for the role.'

Kate relaxed visibly and for a few moments the two women sat in companionable silence, relieved to have found answers to what might have been major problems. But still Kate could not help wishing she had someone of her own flesh and blood to see her married.

As if reading her thoughts, Mrs Herriot broke the silence by asking, 'Kate, wouldn't this be a good time to try and make peace with your family? Didn't you say your adoptive father had a brother? I'm sure he'd be proud to give you away. A wedding might be just the thing to bring you all together again.'

Kate shook her head silently. How could she begin to explain their absolute betrayal, her mother's attempt to force her into marriage with the boy who had raped her?

'But think how nice it would be to have them all at the wedding. I'm sure they would be glad of the chance to – '

Mercifully, Mrs Herriot was interrupted by Tom and his father, who chose that moment to come noisily into the room, still debating some contentious issue.

'I don't agree. You young people are all the same. Too impatient, always wanting to change things. There's nothing wrong with the old ways. They were good enough for my father, they're good enough for me and – '

'They should be good enough for you.' Mrs Herriot finished her husband's sentence for him, laughing as she linked her arm through his and steered him towards a chair.

Tom caught Kate's eye and winked at her, bringing a smile to her face again. 'Everything okay?' he asked, perching on the arm of her chair.

'Aye,' she nodded. 'We've been talking about the wedding. I never realised there was so much to be organised.'

'I hope Mother's not frightened you, Kate,' Tom said grinning at his mother. 'The truth is that she just loves organising things and she gets carried away sometimes. Ask my father.'

Henry Herriot grunted. 'She's the only woman I know who can make the arrangements for an old folks' whist drive look like a world war battle campaign. Mind you,' he confided, making a pantomime of whispering in Kate's direction, shielding his mouth with his hand and fairly bawling the words, 'It gives Tom and me a couple of days of peace and though I say it myself, my wife is damned good at that sort of thing. Best to let her get on with it, lass, and leave yourself free to enjoy it all.'

'Now then, Henry, don't pressurise her. I'm sure she wants to arrange things for herself. I just want you to know that I'm here if you need me, Kate.'

Kate laughed, 'Oh, I'm going to need you. I'm sure of that already.'

'And what you need right now is to get home or you'll never be fit for work tomorrow.' Tom was on his feet, grasping her hand and pulling her upright.

Startled, Kate managed to mumble her thanks before he dragged her from the house, their invitations to return ringing in her ears.

'What was that all about?' she asked as he sent the car bowling along the road.

He glanced at her, then shrugged, not even suspecting what had taken place between his mother and Kate while he and his father put the world to rights over a glass or two of port. 'I thought it was time to get you out of there. Once Mother gets started there's no holding her back. She'd have had you working out the guest lists and choosing the colour of the buttonholes in another minute.'

Kate smiled, happy to have solved the biggest of her problems without the need to worry Tom about them. 'I'm just relieved she's so pleased about it all. And I do need someone to help me, Tom. I haven't got a clue about weddings.'

He signed in obvious relief. 'That's all right then.' Drawing the car to a halt in a shaded spot he switched off the engine and slid his hand along her shoulders. 'Now then, what about me?' he teased. 'I'm starting to feel quite neglected. I'll swear you've not looked at me more than twice today.'

'No, and I'm not going to look at you now,' she chuckled, turning her face to him and closing her eyes as her lips met his.

TWENTY-FOUR

'My, lass, and you're looking a proper treat, so you are.' Mrs Traynor glanced up from her ironing and smiled at her young lodger. 'You and Tom off out, are you?

'Aye,' Kate agreed, croaking the single word through a dry mouth and tight throat.

Her landlady, fully occupied in ironing the weekly wash, failed to notice the girl's pale cheeks and restless manner and was anxious only to get Kate out of the house so that she could get on with her chores. Her weekly routine was already upset by the rain which had poured down on Monday, delaying the wash and setting everything back by a full day. By Wednesday morning the laundry should have been disposed of, leaving the afternoon to be spent comfortably in a fireside chair with the wireless for company and some mending to occupy her hands. If Kate sometimes spent her free half-day in the house then it was pleasant to have a bit of company, but not today, not when the sheets had been caught in a downpour which had brought all the smuts down with it, leaving them black-speckled and smelling of soot and denying her the satisfaction of folding and pressing crisp, fresh-smelling linen.

'Off you go then, lass. Don't keep the laddie waiting.'

Even though it was a now a full fortnight since the night at Tom's house when she had known, deep in her heart, what she must do, and even though she had thought of little else in the intervening days and nights, still Kate wondered whether she was doing the right thing.

Even so her steps never faltered as she made her way steadily to town, then on, starting up a long gentle hill lined with the grey stone terraces which characterised Inverannan. Half-way up the hill, just before the terraces gave way to semi-detached villas and a new stratum of society, was the crossroads on one corner of which stood a busy general store.

Kate had got this far before, had come one day and walked past, very slowly, pretending a great interest in the window display. On that occasion she had had no intention of going inside, but had merely used the exercise as a building block towards what she must do today. Now she hesitated, her nerve almost failing. For a moment she was tempted to turn back, to return to her room and simply write to her natural mother. She dismissed the idea immediately, unable to ignore the feeling that this was something she must do in person.

Crossing the road slowly, she peered inside. She saw a man, his features hidden in the shadows behind the counter, and working with him, a woman. Kate stared, unaware that she was blocking the doorway. Could this be her real mother? The woman who had given birth to her, and then given her away as though she was worthless?

'Make up your mind, lass. Are you going in or coming out? Either way there's not room for both of us in the doorway, so I'd be obliged if you'd shift yourself so's I can get in to buy my baccy.'

'Sorry . . . I wasn't thinking . . .' Kate found herself being propelled into the shop by a determined man of advancing years, walking nimbly despite the aid of a rough-hewn walking stick. Judging from the way he was greeted he was clearly a regular customer.

She hovered in the background, watching as he was served with an ounce of loose tobacco.

'I'll enjoy that tonight,' he said, taking the paper-wrapped package. 'Aye, and that's all I have to look forward to at nights these days.'

'Och, away wi' ye! I've seen you down at the Glen Tavern, chatting up all the young lassies.' The woman who had served him laughed loudly.

'Aye, there's some braw, bonny lassies get in there on a Saturday night right enough. And there's always one that's happy enough to sit on an old man's knee,' he cackled horribly. 'And let me tell you, I may be getting on in years but I'm in fine working order yet. So, if you ever get fed up wi' that man o' yours, I'll be right happy to warm ye're bed fir ye.'

'Ye never know, I might just take ye up on that one o' these days,' the woman responded brazenly.

'Well, ye know whit they say?'

'What do they say?'

'There's many a braw tune played on an auld fiddle,' he responded, leering at her before turning away, chuckling to himself. Kate, who had never before heard such blatantly suggestive conversation in so public a place, couldn't help staring at him, but recoiled in shock at the lewd wink he gave her on his way out.

'Aye?' The woman behind the counter now fixed her attention on Kate.

'I . . . eh . . . I was just wanting – four rashers of bacon.' She blurted the first thing that came into her head. Surely this awful creature couldn't be her mother.

'Streaky or back?' The woman asked with barely concealed impatience.

'Back.'

The woman heaved a flitch of bacon on to the slicing machine. 'How dae ye want it?' she yelled at Kate over the whirr of the machinery.

'Medium.' Kate watched closely as the woman worked, searching for some sort of family resemblance, praying she wouldn't find it. Certainly there was no similarity in colouring. This woman was blonde, though judging by the dark roots, that blondeness owed much to the application of peroxide, and her skin was almost tawny. Kate, in contrast, had the dark hair and fair skin of her celtic ancestors. There was an earthiness, a coarseness about the other woman which made Kate instinctively dislike her. But there was only one way to find out whether there was a family link.

As if sensing Kate's antipathy, the woman thrust the wrapped rashers at her and barked the price. Wondering what on earth she was going to do with them, Kate gave her the correct money, then asked, 'Are you Mrs Laing?'

The astonished chortle sent a shiver of relief down Kate's spine. 'Do I look as if I'm married to a Member of Parliament?'

Since Kate could see no way of answering this honestly without causing offence, she remained silent.

'Anyway, what's it to you who I am?'

Kate was irritated by the antagonistic challenge in the other woman's voice. But not all of Hough's customers were polite and they even had an occasional complaint which, in her more senior capacity, she was now expected to deal with. Drawing on this experience, she forced herself to stay calmly polite and even managed to fix a smile to her lips. 'I'm sorry, I didn't mean to be rude. But it is Mrs Laing I want to see and I thought you might be her.'

Luckily for Kate the other woman chose to see this as flattery. 'I wouldn't mind if I was,' she confided, immediately assuming that this young girl had come about the job which was advertised in the window. 'All that money.'

'Do you know when she will be in the shop?' Kate asked.

'Couldn't say. Sometimes she's here at six in the morning, other days she comes in last thing at night. And then again, she might not come in at all.

'Mind you, if it's the job you're after, it's not Mrs Laing you should be talking to but her brother, Mr McPherson. He's the manager here.'

'Her brother!' Kate exclaimed excitedly. 'I didn't know she had a brother.'

The other woman was eyeing her suspiciously now. 'What difference does it make to you if she's got a brother or not?'

'Well . . . it's just that if she's got a brother and he's the manager here, then, like you said, I could speak to him instead.' Kate knew she was waffling. 'Is he in?'

'Through the back.' The woman jerked her head in the direction of a closed door.

'Could you ask him if he'll see me?'

The woman stared at Kate for a few more seconds, then shrugged and made her way to the back of the shop. She found Matty swinging back on his chair, his feet propped on the table, a cigarette dangling from his mouth. 'There's a young lass out there asking for you,' she told him.

Matty was instantly alert. 'What kind of young lassie?' he asked warily.

'What do you mean, what kind?' she retorted. 'The usual kind, of course. Two legs, two arms, one head – '

'All right, Muriel! Don't try getting smart with me. You know fine what I meant.'

'Och, don't fret yourself,' she retaliated quickly. 'She's o'er smart to be one of the wee scrubbers you like to pick up.' She marched back to the door. 'She's here about a job,' she called back as she banged her way into the shop.

Matty got to his feet, stubbed his cigarette out, made a superficial attempt at tidying himself up and followed her.

'That's her.'

Matty looked in the direction indicated and wished he had taken the time to run a comb through his hair. He made up his mind there and then to offer her the job, whoever she was. Three weeks from now he'd have her bringing him breakfast in bed. He felt himself hardening at the thought, a circumstance which forced him to stay behind the modest shelter of the counter.

'Well, you're keen right enough. That advertisement only went in the window ten minutes ago. I wasn't expecting anyone until tomorrow. Still, now you're here, come on through and we'll have a wee talk.'

Wisely deciding to keep silent about the true nature of her business until they were somewhere more private, Kate followed him into the store room.

'Right then, sit yourself down, lass.' Matty indicated the wooden chair he had so recently vacated and Kate sank on to it, wondering how to begin, what to say to this man who was watching her a little too closely, his eyes frequently falling to parts of her anatomy that she preferred to keep for Tom's exclusive appreciation.

'I think I should explain – ' she started.

'First things first,' he interrupted her. Picking up a chewed pencil, which he held poised and ready over the first page of an unused but grubby notebook, he prompted her. 'Name?' Then, when she didn't answer immediately, he sighed. 'Come on. I haven't got all day.'

'Kate. Kate Brebner.' She watched as he scribbled it in the book.

'Well, Kate Brebner, have you any experience of working in a shop? It's hard work, mind, and I've no time for slackness, or carelessness. You'll be on your feet every minute of the day for there's always plenty to be done in a shop like this. If I tell you to do something, you do it at once, no matter what it is. I'll not put up with lateness or untidiness and I'll not have you talking back to me. I'm in charge here and you'll treat me with respect. If you want to work here you'll have to convince me you can pull your weight. Aye, and one more thing, if you're ever tempted to help yourself from the till, any shortages come out of your wages. I'll not have dishonesty. Not in this shop.' It was a tactic he had used before, one which successfully frightened away all but the genuine workers or the truly desperate.

He looked up at Kate now, his dark complexion and hooded eyes giving him a sinister appearance in the dimly lit store room.

But Kate was too angry to be frightened. To Matty's astonishment, she surged to her feet and stood towering over him, her eyes blazing fury. When she spoke, her voice was icy with disdain, though it was taking all her self-control not to scream her rage at him. 'How dare you suggest I might be dishonest? I have never stolen anything in my whole life and I never will. Nor am I afraid of hard work – I am well used to that. And I am not interested in your stupid job. I already have a very good position. I am Senior Sales Assistant at Hough's of Inverannan and I have no intention of looking for a new post, especially not in a place like this.'

'Then what the hell do you want?' he asked, half-angry, half-aroused by her fury, which promised a passionate nature under that prissy exterior.

'I was trying to tell you.' Kate was aware that this wasn't at all the way she had planned it. This man was her uncle and she was already arguing with him. It was no way to start a new relationship. Taking a deep breath, she paused for a second, then deliberately fixed a smile to her face. 'We seem to have made a bad start, don't we? Do you think we could try again?' He shrugged, but undeterred she went on, holding out her hand. 'Good afternoon, Mr McPherson, my name is Kate Brebner.'

Never one to turn down a friendly advance from a pretty woman, he took her hand and held it for a moment longer than was necessary. 'Matthew McPherson.'

Pulling her hand away and resisting the impulse to wipe his

sweat off, she went on. 'I really want to speak to your sister, Mrs Laing.'

'Ah. But not about a job?'

'No.'

'Well, as you can see, she's not here.'

'When will she be here?' Kate persisted.

'Hard to say.' Matty's instincts warned him that there was something interesting going on here and until he found out more there was no way he was going to let this girl see Meggie.

'It's very important.'

'Something to do with her husband, the local MP?' Matty wondered if she and Oliver had been having an affair. If so, then this was something he could use to his own advantage.

'This is between me and Mrs Laing. If you could just arrange for me to see her?'

Matty adopted his most earnest tone. 'Look, Kate – is it all right if I call you Kate?' She nodded. 'Kate, try to understand, my sister is an important lady in this town. Her husband is an MP and she is a successful businesswoman in her own right. You must see that I can't ask her to meet you unless you tell me what this is all about.'

Kate shook her head, not realising that despair was nakedly exposed on her face. 'It's personal,' she whispered.

Matty tried again. Reaching over the table, he took her hands gently. 'Sit down, Kate, and listen to me.'

She subsided on to the hard chair wondering what to do now. To walk up to the Laings' front door and boldly announce herself was clearly out of the question. Anyway, she didn't know their address.

'You know, Kate, Meggie and me are very close.'

'Meggie?' She looked directly at him now.

'Aye,' he chuckled. Meggie, that's what she's always been to me.' So the girl didn't know his sister that well, then. Everyone knew her as Meggie.

'Oh.'

'Aye, well, like I say. Meggie and me are close. Always have been. She trusts me, that's why I'm her business partner. I'm in charge of the shops. I make sure she gets the best staff, honest and hard-working. And that's why you'll need to tell me what you want with her. I'll not take the chance on anyone upsetting my sister.' He watched her closely for a moment. 'Now then, what's it to be? Are you going to tell me what you want or are you going to go home and stay away from her? And don't think you can contact her at home either. Remember, her husband's an M.P. They get all kinds of nutcases knocking at their door. You wouldn't get a foot over the doorstep.'

Kate gazed at the strangely reptilian face, wondering if she could truly trust him, knowing that he was her best chance of contacting her mother.

Just at that moment the door from the shop crashed open and Muriel poked her head through. 'There's a queue a mile long out here. I can't do it all myself!'

Matty frowned angrily, but even Kate could hear the mutterings from his impatient customers. 'I'm sorry, I'm keeping you from your work,' she said.

He smiled at her, his whole face lightening. 'Aye, I'd best get out there. We're maybe not as big or posh as Hough's, but we still treat the customer right. And they soon let us know if we don't.' He took a white apron from the back of the door and tied it round him. 'Look, we haven't finished, have we? Why don't you let me buy you dinner tonight? Then you can decide whether to trust me or not.' It was said with apparent artlessness and accompanied by another of those transforming smiles.

Kate thought for a brief moment, then, tempted by the opportunity to get to know more about this newly-discovered uncle, nodded. 'All right.'

'Eight o'clock? Shall we say outside Hough's? I'll book a table at the City Hotel,' he said, trying to impress her now.

'Eight o'clock will be fine,' she told him. 'But not the City. It's too . . .' Public was the word she was looking for. She and Tom often had a drink there before going on somewhere else. Even though this was an innocent appointment, the last thing she wanted was for someone to recognise her and for word to get back to Tom that she had been dining with another man.

To her relief, Matty laughed. 'Too stuffy, that's what you're meaning and I think so too. I'll get us in at that new place near the Glen. It's supposed to be good.' Small and dark and cosy, just the thing for what he had in mind.

'That'll be fine,' Kate agreed easily, never for a moment suspecting what was going through his mind.

He shepherded her through the shop under the curious eyes of his queuing customers, who waited until Kate was safely off the premises before launching their attack.

'Aye, aye,' someone teased. 'What's this then?'

'No wonder you've not got the time to serve us, lad. Found something more interesting to do in the stock room, eh?' a second male voice chimed in.

'Mr Davison!' A woman at the front of the queue issued a loud reproof and the men subsided into shamefaced silence.

'Just a lassie after a job, that's all,' Matty smirked.

'Any good?' Muriel asked.

'Not for working in here, no. But in other ways, quite promising I think,' he told her maliciously.

'Bastard,' she snarled furiously as they both turned away from the counter to collect items from the shelves.

'Aye,' he agreed equably. Then, digging his fingers viciously into her forearm, he hissed in her ear, 'And that's why you can't stay away from me, isn't it? Well, now you've got some competition so you'll just have to work extra hard at being nice to me. If you want to keep your job.'

With three kids and an absent husband she could only lower her head, blink away the tears and turn back to her customers.

For the second time that day, Kate left her landlady under the false impression that she was going to meet Tom.

She arrived outside Hough's just as the town hall clock chimed eight. Seeing no sign of Matty McPherson, she stepped back into the shelter of the shop doorway, hoping to make herself inconspicuous. In Inverannan nice girls did not hang about the streets on their own.

Her heart thumping painfully, she wondered whether he was actually going to turn up. In any case, it was appallingly bad mannered of him to be late.

Carefully concealed in the entrance to a narrow wynd ten yards further down the road, Matty watched her. Though he had arrived a good five minutes before her there was no way he would let her know that. Women waited for Matty Mc-Pherson, not the other way round, and he wanted time to study her. She was a pretty enough lassie, that was for sure. Pretty enough to tempt any man. If she had been involved with Oliver, what did she hope to gain by approaching Meggie? Money to keep the story quiet? She could even be pregnant by him. Or maybe it was a simple act of revenge from a jilted lover. Whatever it was, Matty was confident that he could use Kate to his own advantage, to drive another wedge between his sister and her husband. She might even be the means of getting Oliver out of Meggie's life once and for all. And then that only left Meggie herself between him and full ownership of the business. He felt the familiar thrill of pleasure at the thought, but this wasn't the time to be making plans for his sister's future. Unhurriedly extracting the very last breath of smoke from the stub of his cigarette, Matty flicked the butt into the gutter and strolled casually up the road.

Growing more agitated with each passing minute, Kate could

barely stand still. Even in the partial protection of the doorway, the October wind was cold enough to make her shiver and was whipping though her carefully arranged hair. She turned to check her appearance in the shining glass of the windows and suddenly became aware of someone standing very close behind her. Looking up, she saw Matty's dark face reflected beside her own pale one and felt a momentary shudder of something close to fear running through her. But when she turned round, she saw he was smiling, his face open and friendly with nothing at all threatening in his manner. Putting her reaction down to nerves, she smiled back.

'I hope you're hungry,' he said, cheerfully. 'I've a table booked for eight-thirty.'

Kate couldn't tell him that the very thought of food made her feel sick. She fell into step beside him as he started off down the High Street.

They walked briskly, both eager to escape the sharp wind that whistled up the closes. Kate, fully occupied in preventing her skirt from moulding itself to her legs and creeping inelegantly above her knees, was glad that he restricted his conversation to undemanding small talk.

The restaurant he had chosen was a small, newly-opened establishment near to the town's picturesque park, at the bottom of the High Street. After the chill wind, the dining-room looked snug and inviting. Kate settled into her seat at a table in a fairly secluded corner, glad that it afforded a degree of privacy for what she had to say.

Across the table, Matty eyed her appreciatively. The deep blue of her best, fine woollen frock complemented her dark hair and the wind had added colour to her cheeks and a sparkle to her eyes. His gaze wandered down to her modest cleavage, just visible at the scooped neckline. In his imagination his hand slipped down the front of her dress and massaged a firm breast. He wondered if Oliver Laing already knew the feel of her flesh. He hoped so: such potentially damaging information about a Member of Parliament could be worth a great deal of money.

'Sir.' A waiter handed him a menu, destroying the image, and Matty dragged his errant eyes back to her face just as Kate looked up at him. He licked his lips and smiled, oozing charm, then glanced quickly at the menu before shutting it decisively and handing it back.

'Wine, I think,' he said and not waiting for her to agree, turned to the waiter. 'A bottle of your house white.' No point in laying out too much cash. She probably wouldn't know one wine from another and he would much have preferred a pint of heavy. 'And two medium rump steaks with all the trimmings,' he went on, without bothering to consult Kate for her preferences. In truth Matty hadn't recognised most of the dishes on the menu and with no wish to expose his ignorance had opted for the one thing he was familiar with.

'Yes, sir.' The waiter's response was heavily laced with sarcasm. He'd met oafs like this often enough to see through Matty's ploy. He smirked but quickly straightened his face and hurried away at the menacing look that Matty levelled at him.

He returned within a minute and filled their glasses. Matty waited until he had gone, then raised his towards Kate. 'To us,' he suggested.

Kate raised her own glass in answer, then shuddered as the acidic liquid swamped her taste-buds.

Matty smiled and took another sip from his own glass, rolling the astringent wine around his mouth as if it was the very best champagne. 'Don't worry,' he said patronisingly, his face creased in a display of false concern as he enjoyed this chance to impress her. 'Dry wine is an acquired taste. Difficult to enjoy if you're not used to it.'

Kate flushed, but bit back the sharp reply. She picked up her glass and took another vinegary mouthful. 'It's fine,' she lied.

She had drunk wine often enough with Tom to know that this was very poor stuff indeed.

'Good.' He leaned over and topped up her glass, letting his hand brush against hers as he did so.

They talked about nothing in particular until the meal was served. Matty tucked his napkin into his collar and shoved a mouthful of steak into his mouth before suddenly asking, 'So, Kate, tell me why you want to see my sister?' His eyes fastened themselves on her face.

Kate hesitated, feeling uncomfortable with him, a sensation that increased when she looked into those dark eyes: fathomless black pools in which any expression was hidden by heavy lids. Permeating everything, she sensed a raw power about him, a naked sexuality that repelled and attracted in equal amounts. Confused, she looked away and pretended an interest in her food.

Somehow she had to persuade him to arrange a meeting with his sister. The one thing she did know was that she couldn't tell him the truth. Even though this man was probably her uncle it was entirely possible that he didn't know that his sister had given birth to an illegitimate child. To start their relationship by betraying such a terrible secret would not help her chances of success – even if he chose to believe her. But she had had all afternoon to think this through and had already concocted a flimsy story for him.

'Well?' he prompted her, his curiosity about what this intense young woman could possibly want with his sister almost over-whelmed by the desire to kiss her, to thrust his tongue into her mouth, to feel the softness of that inviting body. Sweat broke out on his brow and trickled down his temple.

Kate was too absorbed in trying to make herself sound convincing to notice. 'I want to ask her advice,' she said.

'Advice?' Matty repeated. 'About what?'

'About having my own shop,' she went on.

'Och . . .' He laughed. 'Is that all? Well, I can tell you everything you need to know about that.'

'No!' She knew she had said it too loudly, saw the way his brows shot up and the dark eyes widened momentarily.

'No?' he repeated wondering if he had been wrong about her after all. There was something in Kate's manner, a certain naïvety which seemed to make his more lurid speculations about her possible relationship with Oliver Laing unlikely. He was aware of a rush of temper as he saw the lucrative possibilities fade away, leaving him with nothing more than a hefty restaurant bill.

Kate knew that she was letting the opportunity slip away from her. Desperation drove her on. 'Och, you're going to think this is ridiculous,' she said, trying to lie convincingly. 'But the thing is, your sister is so successful. Everyone in Inverannan knows how well she's doing. You know, running the shops, and then there's all the work she has to do because she's the wife of an MP, and looking after a wean as well . . .' She paused expectantly, but there was no reaction from Matty. 'Anyway, there was that bit in the paper about her the other day and I read it and thought . . . You see, I've always wanted a shop of my own but it's hard for a woman to do something like that and . . . och, I just wanted some advice . . . from another woman.'

Matty filled his mouth with the last chunk of steak and looked across at Kate, who was watching him with a pleading smile hovering round her mouth. Perhaps he might get something out of the evening yet. 'I suppose I could ask her,' he suggested, allowing a hint of uncertainty to creep into his voice. 'But she might not agree to see you. She's very busy, what with the shops and – '

'But if you asked her . . .' Kate interjected eagerly.

'I'll have to think about it. Look, let's just enjoy the food, then we'll talk about it some more while I see you home.' He emptied the remains of the wine into her glass and transferred his whole attention to his meal.

When they emerged into the cold night air an hour later, Kate, her stomach aching with the acid effects of the wine, still didn't know whether the evening had been a success or a failure.

Matty, disappointed that there was nothing more to Kate than a desire to emulate his sister in business, was determined to get more than a piece of steak and some soggy vegetables in return for the money he had spent on her.

'Put your arm through mine,' he offered as they started to walk up the street. When she made no move to accept his arm, he said with a soft laugh, 'It's cold, Kate, if we walk close together we'll be warmer.'

Reluctantly she slipped her arm though his and allowed him to draw her close to him. She had to admit that it was warmer this way.

'Tell me about your plans for a shop of your own, then,' he encouraged her as they passed by Hough's.

All the way to Netherton Kate told him of her imaginary ambition, wondering at her ability to lie so fluently.

'And you still want me to ask Meggie to meet you?' he asked as they approached the railway bridge that spanned the only road into the warren of streets where Kate lodged.

'Aye.' Kate's breath emerged as a white cloud in the freezing night air. 'Do you think she will agree?'

'Well, she might,' he said, stopping in the dark shadows of the tunnel under the bridge itself. 'It depends on me really.'

'But you will ask her?' She faced him now.

'Whatever happens, have you enjoyed yourself tonight, Kate?' he asked, his voice soft in the cold darkness.

'Aye. Thank you,' she told him, wanting only to know what he was going to do and then to get home to the warmth of

Mrs Traynor's cosy house and her own snug bed. Still, so much depended on Matty that she couldn't afford to upset him.

'You're cold,' he said, pulling her closer to him.

'Not really.' She denied it, despite her freezing hands and icy feet.

'I will have a word with Meggie,' he promised her, knowing she would be grateful.

'You will! Och, that's wonderful. Thank you, Matty,' she beamed at him through the frosty air.

'Aye, and whatever she says, I've had a great time tonight, Kate,' he told her, slipping his arm round her shoulder and trying to pull her even closer.

Kate stiffened and tried to keep a safe distance between them, suddenly aware of the fact that she was very much alone with this strangely powerful man. 'I think I should be going home now,' she said.

'Och no, Kate, not yet,' he said, yanking her towards him. 'We've had a good time, haven't we? And you're a smashing lass, Kate, so you are. Right bonny.' To Kate's horror he squashed her up against the wall and tried to kiss her, missing her mouth but slobbering wetly all down the side of her cheek.

'Stop it,' she yelled and shoved him away.

It had never occurred to Matty that she might not welcome his advances. Now he looked at her with a startled expression on his face. 'I thought you liked me,' he said.

'I do . . . but not like – '

The rest of the sentence was lost as he tried to kiss her again, pressing her hard against the filthy wall as his face smothered hers. A hand grappled frantically with the buttons of her coat and his breathing was fast and ragged in her ear.

'No! Stop it! *Stop it!*' she screamed.

He raised his head and muttered, 'Och, you're a braw-looking lassie, Kate.' A wee bit of flattery usually did the trick. His mouth sank to her neck, fastening on the delicate skin like a leech while he ground his pelvis into hers. 'Come on, Kate, please. Just a wee feel, eh? Please? Och, you're smashing, so you are. Come on, give me your hand.'

'*No!*' She recoiled in horror but, pinned against the wall, could only twist her arm away.

His face was still burrowing around her neck but he lifted it again to ask, 'Why not? Come on, Kate.' Why, he wondered, did some lassies need to pretend they didn't want it? They all gave in in the end. Not that a wee bit of resistance didn't make it all the sweeter, but Kate was taking it too far. He was already so hard that he was in pain. One touch from her would send a glorious explosion rocking though his groin . . . just one touch. He fumbled for her hand again.

Kate could not fail to realise that he was highly aroused and knew she had to take drastic action if she wasn't to find herself in serious trouble again. Desperately she grabbed his ears and twisted then until he roared in pain. She waited until he raised his head and then, her hands still firmly on his ears, 'Because you are my uncle,' she told him, fighting to keep her voice even.

Matty froze. For a moment he stood, his body rigid. Then it was as if the life drained out of him and he sagged away from her. 'Your uncle?' His voice was harsh with shock, but not for a moment did he disbelieve her.

'I didn't want to tell you yet,' she said, her voice shaking with outrage. But some of her anger was directed at herself as she realised how foolish she had been to allow herself to get into this dangerous situation with a man she hardly knew. No wonder he had made such unflattering assumptions about her when she had behaved so stupidly.

Matty straightened, ran his fingers through his hair, took a deep breath and turned back to her. 'How do you know?' he asked, his breathing still ragged.

There, in the dark and damp tunnel where neither could see

the other, her words clipped, her voice taut with anger, she told him. When she had finished he stood in silence for so long that she began to panic, not knowing what would happen next.

Matty was glad of the darkness. Even he, practised deceiver that he was, couldn't trust his face not to betray his emotions. This girl was Meggie's daughter; enough of what she said tied in with what he already knew to make him believe her. And it would be obvious to any fool that she must be hoping for some sort of financial gain – a share of the money that should, by rights, be his. He could hardly believe that he had been gullible enough to fall for her lies; that act of innocence she had put on for his benefit. Well, if she thought she could just turn up and lay claim to anything that was rightfully his, just when he was starting to lay plans for taking over the whole of the business, she could think again. She had chosen the wrong man when she decided to make a fool of Matthew McPherson.

Her voice came through the darkness. 'Aren't you going to say anything?'

He collected himself. What he needed now was time, time to think things through and decide what to do. Time to find a way to keep Meggie and Kate apart, to stop this girl worming her way into his sister's affections. But it had to be done in a way which would not arouse her suspicions. If she even began to suspect that he was actually working against her she would make a direct approach to Meggie and then he could lose everything.

'Come on,' he snapped. 'It's cold in here, we'll both catch our deaths.' He walked slowly out of the tunnel and Kate followed.

In the half light from the moon they looked at one another, both feeling awkward.

'So I'm your uncle, then?' he said at last.

'I think so.'

'You should have told me. I'd never have tried to . . . you know . . .'

'Aye. I know. I'm sorry.'

'So am I.'

'Forget it.' It was curtly said.

'Why didn't you tell me the truth? Why did you have to lie to me?' He sounded angry now.

'Because I wasn't sure if you knew.'

'Knew what?' he bawled it at her.

'About the baby.'

He grunted. 'Of course I knew. I told you. Meggie and me are very close.'

'Will you tell her?'

'About you? Aye, I don't keep secrets from Meggie.'

'Do you think she'll agree to see me?' Kate asked anxiously.

'I wouldn't like to say. After all, she's her husband to think of. She never told him about the bairn,' he said, spinning the first thread in the web of lies with which he would try to protect his own position.

'I've not made a very good job of this so far, have I?' Kate sighed. 'Maybe I'd be better to write to her after all.'

'And risk Oliver seeing the letter? She wouldn't thank you for that.'

'That's why I thought it was better this way.'

'Go home, Kate. It's late and we're both tired.'

'So you won't help me?' she said, turning away.

He watched her walk slowly up the road until she was illuminated by the first of the old street lights. 'Come to the shop next Wednesday afternoon,' he called to her retreating back. 'I'll maybe have some news for you then.'

She spun round, her face wreathed in smiles, ready to forgive him. 'Thank you,' she called back. 'Thank you, Matty.' Then she turned again and ran up the road.

Matty walked back towards the town. With or without his help, he thought as he was swallowed up by the darkness of the tunnel, it was clear that she was still set on contacting Meggie. Much better to appear to help her. To stay in control.

TWENTY-FIVE

'Are you sure you don't mind?' Meggie asked anxiously.

'Of course I don't,' Matty reassured her a little too eagerly. 'It's about time you had a few days in London.'

'I suppose it is, but this shop is busy just now and I know you're short-staffed.'

'Will you stop worrying?' he said, grinning at her. 'Now you've made me your partner you can rely on me to look after things for you. Not that you couldn't before,' he added hastily. When she still seemed uncertain, he went on: 'Unless me being a partner hasn't really changed things. Unless you still don't trust me.'

'Och, for goodness sake!' She glared at him. 'Why do you have to say that every time you don't get things your own way?'

'Aye, well, you can't blame me, can you?' he retorted sharply. 'There was a time when you thought I was stealing from you.'

'And I was right. You were.' She faced him angrily.

He flushed and looked away, knowing he had made a mistake. Once his much tried and tested formula would have swamped her with guilt, but Meggie was a much stronger character now than she had been even a year ago and no longer susceptible to his accusations. 'All right,' he muttered. 'But I don't do that sort of thing now. I've more sense.'

She sighed. 'Och, I know. I'm sorry, Matty. It's me. I'm in a lousy mood. Take no notice.'

'Want to tell me what's wrong?' he asked, sitting down at the store room table to wait.

She grimaced, then sank wearily into the seat opposite him. Looking at her, Matty was aware for the first time that Meggie was no longer a young woman. Though still beautiful, there were lines down the side of her mouth that he hadn't noticed before, and, just visible at her temple where she had pushed her hair behind her ears, were the first strands of grey.

'The truth is, I don't really want to go to London,' she told him. 'I was half hoping I could find some reason for getting out of it.'

'But you'll have a good time down there. The theatres, the shops, the restaurants. Take the chance to enjoy yourself for a couple of days.'

'Not much chance of that. This is one of those stuffy formal dinners where the men talk politics and the women make catty remarks about one another. Ugh!' she shuddered expressively.

'It doesn't sound much like fun,' he agreed.

'It's not, but Oliver will never forgive me if I don't go.'

'When are you leaving?'

'On the early morning train.'

'Tomorrow?'

She nodded.

'And coming back on Thursday?'

'No. The dinner's not until Thursday night, but since I can't get out of going I thought I would take the chance to spend some time with Oliver. After all, in the four months since he was elected I have only made the effort to go down there once before. He's not expecting me so soon so it will be a surprise for him. He must get fed up in that pokey little flat all on his own.'

Matty had doubts about Oliver's loneliness but wisely remained silent.

'I don't like leaving Ellen, though,' she went on.

'Why?' Matty's face was instantly full of concern. 'What's the matter with her?'

'Nothing. I'll just miss her, that's all.'

'Well, that's natural enough,' Matty told her, squeezing her hand across the table. 'She's a proper little charmer, that one. Everyone wants to make a fuss of her.'

'Aye,' Meggie responded bitterly. 'Everyone except her father.' Unwilling to pursue such a painful subject, and already regretting that she had let her guard slip, she stood up. 'Are you sure you don't mind?' she asked again.

'How many times do I have to tell you? And don't worry about Ellen. She'll be fine. You know you can trust Jessica to look after her while you're away.'

Meggie knew he was right. Jessica, who helped to look after Ellen, was utterly reliable and genuinely fond of her little charge. 'All right . . . all right,' she laughed faintly. 'And there's nothing I should know before I go?'

Kate's face suddenly imposed itself on Matty's mind, appearing as a younger version of his sister, the resemblance startlingly obvious now. 'I . . .' he mumbled, uncharacteristically disconcerted.

Meggie had seen the momentary confusion. 'Is there something, Matty?' she asked.

Matty recovered quickly. 'No. I was just thinking about the vacancy here, that's all. I could do with the extra help, Meggie. Do you mind if I go ahead and start someone?'

She hesitated. Matty didn't seem to have the knack of choosing suitable staff. But she really hadn't got time to see to it herself. 'No,' she told him. 'You're my partner and you're the one who will have to work with whoever you choose. You do it.'

She knew at once that she had pleased him. He beamed a rare full smile at her, lighting his whole face, making him look much more attractive. If only he could smile like that more often, learn to take himself a little less seriously, then he might find himself a wife. And that, she thought, picking up her bag and leaning over to kiss his cheek, would be the making of him. You only had to see him with Ellen to understand that what Matty really needed was a family of his own.

'See you on Friday then,' he said, ushering her to her car.

'Saturday,' she corrected him on impulse. 'I might as well travel back with Oliver.' And that should stop him complaining that she never had time for him, she thought, waving at her brother as she drove away.

Almost exactly twenty-four hours later, Meggie stepped out on to the station platform, feeling tired and grubby. The journey to London had taken a full twelve hours and she had spent them jammed in a compartment with four men, all of whom smoked incessantly, and a woman with an undisciplined toddler and a baby who had screamed until it was sick. Unfortunately it had been sick on her seat, as she discovered on returning from a very necessary visit to the Ladies at a dark and dreary station somewhere in northern England. The mother had grudgingly swabbed the worn plush fabric with a suspicious piece of terry towelling, but within five minutes of resuming her place Meggie was uncomfortably aware of rising damp and could only pray that her navy-blue skirt would not show too obvious a mark.

Now, her bladder bursting, her head thumping, she looked vainly for a porter to help her with her heavy case. Failing, she picked it up and joined the throng of people shoving their way through the barrier.

With difficulty she hoisted her case through the turnstile which guarded the Ladies toilets and then dumped it outside a cubicle door. Emerging, she realised that her case was no longer where she had left it. Looking frantically around her she saw a girl, so small that she could hardly keep the case from dragging along the ground as she hauled it over the tiled floor. Furiously Meggie ran after her, catching her as she struggled to get through the revolving metal bar which blocked the exit.

'That's my case,' Meggie shouted, grabbing the young thief by the shoulder. 'Put it down! Now!' She got her fingers round the child's wrist and was surprised how thin and fragile it felt. Vainly she looked around for help. The crowd surged past, not a single person showing any interest in her plight.

The girl turned and looked up at Meggie, a cheeky, unrepentant grin on her grimy face. Then, in one fluid movement, she abandoned her grip on the case, kicked Meggie on the shin and vaulted over the barrier. Safely on the other side, she turned and aimed a gob of spittle at her astounded victim before running off into the crowd.

Infinitely saddened, Meggie lifted her case and went back to stand in front of a basin. Rummaging in her handbag, she found two aspirin tablets and swallowed them, washing them down with water cupped in her hand. Reluctantly she straightened and faced the mirror. Well, she thought, looking at herself without pleasure, if she turned up on Oliver's doorstep looking like this he would get a surprise all right. But not one he was likely to appreciate. Giving herself a mental shake she set to work.

Few street urchins would have had the courage to try and take advantage of the confident and smartly-dressed woman who emerged from a taxi outside Oliver's Westminster flat three-quarters of an hour later. A wash, a change of clothes and a dozen kirby grips had joined forces with Max Factor to bring about a vital transformation in Meggie. Her headache had subsided to a manageable niggle and she felt altogether more cheerful and ready for the meal she had booked before leaving home that morning.

The flat was on the top floor of what must once have been a spacious town house. Determined to surprise her husband, she did not ring the bell beside his name on the list by the door, but, fumbling with the unfamiliar keys, let herself in and hauled her case up three flights of stairs. Outside his door she paused, giving herself the chance to get her breath back, then listened carefully, trying to discover whether he was in or not. From inside the flat came the muffled strains of music, some-thing classical that she recognised as one of his favourites. Smiling, determined to make the most of her unwanted break, she inserted the key in the lock, careful to make as little noise as possible. The door swung open silently. Meggie pulled her case in and closed the door behind her.

The flat was compact but well designed. The bathroom was in the hall just inside the front door and all other rooms led off the sitting-room, the door to which was half open. She tiptoed into the room, surprised at how smart it looked, much improved from when she had first seen it, a month or so after Oliver had signed the lease. Then it had been furnished with pre-war odds and ends, functional, adequate and cheerless. Now the place looked as though it had come straight from the pages of a glossy magazine, with modern sofas, thick carpets and contemporary pictures on the freshly-decorated walls. She wondered why he hadn't mentioned having all this done, especially as it had obviously been a very expensive transform-ation, but then, almost at once, felt ashamed for harbouring such thoughts. After all, Oliver spent more time here than he did at home. It wasn't fair to expect him to live in a hovel while she was free to enjoy the luxury of the family house.

It was obvious that Oliver was at home, but in which room she could not immediately tell. She stopped and listened again, hearing nothing, then, not wanting to lose the element of surprise, crept carefully towards the bedrooms. Both were empty, though his suit jacket was tossed casually across the bed.

She walked towards the kitchen door and was rewarded by the sound of movement. Reaching the doorway she stopped and listened again, hearing only the faintest of rustling noises. Slowly she stepped into the room, her mouth already forming the words of greeting.

They died in her throat, emerging as a choked gasp. There, his back to her, stood Oliver, wrapped around a woman who, even as Meggie watched in speechless horror, worked her leg teasingly between his thighs, in a gesture so easily familiar that Meggie knew instantly that this was a scene which had been enacted many times before.

'You bastard!' Meggie was not aware of having crossed the room as she found herself hauling at his shirt. Oliver jerked round, and the expression on his face would have been comical had the situation not been so desperate. The girl, her eyes wide with shock, stood with her back to the sink, her blouse open to the waist, her heavy breasts exposed. Her mouth forming a red circle of shock, she struggled to cover herself with one hand and thrust Oliver away from her with the other. Stumbling, Oliver turned towards his wife with his still-erect penis jutting from his gaping fly.

For a moment husband and wife faced each other in mutual horror. But Oliver was the first to recover. While Meggie fought a wave of sickening dizziness he made himself decent and bundled the girl from the room.

'Get out,' he hissed.

She glared at him but then picked up her shoes and flounced away. He heard the door slam as she went out of the flat.

Running a hand through his hair, he sagged forward in the doorway, his body weight dragging on his hands, which clutched at the door-frame as he prepared to face his wife's anger.

'What the fuck are you doing here?' he snarled, furiously.

But Meggie was beyond speech. Her heart was beating violently enough to burst through her ribs, her breathing was fast and shallow and she felt sweat break and run down her back as her head spun. A sudden, bitter rise of fluid to her mouth sent her to lean over the sink, where she retched miserably.

He waited until she had stopped heaving, then put an arm around her trembling shoulders, steered her to a chair and offered her a glass of water.

Not looking at him, she took the glass and sipped at it, her hand deceptively steady compared with the turmoil in her mind.

'What the hell do you think you were doing barging in without so much as having the courtesy to knock?' he raged at her.

Just, Meggie thought furiously, as if this sorry mess was her fault. 'I thought I would surprise you,' she said coldly. 'And I did, didn't I, Oliver?'

'I wasn't expecting you until tomorrow.'

'And by turning up early I spoiled your fun? Is that what you're trying to say?' She hissed the words at him.

'No!' Meeting his wife's eyes for the first time that day, Oliver had the feeling that she saw right through him, that she knew exactly what he was going to say next. He did the only thing he could and met her scorn with attack. 'All right then, yes. And if you had just stuck to our arrangements you would never have been any the wiser.'

'Not for the first time, I suppose?'

'No, Meggie, not for the first time,' he agreed, the ice in his voice matching her own. 'And don't look so outraged,' he went on, his tone changing to open derision. 'It's what happens when a man is forced to spend too much time on his own.'

'No one forced you to come to London, Oliver,' she retorted.

'But this is where my career is. If you had been any sort of wife you would have come here with me and this need never have happened. But you weren't prepared to do that for me, were you, Meggie? Oh no, you had to stay in Scotland with your bloody shops.'

'I stay in Scotland because of our daughter, Oliver,' she corrected him quietly.

'Ellen wouldn't know the difference between Inverannan and Calcutta,' he said cruelly.

'She would know she wasn't near her friends any more – people who care about her, like Robbie and Matty and Sally. People who care more about her than her own father does!'

'And it's a pity you don't care about me in the same way, isn't it, Meggie?'

'I see! So this is all my fault, is it?' she screamed at him. 'I make an effort to come all the way down here, thinking I would surprise you, that we could spend some time together for once, have dinner. And I get here to find you with another woman. And it's my fault!' She got up from the table and ran from the room, getting as far as the front door before he stopped her.

'Meggie . . .' he put a hand on her arm.

'Don't touch me! Don't you dare touch me!' She picked up her case and grappled with the door-catch.

Oliver took his hand from her arm and stepped round her, leaning his weight against the door. 'Can't we talk about this?' he asked.

'You've said all I want to hear,' she retorted furiously, tugging fruitlessly at the door. 'Get out of the way, Oliver.'

'And where will you go, Meggie? It's too late to go home tonight.' There was a sneer in his voice now.

In that moment Meggie hated him, saw him suddenly for what he had become: a self-satisfied, conceited man who cared only about himself. She knew too that whatever she had once felt for him had withered and died long before the night's sordid events. Somehow the other woman seemed less important, almost a natural culmination of events, a symptom rather then a cause of their failed marriage – a marriage she was suddenly desperate to escape from.

'London has never been short of hotels. I'll find somewhere,' she told him. 'Then you can go and find someone else to keep you company for the night. I'm sure there are plenty of women who will be only too willing to oblige a Member of Parliament. Don't worry, Oliver, you can do what you want. It's no concern of mine any more. And if you have anything else to say, say it through my solicitor. You'll be hearing from him. Now, let me out.'

Oliver saw his hopes for a junior minister's post shrivel as in those few words his wife put an end to his burgeoning career. Though the British people were more open-minded than they had been before the war, divorce was still frowned upon. And, he realised with growing panic, even if the more sophisticated people he now consorted with in London sympathised with his predicament, the sternly Protestant electorate in Inverannan would be outraged.

Sagging back against the door, still blocking her exit, he brought his hands up to cover his face and managed a sob that was not completely contrived. 'Meggie, what can I say? I'm sorry. I truly didn't mean to hurt you. I'm just . . . just so lonely, Meggie.'

Meggie watched her husband silently and without sympathy, not believing a word he uttered.

'Please,' he begged. 'Don't leave me, Meggie. I need you.'

'You seem to have managed very well without me so far, Oliver.'

'But I haven't, have I? That's the whole point, isn't it? That's why I've been behaving the way I have. Because I miss you, Meggie.'

Still Meggie watched him impassively and Oliver was forced to go on.

330

'Meggie, please! You can't leave me. Think what a divorce would do to my career.'

Meggie astounded herself by laughing. 'Now we have the truth,' she said triumphantly. 'You don't care for me any more than I care for you. All you are worried about is what the scandal of a divorce would do to your position as an MP.'

Oliver knew he had made the mistake of underestimating his wife. 'No.' He tried to deny it and almost lost his temper again when he saw the smile which was still playing around her mouth, as if she was making fun of him.

'Don't lie to me, Oliver,' she said coolly.

'If you don't believe me, then at least think what it would mean to you,' he countered, drawing on all the skills he had learned in the debating chamber. 'We've both got too much at stake.'

Meggie did think, viewing the prospect of running her own life again with an unexpected frisson of excitement. There was no hint of that in her reply. 'I see so little of you, Oliver, that I might as well not be married,' she said. 'And when we are together we barely talk – unless it's to argue. I don't think I would miss that.'

'No.' He was as cool as she now and both recognised a new element in their relationship: a detachment, a lack of emotion, strange and unexpected after so traumatic an evening. 'But you would miss the respect you get because of who I am.'

She snorted her derision. 'You have an inflated idea of your own importance. People respect me because of who *I* am, not because I happen to be your wife.'

'You're wrong.' He moved away from the door now and she made no attempt to leave. 'If we divorce my career at Westminster is finished, that's certain. But you will suffer too. And so will Ellen,' he added craftily.

'Of course she won't.' She denied it quickly, but her voice had lost that edge of calm.

'Can't you just imagine it, Meggie?' he asked, circling her, almost teasing her now. 'It would be in all the national papers, of course, and they would have a field day, wouldn't they? They'd drag everything up. I can see the headlines now. "Crippled MP and wife to divorce." That business with my leg would be brought up again and there'd be no way to keep Matty's name out of it. And they would be bound to bring Ellen in somewhere, wouldn't they? And what about your past, Meggie? Do you think that no one in Inverannan knows about you? All the publicity might jog someone's memory, remind them of what you used to be. The papers would pay good money for a story like that and there are folk who would jump at the chance to make a pound or two these days. "*MP divorces exprostitute wife.*" How does that sound, Meggie?'

Meggie felt the colour draining from her face. 'They wouldn't – '

'Oh yes they would,' Oliver assured her, a gleam of triumph shining from his eyes.

Slowly Meggie put her case back on the ground. 'Let's talk,' she said, her voice low and sad as she turned back towards the sitting-room.

Kate hurried up the hill towards the corner shop, her heart pounding with excitement, the normal weariness after a full day's work quite forgotten in the anticipation of meeting her real mother at last. Though the shop should have closed half an hour ago, she could see the lights were still on, as if to welcome her. Outside, she paused for a moment and patted her hair into place, doing her best to make sure she was presentable for this momentous meeting. At that moment she was no longer wondering what her mother would be like. Her overwhelming concern was with the impression she would make on this unknown woman. She was determined to make her mother proud of her.

The shop door was locked. Kate felt a momentary stab of disappointment, but then told herself that of course the door had to be locked, or the place would still be attracting customers, customers who would be a very unwelcome intrusion on what would surely be an emotional reunion. Peering into the shop, she saw no sign of life – but they wouldn't wait for her in the shop, would they? Much more likely that they would stay in the back room, or even upstairs in her uncle Matty's flat.

Taking a deep breath, Kate knocked loudly on the door, then waited. Nothing happened. But of course, she told herself, if they were upstairs they wouldn't be able to hear. She knocked again, even louder this time, but still with no result. Puzzled, she stepped back and looked up at the upstairs windows. They were all in darkness. Strange, because Matty himself had told her to come here tonight. But of course! She should go to the back door. She couldn't think why she hadn't gone there in the first place. Quickly she made her way round, let herself in through the high wooden gate, crossed the small yard and hammered on the back door. She was rewarded almost at once by the sound of the key turning in the lock as the door opened to reveal Matty, still in his work apron.

'Hello.'

She smiled at him warmly and was puzzled when he frowned slightly before saying, 'You'd better come on in.'

She stepped inside and followed him along a short passage and into the store room, looking round expectantly, instantly disappointed to realise there was no one else there.

'Sit down, Kate. I've just made a pot of tea – would you like a cup?'

She shook her head, knowing her throat was too tight to swallow anything. 'No thanks.'

He seemed to take for ever to pour himself one. When he

did eventually settle himself on the other side of the table, his face was unsmiling.

'I have come on the right night, haven't I?' she asked, wondering if she could possibly have made a mistake about something so important.

'Oh aye,' he assured her. 'You're right enough.'

'Is my mother here?' she asked, letting her eyes travel round the room again, even though she knew they were alone.

Matty sighed. 'Kate, I never told you Meggie would be here tonight.'

'But I thought . . .' Kate had assumed that as soon as her mother knew about her she would waste no time in coming to meet her. Her eyes flooded with tears of bitter disappointment.

'Kate . . .' Matty patted her hand across the table. 'I'm sorry, lass, but these things take time. You have to give her a chance to get used to the idea.'

Kate blinked back her tears, determined not to let herself down in front of her uncle. 'You told her about me?'

He nodded. 'Aye.'

'And what did she say?' she asked, eager for any piece of information.

Matty shook his head and looked uncomfortable. 'Like I say,' he muttered. 'You have to give her time to get used to the idea.'

'You mean she wouldn't meet me?' Kate felt a knot of pain tie itself in her stomach.

'No, she won't meet you.'

'Not ever?' Kate persisted miserably.

Matty played his part to perfection, a fine blend of loyal brother and affectionate uncle. 'I wish I had better news for you, hen, but the truth is she was a bit shocked, you turning up out of the blue like you did.'

'But when she's had time to get used to the idea, do you think she will meet me then?' Kate persisted.

Matty looked grave and held Kate's hand tightly. 'I didn't want to have to tell you this, Kate, but . . . well, I'm an honest sort of bloke and I'm not happy telling lies.'

'Yes?' she encouraged him bleakly.

'The truth is, Kate, that Meggie says she won't meet you. Try to see it her way, lass. Meggie had you when she was just a bairn herself.' He raised her hand and clasped it between both of his, looking into her eyes as he spoke. 'She thought she'd put it all behind her and all she wants to do is forget about it. It was a very unhappy time for her, Kate.'

'I only want to meet her.'

'I know. But it would be so hard for her, can't you see that? It would make her live through it all again.'

'Doesn't she even want to know what I'm like?' Kate whispered.

'No. She feels it's best left alone.'

'I don't believe you!' Kate jerked her hand away and got to her feet, turning so that he wouldn't see the tears which were filling her eyes. 'No one could be that cruel.'

Matty was beside her in an instant, all concern. 'It's not cruelty, Kate, well, not deliberately. Meggie's frightened.'

'Frightened? Of me?'

'No, Kate, not of you. Meggie's frightened that her husband will find out. If he does, this could destroy her marriage.'

'But I wouldn't do that. I wouldn't hurt her. All I want to do is meet my real mother.'

'No, Kate. I'm sorry, but the answer's no.'

She turned away, her shoulders heaving. Matty waited for a few seconds, then put his arms round her and drew her to him. She stiffened but then lowered her head against his chest.

'But we'll keep in touch, won't we?' she asked, her voice muffled by tears.

'Aye, we'll keep in touch. After all, you're my niece,' he said, dropping a kiss into her hair. 'And,' he went on, deliberately kindling a new spark of hope within her. 'You never know, one day Meggie might feel ready to meet you. I won't let her forget about you, I promise you that.'

Kate raised a tear-stained face and did her best to smile at him. 'Thank you, Uncle Matty.'

TWENTY-SIX

'For goodness sake, lass! You're all fingers and thumbs the day.' Mrs Donald's infallible nose for inefficiency brought her to the door at the very moment that Kate let a scoop of best tea droop in her hand, sending the leaves cascading over the store room floor.

'And you, Christina Duncan.' She rounded on the young girl who had started work at Hough's only the day before. 'There's nothing to laugh at in such wastefulness. Away and fetch the brush and pan and sweep up every last speck of tea from this floor.'

'Not much of an example to the young lassie, is it, Kate?' she commented acidly as Christina hurried away.

'No, Mrs Donald. I'm sorry. I don't know how I could be so clumsy.' Kate had flushed to the roots of her hair to be rebuked in front of the girl she was supposed to be training. To her shame, tears were pricking at the back of her eyes.

'Aye, well, be more careful in future.' Mrs Donald watched sternly as Kate brushed stray specks of tea from her apron, but to be fair it was most unlike Kate to make such a silly mistake. And if she wasn't mistaken, the girl was close to tears. Waiting until the young trainee had gone outside to empty the shovel in the bin, she asked, 'Is everything all right, Kate? I'm thinking you're not quite yourself today, lass.'

Kate smiled ruefully. 'I've a wee bit of a sore head,' she admitted.

'Aye, I thought as much. Och, it's quiet enough this morning, away upstairs and have yourself a nice cup of tea and

337

half an hour of peace and quiet. That'll make you feel better. Best take an aspirin too.'

'I – ' Kate opened her mouth to protest.

'Now don't argue, lass. There's a long day ahead and you'll not be much use to me if you're not feeling well. Off you go now. I'll look after Christina until tea break.'

Kate made for the stairs gratefully enough, for her head was aching horribly – the result of a long, sleepless night.

The attic room where they took their breaks was empty, the silence broken only by the hissing of the tea-urn and the muted noise from the street far below. Helping herself to a cup of the strong brew, she settled herself at the table, rested her head in her hands and closed her eyes.

'Kate. Are you all right?'

She looked up with a start as Tom came in to the room. 'Aye.' She did her best to smile at him, but much as she loved him, she would rather have had these few minutes to herself.

'Mrs Donald said you weren't feeling well,' he said, coming to sit beside her, his face creased with concern.

'Och,' she shrugged dismissively. 'It's nothing. Just a wee bit of a sore head, that's all.'

'And you weren't well last night. Maybe you should have a word with the doctor. We don't want you coming down with something.'

'It's just a sore head, Tom!' she snapped at him crossly.

'Aye, and a sore temper too,' he retorted, hurt.

Immediately her eyes filled with tears again, and this time, to her absolute dismay, they trickled over her cheeks. Furious with herself, she rubbed at her eyes, but it was too late.

'Has someone upset you, Kate?' Tom asked, his anger instantly forgotten. 'If it was Mrs Donald, take no notice. You know she's not half as bad as she sounds.'

She shook her head and mumbled, 'It's not Mrs Donald. She's been right kind.'

'Then what is it?' He slid along the bench until he could put an arm round her shoulders.

She shook her head. 'It's nothing, Tom, and it's time I was getting back to work.'

'You can't go into the shop looking like that,' he teased her gently, stroking the hair back from her tear-stained face. 'You'll have everyone talking.'

And that, she knew, was true. She gave a half smile and sipped at her tea.

'Come on then, get it off your chest. I know something's bothering you.' He spoke lightly but inside he was worried about her. Kate was not given to tears and was certainly not a moody person. This silent misery was totally out of character for her. He gave her a little hug.

Kate tensed, fighting to control the tears which were welling up inside her. But it was a hopeless battle. The disappointment of the previous night overwhelmed her.

'Kate, please! Tell me what's wrong.' Tom had never felt as useless as he did when she turned into his shoulder and sobbed.

'I'm just so . . . so unhappy,' she choked though streaming tears.

Something in Tom's stomach tightened and dread made his whole body tense. 'Unhappy?' he repeated, stunned to think he had known nothing of her true feelings. Without realising he was doing it, he drew away from her a little.

As miserable as she was, Kate felt his withdrawal. Looking up at his face, she saw the tight lines around his mouth, the shocked expression in his eyes, and knew at once what he was thinking. 'No!' she gasped, her own pain instantly relegated to second place. 'Not unhappy with you, Tom.'

He wouldn't look at her. 'You don't need to try to protect me, Kate. I don't want to make you miserable. If that's the case then you'd better tell me now.'

She slid along the bench until her body was touching his

again, then took his hand and kissed his strong fingers. 'Don't be so stupid, Tom Herriot,' she said, sniffing back the last of the tears.

'Well, if it's not me, what is it?' he asked, looking up at her, his face puzzled.

Kate sighed, but knew she had to tell him everything. 'Last night?'

He nodded.

'I lied to you, Tom. I didn't have a headache. I went to meet someone.'

It only took two or three minutes to tell him what had happened. So few words to try and justify the deep, black misery that had engulfed her since last night.

'I just feel so hurt,' she ended lamely. 'So hurt.' Fresh tears glistened in her eyes. 'How could she?'

'I thought you had decided not to try and trace your family. Why didn't you tell me what you were going to do, Kate? I could have come with you.'

She shook her head miserably. 'I thought it was something I should do on my own.'

'Why?' His voice was tight with bewilderment.

'You don't understand, Tom!' she cried. 'It was meeting your mother. She . . . she's . . .'

'Has mother upset you?' he asked sharply.

'No! Of course not, Tom. She's wonderful,' she said wistfully.

'Ah . . .' Now he was beginning to understand and his heart ached for her.

'I wanted to surprise you . . . to be able to introduce you to *my* mother . . . to have a proper wedding . . . a proper family . . .'

'You *will* have a proper family, Kate. You and me, we'll make one of our own,' he promised her.

Silently he pulled her close to him, resting his head on hers as it leaned against his chest. They sat like this, she comforted just to be close to him, until a sudden thumping of feet on the stairs caused them to jerk apart. a conspicuous space between them as the first of the assistants came upstairs for their mid-morning cup of tea.

'Best get back downstairs,' he whispered. 'We'll talk about it some more tonight.'

She nodded and they walked out together, very conscious of the sudden silence and of several pairs of eyes on their backs.

'Well,' Tom said, bringing the ghost of a smile to her pale face. 'That'll give them all something to talk about.'

'I've been thinking,' Tom said as they sat together in his mother's front room that evening, a privacy allowed to them now that their relationship was official. 'Why don't you write to your mother?'

'What good would that do?' she asked despondently. 'She's made her views pretty plain.'

'Aye,' Tom agreed. 'But it's easy for her to say she doesn't want to meet you when she's had no real contact with you, isn't it? If you were to write to her, tell her a little bit about yourself, give her your address . . . well, maybe she'd have to think again.'

'I don't know. I suggested that to my uncle but he doesn't think it's a very good idea.'

'You've nothing to lose, Kate. And I don't believe she isn't curious about you. Your uncle's likely right. She'll be worried about her husband finding out. If you were to make it clear that you didn't want to cause her any trouble, that you just want to meet her – '

'But what if he sees the letter? Anyway, I don't know her address.'

'I hadn't thought of that. But her husband's an MP, isn't he?'

'So?'

'So he must spend most of his time in London. Chances are

he won't even know she got a letter if we make sure it gets there mid-week.'

'I suppose so, but we still don't know where she lives.'

'He's an MP, Kate,' Tom said impatiently. 'It'll be easy to find out where they live. I'll ask Mother. Some of her friends will know. They all vote Tory.'

Before she had the chance to stop him, he was on his feet and out of the room. Five minutes later he was back, a triumphant grin on his face. 'Easy,' he laughed.

'You know where she lives?' she asked eagerly, a bubble of excitement back in her chest.

'Well, not exactly. But Mother knows someone who does.'

At midnight, when Mrs Traynor made the first of her customary three nightly visits to the bathroom, she was surprised to see light still filtering out from under Kate's door.

'Goodnight, lass,' she called as she recrossed the landing, wrapped in a long nightdress and a threadbare dressing-gown which had belonged to her late husband. 'Don't be staying up too long, mind, or you'll be o'er tired in the morning.'

'I won't,' Kate called back. 'Goodnight, Mrs Traynor.'

Frowning with concentration, Kate returned to the letter which had demanded her full attention for the last hour and a half. The crumpled sheets of paper which littered her bedspread bore witness to the difficulty of her task, but at last she felt that she had done the best she could. Folding the two sheets carefully, she inserted them in an envelope then slipped it in her bag where it would wait for the address which Tom's mother would supply.

Then she slipped off the cardigan which had kept her shoulders warm and tucked her feet under the covers. Within five minutes she was sound asleep.

★

'Letters!' Ellen slithered down the last stair and made her lolloping way across the hallway, where she swooped gleefully on the letters which had plopped on to the mat as she came downstairs. She returned, waving them triumphantly at Meggie.

'Thank you.' Meggie laughed with her daughter, then scooped her up and bore her off to the kitchen for breakfast, pausing only to prop the mail on the sitting-room mantelpiece.

It was evening before she returned to the room, the front of her dress still damp from bathing Ellen. She sank into a chair and closed her eyes for a few moments, content just to savour the peace and quiet.

Her day, as always, had been busy. Although she had Jessica to help with Ellen, Meggie liked to spend as much time as possible with her daughter and it was largely through her efforts that Ellen was progressing beyond everything predicted for her at birth. She would never be normal, would always need help and support, but most importantly of all was obviously a happy and contented little girl. But in between caring for her daughter, running the shops and playing her part as an MP's wife, Meggie had few minutes to call her own.

As she opened her eyes now she was aware of the letters on the mantelpiece which seemed to stare down at her reproachfully. They would, she knew, be for Oliver, mostly from constituents writing to canvas his help or support on some matter or another and it fell to her to reply to them on his behalf, a task which would take at least two more precious hours from her.

She would resent this chore less if Oliver showed any sign of appreciation, but they barely communicated these days, living almost completely separate lives, he for the most part in London, she in Inverannan. To the outside world they seemed a contentedly married couple; only those people close to them knew what a sham their marriage was. It was a pretence they had entered into from mutual necessity, he in order to protect his career, she to guard her reputation. But it was a situation that Meggie was finding increasingly unbearable and if it weren't for the unwavering support of her friends and the innocent love of her daughter, she sometimes thought she would have cracked under the strain.

Sighing, she settled herself at the small writing desk and slit the first letter open. If she was diligent she should get through most of these before Robbie arrived. Thinking of him brought a dreamy smile to her face. It was uncanny, the way he had seemed to know that she and Oliver had reached some sort of turning-point in their marriage. He had turned up on her doorstep, on the very night that she had returned, distraught, from London and they had sat up talking long into the night. It was as it had always been with him, as though they had known each other all their lives. Now he knew everything about her, more even than Oliver knew, and she felt comforted to realise that he thought no less of her for it, to understand that she had his unqualified support. Though they were at their most relaxed in each other's company there was still the strange contradiction of electric tension between them; the unspoken acknowledgement of the dangerous spark which, if ignited, would light a fire which would be impossible to control. She treasured those evenings when he arrived to spend an hour or two with her before kissing her chastely on the cheek and going off to his own home and family.

Still smiling, she scanned the first letter, a plea for support from a voter who was embroiled in a dispute with a neighbour. Meggie penned a tactful reply and turned to the next missive, the smile turning to a frown of concentration as she tried to get the task completed before Robbie's arrival.

Just under two hours later she had only one letter left. Not even bothering to look at the outside of the envelope, she tore it open and began to read. Anyone watching her would have

344

seen the quick flush, followed by an equally dramatic draining of colour from her face. For several minutes she sat as if frozen, though her whole body throbbed to the wild beating of her heart. When the doorbell rang she failed to hear it, nor did she register Jessica's rapid footsteps as she ran downstairs from her room. The door behind her opened and still Meggie sat staring blindly at the piece of paper in her hand.

Jessica smiled at Robbie as she ushered him into the sitting-room, then she quickly closed the door on him and hurried back to her own room. She lived at close enough quarters with the Laings to know that they could barely tolerate being in the same room together. Despite the thick walls she had overheard enough to know just what, or rather who it was that occupied Mr Oliver Laing's time and attention in London. She knew too that there was no serious impropriety in Mrs Laing's relationship with the other Mr Laing, but a body would need to be blind and insensitive not to realise how they felt about each other. And good luck to them too. In Jessica's view a lady as kind and generous as Mrs Laing deserved a little happiness in her life and as far as she could see there was no hope of that with her husband.

'Still busy, Meggie?' Robbie came to stand behind her, expecting her usual smile of welcome and was disappointed when she didn't even turn round. 'Meggie?' He placed a gentle hand on her shoulder.

Meggie jumped violently and the sheet of paper she had been holding fluttered down to the desktop. She was facing him now and he was shocked by her pallor as she stared up at him, her eyes wide, her mouth slightly open.

'Meggie! What on earth's the matter? You look as if you've seen a ghost.'

She shook her head slightly, as if trying to jolt herself back to life, but though she tried to speak, words simply would not come.

Robbie took her hands and gently pulled her to her feet. 'But you're frozen!' he exclaimed, feeling her hands in his like ice. 'Are you ill, Meggie? Look, come and sit by the fire and get warm.' He led her, unprotesting, to the fireside and settled her in a chair, then hurried to the tray of drinks on the sideboard and poured her a small measure of brandy. 'Here, drink this then get yourself off to bed. If you're no better in the morning I'll ask the doctor to call round.' He clasped her hands around the glass and after a moment or two she sipped at the tawny liquid, coughing slightly as it caught the back of her throat.

He watched while she drank, then put a hand to her forehead, testing her temperature as he might have done for his children. 'At least you don't feel feverish.'

'I'm not ill, Robbie.' At last she found her voice.

He frowned, then pulled a chair up close to hers. 'Then what is it, Meggie? You look dreadful. Something's obviously upset you.'

She shivered, then sipped again at the brandy, which was already having its effect. 'I've had a letter.'

Judging from her appearance, it could only have contained bad news. 'Oliver?' he asked, jumping to the most obvious conclusion.

She shook her head. 'No.' She took a deep breath. 'It was from my daughter.'

Now it was his turn to look blank. 'Your daughter?' he repeated. 'Ellen?'

'The daughter I gave away,' she whispered.

He was beginning to understand. The muttered profanity was an indication of his own shock. 'After all these years?'

Again she nodded.

Robbie was at a loss to know what to say, unable to decide whether her traumatised reaction was one of joy or despair. 'What does she say?' he asked.

'She wants to meet me.' She spoke as if in a half trance, her eyes unfocused.

'And is that what you want, Meggie?'

Abruptly she was back with him, her eyes searching for his, desperately looking for reassurance and understanding. 'I don't know, Robbie. I just don't know.'

Sal, in whom Meggie also confided, had very definite views. 'She's your daughter, Meggie. Surely you want to meet her?'

'Yes! Of course I do, Sal.' Now that she had recovered from the initial shock, Meggie's own feelings were equally strong. 'But what about Oliver?'

Sally pulled a face. 'What about Oliver? He never considers *your* feelings. In any case, Meggie, it's not as if he doesn't know you had a child.'

'But he doesn't know who her father was.'

The two friends stared at each other as the true import of the situation came home to them. 'Perhaps she won't even ask about her father.'

'Of course she will. If she's taken the trouble to find me after all this time it's because she wants to know about her parents. In her place, wouldn't you want to know?'

'Aye,' Sally admitted. 'But that doesn't mean Oliver has to find out.'

They sat, each deep in thought. It was Meggie who finally broke the silence. 'It's strange,' she mused. 'But in my mind she has always been a baby. Just the way she was when she was new-born. I've never forgotten her, Sal. Often when I look at Ellen I think about the daughter I gave away.'

Sally smiled back at her. 'You will never rest now, Meggie. Not until you've met her, seen what sort of a person she's grown into.'

'I know,' Meggie replied thoughtfully.

347

Meggie arrived at Matty's flat just as he was closing the shop for the day.

'Didn't expect to see you down here tonight,' he said, locking the door behind her and yanking down the blind.

'Have you got time to talk to me, Matty?' she asked.

He shrugged. 'I've always got time for you, Meggie. Why? Has something happened?' Now he came to look at her closely he realised that she was pale, her eyes ringed with dark shadows. 'Have you and Oliver been arguing again?'

'No.' Her answer was abrupt and Matty felt a moment of panic as he began to suspect the cause of her distress. He instantly jumped to the wrong conclusion. If Kate had somehow made contact with Meggie he could be in serious trouble. He would have to think of some plausible way of explaining why he had not told his sister about his meetings with Kate, and quickly.

'Meggie, look, don't get upset, I can explain – '

She interrupted him. 'Can we go upstairs, Matty? Something's happened and I need your advice, but I don't want to talk about it down here and to tell the truth I could use a drink.'

He let out a whistling breath of relief, realising that he had very nearly betrayed himself unnecessarily. Meggie was upset, that was obvious, but there was nothing in her manner to suggest that she was angry with him. 'Sure, come on up.'

'Read that.' She handed an envelope to him as he gave her a small measure of neat whisky, then settled herself in one of his shabby easy chairs while he read through the two-page letter.

'Well, well. There's a turn up for the books,' he said, not meeting his sister's eyes.

Meggie was too preoccupied to notice the lack of surprise with which Matty absorbed the letter's contents.

'I have decided to meet her, Matty. I want to know what she's like.' Meggie's voice had a ring of excitement to it now. 'I'll just need to be very careful and make quite sure Oliver doesn't find out, at least not to start with.' But she couldn't tell her brother why she was so frightened. Terribly mistaken, she thought she had succeeded in keeping the name of her first child's father a secret from her brother.

'Aye,' Matty agreed readily. 'That could cause a whole lot of trouble.' She looked at him sharply, wondering just how much he did know, but his next words reassured her. 'No man likes to be reminded that his wife has had an illegitimate bairn to another man. Especially a man in Oliver's position.'

'I might have to tell him, Matty. If things work out well with Kate.'

Matty handed back the letter, immensely relieved that Kate had made no mention of her abortive attempts to arrange a meeting with her mother through him. Little bitch, going behind his back as if she didn't trust him. She would need to be taught a lesson she wouldn't forget in a hurry. 'Be careful, Meggie,' he warned. 'You don't know anything about her.'

'She's my daughter, Matty.'

'So she is, but you've not had the raising of her. For all you know she could hate you for abandoning her.'

This possibility had already occurred to Meggie, but she, like Robbie and Sally, believed it unlikely. There had certainly been no hint of animosity in the girl's letter, which had been no more than a brief description of her life, along with the simple request for a meeting. 'I don't think so, Matty. Why are you being so negative? All she wants is to meet her real mother. Surely she has the right to ask that much of me?'

He sighed heavily. 'Och, Meggie, I'm sorry, but I'm just trying to watch out for you. You're too involved to see the trouble this could cause. I daresay she's a decent enough lass, but we don't *know* that for sure. For all you know she might want something from you. After all, you and Oliver are well known in this town. Everyone knows you've got a bob or two. Maybe she thinks you'll give her some money. Or maybe she's got her eye on the business.'

'Matty!' Meggie was horrified.

'Like I say. You don't know. All I want is for you to be careful. I don't want you to get hurt, Meggie.' He looked into her eyes, giving an impression of deep sincerity.

She smiled at him. 'Thanks, Matty. I understand what you mean, but nothing you can say will stop me meeting her now.'

He sighed. 'All right. But don't do anything rash. And don't meet her at the house.'

'Where then?'

'I'll tell you what we'll do!' he exclaimed as a new plan began to form in his twisted mind. 'Her address is on that letter. I'll nip down there after work. Have a word with – '

'I'll come too,' she interrupted him eagerly.

'No. Listen to me, Meggie. I'll go down there after work, introduce myself, have a wee chat. Then I'll arrange for her to come up to the shop one night. How about that?'

Now that Meggie thought about it, his idea made sense. She would feel better knowing Matty was on hand for this first meeting. 'All right,' she agreed. 'But go now please, Matty. Ask her to come here tomorrow.'

Standing up to put the kettle on, Matty couldn't hide the smirk of victory which twisted his lips. What might have been a very nasty situation could still turn out well after all.

TWENTY-SEVEN

Matty walked quickly, eager to put the final touches to his plan. Reaching the street where Kate lodged, he counted along the houses until he reached Mrs Traynor's freshly scrubbed doorstep. He paused for a moment and pulled his coat collar higher round his neck, thankful for the chill weather which made his heavy coat and scarf seem a matter of common sense rather than the disguise they really were. He looked around with the furtive glance of the criminal. He was not unknown in these parts and he wanted no one to recognise him and go tittle-tattling about him to his niece. For the moment it was vital that she trusted him.

A sharp knock on the door brought instant sounds of movement from within.

'Yes?' Mrs Traynor eyed him without pleasure, thinking he looked shifty.

'Mrs Traynor?' he asked, briefly doffing his hat, trying to impress her.

'I am,' she replied. An instinctively good judge of character, there was something about this man she distrusted.

'I've come to have a wee word with Kate,' he said, smiling determinedly despite the sour expression on her face.

'She's not in.'

'Oh.' He pretended confusion, though he had deliberately planned to arrive while Kate was safely at work. 'I've a message for her. Maybe I could just come in for a wee minute?'

'Whatever it is you have to say, I'll hear it just as well on my 'doorstep,' she retorted, shoving the door forward against his encroaching foot.

'Well . . . it's private you see.' And the longer he stood here the greater the chance of someone seeing and recognising him.

'Then you'd best come back.'

'Maybe I could wait?' he suggested

'The street's a public highway. I can't stop you waiting there.'

'Will she be long?'

Mrs Traynor's patience evaporated. 'And what's it to you?' she demanded. 'If you want to speak to Kate then come back the morn's night, after seven.'

Matty, seething inside, managed to keep up the pretence and shook his head sadly. 'It'll not keep. Maybe you could tell her her uncle Matty called?' He was amused to see the change in her expression and prepared to step inside the house.

'Her uncle Matty?' Mrs Traynor's gaped her astonishment, but Matty would have been far from flattered had he been able to read her thoughts. Kate had confided in her, of course, but to hear the lassie talk you'd have thought her uncle was a well set-up, smart gent, what with him being brother-in-law to an MP. Fifty years of living in Inverannan's poorest area had given Mrs Traynor an unerring instinct for good and bad. And unless her powers were finally failing this young man fell soundly into the latter category. You only had to look into those hooded eyes to see that he was hiding something. Uncle or not, nothing would induce her to invite him into her home. 'I'll tell her you called.'

Matty knew he had stood on her doorstep for longer than was prudent and admitted defeat. It was a pity, he thought angrily, that he had lost contact with so many of his old mates or he might have arranged for this miserable old crone to be taught a lesson. Few people insulted Matty McPherson and got away with it. 'Perhaps you could give her a message,' he suggested, forcing his face into a wooden approximation of a charming smile which simply reinforced Mrs Traynor's opinion of him.

'Well? Get on with it,' she snapped. 'The longer you stand there the more cold air's coming into my house.'

Matty abandoned all attempt at civility. 'Just tell her to come to the shop. I've some news for her.'

'Right.'

The door closed with a sharp bang. Matty kicked out at it in temper, forgetting he had his best shoes on instead of his usual workboots. He hobbled off up the street on bruised toes.

'Not what I expected, your uncle Matty,' Mrs Traynor said once she had delivered his message.

Kate, her heart full of joyful expectation again, was too happy to hear the implied criticism. 'He's been wonderful,' she said, turning to beam at Tom, who had seen her home after an evening with his parents, going over the plans for the wedding. 'Do you think she's changed her mind?'

'Well, I wouldn't get too excited about it yet,' he cautioned. 'But there must be some good reason for him asking you to go up there tomorrow.'

'Yes, young man, and there's an even better reason for you taking yourself off home. It's after eleven o'clock and high time all decent folk were in their beds.' Mrs Traynor took the sting out of her words by smiling, but then added, 'Five minutes, Kate,' as she started up the stairs. 'Goodnight then.'

'Goodnight,' they replied in unison, grinning at one another. They waited until they heard the click of her bedroom door before falling into each others' arms.

Exactly seven minutes later, Mrs Traynor heard the front door close and Tom's car splutter into life.

What it was to be young and in love, she thought, smiling nostalgically as she recalled her own mother saying much the same things to her when she had been winching. And now her husband was dead and buried and she was left on her own. Aye, she thought, settling into bed, it was good to have young 'uns around the house again. She'd grown fond of Kate and was truly happy that she had found herself a decent young man who obviously thought the world of her. But she would miss her when she got married. Oh, how she would miss her . . .

And she drifted off to sleep.

'I'll wait here,' Tom said, drawing the car into the kerb and switching off the engine.

'No! Come in with me,' Kate insisted. 'I'd like you to meet my uncle Matty.' She said it with relish, enjoying the novelty of having a real uncle, someone with whom she had a genuine blood tie.

'All right,' Tom agreed eagerly. He was anxious to meet Kate's new relation, especially after Mrs Traynor's barely concealed antipathy.

Hand in hand, they walked to the shop door and finding it open, went inside.

'Kate!' Matty hurried from behind the counter, beaming at her.

'Uncle Matty, this is Tom. Tom this is my uncle Matty.' She introduced them proudly.

Matty slid his eyes over the other man and quickly looked away, hiding his irritation under lowered lids. On her own, Kate would have been easy to deal with, but this young man was an unknown factor, a complication he hadn't foreseen. He would have to be careful.

Tom, aware of Matty's hostile appraisal, kept his face carefully inscrutable and made no comment whatsoever.

'Well then, let me lock up and we'll go on upstairs.' Matty busied himself with the locks, then ushered them behind the counter, through the store room and up the steep stairway which led to his flat.

Tom brought up the rear, surprised to see how dingy the rooms were. What sort of person would live in such a dreary place as this, he wondered. Not like a real home at all, he thought, taking in the worn settee, the threadbare patch of carpet and faded, old-fashioned wallpaper. Even a fresh coat of paint would have helped. It couldn't be that Kate's uncle couldn't afford to smarten it up a bit. He watched Matty more closely, feeling increasingly that there was something odd about this man who steadfastly avoided making eye-contact.

Matty hastily gathered up dirty cups and plates from the floor, cleared newspapers off the chairs and invited them to sit.

Kate perched on the very edge of the chair, clearly nervous. Tom sat back, crossing his long legs, then reached over and took Kate's hand, giving it a light squeeze of support.

Matty watched, the expression on his face dangerously close to a sneer, which rapidly changed to a smile when he realised Tom was watching him. 'You got my message then?' he enquired, remaining standing.

'Yes. Thanks.' She waited in vain for him to go on. There was a moment or two of awkward silence before she asked, 'Have you got some news for me, Uncle Matty?'

He looked at her, his face grim. 'I've been to see Meggie.'

Kate's face broke into a huge smile. 'She's going to meet me! I knew she would.' She twisted round to face Tom, 'I knew that could be the only reason for Uncle Matty to ask me to come up here again.'

But there was no answering smile from Tom. In fact he didn't even meet her shining eyes, so intent was he on watching Matty. His hand on Kate's tightened fractionally. 'Let's hear what your uncle has to say, Kate.'

The understated warning was enough to freeze the smile on her face. Slowly she turned back to Matty. 'She has changed her mind, hasn't she? She will meet me now, won't she?' But it sounded more like a plea than a question.

Matty's instinctive reaction to her tortured questions was to smile. His sadistic, twisted mind held no room for compassion. In fact, he was enjoying her distress. It took every ounce of concentration to maintain the façade of a concerned and caring uncle. 'No, Kate. My sister has not changed her mind, and is never likely to.' He sighed heavily. 'Och, I wish I didn't have to tell you this, but, well I thought it best to be honest with you. It wouldn't have been fair to say nothing and have you living in hope of meeting her one day.'

'Then what has happened? I don't understand.'

Matty sighed again, then sat abruptly in a chair and ran his fingers through his hair, seeming agitated and upset. 'I feel right bad about this, lass. If I had just left things as they were for a wee while – '

Sensing Kate's increasing distress, Tom intervened. 'Perhaps you could just tell Kate the facts?' he suggested coldly.

Still avoiding the other man's eyes, Matty made a show of pulling himself together. 'Aye,' he agreed. 'You're right, Tom. Best just to say it straight out, eh?'

Tom kept hard, watchful eyes on Matty, wanting to give this man a piece of his mind for putting Kate through such an ordeal. Whatever it was he was trying to say was obviously going to hurt Kate and her uncle was making it worse with every passing second.

Tom's impatience communicated itself to Matty, who saw the way the other man was now sitting on the edge of his seat, as if in another moment he would be at his throat. 'Your mother,' Matty said, emphasising the word slightly, 'will never agree to meet you. In fact,' – here he paused and seemed to search for words – 'in fact she has asked me to tell you to stay away. She doesn't want you to try and make contact with her ever again.'

Kate gasped. 'Why? I don't want to make trouble for her. Doesn't she understand that? Didn't you tell her?'

'Aye, of course I did. And that's where I went wrong. Och, Kate, lass, I feel I've let you down.'

'No,' she murmured, feeling obliged to respond to the sorry way he was looking at her.

'Aye, I have. I went up to talk to her about you again, see. I thought she was being stupid, selfish really. I didn't see what harm it would do for the two of you to meet. I told her what a braw lassie you were, said she could be proud of you. I suppose I said too much, but well . . . you're my niece after all, aren't you? I felt I had the right to speak out. Och, but she was angry. I've never seen her like that, Kate. Never in all my life have I seen her like that.' He shook his head and subsided into silence.

Kate was determined not to make a fool of herself this time and looked up bravely. 'Thank you for trying, Uncle Matty.' She managed to smile and added, 'At least I've got you, so it's not all bad, is it?'

To her astonishment Matty shook his head. 'No, lass. She made me promise not to see you again and I had to agree.'

'But that's not fair!' she protested, angry now.

'Try to understand, Kate. Meggie and me, we're very close. She was like a mother to me when we were weans and now, well, now I try to watch out for her. I couldn't let her down now, Kate.'

Kate stormed to her feet and Tom rose with her, half frightened of what she might do next. 'So that's it, is it?' she demanded. 'You don't want anything more to do with me? You and my mother . . . *your sister* . . . are going to pretend I don't exist.'

'Come on, Kate. We don't need to stay here a minute longer.' Tom tried to draw her away. For a moment she resisted, then allowed him to pull her towards the door, his arm protectively round her shoulders.

Kate glared at Matty for a moment longer, but as she turned

to leave the room he said, 'She gave me something to give to you.'

She stopped at once and very slowly turned to face him. Tom let go of her and allowed her to walk towards her uncle's outstretched hand. 'She sent me something?' A memento, some small sign – despite all he had said – of hope for the future?

Matty's closed hand drew her on and he waited until she was very close to him before he uncurled his fingers.

Kate stared, appalled by what she saw. She threw one desperate glance over her shoulder to Tom who crossed the room quickly.

'Money?' he said, shock as clear in his voice as it was in Kate's face.

'She sent me money?' Kate almost screamed the words.

'Aye,' Matty said, thrusting a roll of banknotes at her. 'But only if you agree to stay away from her.'

Kate reached out and took the notes from his hand, counted them, then waved them furiously under her uncle's nose. 'Fifty pounds? Fifty pounds! That's what I'm worth, is it? Fifty lousy pounds.' She screwed the notes up, flung them at his feet and stormed to the door. 'Well, you can keep your money. I don't want it. Not even if you gave me a *million* pounds. You don't need to pay me to stay away from you. I never want to see you again. And you can tell that to my mother too. I'm *glad* she gave me away.'

With that she ran out of the room. Tom lingered only long enough to offer one insult. 'You bastard,' he snarled. 'You fucking bastard.'

Matty met Tom's blazing eyes with his own fathomless ones, his mouth lifting in a smile. 'You got that wrong,' he sneered. 'She's the bastard, not me. And as for fucking . . . well, I guess you know more about the sort of girl she is than I do.'

Tom launched himself across the room, but before he had taken more than two paces Matty had armed himself with the poker and stood brandishing it in front of him, willing Tom on.

'Tom!' From the bottom of the stairs, Kate yelled at him.

He hesitated. He was no coward but knew he would stand no chance against a stockily built man wielding a heavy weapon and what's more, Kate needed him. Abruptly he turned and ran down the stairs to where she waited. Matty's mocking laughter floated after him.

'What were you doing?' she demanded angrily.

'Nothing,' he snapped.

'Just take me home,' she said. 'Please, take me home.'

Still shaking with anger, he hugged her briefly and led her out of the back door, through the yard and back to the relative comfort of the car.

Upstairs Matty dropped the poker and fell to his knees, gathering up the scattered pound notes. Smiling to himself he shrugged his jacket on, shoving the money into his inside pocket where it joined the other hundred and fifty pounds he had taken from the till. Enough, he thought, letting himself out and heading in the direction of the Glen Tavern, to keep him in beer and cigarettes for quite a while.

'Come away in out of the cold, Matty.' Meggie ushered her brother into her house, pecked him quickly on the cheek and led him to her cosy sitting-room.

'Where's Ellen?' he asked, deliberately forestalling her own anxious questions.

'In bed!' Meggie snapped but then, seeing his genuine disappointment, added, 'But I've only just taken her up. I don't think she'll be asleep yet.'

Matty took his coat off and dumped it untidily on the nearest chair, then hurried off upstairs. Meggie picked it up and took it out to the hall stand, smiling indulgently as she heard her daughter's squeals of delight. Her own impatience to hear

Matty's news would have to be contained for a little longer, but she couldn't really grudge either of them these few minutes of enjoyment. It was Matty's loving, patient and infinitely gentle attitude to Ellen that had, more than anything else, influenced Meggie's decision to bring him into the business with her. Ellen had highlighted an aspect of Matty's character which Meggie believed to be totally natural: unassailable proof that the selfish, corrupt and violent young man had finally been replaced by someone who deserved both love and trust.

Upstairs, Matty tickled his little niece's ribs, reducing her to helpless giggles, then picked her up and hugged her close, feeling a fierce, possessive love for her. He cradled her until she was calm again and sleep began to claim her. Watching her, he knew that if anyone ever harmed her, he would kill them with his own bare hands. One day, he thought, kissing her face and laying her back in bed, it would be just her and him. The way it should have been with Meggie, but better, because Ellen would know nothing of the past. Ellen would be his in a way that his strong-willed sister would never be. And unlike Meggie, Ellen, who would never do more than babble like a three-year-old, could never betray him.

While the little girl smiled sleepily up at him with drowsy, trusting eyes, Matty stroked her hair, then straightened her nightclothes, which had rumpled up, exposing pink, flawless skin to the evening air. His broad fingers were surprisingly gentle as he pulled her vest down. But the tender scene was desecrated as Matty's hand settled on the plump mound of warm flesh at the top of her chubby legs, his fingers exploring her innocence in an unspeakably vile act of perversion. After a moment he moved his hand away and anchored the vest firmly under the elasticated top of her trouser bottoms before tucking the covers in around her. Her thumb firmly in her little mouth, her index finger curled round her nose, her lashes curling on her cheeks, Ellen murmured sleepily, her trust intact. Matty kissed her again and tiptoed from the room.

Meggie, her nerves stretched to breaking point, had spent the last fifteen minutes pacing the floor in an agony of impatience, completely unaware of the gross betrayal that had taken place in her daughter's bedroom. 'You'll have got her so excited that she won't be able to sleep,' she accused her brother when he finally joined her in the sitting-room.

'She's fine,' he assured her. Grinning widely, he settled himself in the most comfortable armchair and picked up the paper, seemingly in no hurry to end her suspense. She almost screamed at him, then realised, just in time, that he was teasing her.

'You're horrible, Matty,' she hissed, her aggravation only partly feigned. 'You know fine that I've been waiting all day to know what happened.'

Matty's cheerful expression disappeared instantly.

'Well?' she demanded.

He sighed heavily and shifted in his seat, carefully avoiding meeting her eyes. 'I went to see Kate,' he prevaricated. 'Like we agreed.'

'And?' She crouched down in front of him, eager not to miss a single thing.

He shook his head and she wanted to yell, to hit him, to shake the words from him.

'Matty!'

'I wish it wasn't me who had to tell you this.' He kept his head lowered.

Meggie knew she was breathing too fast, felt her head start to spin with the certain knowledge of impending disaster. She stood up and walked over to the window, then back again in a desperate attempt to relieve the unbearable tension. 'Just tell me what she said, Matty.'

'Don't say I didn't warn you.'

Meggie felt the last ounce of hope drain from her body, and all her energy with it. 'Tell me,' she begged, her voice a strangled whisper.

Matty, glancing up to better appreciate the full effect of her distress, felt not one bit of sympathy for his sister's anguish. At last, here was his chance to even the score, to watch her suffer, just as he had suffered in the past, and he was relishing every moment. The time wasn't far away now when he would finish her off altogether. Fate itself was conspiring to help him. Kate, Meggie's own daughter, was giving him the opportunity he had been waiting for. When the scandal broke, when the newspapers began to run stories which exposed Meggie's past, destroying her own reputation and ending her husband's career, who would be surprised if she was unable to face the scorn of her home town? Who would question a verdict of suicide in the face of such disgrace, such appalling shame? Then he would be the one with everything and she . . . she would have nothing, would be nothing. Half-formed plans raced through Matty's excited brain, but nothing of this showed in his sombre expression as he spoke. 'It's just what I was afraid of,' he told her, getting up and putting a treacherous hand on her shoulder. 'She's just out for all she can get. Aye, she's a sly one right enough.'

'But she wrote to say she wanted to meet me! I don't understand!'

'She's bitter, Meggie. Like she said in her letter, she went to live with farming folk and och . . . I don't know, maybe they turned her against you, but the truth is, she hates you. She didn't say what happened exactly, but they threw her out. I think there was a lad involved somewhere. But . . . well, nobody throws a young lassie out on the street unless they've good cause, do they?'

'You mean she's nowhere to live?' Meggie's easy sympathy

was aroused, and Matty realised he was in danger of overplaying his hand.

'She found herself lodgings – right rough they are too, but she's happy enough there. The thing is, Meggie, she knows who you are and she reckons she's on to a good thing.'

'But if she needs help, Matty . . .'

'Now just you listen to me, Meggie.' Matty was all masterful concern. 'She came looking for you deliberately, just to see if there was anything in it for her. She admitted it to me! Right brazen she is. And she struck lucky. She knows all about you, all about the shops, everything. She's not interested in *you*, Meggie. What she wants is your money.'

Meggie shook her head. 'I can't believe that. How could she have known?'

'She went to see old Carlyle. From the workhouse. Remember him?'

Meggie couldn't suppress a shiver as she nodded.

'A right evil bastard he was. He's working for the council now, in the records office. And he was only too happy to tell her all she wanted to know about you. The shops, Oliver, everything.'

'But she can only have gone to him to try and find out more about me. Isn't that what anyone in her position would do?'

'Aye,' he conceded. 'She wanted to find out about you, right enough. She wanted to find out how much you are worth – to find out how much she could milk you for.'

'Matty!' Meggie was appalled.

'It's the truth, and the sooner you start believing it, the better it will be for you, Meggie.'

'But why, Matty? If she had just come to see me I would have told her anything she wanted to know. If she had needed help, I'd have given it. You know that.'

Now Matty played his trump card. 'She's nothing but a dirty

little blackmailer, Meggie. She threatened to make a lot of trouble for you and Oliver. She wanted two hundred pounds to keep her mouth shut.'

Meggie gawped at him, hardly able to believe what she was hearing. 'She's trying to blackmail me? But why? Why does she want to hurt me? I only did what I thought was best for her.'

'You gave her away, Meggie. She'll never forgive you for that. And she meant what she said. It would be easy for her to make sure word got round that you had an illegitimate daughter. Especially in a wee town like this. You know how folk like a bit of gossip. Oliver's career would be ruined by any hint of scandal.'

For the second time that year, Meggie's past returned to threaten her future. With a choked cry she collapsed into the nearest chair and stared blankly at the fire.

'Never mind, Meggie. You're better off without her,' was Matty's heartless attempt at comfort.

'I still can't believe she would really take money from me.' Meggie was almost talking to herself. 'Maybe if I just met her – if I could only make her see that I did what I thought was best for her.'

'Too late,' he said with an air of finality.

'How can it possibly be too late?' she demanded. 'I'll write back . . . ask her to come and meet me somewhere. Perhaps she was hurt because you went, not me. I knew I should have met her myself.'

'I've given her the money.'

Meggie stared at him. 'You gave her two hundred pounds?'

He nodded.

'And she took it?'

'It's what she asked for, Meggie. It's what she demanded in exchange for keeping quiet. I had to give it to her, Meggie. It was the only way. She meant what she said. She would have gone to the papers. I had to protect you, Meggie.'

Meggie got up and walked back to the window, staring out over the dark garden, her back to him. When at last she turned round, her eyes were suspiciously bright. 'It doesn't make any sense,' she said. 'Even if she just wanted me to give her money, she must have been curious about me. Surely she would have wanted to meet me, just once.'

'I'm sorry, Meggie, but I don't think so. I offered to bring her to meet you but she wouldn't come.'

Meggie sighed.

'And I'm glad she wouldn't!' Matty asserted loudly, making Meggie look up in alarm. He put his hands on her shoulders, and looked into her eyes as he said. 'Meggie, I've not been able to do much to repay you for everything you've done for me, but at least I was able to stop you getting too badly hurt. I've taken care of her for you. I threatened her with the police; she'll be too scared to try any more of her tricks. She's leaving Strathannan and we'll never hear from her again. You've got to trust me, Meggie. It's for the best.'

She searched his eyes for a moment, then looked away, murmuring, 'I still wish I could have seen her, just once.' Then, glancing up at him again she asked, 'Is she pretty, Matty?'

He dropped his hands from her shoulders and moved away with a shrug. 'I suppose she would be if she made an effort to tidy herself up a bit. Bit common really.'

Meggie turned away and this time didn't look round until Matty, eager to get to the pub for a few celebratory pints, started to leave. He was almost at the door before she stopped him. 'Matty?'

'The money, Matty. Where did it come from? How did you pay her?'

'Och, that! I took it from the till.'

TWENTY-EIGHT

'Well, it doesn't make any sense to me,' Sal insisted. 'Why would she go to all the trouble of tracing you and then refuse to meet you?'

Meggie, her face bearing signs of strain, shrugged helplessly. 'That's what I said, but the truth is she doesn't want me, Sal. She wants my money.' And how it hurt to put that in words.

'I still don't understand.' Sally, who came from a large, poor but deeply loyal family simply couldn't accept what she had heard. 'It's not natural, Meggie. Something's not right.'

'It's clear enough to me.' Meggie was infinitely saddened and depressed by the whole thing.

'But think about it, Meggie!' Sally, worried about her friend's uncharacteristic behaviour, tried to shock her out of this apathetic acceptance of her daughter's cruel rejection. 'Put yourself in her place. Would you go to all the trouble of tracing the mother you had never known and then refuse to meet her? Of course you wouldn't!' she went on before Meggie had the chance to answer. 'Even if you had no intention of trying to build a relationship, you would still want to meet her. Even if it was just the once, just to see what she was like.'

'But she wasn't interested in me, all she wanted was money. And why should she want to meet me after what I did to her?'

'You did the very best you could for her, Meggie,' Sally said sternly. 'Anyway, she can't have had any way of knowing you had any money when she first started to look for you.'

'No,' Meggie agreed thoughtfully. 'I might have been living in a slum for all she knew.'

'Exactly!' Sally cried, feeling she was getting somewhere at last. 'So we know that, at least to start with, it was you she was looking for.'

'But how do we know that she wouldn't have tried to make contact if she'd discovered I was dirt poor?'

Sally could have screamed with frustration. Meggie seemed determined to believe that her daughter had no interest in her as a person, had simply seen her as an opportunity to get some easy money, that she had been prepared to inflict dreadful harm on Meggie and her family in order to get what she wanted.

'We know in here, Meggie!' She practically screamed the words, leaning forward and hitting her breastbone with her fist. 'In here! I think there's more to this than you've been told, and if you won't do anything about it, then I will.'

'There is nothing anyone can do, Sally. She took the money. That's proof enough for me.'

'Aye, or so Matty says,' Sally commented acidly. 'I think you should have another word with that brother of yours. I don't think he tried very hard to get Kate to meet you.' This was a very much diluted version of what Sally actually thought of Matty McPherson, but she knew from long experience that Meggie was deaf and blind where her brother was concerned. Even Sally had to admit that Matty was being careful these days. And she knew why, though it was doubtful that Meggie realised just how far Matty would go to protect his own interests. Matty would have seen Kate as a threat, just as he had seen Oliver as a threat all those years ago. And look what had happened there. Oliver's wooden leg was a permanent reminder of Matty's jealousy. 'Have you ever stopped to think that Matty didn't want you and Kate to meet? Perhaps he felt she was a threat to him.'

'That's typical of you, Sally Sandys,' Meggie rounded on her friend furiously. 'You have never liked Matty and you never will.'

'With good reasons!' Sally retorted. 'And you would do well to remember some of them, Margaret Laing.'

Meggie got up and started gathering the cups and saucers together, an obvious sign that Sally had, for once, outstayed her welcome.

Sally grabbed her coat and left the house without saying goodbye. There was anger in every movement as she stalked away up the drive, but it wasn't Meggie who was the target of her temper.

Tom Herriot brought his car to a smooth halt, relieved that the sturdy hedge which protected the garden from prying eyes would also hide his car from those inside the house. For a few moments he sat, going over in his mind all the things he wanted to say to the woman who lived here. The woman whose selfish and hurtful actions had turned his bubbly, happy fiancée into a sad, morose creature who could no longer find any pleasure in her wedding plans. Only last night Kate had shocked his own mother by declaring that she would get married in the little Netherton Kirk, a bleak, cold place. When asked why, she had repeated that a wedding was supposed to be the bride's big day, and as she had no family who cared about her, anything grander would be a waste of money. She added that instead of the usual reception, all she wanted was a meal for herself, Tom and Tom's parents at the City Hotel. Given the mood she had been in lately, Tom was relieved that she hadn't chosen to dine at the Glen Tavern.

His mother, who had nothing but sympathy for Kate's dreadful experience, had advised him to wait a little, to give her time to come to terms with the heartless rejection, but Tom, furiously angry with the Laings, had other ideas. If he could do nothing else for Kate, he could at least offer her the satisfaction of knowing that he had given her mother a piece of his mind.

Thinking back over recent events was enough to bring his anger to simmering point again. He got out of the car and strode purposefully up the drive, put a finger on the doorbell and left it there until he heard hurried footsteps in the hall.

'Do you mind!' Jessica regarded him with outrage.

'Are you Mrs Laing?' he demanded, too wound up to realise that this girl was far to young to be Kate's mother.

'No I am not. Who wants her?'

'Tom Herriot.'

She shut the door, leaving him fuming on the doorstep. His finger was poised over the bell again when the door opened once more. 'Mrs Laing is not very well. She's not seeing anyone today.'

'She'll see me,' he said, pushing his way inside.

Meggie, reading to Ellen, looked up in astonishment as a wild-eyed young man burst into her sitting-room.

Gently dislodging Ellen from her lap, she stood up. 'If it's my husband you're looking for I am afraid he won't be home until Friday night,' she told him, assuming he was some disgruntled voter looking for his MP.

'Mummy.' Ellen tugged at her skirt, impatient for her story to be continued.

'In a minute, Ellen.' Meggie smiled at her before turning frosty eyes on the intruder. 'Perhaps you could come back, Mr . . .?'

'My name is Herriot. Tom Herriot. I am Kate Brebner's fiancé.' He was pleased to see the rather haughty expression on her face disappear, to be replaced by one of shock.

'I can ring for the police, Mrs Laing,' offered Jessica from the doorway.

'No!' Meggie spoke sharply.

Ellen slipped from the settee and, understanding that her mother would not be finishing the story, offered the book to Tom, her eyes wide with childish appeal.

Meggie's instant, protective reaction was to draw the child away. Strangers were often repelled by Ellen, who despite her wonderful progress, was clearly not as other children. The little girl had often been confused and hurt by the reactions of adults who were unable to hide their disgust. But before she could reach her daughter, Tom had accepted the offered book. Crouching down so he was on a level with the child, he smiled at her and turned a few pages, pointing to the colourful pictures and reading a few lines to her.

Meggie did not interrupt, but beckoned to Jessica who gently took Ellen's hand, 'Say goodbye to the kind gentleman,' she instructed, drawing her charge firmly away.

Ellen's face broke in to a dimpled smile as Tom handed the book back and winked at her.

'Bye bye, Ellen,' he said.

'Bye bye. Bye bye. Bye bye,' she sang, waddling clumsily but happily alongside Jessica.

Tom and Meggie both watched as the child left the room. Tom, who had a cousin with similar afflictions, had reacted quite naturally to Meggie's daughter and, in so doing, had prevented his immediate ejection from the Laing household. But the look Meggie now aimed at him was full of dislike.

'So, you are Kate's fiancé?' she asked coldly.

'Yes.' His voice too was stiff with antipathy.

'I'm surprised you've got the cheek to show yourself at this house.' She spat the words at him, assuming they had been in this together. 'What does she want now?'

'The same as she wanted before,' he said, knowing that if he was going to get anywhere he would need to keep a careful hold on his temper. 'All she wants – '

'Oh, I know what she wants,' Meggie interrupted him heatedly. 'Well, you can tell her that she'll get nothing more from me. I am not afraid of her. And I won't give in to threats, do you hear me?' she roared at him. 'She can run with her tales to my husband. I don't care. He knows everything, so there is nothing she can do to hurt me.' And if she had dealt with this herself the first time round instead of leaving it to Matty, this young man would have known better than to come here today, trying to extract more money from her. 'It's blackmail, you know,' she yelled at his slack-jawed face. 'I could have the police on you for this. And that's exactly what I will do if you ever come near me again.' She ended triumphantly and waited for him to go. He had obviously been expecting her to be an easy target: he was totally stunned by her reaction. Well, she had shown him that Meggie Laing was nobody's fool.

Tom blinked in bewilderment. This wasn't at all how he had planned things. *He* should have been shouting at *her*, not the other way round. Something wasn't quite right here, but he was too shocked to know what it was. Belatedly he drew himself up for the attack. 'You could have the police on me? *You're* the one who should be locked up for the way you've behaved to Kate. You've ruined her life, made her miserable. Are you happy now?'

There was such disapproval in the young man's face that Meggie felt she had to defend herself. 'How dare you come here and judge me? I did what I thought was best for her and I'd swear to that on the Bible. Don't you think it hurt me too, to give away a baby? Believe me, you could never even begin to imagine how I felt.'

Again Tom had that sense of something out of line, of something not quite right. 'Then why did you try to pay her off?' he asked.

Meggie stared at him, her blood rushing round her body so fast she could hear it in her ears, felt her head would burst with anger. 'Pay her off? Is that what she told you?' But now she too felt they were missing something vital.

'How could you do it?' Tom asked. 'All she wanted was a hour of your time. But you couldn't even spare her that much.

It was easier to send her fifty pounds and tell her never to come back. Can you imagine how that made *her* feel?'

The rushing in Meggie's ears increased in volume until it was all she could hear. The room tilted dangerously and she staggered a little.

Tom rushed to her side and guided her to a chair. 'Can I get you anything?' he asked anxiously, feeling more bewildered by the second. This wasn't the reaction of the heartless woman Kate's uncle had described.

'No . . .' Meggie closed her eyes for a moment and forced her body into submission. In a moment her head began to clear and the room regained its normal stability. 'I'm sorry. I don't know what . . . it's the shock, I suppose.'

'Yes.' Tom, feeling totally useless, had spotted three decanters on a tray by the window and advanced on them eagerly. He identified the brandy and poured a generous measure into a whisky glass. 'I think this might help,' he said, offering it to her.

She accepted it gratefully. 'Perhaps you should have one for yourself,' she suggested, more herself now. 'I think we both need it.'

Gratefully he poured a more modest measure of whisky for himself and drank most of it in a quick gulp. 'Thank you,' he said stiffly.

Meggie was in charge now. Looking at this obviously confused young man and remembering his natural kindness with Ellen, she couldn't believe that he had been involved in blackmail. Perhaps she was being irrational, and certainly it couldn't be wise to allow him to remain alone with her, but now she had time to really look at him, she realised he was well mannered, smartly dressed and obviously educated. Above all, he was clearly as shocked and bewildered as she was herself. No, he didn't seem at all the type who would resort to blackmail. She felt a sudden wave of pity for him. If he was engaged to

Kate then it seemed she was using him in the worst possible way. Fleetingly she recalled Sally's warning about Matty, but instantly dismissed it, preferring to believe anything rather than face the possibility that Matty had betrayed her again.

'Perhaps you should tell me everything Kate has told you about me?' she suggested.

Tom nursed his warm glass, then tipped the rest of the whisky into his mouth before starting his story.

Meggie listened in growing dismay, feeling that the bottom was falling out of her world again. 'You think I offered her money to stay away?'

He nodded. 'I can see that Kate turning up must have been a terrible shock for you, but to offer her money! Can't you understand how much you hurt her?'

'Yes, I can see she would be hurt, but I'm sorry to have to tell you that she has not been honest with you. I didn't offer money to Kate – she demanded it from me.'

Tom eyed her angrily again. 'Are you accusing me of lying?' he demanded. 'You can't get out of it that way. I was there. I went to see your brother with Kate. I was there when he gave her the money. Fifty pounds! And you know as well as I do that she didn't take it. It's not your money that she wants.'

Meggie felt the room tilt in warning again and waited a second or two before replying. 'I listened to you, Tom. Will you now hear me out?'

He nodded.

She told him everything, noting his shock when she described her past. 'So you see, Tom, it was impossible for me to keep Kate. I did what I thought was best for her but it hurt me more than anyone will ever understand. When she wrote to me I was . . .' – she searched for a word to adequately describe her feelings, failed and whispered, 'overjoyed. I so much wanted to meet her. To have a second chance. Can't you see that I would never have asked her to stay away from me?

And, as for trying to buy her off with money – any amount of money . . .' She faltered and shook her head mutely as emotion prevented further speech.

'I'm sorry,' he began, knowing he was expected to say something but also unable to find suitable words.

'Please, Tom, go back and tell Kate that if she can forgive me for what's happened, I should like the chance to meet her more than anything in the world.'

She was so obviously sincere that Tom couldn't immediately reply. To cover his own emotional state he tipped the empty whisky glass to his lips and pretended to drain it. When he spoke his voice was unsteady. 'I know that Kate wants that with all her heart,' he told Meggie.

'I want you to go and see him, Robbie.' Less than five minutes after Tom had left her house, Meggie had summoned Robbie, turning instinctively to him for help. A second phone call had brought Sally and Ronnie, and all four were now in deep discussion.

'It will be a pleasure.' Robbie got to his feet, his grim face signalling his intent. 'I'll give the little bastard something to think about.'

'No,' Meggie cried. 'I don't want you using violence of any sort. Just tell him to get out of the shop, out of the flat and out of my life. He's got until next Friday. Tell him – ' she hesitated over the fateful words, but this time Matty had wounded her too deeply – 'tell him I never want to see him again. And this time I mean it.'

'Och, Meggie,' Sally hugged her distraught friend. 'I'm sorry. I really am.'

'I know, Sal. And I'm sorry for what I said to you the other night. I wish I'd listened to you.'

'That doesn't matter, Meggie. The important thing is to make things right between you and Kate.' Sally had never made any secret of her deep dislike of Meggie's brother, but even though she had been proved right she would have given much to have been wrong this time.

'Tom is going to talk to her and let me know what she says.'

'And in the meantime we have Matty to sort out,' Robbie reminded them. 'Best to get it over with before he has the chance to do any more damage.'

'Aye. I'm with you there.' Ronnie spoke for the first time. 'We'll go together.'

'I can do this on my own.'

'No, Robbie, Ronnie's right. Both of you go. It's safer that way.' It was as if years of blindness had fallen away, leaving her a clear sight of her brother for the first time. More than anyone else in that room, though they all knew what Matty had done to Oliver, Meggie understood that her brother was a murderously dangerous man. Her hands were wet with fear at the thought of what he might do to Robbie if he had been foolish enough to tackle him on his own and there was no doubt that Robbie, though never a violent man, was angry enough to relish the thought of tackling Matty single-handed.

Sally didn't miss the look that passed between Meggie and Robbie. It was blindingly obvious that they were in love. If they weren't careful Oliver would realise it too and then Meggie's life would be in an even greater mess than it was now. Or would it? Perhaps that would be the best thing for everyone: none of the three was happy the way things were. Her husband's voice recaptured her attention.

'Matty's a vicious thug, Robbie. I'm sure you can hold your own with the best of them but even I wouldn't take him on on my own. We all know what he can do, we've only got to think of what happened to Oliver. Unless you want to risk ending up like that, or worse, you'd best let me come with you.'

'Robbie, please,' Meggie pleaded. 'I know you only want to

375

help me but I'd never forgive myself if anything happened to you.' Again there was that revealing look between the two of them and this time Ronnie saw it too. 'Take Ronnie with you.'

Robbie shrugged. 'All right.'

'Meggie?' Sally asked. 'What will you tell Oliver?'

'The truth,' Meggie said.

'Good.' Sally hugged her friend tightly. 'And don't worry. Everything will work itself out, you'll see. Look, I'd better be getting home too. I've left my mum with the kids.'

Meggie nodded, though she would dearly have liked to have her friend's company until the men returned.

Seeing the tense expression on Meggie's face, Robbie put his arms around her, then, as if unaware of the others in the room, kissed her softly on the mouth. 'Try not to worry. We'll take care of it. I'll be back here as soon as I can.'

'All right.'

They left the house together and she followed them to the doorway, then stood watching as they walked away.

'Robbie,' she called after them, the urgency in her voice causing all three to stop and look at her. 'Don't hurt him,' she begged, her voice cracking on a sob. 'Please don't hurt him.'

Meggie and Robbie faced each other silently, ten yards between them, then almost imperceptibly he nodded, turned away and walked quickly to his car.

'Wait for me.' Sally caught up with the men.

'I'll drop you off first,' Ronnie said.

'Oh no you won't, Ronnie Sandys,' she insisted in the tone of voice which he knew better than to argue with. 'I'm coming with you.'

Matty was so absorbed in what he was doing that the sound of persistent hammering at the back door made him jump. Angry at the disturbance, he ignored it and went back to his task. He had never been any good at writing, and composing a suitable letter to the editor of the local paper had left him with a grinding headache. But at last he was satisfied with the result and impatient, now that he had dealt with Kate, to put the final stage of his plan into effect. In another two or three weeks Meggie's marriage would be over, Oliver's career would be in ruins and she would be the talk of the burgh, unable to show her face in public for fear of being recognised. And the best thing was, every word of what he had written was true, the facts checkable. No wonder she would feel unable to go on. The exact manner of her death was something he was mulling over. Pills, perhaps, or something more dramatic, like a deliberate crash in her car. He smiled, licked his lips in anticipation, then folded the paper and put it in an envelope, aware as he did so of the continued banging on his door, of raised voices outside.

Shoving the envelope into his jacket pocket, he went downstairs to investigate the row.

'Open up. I know you're in there!'

Matty recognised Ronnie Sandys's voice. He opened the door a crack and stumbled backwards as Ronnie threw all his weight against it. 'What do you want?' he demanded, recovering quickly.

'You, you little shit.' Ronnie had him by the throat and slammed him against the brick wall.

'Not here, Ronnie.' Strong arms hauled Ronnie back, turned Matty round and shoved him towards the stairs. Someone grabbed his arm and brought it painfully up across his back, forcing him up the stairs.

'Right!' Matty's arm was dropped and he was given a mighty push which sent him sprawling though his own front door, landing on his knees on the sitting-room carpet. 'Get up.'

Matty stood, his face a mask of dark defiance as he stared at his unwelcome guests. 'What the fuck do you want?' He spat the words.

'We want you out of here.' Robbie stood right in front of him.

'Yeah?' Matty sneered.

'Yes.' Robbie took a single step closer, the threat plain.

'You can't make me do anything.' Matty held his ground, but not for long. Robbie's hand grabbed the side of his collar, twisting it round his neck so he could hardly breathe.

'Don't be so sure,' Robbie rasped.

From behind her husband, Sally Sandys stepped forward. Matty, held immobile by Robbie, followed her with eyes that were protruding from his face. She stopped, a look of utter abhorrence on her face as her eyes raked him from the top of his sweating head to the tips of his scruffy boots. 'I always knew you were a little bastard, Matty. Just what Meggie ever did to deserve a brother like you, I don't know. She would have given her life for you. Did you know that?'

She stopped, waiting for an answer, and Robbie increased the pressure on Matty's shirt collar, forcing a strangled grunt.

'She never gave up on you, Matty. Even when everyone else was telling her what a little shit you were, she still believed in you. And look where it got her.' She stopped again, her face so full of hatred that Ronnie, watching, shuddered.

'We know what you did, Matty. We know all about what you said to Kate. How you tried to keep her and Meggie from meeting. Meggie knows too. And this time you've gone too far, because she will never forgive you, Matty. Never.'

Unable to turn his head away, Matty closed his eyes, repelled by the sheer force of her loathing. Sally screamed at him, tears running down her face.

'Meggie's my friend! I couldn't love her more if she was my own sister. Her only fault is she tries to see the best in folk. She deserves a better life than the one she's had, and she might

378

stand a chance of that once you are out of the way.' She stepped close to him and waited in silence until he opened his eyes. Very deliberately she spat, catching him on the eye. Then she stepped back, snorting her derision. 'You're not even worth that much, Matthew McPherson. I hope you rot in the hottest part of hell.'

Ronnie, seeing his wife cover her face with her hands, sobbing in earnest, gently pulled her away.

Robbie, his arms aching with strain, let go of Matty's collar and the younger man reeled away choking, gasping for air.

'You've got a week,' Ronnie told Matty. 'Leave the keys on the shop counter. 'And don't even think about trying to contact Meggie. She never wants to set eyes on you again.'

Matty, short, stocky and out of condition, knew he stood no chance against the burly Ronnie and the superbly fit Robbie. But what had really upset him was the vicious tongue-lashing that Sally had served up. It was demeaning to be spoken to like that by a woman. He'd have dearly liked to stick a fist in her face, yet he knew that Robbie Laing and Ronnie Sandys were praying he would try something like that, just to give them the excuse they needed to give him a really good going over.

As if reading his mind, Ronnie grabbed him by the collar and pulled him close. 'And think yourself lucky you're not in bits on the floor,' he growled.

'Aye,' Robbie added. 'But you've Meggie to thank for that. She didn't want you hurt. If it had been up to me you'd not have a whole bone in your body.' Never a violent man, Robbie was discovering a side of himself that he didn't much like.

Ronnie tugged at the other man's collar until Matty's feet left the ground, then dropped him suddenly.

Matty stumbled and almost fell. 'You've all said what you had to say. Now get out,' he roared in a belated attempt at bravado.

'We're going,' Sally sneered. 'But you make sure you're out of here by Friday.'

'Or what?' Matty challenged, feeling safer now he knew they intended no serious harm.

Ronnie rounded on him so fast that the others were left staring at each other. 'Or,' he snarled, shoving Matty hard against the wall. 'I will be back with some friends, and if that happens, you can be sure that you'll leave here on a stretcher.'

Matty had no reason to doubt him and cowered against the wall.

'Come on, let's get out of here.' Robbie felt contaminated by Matty. He couldn't get away from him fast enough.

Matty waited until he heard the back door slam, then straightening up, he walked thoughtfully through to his bedroom. So they thought they'd beaten him, did they? Well he had one ace left. One damning piece of evidence which would ruin Meggie.

Reaching up to the very back of his wardrobe shelf, he drew down a small, suede-covered box.

Sitting on the edge of his bed, he stroked the velvety material with his fingertips, his face contorting into an ugly, grimacing smile as he contemplated the damage this one small item would do.

And as for the letter to the press, well, that could be sent from anywhere in the country. Better for him if everyone thought he was out of the area when Meggie died.

Matty McPherson would show them all that he wasn't a man to be crossed.

TWENTY-NINE

'Oliver!'

'Hmm?' He didn't bother to look up from the papers he was studying.

'We have to talk.' It was an unwritten rule in the household that she allowed him to complete any unfinished work as soon as he returned home on Friday night, but Meggie had been gearing herself up for this moment ever since she had become aware of Matty's perfidy forty-eight hours previously and could wait no longer. The strain she was under was obvious in her pale face and violet-ringed eyes, though Oliver's gaze had not rested on her for long enough to register anything more than her physical presence.

With exaggerated care, Oliver gathered his papers together, replaced them in his case and, bringing his hands together, looked across to where she sat, perched on the edge of her chair. 'Well?' It was hardly encouraging. His constituents would get a better welcome, she thought, amazed at how pompous he had become since entering parliament. Her momentary hesitation gave him the opportunity to jump to the wrong conclusion. 'If you are going to berate me again about where I go and who I go with while I am in London, Meggie, then you might as well save your breath. I don't feel inclined to discuss it.'

She raised her eyebrows. 'I am very well aware of how you fill your time, Oliver, and frankly it no longer bothers me.' It was true. Any emotion she might have felt for her husband had long since burnt itself out. What she felt for him now was precisely nothing. She didn't love him; she couldn't hate him. The best she could rise to was a faint contempt for the self-important buffoon he was fast becoming. The remnants of boyish charm which had done so much to secure his majority had vanished, suffocated by his own expanding ego. The straining waistcoat buttons on his pin-striped suit drew attention to his ballooning paunch and the half-moon glasses were nothing more than an affectation, designed to give an impression of intellect. She noticed too that he had been working on his accent, striving unsuccessfully to hide his roots. The down-to-earth Strathannan people would not appreciate that, but it would be no good trying to suggest as much to him.

'Then say what you have to say and let me get on with my work.' He swung back on his chair and hitched his thumbs into his waistcoat pockets. She found herself hoping that the chair would slip, landing him in an undignified heap on the floor.

Meggie, who had been rehearsing her speech ever since she woke that morning, abandoned it and simply related the chain of events which had rocked her world.

When she was finished he tipped his chair forward very slowly and looked at her for a long time over the top of his glasses, very much as though he were the headmaster and she the wayward pupil. 'This is your problem, Meggie,' he told her at last. 'You deal with it. But I warn you now, if one whiff of this gets out, if there is the slightest hint of scandal, I shall divorce you. I think an illegitimate daughter will be ample grounds.'

The tension went out of Meggie and she sagged back in her chair, toying with her knife. Why, she asked herself, had she expected any other reaction? Oliver's response had been as predictable as rain in spring. He was concerned only with the way things might affect him, was completely oblivious to his wife's feelings. Meggie found that she didn't care how it might rebound on Oliver. So what if word got out and everyone knew his wife had had an illegitimate daughter? She wasn't the only woman in the world to have been caught out. And right now the only thing that mattered to Meggie were her children: Kate, this unknown daughter who was poised to enter her world at last, and Ellen, the loving, affectionate child whose future was so uncertain. And if it all ended in divorce from Oliver? What would happen to them then? She closed her eyes, tried to think of something else, frightened to let her mind run on to the conclusion it reached for. But somehow Robbie was there, in her mind, stubbornly refusing to move.

Unable to summon the energy to try to discuss it with him, she got to her feet and gathered her things together. 'If that's all you have to say then I might as well go to bed.'

'Yes.' He poured himself another whisky from the bottle by his elbow, got out another sheaf of papers from his case and didn't look at her again.

Though they slept in separate bedrooms it was more than mere coincidence that brought them to the breakfast table at the same time on the Saturday morning. When he was in his constituency for a weekend there were many demands on Oliver's time and he was always up before seven-thirty. Meggie, detached though she was from him as a person, felt duty-bound to play her role and rose with him to prepare breakfast while he shaved and dressed. They ate together too, though he was always hidden behind the *Courier*, catching up on local news while she immersed herself in the dailies, a convenient way of avoiding conversation.

A sharp and prolonged ring on the bell made them both look up. Meggie, assuming it was an early caller for Oliver, rose and went to open the door. There was no one there, though she thought she caught a glimpse of someone disappearing through the drive gates before the hedge hid him from view. Perplexed, she shut the door. Only then did she see the envelope which had fallen to the floor. She added it to the morning's post which sat on the hall shelf and took it through to the dining-room.

'Who was that?' Oliver asked without looking up.

'Someone put an envelope through the letter box.' She picked it up and examined it. The envelope was a sturdy one and obviously contained a small box of some sort. Intrigued she turned it over and examined the address, but all it said was '*Oliver Laing, MP*', with the word '*Private*' printed in red ink across the top of the envelope. 'Looks interesting. Shall I open it?'

'No.' He reached across and took the pile of envelopes from her. Despite the fact that Meggie opened and dealt with his mail while he was in London, Oliver insisted on opening everything himself when he was at home. Meggie didn't mind that, but she did object to the detailed instructions he then insisted on giving her on how to deal with each letter – as if she didn't cope with it all perfectly adequately when he wasn't there.

He slit the envelopes with fussy precision, deliberately, she thought, leaving the special delivery until last. Then he assigned each letter to one of two piles, urgent and non-urgent. At last he turned to the large envelope and withdrew a small suede-covered box. Placing it on the table he thrust a hand inside the envelope and pulled out a single sheet of paper. He scanned it as he had scanned the others. She watched, curious to know what was in the box, which looked like a jewellery case, wondering who could have sent it. Probably, she thought, it was from one of his lady friends. If so his reaction could be interesting. He certainly looked far from pleased. Oliver smoothed out the sheet of paper, laid it on the table and read through it again, this time with total concentration. By the time he had finished his face was puce.

'Something wrong, Oliver?' she asked with wry amusement, wondering, if her guess was right, how he would explain it away.

He ignored her and picked up the box, clicking the lid open and staring intently at what was inside. When he finally looked up at his wife the expression on his face made Meggie's heart thump with terror. Never before had he looked at her with such hatred.

'What is it?' she asked, thoroughly alarmed.

In answer he tore something roughly from the case and hurled it across the table at her. It slithered to a halt beside her hand.

She recognised it immediately. With the breath frozen in her chest, Meggie picked up a delicately worked bracelet. It was of gold links studded alternately with jet and diamonds, an unusual and unforgettable thing. The memories it brought drained her face of colour.

It had been a gift from Wallace, Kate's father, given to her not long after they met. Feeling betrayed when he appeared to reject her on discovering her pregnancy, she had returned it to him. Many years later, when she had met and fallen in love with Wallace's son, Oliver, and Wallace himself was dying, he had returned it to her, giving her marriage to Oliver his blessing but swearing her to secrecy about their own relationship. Wallace had been a wise and generous man, the first of the Laings to capture her heart, and he had known that Oliver would never come to terms with the fact that his own father had fathered Meggie's illegitimate child. It was a secret that Wallace had taken with him to the grave and one that Meggie would never have betrayed. But now, here in the crudely printed letter which accompanied the bracelet, was the truth she had hoped to hide for ever, the one secret that she and Oliver did not share.

Appalled, she glanced up at her husband. Even from where she sat she could see he was shaking with outrage.

'Read it!' he bawled at her. 'Read it.'

Meggie read it through carefully, wincing at the crude names the writer had used to describe her relationship with Wallace, cheapening something that had saved her from a hopeless future and given her back her self-respect.

'Turn it over,' Oliver screamed at her.

On the back there was another, single paragraph, threatening to take the story to the press, a move which was sure to destroy Oliver's career. And destroy Meggie too. An illegitimate child was one thing, not easy to live down, but at least not unique. But to have borne a child to your husband's father. Meggie knew that the shame would destroy everything: her marriage, her home, her family, her friends; it would have repercussions on Ellen, perhaps even on her nephew and niece. It would certainly destroy any hope she might have for a lasting relationship with Kate, the offspring of her relationship with Wallace Laing. And what hope, she wondered, her heart thudding in anguish, could she have of building a new life with Robbie, the third Laing man she had loved, should this become public? Not even he, loyal though he was, could be expected to brave the public censure their relationship would attract if all this became common knowledge. Through her mounting despair, Meggie realised that the one thing she had clung on to while her marriage disintegrated around her was the unacknowledged dream that one day she and Robbie would be together. Now that dream was destroyed, taking all hope for the future with it. It was as if a screen of black gauze had fallen between her and the rest of the world, condemning her to a life of loneliness and misery. Who could hate her enough to want to destroy even her faintest hopes?

Even as she asked herself that question, and even though the letter was unsigned, the writing unrecognisable, she knew who had written it. Apart from herself, there were only three people still alive who knew the whole truth about Kate's parentage: Sally, Ronnie and – although, until now, she believed she had kept the truth from him – Matty. The bracelet had disappeared on the day Matty vanished after his appalling attack on Oliver. When he returned to Inverannan after the war she had asked him about it and he had admitted taking it, telling her he had sold it. Now she knew he had been lying, as he had lied to her about so many things.

Lost in her own terrible thoughts, she wasn't aware that Oliver had risen from the table until he dragged her forcibly from her seat.

He stared down at her, her face almost purple, his whole body shaking. 'Who wrote this?' he roared. 'Who knows enough about you to be able to write something like this?'

'It was Matty,' she said, no longer feeling the need to defend him.

'Matty.' He hissed the name, his grip tightening on her until she cried out in pain. Even though she saw the blow coming she could not move away. It caught her across the mouth, his signet ring cutting her lip. Again he hit her, this time catching her cheekbone. 'Slut!' he hissed again. 'You slept with my own father! You had a child by my father and then dared to marry me. It's . . . it's perverted, filthy.' She could see that he meant every word, that in his eyes she was tainted, as untouchable as a leper. 'And he . . . my own father . . . passed you on to me when he had finished with you. How you and he must have laughed about me, poor gullible fool that I was.'

'You don't understand,' she pleaded. 'It wasn't like that. Think what you like about me, Oliver, but your father was a good man.' Even now, though she knew he hated her, she couldn't bear to have him think ill of his father.

He hit her again, so hard that for a moment everything went dark and her head spun wildly. She was aware of a deep, throbbing pain in her skull.

'Don't you dare to speak to me about my father.' A man Oliver had loved and revered, his memory now sullied for ever. For a moment longer Oliver held his wife, forcing her to stay upright, then suddenly he released his grip on her and she crumpled to the floor, sick and dizzy.

He stood looking down on her, his expression one of absolute loathing. 'You will be hearing from my solicitors. I want a divorce, but first I want you and that imbecile daughter of yours out of this house before I come home next weekend.'

Meggie fought desperately to control her reeling senses and managed to say, 'Ellen is your daughter, Oliver.'

Turning away from her, his fury sated, he limped to the table and gathered his papers together. Picking up the bracelet, he tore it apart, ripping at it again and again before throwing the twisted remains at her.

Meggie hung her head, unable to watch the disgust in his face, but cried, 'Turn your back on me if you like but I won't let you deny your daughter.'

But she was talking to empty space. The front door slammed and Oliver walked out of her life.

Perhaps half an hour later she picked her aching body up off the floor. Slowly, her head thumping, her stomach churning, she pulled herself upstairs, thankful that Jessica had the weekend off and had not witnessed her degradation. Quietly she crept into Ellen's room and gently knelt down on the floor, looking at the innocent, sleeping child. 'It's just you and me now,' she murmured, stroking her daughter's downy cheek. 'Just you and me.'

Then, wincing with pain, she got up and quietly began to take some clothes from the wardrobe. In her own room she did the same, taking just enough to get her through the next couple of days. There would be time later to take the rest of their things.

That done, she made a phone call, then went back upstairs to lift Ellen gently from bed, wrapping her in a nest of blankets.

Minutes later she heard a car screeching to a stop outside. Carefully, still dizzy from the blow to her head, she carried the child downstairs and opened the front door.

For a moment Robbie stared in mute horror at the livid bruises on her face, the split and swollen lip and the purple, puffy eye.

'What the hell . . .?' He started to speak but Meggie shook her head.

'Later,' she whispered, offering her waking daughter to the man she loved.

'Unc . . .' Ellen murmured drowsily, snuggling happily into the strong, reliable arms of the man she too loved.

'Please, Robbie, don't say anything. Not yet. Just take us away from here. Please,' Meggie begged.

His face stiff with anguish, Robbie could only nod as he led her to his car.

Just over a week later Meggie unlocked the door to the corner shop and stepped inside, half frightened of what she might find.

'Well, at least he's not wrecked the place,' Robbie said, voicing her innermost fear.

'He hardly needed to,' she replied. 'He couldn't do any more harm than he already has.'

Slowly she went behind the counter and opened the till, finding it empty as she had expected. Behind her the cigarette shelves were almost bare too.

She slammed the till shut and sighed. 'I still can't believe Matty told me so many lies, Robbie. I was so proud of him! I thought he'd fought in the war. But all the time he was in Drumlinnie. How could I have been so stupid?'

'You weren't stupid, Meggie, just loyal. And Matty is a very good liar.'

She sighed. 'I wonder where he is now?'

'Does it matter?' he asked. 'He won't be coming back here, I can promise you that.'

She rounded on him quickly. 'How can you be so sure, Robbie?'

He shrugged. 'I am. Let's just leave it at that, shall we?'

She stared at him. 'No . . . please,' she whispered, half to herself, and he looked up sharply.

'I know what you're thinking, Meggie and no, I didn't so much as lay a finger on him, and nor did Ronnie. I promised you I wouldn't hurt him and I don't break promises.'

'I know.' She looked away for a moment, ashamed to have doubted him. 'But I do think you know where he is.'

'It doesn't matter where he is, Meggie. Just trust me when I say he won't be coming back to Strathannan.'

'Don't you understand, Robbie?' she cried. 'Matty went away once before and I thought I'd never see him again. But he came back! How can I be sure he won't do the same again? He nearly destroyed me and I will never feel safe until I am absolutely certain that he won't come looking for me.'

Robbie looked at her for a moment, obviously considering his course of action. Then, reaching his decision, he came and stood in front of her. 'I never meant to tell you this, Meggie, but I suppose I never understood how frightened you would be.'

'Tell me what?'

'Matty has gone to Canada.'

'Canada? But how? They won't take him, not with a criminal record.'

'It's all arranged. He sails next week and in the meantime

he's in lodgings in Southampton, with someone to keep an eye on him to make sure he gets on the ship. Actually he jumped at the chance to leave the country.'

'But how, Robbie? Even you can't have fixed that.'

'No,' he agreed. 'But a Member of Parliament can.'

'Oliver? But why would Oliver help me?' she asked.

'Och, he's not helping you, Meggie. He's looking after his own interests. He's scared silly of what Matty might say to the press about you and Wallace. I suggested a way out and with just a little encouragement from me he was pulling every string he could get his fingers round.'

'Encouragement?'

He shrugged. 'I asked him what the local Conservative Party would think of him if I let it slip that he beat his wife.'

'Oh Robbie, you couldn't! It would be awful. I'd hate everyone to know . . .'

'Of course I wouldn't!' he laughed. 'But Oliver doesn't know that, does he?'

Now Meggie laughed too. Reaching up, she put her arms round Robbie's neck and kissed him on the lips. 'You are a miracle worker, Robbie Laing.' But she stepped away again as he started to pull her into his arms.

He smiled ruefully but let her go. 'And it's going to take a miracle to get this place fit for you to live in. Let's go upstairs and see what needs to be done.' He led the way, opening the door and peering inside to check everything was in order before allowing her in.

She sighed, thinking how grim and dark it all was. 'A coat of paint and some decent furniture and it will be fine,' she said without conviction.

Robbie put his arms around her and held her close, kissing her head then raising her face and kissing her again, on the lips. This time she didn't move away.

'You don't have to live here, Meggie. There is plenty of

room for you both with me.' He repeated the offer he had made several times in the last week.

She smiled up at him, awed by the strength of her feelings for him. It was as if Oliver had finally released her, freeing her to discover just how much she loved Robbie. But it was a love that was, as yet, unconsummated. 'I know. I'm grateful to you for letting Ellen and me stay with you for the last week, but I have to have a place of my own, Robbie.'

'Why, Meggie? You and Ellen will be miserable here. If you won't think of yourself then think of her. This is no place for a child. Where will she play? Who will look after her while you work?'

She shook her head and moved slightly away from him, not trusting herself to make a sensible decision while she was in his arms. 'I don't know, Robbie.' Her overriding concern had been to pack her things, to get herself and Ellen out of the house before Oliver could return. She had turned to Robbie instinctively for help, but she knew she couldn't remain under the same roof as him for much longer without giving rise to the sort of gossip she was so anxious to avoid. Once people started speculating, the whole dreadful story might come out after all. 'Perhaps Jessica could come in every day.' But Jessica was used to better things and, just as important, needed somewhere to live. Though she would miss Ellen dearly, she was desperately searching for another live-in position.

'Sit down, Meggie. I want to talk to you.' He led her to the worn and grubby sofa and then sat down beside her, keeping an arm firmly round her shoulders.

'You shouldn't worry about me, Robbie. I can take care of myself. And Ellen too.' She smiled bravely at him. 'This is only a temporary thing. As soon as the divorce is settled I'll look for a decent place to live. I'm not exactly penniless, you know.' Thank goodness, she added under her breath.

'I know that, but it's Ellen I'm worried about at the moment.

You can't have anyone come here to look after her. There isn't enough room for her to play and you will be constantly worried about her.'

'It's the best I can do for the moment, Robbie.'

'But I have a better suggestion.'

'What?' she asked.

'Well, the best thing would be for us to stay as we are.'

She sighed. 'We've already been over this.'

'I know,' he grinned wryly. 'But I love having you both around the place, Meggie. And' – he raised his voice over her repeated objection – 'why not let me hire Jessica to look after Ellen? She's wonderful with Ellen and Ellen loves her. You know how important it is for Ellen to have someone who understands her to look after her.'

'I know, but . . .'

'No buts, Meggie. Forget your pride and let me help you, both of you. Can't you see what a good arrangement it would be? Ellen can come home to you at night, though if you wanted her to stay over, Jessica would be there to look after her so she would be quite safe. Besides, when Avis and Tommy are home in the holidays, Jessica will be able to go on looking after them too. They don't need any more changes in their lives, Meggie.'

'No, you're right.' She almost capitulated, seeing the sense of his argument. 'But I would have to have Ellen home in the evenings, Robbie.'

'Yes. I think you should too. You need to spend as much time with her as you can. But you could bring her to my house in the mornings and fetch her back in the evenings. You won't need to worry about her if she stays with Jessica. Jessica can keep her job, so it helps her too, and you can concentrate on the shops. That's if you're still determined to go back to taking an active role in the business.'

'I have to keep expenses down and someone's got to take over where Matty left off.'

'Yes, I suppose so.' He looked at her closely for a moment then said quietly, 'I do love you, Meggie, you know that, don't you?'

She smiled at him, 'Yes, I know that, Robbie, and I love you too. But I can't come and live with you.'

'We're not children, Meggie. What difference will it make?'

'People will gossip, Robbie, especially when the divorce becomes common knowledge. I just hope the whole story doesn't come out.'

'It won't,' he assured her. 'Oliver will try everything he can to keep the details quiet. That's why he's decided to let you divorce him for adultery. He won't contest it, just so he can avoid that risk.'

'Still, best to keep ourselves out of the spotlight. If anything does come out it could rebound on you and the children. I'd hate to have that on my conscience too.'

'As well as what?' he teased. 'Having the good taste to love Laing men?'

'You know what I mean.'

'Yes I do, Meggie and I wish you'd stop tormenting yourself. You've done nothing to be ashamed of. All your life you've done what you thought was best for other people and look where that got you. It's time to start thinking of yourself.' He kissed her again. 'For now, just agree to me employing Jessica to look after Ellen.'

'I can't ask you to do that, Robbie. *If* I agree to this, I will pay Jessica.'

He sighed in mock exasperation. 'Why did I have to fall in love with such a very stubborn woman? And remember,' he went on quickly, 'this is for for Avis and Tommy too, so I shall at least pay my fair share. Anyway,' he added with deceptive casualness, 'you will have to agree because it will save messing Ellen around again when you *do* move in with me.'

Meggie sighed with irritation, wishing he wouldn't go on about it. Much as she would like to wake with him beside her each morning, he must see it was impossible.

'After we're married, that is,' he added.

She rounded on him, her eyes wide with pleasure.

'You will marry me, Meggie, won't you?'

'Well,' she teased him now. 'It's a bit premature. Better ask me again later, after the divorce.'

'It won't take long, Meggie. This time next year it should all be over.'

Whatever she might have said in reply was stifled by his lips on hers. For the next fifteen minutes they were oblivious to everything.

A thumping on the stairs made them spring apart like guilty schoolchildren. When Sally burst into the room they were sitting with a full foot of space between them, looking decidedly shifty.

Sally chortled gleefully. 'By the look of you two it's a very good job I made all that noise coming up the stairs.'

'Sally!' But Meggie was laughing as she sprang up to welcome her friend.

'Well, it needs a bit of brightening up but Ronnie knows someone who works as a painter and decorator. He'll be here first thing in the morning. All you have to do is choose the paint and paper.'

'But Sal . . .' She knew her friend well enough to suspect that Sally would give her her last penny if she thought it would help, but knew too that although the Sandys were not short of money, they couldn't afford to be extravagant.

'Don't start, Meggie. I know fine that you've not much money right now. But you'll soon have that sorted out. I know you're too proud to let me and Ronnie help you properly but you can't stop us doing this. It's all arranged. Think of it as a house-warming gift. Anyway,' she added, looking around the place with critical eyes. 'You couldn't possibly live in it like this.'

'Thank you, Sally. What would I do without you?' Meggie hugged her friend tightly and the two pairs of eyes were suspiciously bright.

'Och, stop it and grab that bucket. There's work to be done.' Sally pushed Meggie away and Robbie had to suppress a smile when he saw her take a surreptitious dab at her eyes with the sleeve of her blouse. Catching him watching, she flushed, then challenged him. 'There's another bucket downstairs. We need all the help we can get if this place is not to shame us when that decorator arrives.'

'Eh . . . well actually I have to get to work,' he said, glancing at his watch and backing towards the door. 'Oh,' he said, 'before I forget. 'Good luck for tomorrow, Meggie.'

She turned and smiled at him. 'I know everything's going to fine, Robbie. I can just feel it.'

Twenty-four hours later, Meggie sat by the rock pool in the tropical glasshouses which were a feature of the town's large park. She was more nervous than she had ever been in her whole life but the water, trickling over a series of rocks, had a calming effect.

It was quiet in here, most folk who visited the park in winter choosing the tea-rooms rather than the hothouses. And hot was the word, Meggie realised, starting to feel uncomfortable in her heavy winter coat. She looked at her watch again, wishing she hadn't arrived so early. Tom had explained that today was Kate's half day and that she would come straight from work at twelve-thirty, but Meggie had been unable to settle in the flat, which had been invaded by men in white overalls carrying buckets of paint and rolls of wallpaper.

The parkkeeper strolled by for the second time in ten minutes, nodding to her. 'He's wondering what I'm doing here,' she thought, amused at his suspicious expression. 'Perhaps he thinks I'm going to steal the fish or dig up one of his precious plants.' Nerves made her giggle.

Actually he suspected that she had an assignation with her lover, a not unknown occurrence in the sultry hothouses, and something he deeply disapproved of. He saw it as his duty to stop all public displays of affection and made a point of patrolling round suspects with a frequency guaranteed to cool even the hottest ardour. There would be no hanky-panky while he was on duty. Casting another deeply worried frown at her, he plodded on, then stood a little way away where he could still keep a careful eye on her.

He turned at the sound of footsteps on the flagged pathways. Another lady. Well this was a turn-up for the books. The most they usually got in here at this time of year was a couple of pensioners come in to keep warm for the price of the penny in the turnstile. Half the time they fell asleep and he had to rouse them and send them on their way when it started to get dark. Once he had discovered that one old gent had gone for a permanent sleep. And very difficult it had been getting the stretcher through the turnstile. They had kept the sealed doors open for so long that the temperature had dropped alarmingly and he had had to stay late, stoking up the boiler.

He turned and watched the young woman as she walked between the lush greenery. She had slowed down now, almost as if she was about to turn and go back the way she had come. He watched with interest.

Meggie too had heard the light footsteps. She jumped to her feet, wiped her damp palms on her coat and tried her best to stay calm. She could see nothing yet because the pool was slightly off the main walkway, protected by greenery.

But then there was the flash of glossy dark hair that swung

as its owner walked, a glimpse of a dark coat and, all of a sudden, a young girl rounded the corner.

Kate, her heart thumping painfully, came to a sudden and complete halt. Though she had been prepared for this moment, the actuality of seeing her mother for the first time seemed to have a paralysing effect on her limbs.

Meggie too was momentarily overcome. The two women simply stood and stared at each other.

Behind them, unnoticed, the parkkeeper edged ever nearer, driven to unprofessional behaviour by overwhelming curiosity.

'Kate?' Meggie was the first to speak, though the words emerged as a choked whisper.

The girl before her nodded. 'You must be Meggie Laing.' Her voice was equally strangled.

Meggie knew that words were beyond her and simply opened her arms in an instinctive gesture of welcome. After only the faintest hesitation Kate stepped into them.

'My baby,' Meggie whispered. 'My beautiful baby. I never thought I would see you again.' She held Kate away from her, unashamed of the tears which she was helpless to control. Yes, she thought, this was Wallace's child, the resemblance was unmistakable, and yet there was much of herself there too. 'But you are even more lovely now than you were as a baby,' she said.

'You remember me?' Kate asked hesitantly. 'After all this time you still remember what I looked like then?'

'You are engraved on my heart,' Meggie said, her eyes glittering with tears. 'And my heart nearly broke the day I gave you away.' She looked at this beautiful young woman, her heart swelling with love, and said softly, 'I must tell you now, Kate, before we say anything else to one another, that I had no idea what Matty was doing. And I am so very, very sorry that you were hurt. You would always have been welcome in my home, Kate, and in my heart. I can't bear to think that you believed

I didn't want you.' Kate's eyes too filled with tears and she clutched Meggie's hand tightly, unable to speak. It was many moments before they could see well enough to make their way to the bench by the pool.

'We've so much catching up to do,' Meggie said, finding her voice again at last.

'But so much time to do it in,' Kate replied, her voice breaking with emotion, her hand still firmly holding Meggie's.

'Yes,' Meggie agreed. 'The rest of our lives. I want you to know,' she added softly. 'That you can ask me anything you like and I will give you honest answers. I will tell you anything about myself, about my past. And about your father.'

Kate nodded. 'I want to know everything,' she admitted. 'But not yet. I . . . I need to get used to knowing I have a real mother first. It's enough just to be here.' She laughed softly and admitted, 'I'm so excited I'd probably not be able to take in a thing you told me.'

Meggie squeezed her daughter's hand. 'Then why don't you tell me something about yourself, Kate.'

The younger woman smiled. 'I don't know where to start.'

'With something happy,' Meggie said. 'Something to stop these tears before my face gets too puffy. I know. Tell me about Tom.'

She relaxed as she saw the girl's face light up, knew she had chosen the right subject to begin learning about one another. Before long they were deep in conversation: two dark heads bent together, their tears mingling, their hands linked.

From his vantage point behind the ferns the keeper produced an off-white hanky and blew his nose noisily before going on his rounds, unable to intrude a moment longer on such an intimate reunion.

It was two hours later when the two men huddled in the freezing cold on the benches outside the hothouses jumped gratefully to their feet. Both watched anxiously as Kate and Meggie emerged.

Mother and daughter walked slowly towards them, both conscious of tear-stained faces and ruined make-up. The men stood silently, afraid to move, not knowing what to expect.

Kate stood, her head bowed for a moment as she composed herself, but when she looked up her radiant face told its own story.

Meggie, equally emotional still, went to stand by Robbie and taking his hand, simply said, 'Robbie, I want you to meet my daughter, Kate.'

THIRTY

Matthew McPherson strolled around the deck of the ocean liner which was speeding him across the Atlantic, nodding to his fellow passengers who were, like him, taking the bracing sea air after a more than substantial dinner in the luxurious dining-room. Walking slowly towards the stern, Matty leaned against the rail and stared contentedly out at the ship's wake.

He lit a cigar and puffed on it, feeling on top of the world. A nice little ocean cruise was just what he needed. Then, with money in his pockets and a regular income from his legally-acquired share of Meggie's business, plus of course a sizeable bank balance gleaned from his illegally-gained share of the shop's takings, he could afford to spend a month or so in the United States, an experience he had never, in his wildest dreams, expected to be able to enjoy.

And all thanks to Oliver Laing, a very frightened man. And with good reason, Matty thought smugly. For a supposedly intelligent man, Oliver had acted with incredible stupidity. Three thousand pounds, a first class ticket to the USA and the promise of a job in Canada, when he eventually got there, all arranged in double-quick time on the understanding that Matty would take himself to foreign shores, where he could be no threat to Oliver's career. And that, Matty smiled grimly, had been Oliver's fatal mistake.

If Oliver had been actively abetting Matty's evil ambition he could not have devised a better plan, nor one designed to safeguard Matty more thoroughly. For who would suspect a man who was known to be on the other side of the world at the time of his sister's tragic suicide? Matty's plans were unchanged, his evil ambition stronger than ever since Meggie had chosen to turn her back on him in favour of her bastard daughter.

As soon as he got to New York he would post the letter which he carried deep in his jacket pocket. That, along with the copy of Kate's birth certificate which he had requested years ago, should be more than enough to start a furore in the local and national press, ending Oliver's career and sending Meggie into an understandable mental decline from which she would, with his help, never recover. All he had to do was slip quietly back to Britain, pay one last visit to his sister, and then, having left ample evidence of suicide, fly quickly back to the USA and resume his little holiday. Of course the British papers, available in America, would carry news of the scandal involving one of the country's most promising MPs. As soon as Matty read of his sister's tragic death he would have the perfect excuse for returning to Scotland to claim his rightful share of the business – and his little niece.

Yes, he mused, turning to lean with his back against the rail, it couldn't have worked out better. In a matter of weeks he would have what he had always wanted: Meggie's business. Meggie's death – he favoured the dramatic gesture, so would probably slit her wrists open after slipping her a couple of sleeping pills in a drink – would be, beyond all question, suicide. There would be no reason for anyone to suspect foul play. Even if Oliver was suspicious, he himself had bribed Matty to leave the country and would certainly not want to compromise himself further by admitting as much in court. All in all, Matty thought, tossing the cigar butt into the ocean, he was in an invincible position. There were one or two other scores to be settled while he was about it. Robbie Laing, for one, and that shirty little cow, Sally Sandys. Yet even Matty wasn't confident enough to think that the deaths of three close friends would go unchallenged by the law. Pity, because nothing would give him greater satisfaction than to send the whole lot of them to hell. No, he would think of something else for Robbie Laing and Sally Sandys. Accidents to their children; fires in their homes. He sniffed the wind, taking a deep, satisfied breath, knowing he would relish the planning, the little touches which would make these horrible crimes appear to be nothing more than a series of unfortunate accidents.

He turned for one last look at the ocean before retiring to his cabin for the night, reluctant to end the pleasant contemplation which occupied much of his time aboard.

'Pleasant evening.'

Matty turned and nodded briefly to a fellow passenger: a man who, like himself, was travelling alone. It seemed that he too enjoyed a late-night stroll around the decks, for their paths had crossed on both previous nights of the voyage. But though they had exchanged a brief greeting, neither appeared to have the desire for companionship. Tonight, as before, the other man walked on, pausing some yards away and waiting, looking out to sea, until Matty began to walk slowly back towards his cabin. Only then did he turn and watch until Matty disappeared from view.

The days at sea had taken on a pleasant routine. Though the weather was not warm enough for lounging on deck, Matty occupied his time in perfect idleness, emerging from his cabin only for meals and then to spend a large part of every evening in the bar. His nightly strolls around the perimeter of the deck had an unsteady roll that owed more to the quantity of beer he had imbibed than to the swell of the ocean.

Nevertheless, on the fourth night out, the weather was rough enough to deter all but the hardiest from venturing outside.

'I'd not recommend you go out on deck tonight, sir,' a young officer advised as Matty stepped into the gusty wind.

'Just a bit of fresh air before I turn in for the night,' Matty answered pleasantly enough, relishing the thought of the fresh wind in his face after the stuffiness of the bar.

'Take care then. Best stay on this side of the ship where it's more sheltered.' The officer offered a sketchy salute and went about his duties, not seriously concerned. In his experience bad weather seemed to attract a certain type of passenger and even in the worst storms of the winter there were always one or two hardy souls to be found at the stern with the spray in their faces, loving every moment of it. Rarely did the crew intervene and insist on everyone staying below, and then only if the storm was likely to be particularly severe or, more often, if an individual was considered to be a danger to himself.

Matty made his way carefully towards the stern. The strength of the wind startled him, whipping spray into his face, stinging his skin, but he bent into it and walked on. The realisation that he was obviously a good sailor, better than some who had retreated to their cabins early in the evening, drove him on, imbuing him with pride, that wonderful feeling of superiority over his fellows which he was enjoying more and more these days.

Behind him, well in the shadows, another figure followed the same route.

Reaching the rail, Matty tried unsuccessfully to light a cigarette. From behind him the other man emerged and looked quickly round, checking for the unlikely presence of other passengers, then, satisfied that they were unobserved, closed in on Matty.

'Here, take a light from this.'

Matty, who had been unaware of the other man's approach, turned round quickly, then silently applied the glowing tip of the lighted cigarette to his own. 'Thanks.' He turned back towards the ocean, disinclined to talk.

'Rough night.' His companion settled at the rail beside him.

Matty stared silently at the churning sea.

The man turned, putting his back to the ocean and stood smoking his cigarette, his eyes watchful, scanning the darkened decks and curtained portholes for signs of any hidden observer. 'It's too cold for me,' he said at last, straightening up and tossing his cigarette overboard.

Matty saw him move away from the rail and relaxed, glad to be on his own again. A sudden flurry of movement behind him alerted him to trouble but before he could turn around something long and hard had been thrust into his back. He tried to scream as the knife ripped through his rib cage, punctured a lung and came to rest with the tip embedded in his heart, but the sound emerged as a strangled gurgling noise, whipped away by the wind before it was fully formed.

Somehow he managed to turn and face his attacker, but could see nothing of the man's face. Terror overwhelmed him, making the pain insignificant, but he was powerless to resist as he felt himself lifted and balanced for a moment on the ship's rail. Then he was in the air, falling, the spray cold on his face. And then there was the icy clutch of the water, dragging him down, filling him . . . And then there was nothing.

Three days later the bedside phone in Oliver's flat rang. Removing his hand from his secretary's breast, he picked it up and barked, 'Oliver Laing,' annoyed by the badly-timed interruption.

'I have some private information for you.' The voice at the other end was muffled.

Instantly alert, Oliver jerked his head at the girl in an unmistakable gesture of dismissal, underlining it with a non-too-gentle shove with the flat of his hand.

The girl huffed out of bed, gathered up her scattered clothes and disappeared into the sitting-room, slamming the door as loudly as she could.

'Go on,' Oliver said into the receiver.

'Just to let you know that our friend has had to cancel his American trip.'

There was a long pause as Oliver absorbed the information, his whole body sagging with relief. Then he simply said, 'Thank you for letting me know,' and put the phone down.

The slamming of the front door told him that he was destined to spend the night alone, but he settled back among the pillows, put his hands behind his head and closed his eyes, a smile of utter contentment spreading over his face.